I0589551

Brant, Fuller & Co

History of Indiana

containing a history of Indiana and biographical sketches of governors and other

leading men - Vol. 1

Brant, Fuller & Co

History of Indiana
containing a history of Indiana and biographical sketches of governors and other leading men
- Vol. 1

ISBN/EAN: 9783337380519

Printed in Europe, USA, Canada, Australia, Japan

Cover: Foto ©Andreas Hilbeck / pixelio.de

More available books at **www.hansebooks.com**

OF

INDIANA.

SPECIAL EDITION FOR MARSHALL COUNTY.

CONTAINING A HISTORY OF INDIANA AND BIOGRAPHICAL SKETCHES OF
GOVERNORS AND OTHER LEADING MEN. ALSO A STATEMENT OF THE
GROWTH AND PROSPERITY OF MARSHALL COUNTY, TOGETHER
WITH A PERSONAL AND FAMILY HISTORY OF
MANY OF ITS CITIZENS. IN TWO VOLUMES.

VOL. I.

ILLUSTRATED.

MADISON, WIS.;
BRANT, FULLER & CO.
1890.

Democrat Printing Company, Madison, Wis.
Bindery of W. B. Conkey, Chicago, Ill.

CONTENTS.

PART I.—HISTORY OF INDIANA.

PART II.—HISTORY OF MARSHALL COUNTY.

BIOGRAPHICAL SKETCHES.

HISTORY OF INDIANA.

FORMER OCCUPANTS.

PREHISTORIC RACES.

Scientists have ascribed to the Mound Builders varied origins, and though their divergence of opinion may for a time seem incompatible with a thorough investigation of the subject, and tend to a confusion of ideas, no doubt whatever can exist as to the comparative accuracy of conclusions arrived at by some of them. Like the vexed question of the Pillar Towers of Ireland, it has caused much speculation, and elicited the opinions of so many learned antiquarians, ethnologists and travelers, that it will not be found beyond the range of possibility to make deductions that may suffice to solve the problem who were the prehistoric settlers of America. To achieve this it will not be necessary to go beyond the period over which Scripture history extends, or to indulge in those airy flights of imagination so sadly identified with occasional writers of even the Christian school, and all the accepted literary exponents of modern paganism.

That this continent is co-existent with the world of the ancients cannot be questioned. Every investigation, instituted under the auspices of modern civilization, confirms the fact and leaves no channel open through which the skeptic can escape the thorough refutation of his opinions. China, with its numerous living testi-monials of antiquity, with its ancient, though limited literature and its Babelish superstitions, claims a continuous history from antediluvian times; but although its continuity may be denied with every just reason, there is nothing to prevent the transmission of a hieroglyphic record of its history prior to 1656 *anno mundi*, since many traces of its early settlement survived the Deluge, and became sacred objects of the first historical epoch. This very sur-vival of a record, such as that of which the Chinese boast, is not at variance with the designs of a God who made and ruled the universe; but that an antediluvian people inhabited this continent, will not be claimed; because it is not probable, though it may be possible, that a settlement in a land which may be considered a portion of the Asiatic continent, was effected by the immediate followers of the first progenitors of the human race. Therefore, on entering the study of the ancient people who raised these tumulus monuments over large tracts of the country, it will be just sufficient to wander back to that time when the flood-gates of heaven were swung open to hurl destruction on a wicked world; and in doing so the inquiry must be based on legendary, or rather upon many circumstantial evidences; for, so far as written narrative extends, there is nothing to show that a movement of people too far east resulted in a Western settlement.

THE FIRST IMMIGRATION.

The first and most probable sources in which the origin of the Builders must be sought, are those countries lying along the eastern coast of Asia, which doubtless at that time stretched far beyond its present limits, and presented a continuous shore from Lopatka to Point Cambodia, holding a population comparatively civilized, and all professing some elementary form of the Boodhism of later days. Those peoples, like the Chinese of the present, were bound to live at home, and probably observed that law until after the confusion of languages and the dispersion of the builders of Babel in 1757, A. M.; but subsequently, within the following century, the old Mongolians, like the new, crossed the great ocean in the very paths taken by the present representatives of the race, arrived on the same shores, which now extend a very questionable hospitality to them, and entered at once upon the colonization of the country south and east, while the Caucasian race engaged in a similar movement of exploration and colonization over what may be justly termed the western extension of Asia, and both peoples growing stalwart under the change, attained a moral and physical eminence to which they never could lay claim under the tropical sun which shed its beams upon the cradle of the human race.

That mysterious people who, like the Brahmins of to-day, worshiped some transitory deity, and in after years, evidently embraced the idealization of Boodhism, as preached in Mongolia early in the 35th century of the world, together with acquiring the learning of the Confucian and Pythagorean schools of the same period, spread all over the land, and in their numerous settlements erected these raths, or mounds, and sacrificial altars whereon they received their periodical visiting gods, surrendered their bodies to natural absorption or annihilation, and watched for the return of some transmigrated soul, the while adoring the universe, which with all beings they believed would be eternally existent. They possessed religious orders corresponding in external show at least with the Essenes or Theraputæ of the pre-Christian and Christian epochs, and to the reformed Theraputæ or monks of the present. Every memento of their coming and their stay which has descended to us is an evidence of their civilized condition. The free copper found within the tumuli; the open veins of the Superior and Iron Mountain copper-mines, with all the *modus operandi* of ancient mining, such as ladders, levers, chisels, and hammer-heads, discovered by the French explorers of the Northwest and the Mississippi, are conclusive proofs that those prehistoric people were highly civilized, and that many flourishing colonies were spread throughout the Mississippi valley, while yet the mammoth, the mastodon, and a hundred other animals, now only known by their gigantic fossil remains, guarded the eastern shore of the continent as it were against supposed invasions of the Tower Builders who went west from Babel; while yet the beautiful isles of the Antilles formed an integral portion of this continent, long years before the European Northman dreamed of setting forth to the discovery of Greenland and the northern isles, and certainly at a time when all that portion of America north of latitude 45° was an ice-incumbered waste.

Within the last few years great advances have been made toward the discovery of antiquities whether pertaining to remains of organic or inorganic nature. Together with many small, but telling relics of the early inhabitants of the country, the fossils of prehistoric animals have been unearthed from end to end of the land, and in districts, too, long pronounced by geologists of some repute to be without even a vestige of vertebrate fossils. Among the collected souvenirs of an age about which so very little is known, are twenty-five vertebræ averaging thirteen inches in diameter, and three vertebræ ossified together measure nine cubical feet; a thigh-bone five feet long by twenty-eight, by twelve inches in diameter, and the shaft fourteen by eight inches thick, the entire lot weighing 600 lbs. These fossils are presumed to belong to the cretaceous period, when the Dinosaur roamed over the country from East to West, desolating the villages of the people. This animal is said to have been sixty feet long, and when feeding in cypress and palm forests, to extend himself eighty-five feet, so that he may devour the budding tops of those great trees. Other efforts in this direction may lead to great results, and culminate probably in the discovery of a tablet engraven by some learned Mound Builder, describing in the ancient hieroglyphics of China all these men and beasts whose history excites so much speculation. The identity of the Mound Builders with the Mongolians might lead us to hope for such a consummation; nor is it beyond the range of probability, particularly in this practical age, to find the future labors of some industrious antiquarian requited by the upheaval of a tablet, written in the Tartar characters of 1700 years ago, bearing on a subject which can now be treated only on a purely circumstantial basis.

THE SECOND IMMIGRATION

may have begun a few centuries prior to the Christian era, and unlike the former expedition or expeditions, to have traversed north-eastern Asia to its Arctic confines, and then east to the narrow channel now known as Behring's Straits, which they crossed, and sailing up the unchanging Yukon, settled under the shadow of Mount St. Elias for many years, and pushing South commingled with their countrymen, soon acquiring the characteristics of the descendants of the first colonists. Chinese chronicles tell of such a people, who went North and were never heard of more. Circum-stances conspire to render that particular colony the carriers of a new religious faith and of an alphabetic system of a representative character to the old colonists, and they, doubtless, exercised a most beneficial influence in other respects ; because the influx of immi-grants of such culture as were the Chinese, even of that remote period, must necessarily bear very favorable results, not only in bringing in reports of their travels, but also accounts from the fatherland bearing on the latest events.

With the idea of a second and important exodus there are many theorists united, one of whom says: "It is now the generally received opinion that the first inhabitants of America passed over from Asia through these straits. The number of small islands lying between both continents renders this opinion still more probable; and it is yet further confirmed by some remarkable traces of similarity in the physical conformation of the northern natives of both continents. The Esquimaux of North America, the Samoieds of Asia, and the Laplanders of Europe, are supposed to be of the same family; and this supposition is strengthened by the affinity which exists in their languages. The researches of Humboldt have traced the Mexicans to the vicinity of Behring's Straits; whence it is conjectured that they, as well as the Peruvians and other tribes, came originally from Asia, and were the Hiongnoos, who are, in the Chinese annals, said to have emigrated under Puno, and to have been lost in the North of Siberia."

Since this theory is accepted by most antiquaries, there is every reason to believe that from the discovery of what may be called an overland route to what was then considered an eastern extension of that country which is now known as the "Celestial Empire," many caravans of emigrants passed to their new homes in the land of illimitable possibilities until the way became a well-marked trail over which the Asiatic might travel forward, and having once entered the Elysian fields never entertained an idea of returning. Thus from generation to generation the tide of immigration poured in until the slopes of the Pacific and the banks of the great inland rivers became hives of busy industry. Magnificent cities and monuments were raised at the bidding of the tribal leaders and populous settlements centered with happy villages sprung up everywhere in manifestation of the power and wealth and knowledge of the people. The colonizing Caucasian of the historic period walked over this great country on the very ruins of a civilization which a thousand years before eclipsed all that of which he could boast. He walked through the wilderness of the West over buried treasures hidden under the accumulated growth of nature, nor rested until he saw, with great surprise, the remains of ancient pyramids and temples and cities, larger and evidently more beautiful than ancient Egypt could bring forth after its long years of uninterrupted history. The pyramids resemble those of Egypt in exterior form, and in some instances are of larger dimensions. The pyramid of Cholula is square, having each side of its base 1,335 feet in length, and its height about 172 feet. Another pyramid, situated in the north of Vera Cruz, is formed of large blocks of highly-polished porphyry, and bears upon its front hieroglyphic inscriptions and curious sculpture. Each side of its square base is 82 feet in length, and a flight of 57 steps conducts to its summit, which is 65 feet in height. The ruins of Palenque are said to extend 20 miles along the ridge of a mountain, and the remains of an Aztec city, near the banks of the river Gila, are spread over more than a square league. Their literature consisted of hieroglyphics; but their arithmetical knowledge did not extend farther than their calculations by the aid of grains of corn. Yet, notwithstanding all their varied accomplishments, and they were evidently many, their notions of religious duty led to a most demoniac zeal at once barbarously savage and ferociously cruel. Each visiting, god instead of bringing new life to the people, brought death to thousands; and their grotesque idols, exposed to drown the senses of the beholders in fear, wrought wretchedness rather than spiritual happiness, until, as some learned and humane Montezumian said, the people never approached these idols without fear, and this fear was the great animating principle, the great religious motive power which sustained the terrible religion. Their altars were sprinkled with blood drawn from their own bodies in large quantities, and on them thousands of human victims were sacrificed in honor of the demons whom they worshiped. The head and heart of every captive taken in war were offered up as a bloody sacrifice to the god of battles, while the victorious legions feasted on the remaining portions of the dead bodies. It has been ascertained that during the ceremonies attendant on the consecration of two of their temples, the number of prisoners offered up in sacrifice was 12,210; while their own legions contributed voluntary victims to the terrible belief in large numbers. Nor did this horrible custom cease immediately after 1521, when Cortez entered the imperial city of the Montezumas; for, on being driven from it, all his troops who fell into the hands of the native soldiers were subjected to the most terrible and prolonged suffering that could be experienced in this world, and when about to yield up that spirit which is indestructible, were offered in sacrifice, their hearts and heads consecrated, and the victors allowed to feast on the yet warm flesh.

A reference is made here to the period when the Montezumas ruled over Mexico, simply to gain a better idea of the hideous idolatry which took the place of the old Boodhism of the Mound Builders, and doubtless helped in a great measure to give victory to the new comers, even as the tenets of Mahometanism urged the ignorant followers of the prophet to the conquest of great nations. It was not the faith of the people who built the mounds and the pyramids and the temples, and who, 200 years before the Christian era, built the great wall of jealous China. No: rather was it that terrible faith born of the Tartar victory, which carried the great defenses of China at the point of the javelin and hatchet, who afterward marched to the very walls of Rome, under Alaric, and

spread over the islands of Polynesia to the Pacific slopes of South
America.

THE TARTARS

came there, and, like the pure Mongols of Mexico and the Mississippi valley, rose to a state of civilization bordering on that attained
by them. Here for centuries the sons of the fierce Tartar race continued to dwell in comparative peace until the all-ruling ambition
of empire took in the whole country from the Pacific to the Atlantic, and peopled the vast territory watered by the Amazon with a
race that was destined to conquer all the peoples of the Orient,
and only to fall before the march of the arch-civilizing Caucasian.
In course of time those fierce Tartars pushed their settlements
northward, and ultimately entered the territories of the Mound
Builders, putting to death all who fell within their reach, and
causing the survivors of the death-dealing invasion to seek a refuge
from the hordes of this semi-barbarous people in the wilds and fastnesses of the North and Northwest. The beautiful country of the
Mound Builders was now in the hands of savage invaders, the quiet,
industrious people who raised the temples and pyramids were gone;
and the wealth of intelligence and industry, accumulating for ages,
passed into the possession of a rapacious horde, who could admire
it only so far as it offered objects for plunder. Even in this the
invaders were satisfied, and then having arrived at the height of
their ambition, rested on their swords and entered upon the luxury
and ease in the enjoyment of which they were found when the vanguard of European civilization appeared upon the scene. Meantime the southern countries which those adventurers abandoned
after having completed their conquests in the North, were soon
peopled by hundreds of people, always moving from island to
island and ultimately halting amid the ruins of villages deserted
by those who, as legends tell, had passed eastward but never returned;
and it would scarcely be a matter for surprise if those emigrants
were found to be the progenitors of that race found by the Spaniards
in 1532, and identical with the Araucanians, Ouenches and Huil-
tiches of to-day.

RELICS OF THE MOUND BUILDERS.

One of the most brilliant and impartial historians of the Republic
stated that the valley of the Mississippi contained no monuments.
So far as the word is entertained now, he was literally correct, but

in some hasty effort neglected to qualify his sentence by a reference to the numerous relics of antiquity to be found throughout
its length and breadth, and so exposed his chapters to criticism.
The valley of the Father of Waters, and indeed the country from
the trap rocks of the Great Lakes southeast to the Gulf and southwest to Mexico, abound in tell-tale monuments of a race of people
much farther advanced in civilization than the Montezumas of the
sixteenth century. The remains of walls and fortifications found
in Kentucky and Indiana, the earthworks of Vincennes and
throughout the valley of the Wabash, the mounds scattered over
Alabama, Florida, Georgia and Virginia, and those found in Illinois, Wisconsin and Minnesota, are all evidences of the univer-
sality of the Chinese Mongols and of their advance toward a comparative knowledge of man and cosmology. At the mouth of
Fourteen-Mile creek, in Clark county, Indiana, there stands one of
these old monuments known as the "Stone Fort." It is an
unmistakable heirloom of a great and ancient people, and must
have formed one of their most important posts. The State Geologist's report, filed among the records of the State and furnished
by Prof. Cox, says: "At the mouth of Fourteen-Mile creek, and
about three miles from Charleston, the county-seat of Clark county,
there is one of the most remarkable stone fortifications which has
ever come under my notice. Accompanied by my assistant, Mr.
Borden, and a number of citizens of Charleston, I visited the 'Stone
Fort' for the purpose of making an examination of it. The locality
selected for this fort presents many natural advantages for making
it impregnable to the opposing forces of prehistoric times. It
occupies the point of an elevated narrow ridge which faces the
Ohio river on the east and is bordered by Fourteen-Mile creek on
the west side. This creek empties into the Ohio a short distance
below the fort. The top of the ridge is pear-shaped, with the
part answering to the neck at the north end. This part is not
over twenty feet wide, and is protected by precipitous natural walls
of stone. It is 280 feet above the level of the Ohio river, and the
slope is very gradual to the south. At the upper field it is 240 feet
high and one hundred steps wide. At the lower timber it is 120
feet high. The bottom land at the foot of the south end is sixty
feet above the river. Along the greater part of the Ohio river
front there is an abrupt escarpment rock, entirely too steep to be
scaled, and a similar natural barrier exists along a portion of the
northwest side of the ridge, facing the creek. This natural wall

is joined to the neck of an artificial wall, made by piling up, mason
fashion but without mortar, loose stone, which had evidently been
pried up from the carboniferous layers of rock. This made wall, at
this point, is about 150 feet long. It is built along the slope of the
hill and had an elevation of about 75 feet above its base, the upper
ten feet being vertical. The inside of the wall is protected by a
ditch. The remainder of the hill is protected by an artificial stone
wall, built in the same manner, but not more than ten feet high.
The elevation of the side wall above the creek bottom is 80 feet.
Within the artificial walls is a string of mounds which rise to the
height of the wall, and are protected from the washing of the hill-
sides by a ditch 20 feet wide and four feet deep. The position of
the artificial walls, natural cliffs of bedded stone, as well as that of
the ditch and mounds, are well illustrated. The top of the enclosed
ridge embraces ten or twelve acres, and there are as many as five
mounds that can be recognized on the flat surface, while no doubt
many others existed which have been obliterated by time, and
though the agency of man in his efforts to cultivate a portion of
the ground. A trench was cut into one of these mounds in search
of relics. A few fragments of charcoal and decomposed bones, and
a large irregular, diamond-shaped boulder, with a small circular
indentation near the middle of the upper part, that was worn quite
smooth by the use to which it had been put, and the small pieces
of fossil coral, comprised all the articles of note which were revealed
by the excavation. The earth of which the mound is made resem-
bles that seen on the hillside, and was probably in most part taken
from the ditch. The margin next to the ditch was protected by
slabs of stone set on edge, and leaning at an angle corresponding to
the slope of the mound. This stone shield was two and one-half
feet wide and one foot high. At intervals along the great ditch
there are channels formed between the mounds that probably served
to carry off the surplus water through openings in the outer wall.
On the top of the enclosed ridge, and near its narrowest part, there
is one mound much larger than any of the others, and so situated
as to command an extensive view up and down the Ohio river, as well
as affording an unobstructed view east and west. This is designated
as 'Look-out Mound.' There is near it a slight break in the cliff
of rock, which furnished a narrow passage way to the Ohio river.
Though the locality afforded many natural advantages for a fort or
stronghold, one is compelled to admit that much skill was displayed
and labor expended in making its defense as perfect as possible at

all points. Stone axes, pestles, arrow-heads, spear-points, totums, charms and flint flakes have been found in great abundance in plowing the field at the foot of the old fort."

From the "Stone Fort" the Professor turns his steps to Posey county, at a point on the Wabash, ten miles above the mouth, called "Bone Bank," on account of the number of human bones continually washed out from the river bank. "It is," he states "situated in a bend on the left bank of the river; and the ground is about ten feet above high-water mark, being the only land along this portion of the river that is not submerged in seasons of high water. The bank slopes gradually back from the river to a slough. This slough now seldom contains water, but no doubt at one time it was an arm of the Wabash river, which flowed around the Bone Bank and afforded protection to the island home of the Mound Builders. The Wabash has been changing its bed for many years, leaving a broad extent of newly made land on the right shore, and gradually making inroads on the left shore by cutting away the Bone Bank. The stages of growth of land on the right bank of the river are well defined by the cottonwood trees, which increase in size as you go back from the river. Unless there is a change in the current of the river, all trace of the Bone Bank will be obliterated. Already within the memory of the white inhabitants, the bank has been removed to the width of several hundred yards. As the bank is cut by the current of the river it loses its support, and when the water sinks it tumbles over, carrying with it the bones of the Mound Builders and the cherished articles buried with them. No locality in the country furnishes a greater number and variety of relics than this. It has proved especially rich in pottery of quaint design and skillful workmanship. I have a number of jugs and pots and a cup found at the Bone Bank. This kind of work has been very abundant, and is still found in such quantities that we are led to conclude that its manufacture formed a leading industry of the inhabitants of the Bone Bank. It is not in Europe alone that we find a well-founded claim of high antiquity for the art of making hard and durable stone by a mixture of clay, lime, sand and stone; for I am convinced that this art was possessed by a race of people who inhabited this continent at a period so remote that neither tradition nor history can furnish any account of them. They belonged to the Neolithic, or polished-stone, age. They lived in towns and built mounds for sepulture and worship and protected their homes by surrounding them with walls of earth and stone. In some of these mounds specimens of various kinds of pottery, in a perfect state of preservation, have from time to time been found, and fragments are so common that every student of archæology can have a bountiful supply. Some of these fragments indicate vessels of very great size. At the Saline springs of Gallatin I picked up fragments that indicated, by their curvature, vessels five to six feet in diameter, and it is probable they are fragments of artificial stone pans used to hold brine that was manufactured into salt by solar evaporation.

"Now, all the pottery belonging to the Mound Builders' age, which I have seen, is composed of alluvial clay and sand, or a mixture of the former with pulverized fresh-water shells. A paste made of such a mixture possesses, in high degree, the properties of hydraulic Puzzuoland and Portland cement, so that vessels formed of it hardened without being burned, as is customary with modern pottery."

The Professor deals very aptly with this industry of the aborigines, and concludes a very able disquisition on the Bone Bank in its relation to the prehistoric builders.

HIEROGLYPHICS OF THE MOUND-BUILDERS.

The great circular redoubt or earth-work found two miles west of the village of New Washington, and the "Stone Fort," on a ridge one mile west of the village of Deputy, offer a subject for the antiquarian as deeply interesting as any of the monuments of a decayed empire so far discovered.

From end to end of Indiana there are to be found many other relics of the obscure past. Some of them have been unearthed and now appear among the collected antiquities at Indianapolis. The highly finished sandstone pipe, the copper ax, stone axes, flint arrow-heads and magnetic plummets found a few years ago beneath the soil of Cut-Off Island near New Harmony, together with the pipes of rare workmanship and undoubted age, unearthed near Covington, all live as it were in testimony of their owner's and maker's excellence, and hold a share in the evidence of the partial annihilation of a race, with the complete disruption of its manners, customs and industries; and it is possible that when numbers of these relics are placed together, a key to the phonetic or rather hieroglyphic system of that remote period might be evolved.

It may be asked what these hieroglyphical characters really are. Well, they are varied in form, so much so that the pipes found in the mounds of Indians, each bearing a distinct representation of some animal, may be taken for one species, used to represent the abstract ideas of the Mound Builders. The second form consists of pure hieroglyphics or phonetic characters, in which the sound is represented instead of the object; and the third, or painted form of the first, conveys to the mind that which is desired to be represented. This form exists among the Cree Indians of the far Northwest, at present. They, when departing from their permanent villages for the distant hunting grounds, paint on the barked trees in the neighborhood the figure of a snake or eagle, or perhaps huskey dog; and this animal is supposed to guard the position until the warrior's return, or welcome any friendly tribes that may arrive there in the interim. In the case of the Mound Builders, it is unlikely that this latter extreme was resorted to, for the simple reason that the relics of their occupation are too high in the ways of art to tolerate such a barbarous science of language; but the sculptured pipes and javelins and spear-heads of the Mound Builders may be taken as a collection of graven images, each conveying a set of ideas easily understood, and perhaps sometimes or more generally used to designate the vocation, name or character of the owner. That the builders possessed an alphabet of a phonetic form, and purely hieroglyphic, can scarcely be questioned; but until one or more of the unearthed tablets, which bore all or even a portion of such characters, are raised from their centuried graves, the mystery which surrounds this people must remain, while we must dwell in a world of mere speculation.

Vigo, Jasper, Sullivan, Switzerland and Ohio counties can boast of a most liberal endowment in this relation; and when in other days the people will direct a minute inquiry, and penetrate to the very heart of the thousand cones which are scattered throughout the land, they may possibly extract the blood in the shape of metallic and porcelain works, with hieroglyphic tablets, while leaving the form of heart and body complete to entertain and delight unborn generations, who in their time will wonder much when they learn that an American people, living toward the close of the 59th century, could possibly indulge in such an anachronism as is implied in the term "New World."

THE INDIANS.

The origin of the Red Men, or American Indians, is a subject which interests as well as instructs. It is a favorite with the ethnologist, even as it is one of deep concern to the ordinary reader. A review of two works lately published on the origin of the Indians treats the matter in a peculiarly reasonable light. It says:

" Recently a German writer has put forward one theory on the subject, and an English writer has put forward another and directly opposite theory. The difference of opinion concerning our aboriginals among authors who have made a profound study of races is at once curious and interesting. Blumenbach treats them in his classifications as a distinct variety of the human family; but, in the threefold division of Dr. Latham, they are ranked among the Mongolidæ. Other writers on race regard them as a branch of the great Mongolian family, which at a distant period found its way from Asia to this continent, and remained here for centuries separate from the rest of mankind, passing, meanwhile, through divers phases of barbarism and civilization. Morton, our eminent ethnologist, and his followers, Nott and Gliddon, claim for our native Red Men an origin as distinct as the flora and fauna of this continent. Prichard, whose views are apt to differ from Morton's, finds reason to believe, on comparing the American tribes together, that they must have formed a separate department of nations from the earliest period of the world. The era of their existence as a distinct and insulated people must probably be dated back to the time which separated into nations the inhabitants of the Old World, and gave to each its individuality and primitive language. Dr. Robert Brown, the latest authority, attributes, in his " Races of Mankind," an Asiatic origin to our aboriginals. He says that the Western Indians not only personally resemble their nearest neighbors—the Northeastern Asiatics—but they resemble them in language and traditions. The Esquimaux on the American and the Tchuktchis on the Asiatic side understand one another perfectly. Modern anthropologists, indeed, are disposed to think that Japan, the Kuriles, and neighboring regions, may be regarded as the original home of the greater part of the native American race. It is also admitted by them that between the tribes scattered from the Arctic sea to Cape Horn there is more uniformity of physical features than is seen in any other quarter of the globe. The weight of evidence and authority is altogether in favor of the opinion that our so-called Indians are a branch of the Mongolian family, and all additional researches strengthen the opinion. The tribes of both North and South America are unquestionably homogeneous, and, in all likelihood, had their origin in Asia, though they have been altered and modified by thousands of years of total separation from the parent stock."

The conclusions arrived at by the reviewer at that time, though safe, are too general to lead the reader to form any definite idea on the subject. No doubt whatever can exist, when the American Indian is regarded as of an Asiatic origin; but there is nothing in the works or even in the review, to which these works were subjected, which might account for the vast difference in manner and form between the Red Man, as he is now known, or even as he appeared to Columbus and his successors in the field of discovery, and the comparatively civilized inhabitants of Mexico, as seen in 1521 by Cortez, and of Peru, as witnessed by Pizarro in 1532. The fact is that the pure bred Indian of the present is descended directly from the earliest inhabitants, or in other words from the survivors of that people who, on being driven from their fair possessions, retired to the wilderness in sorrow and reared up their children under the saddening influences of their unquenchable griefs, bequeathing them only the habits of the wild, cloud-roofed home of their declining years, a sullen silence, and a rude moral code. In after years these wild sons of the forest and prairie grew in numbers and in strength. Some legend told them of their present sufferings, of the station which their fathers once had known, and of the riotous race which now reveled in wealth which should be theirs. The fierce passions of the savage were aroused, and uniting their scattered bands marched in silence upon the villages of the Tartars, driving them onward to the capital of their Incas, and consigning their homes to the flames. Once in view of the great city, the hurrying bands halted in surprise; but Tartar cunning took in the situation and offered pledges of amity, which were sacredly observed. Henceforth Mexico was open to the Indians, bearing precisely the same relation to them that the Hudson's Bay Company's villages do to the Northwestern Indians of the present; obtaining all, and bestowing very little. The subjection of the Mongolian race represented in North America by that branch of it to which the Tartars belonged, represented in the Southern portion of the continent, seems to have taken place some five centuries before the advent of the European, while it may be concluded that the war of the races which resulted in reducing the villages erected by the Tartar hordes to ruin took place between one and two hundred years later. These statements, though actually referring to events which in point of time are comparatively modern, can only be substantiated by the facts that, about the periods mentioned the dead bodies of an unknown race of men were washed ashore on the European coasts, while previous to that time there is no account whatever in European annals of even a vestige of trans-Atlantic humanity being transferred by ocean currents to the gaze of a wondering people. Towards the latter half of the 15th century two dead bodies entirely free from decomposition, and corresponding with the Red Men as they afterward appeared to Columbus, were cast on the shores of the Azores, and confirmed Columbus in his belief in the existence of a western world and western people.

Storm and flood and disease have created sad havoc in the ranks of the Indian since the occupation of the country by the white man. These natural causes have conspired to decimate the race even more than the advance of civilization, which seems not to affect it to any material extent. In its maintenance of the same number of representatives during three centuries, and its existence in the very face of a most unceremonious, and, whenever necessary, cruel conquest, the grand dispensations of the unseen Ruler of the universe is demonstrated; for, without the aborigines, savage and treacherous as they were, it is possible that the explorers of former times would have so many natural difficulties to contend with, that their work would be surrendered in despair, and the most fertile regions of the continent saved for the plowshares of generations yet unborn. It is questionable whether we owe the discovery of this continent to the unaided scientific knowledge of Columbus, or to the dead bodies of the two Indians referred to above; nor can their services to the explorers of ancient and modern times be over-estimated. Their existence is embraced in the plan of the Divinity for the government of the world, and it will not form subject for surprise to learn that the same intelligence which sent a thrill of liberty into every corner of the republic, will, in the near future, devise some method under which the remnant of a great and ancient race may taste the sweets of public kindness, and feel that, after centuries of turmoil and tyranny, they have at last found a shelter amid a sympathizing people. Many have looked at the Indian as the pessimist does at all things; they say that he was never formidable until the white man supplied him with the weapons of modern warfare; but there is no mention made of his eviction from his retired home, and the little plot of cultivated garden which formed the nucleus of a village that, if fostered instead of being destroyed, might possibly hold an Indian population of some importance in the economy of the nation. There is no intention whatever to maintain that the occupation of this country by the favored races is wrong even in principle; for where any obstacle to advancing civilization exists, it has to fall to the ground; but it may be said, with some truth, that the white man, instead of a policy of conciliation formed upon the power of kindness, indulged in belligerency as impolitic as it was unjust. A modern writer says, when speaking of the Indian's character: "He did not exhibit that steady valor and efficient discipline of the American soldier; and to-day on the plains Sheridan's troopers would not hesitate to attack the bravest band, though outnumbered three to one." This piece of information applies to the European and African, as well as to the Indian. The American soldier, and particularly the troopers referred to, would not fear or shrink from a very legion of demons, even with odds against them. This mode of warfare seems strangely peculiar when compared with the military systems of civilized countries; yet, since the main object of armed men is to defend a country or a principle, and to destroy anything which may oppose itself to them, the mode of warfare pursued by the savage will be found admirably adapted to their requirements in this connection, and will doubtless compare favorably with the systems of the Afghans and Persians of the present, and the Caucasian people of the first historic period.

MANNERS AND CUSTOMS.

The art of hunting not only supplied the Indian with food, but, like that of war, was a means of gratifying his love of distinction. The male children, as soon as they acquired sufficient age and strength, were furnished with a bow and arrow and taught to shoot birds and other small game. Success in killing a large quadruped required years of careful study and practice, and the art was as sedulously inculcated in the minds of the rising generation as are the elements of reading, writing and arithmetic in the common schools of civilized communities. The mazes of the forest and the dense, tall grass of the prairies were the best fields for the exercise of the hunter's skill. No feet could be impressed in the yielding soil but that the tracks were the objects of the most searching scrutiny, and revealed at a glance the animal that made them, the direction it was pursuing, and the time that had elapsed since it had passed. In a forest country he selected the valleys, because they were most frequently the resort of game. The most easily taken, perhaps, of all the animals of the chase was the deer. It is endowed with a curiosity which prompts it to stop in its flight and look back at the approaching hunter, who always avails himself of this opportunity to let fly the fatal arrow. 1261213

Their general councils were composed of the chiefs and old men. When in council, they usually sat in concentric circles around the speaker, and each individual, notwithstanding the fiery passions that rankled within, preserved an exterior as immovable as if cast in bronze. Before commencing business a person appeared with the sacred pipe, and another with fire to kindle it. After being lighted it was first presented to heaven, secondly to the earth, thirdly to the presiding spirit, and lastly the several councilors, each of whom took a whiff. These formalities were observed with as close exactness as state etiquette in civilized courts.

The dwellings of the Indians were of the simplest and rudest character. On some pleasant spot by the bank of a river, or near an ever-running spring, they raised their groups of wigwams, constructed of the bark of trees, and easily taken down and removed to another spot. The dwelling-places of the chiefs were sometimes more spacious, and constructed with greater care, but of the same materials. Skins taken in the chase served them for repose. Though principally dependent upon hunting and fishing, the uncertain supply from those sources led them to cultivate small patches of corn. Every family did everything necessary within itself, commerce, or an interchange of articles, being almost unknown to them. In cases of dispute and dissension, each Indian relied upon himself for retaliation. Blood for blood was the rule, and the relatives of the slain man were bound to obtain bloody revenge for his death. This principle gave rise, as a matter of course, to innumerable and bitter feuds, and wars of extermination where such were possible. War, indeed, rather than peace, was the Indian's glory and delight,—war, not conducted as civilization, but war where individual skill, endurance, gallantry and cruelty were prime requisites. For such a purpose as revenge the Indian would make great sacrifices, and display a patience and perseverance truly heroic; but when the excitement was over, he sank back into a listless, unoccupied, well-nigh useless savage. During the intervals of his more exciting pursuits, the Indian employed his time in decorating his person with all the refinement of paint and feathers, and in the manufacture of his arms and of canoes. These were constructed of bark, and so light that they could easily be carried on the shoulder from stream to stream. His amusements were the war-dance, athletic games, the narration of his exploits, and listening to the oratory of the chiefs; but during long periods of such existence he remained in a state of torpor, gazing listlessly upon the trees of the forests and the clouds that sailed above them; and this vacancy imprinted an habitual gravity, and even melancholy, upon his general deportment.

The main labor and drudgery of Indian communities fell upon the women. The planting, tending and gathering of the crops, making mats and baskets, carrying burdens,—in fact, all things of the kind were performed by them, thus making their condition but little better than that of slaves. Marriage was merely a matter of bargain and sale, the husband giving presents to the father of the bride. In general they had but few children. They were subjected to many and severe attacks of sickness, and at times famine and pestilence swept away whole tribes.

EXPLORATIONS BY THE WHITES.

The State of Indiana is bounded on the east by the meridian line which forms also the western boundary of Ohio, extending due north from the mouth of the Great Miami river; on the south by the Ohio river from the mouth of the Great Miami to the mouth of the Wabash; on the west by a line drawn along the middle of the Wabash river from its mouth to a point where a due north line from the town of Vincennes would last touch the shore of said river, and thence directly north to Lake Michigan; and on the north by said lake and an east and west line ten miles north of the extreme south end of the lake, and extending to its intersection with the aforesaid meridian, the west boundary of Ohio. These boundaries include an area of 33,809 square miles, lying between 37° 47' and 41° 50' north latitude, and between 7° 45' and 11° 1' west longitude from Washington.

After the discovery of America by Columbus in 1492, more than 150 years passed away before any portion of the territory now comprised within the above limits was explored by Europeans. Colonies were established in Florida, Virginia and Nova Scotia by the principal rival governments of Europe, but not until about 1670–'2 did the first white travelers venture as far into the Northwest as Indiana or Lake Michigan. These explorers were Frenchmen by the names of Claude Allouez and Claude Dablon, who then visited what is now the eastern part of Wisconsin, the northeastern portion of Illinois and probably that portion of this State north of the Kankakee river. In the following year M. Joliet, an agent of the French Colonial government, and James Marquette, a good and simple-hearted missionary who had his station at Mackinaw, explored the country about Green Bay, and along Fox and Wisconsin rivers as far westward as the Mississippi, the banks of which they reached June 17, 1673. They descended this river to about 33° 40', but returned by way of the Illinois river and the route they came in the Lake Region. At a village among the Illinois Indians, Marquette and his small band of adventurers were received in a friendly manner and treated hospitably. They were made the honored guests at a great feast, where hominy, fish, dog meat and roast buffalo meat were spread before them in great abundance. In 1682 LaSalle explored the West, but it is not known that he entered the region now embraced within the State of Indiana. He took formal possession, however, of all the Mississippi region in the name of the King of France, in whose honor he gave all this Mississippi region, including what is now Indiana, the name "Louisiana." Spain at the same time laid claim to all the region about the Gulf of Mexico, and thus these two great nations were brought into collision. But the country was actually held and occupied by the great Miami confederacy of Indians, the Miamis proper (anciently the Twightwees) being the eastern and most powerful tribe. Their territory extended strictly from the Scioto river west to the Illinois river. Their villages were few and scattering, and their occupation was scarcely dense enough to maintain itself against invasion. Their settlements were occasionally visited by Christian missionaries, fur traders and adventurers, but no body of white men made any settlement sufficiently permanent for a title to national possession. Christian zeal animated France and England in missionary enterprise, the former in the interests of Catholicism and the latter in the interests of Protestantism. Hence their haste to preoccupy the land and proselyte the aborigines. No doubt this ugly rivalry was often seen by Indians, and they refused to be proselyted to either branch of Christianity.

The "Five Nations," farther east, comprised the Mohawks, Oneidas, Cayugas, Onondaguas and Senecas. In 1677 the number of warriors in this confederacy was 2,150. About 1711 the Tuscaroras retired from Carolina and joined the Iroquois, or Five Nations, which, after that event, became known as the "Six Nations." In 1689 hostilities broke out between the Five Nations and the colonists of Canada, and the almost constant wars in which France was engaged until the treaty of Ryswick in 1697 combined to check the grasping policy of Louis XIV., and to retard the planting of French colonies in the Mississippi valley. Missionary efforts, however, continued with more failure than success, the Jesuits allying themselves with the Indians in habits and customs, even encouraging inter-marriage between them and their white followers.

OUABACHE.

The Wabash was first named by the French, and spelled by them Ouabache. This river was known even before the Ohio, and was navigated as the Ouabache all the way to the Mississippi a long time before it was discovered that it was a tributary of the Ohio (Belle Riviere). In navigating the Mississippi they thought they passed the mouth of the Ouabache instead of the Ohio. In traveling from the Great Lakes to the south, the French always went by the way of the Ouabache or Illinois.

VINCENNES.

Francois Morgan de Vinsenne served in Canada as early as 1720 in the regiment of "De Carrignan" of the French service, and again on the lakes in the vicinity of Sault Ste. Marie in the same service under M. de Vaudriel, in 1725. It is possible that his advent to Vincennes may have taken place in 1732; and in proof of this the only record is an act of sale under the joint names of himself and Madame Vinsenne, the daughter of M. Philip Longprie, and dated Jan. 5, 1735. This document gives his military position as commandant of the post of Ouabache in the service of the French King. The will of Longprie, dated March 10, same year, bequeaths him, among other things, 408 pounds of pork, which he ordered to be kept safe until Vinsenne, who was then at Ouabache, returned to Kaskaskia.

There are many other documents connected with its early settlement by Vinsenne, among which is a receipt for the 100 pistoles granted him as his wife's marriage dowry. In 1736 this officer was ordered to Charlevoix by D'Artagette, viceroy of the King at New Orleans, and commandant of Illinois. Here M. St. Vinsenne received his mortal wounds. The event is chronicled as follows, in the words of D'Artagette: "We have just received very bad news from Louisiana, and our war with the Chickasaws. The French have been defeated. Among the slain is M. de Vinsenne, who ceased not until his last breath to exhort his men to behave worthy of their faith and fatherland."

Thus closed the career of this gallant officer, leaving a name which holds as a remembrance the present beautiful town of Vincennes, changed from Vinsenne to its present orthography in 1749.

Post Vincennes was settled as early as 1710 or 1711. In a letter from Father Marest to Father Germon, dated at Kaskaskia, Nov. 9, 1712, occurs this passage: *"Les Francois itoient itabli un fort sur le fleuve Ouabache ; ils demanderent un missionaire ; et le Pere Mermet leur fut envoye. Ce l'ere crut devoir travailler a la conversion des Mascoutens qui avoient fait un village sur les bords dumeme fleuve. C'est une nation Indians qui entend la langue Illinoise.*" Translated: "The French have established a fort upon the river Wabash, and want a missionary; and Father Mermet has been sent to them. That Father believes he should labor for the conversion of the Mascoutens, who have built a village on the banks of the same river. They are a nation of Indians who understand the language of the Illinois."

Mermet was therefore the first preacher of Christianity in this part of the world, and his mission was to convert the Mascoutens, a branch of the Miamis. "The way I took," says he, "was to confound, in the presence of the whole tribe, one of these charlatans [medicine men], whose Manitou, or great spirit which he worshiped, was the buffalo. After leading him on insensibly to the avowal that it was not the buffalo that he worshiped, but the Manitou, or spirit, of the buffalo, which was under the earth and animated all buffaloes, which heals the sick and has all power, I asked him whether other beasts, the bear for instance, and which one of his nation worshiped, was not equally inhabited by a Manitou, which was under the earth. 'Without doubt,' said the grand medicine man. 'If this is so,' said I, 'men ought to have a Manitou who inhabits them.' 'Nothing more certain,' said he. 'Ought not that to convince you,' continued I, 'that you are not very reasonable? For if man upon the earth is the master of all animals, if he kills them, if he eats them, does it not follow that the Manitou which inhabits him must have a mastery over all other Manitous? Why then do you not invoke him instead of the Manitou of the bear and the buffalo, when you are sick?' This reasoning disconcerted the charlatan. But this was all the effect it produced."

The result of convincing these heathen by logic, as is generally the case the world over, was only a temporary logical victory, and no change whatever was produced in the professions and practices of the Indians.

But the first Christian (Catholic) missionary at this place whose name we find recorded in the Church annals, was Meurin, in 1849.

The church building used by these early missionaries at Vincennes is thus described by the "oldest inhabitants:" Fronting on Water street and running back on Church street, it was a plain building with a rough exterior, of upright posts, chinked and daubed, with a rough coat of cement on the outside; about 20 feet wide and 60 long; one story high, with a small belfry and an equally small bell. It was dedicated to St. Francis Xavier. This spot is now occupied by a splendid cathedral.

Vincennes has ever been a stronghold of Catholicism. The Church there has educated and sent out many clergymen of her faith, some of whom have become bishops, or attained other high positions in ecclesiastical authority.

Almost contemporaneous with the progress of the Church at Vincennes was a missionary work near the mouth of the Wea river, among the Ouiatenons, but the settlement there was broken up in early day.

NATIONAL POLICIES.

THE GREAT FRENCH SCHEME.

Soon after the discovery of the mouth of the Mississippi by La-Salle in 1682, the government of France began to encourage the policy of establishing a line of trading posts and missionary stations extending through the West from Canada to Louisiana, and this policy was maintained, with partial success, for about 75 years. The traders persisted in importing whisky, which cancelled nearly every civilizing influence that could be brought to bear upon the Indian, and the vast distances between posts prevented that strength which can be enjoyed only by close and convenient inter-communication. Another characteristic of Indian nature was to listen attentively to all the missionary said, pretending to believe all he preached, and then offer in turn his theory of the world, of religion, etc., and because he was not listened to with the same degree of attention and pretense of belief, would go off disgusted. This was his idea of the golden rule.

The river St. Joseph of Lake Michigan was called "the river Miamis" in 1679, in which year LaSalle built a small fort on its bank, near the lake shore. The principal station of the mission for the instruction of the Miamis was established on the borders of this river. The first French post within the territory of the Miamis was at the mouth of the river Miamis, on an eminence naturally fortified on two sides by the river, and on one side by a deep ditch made by a fall of water. It was of triangular form. The missionary Hennepin gives a good description of it, as he was one of the company who built it, in 1679. Says he: "We fell the trees that were on the top of the hill; and having cleared the same from bushes for about two musket shot, we began to build a redoubt of 80 feet long and 40 feet broad, with great square pieces of timber laid one upon another, and prepared a great number of stakes of about 25 feet long to drive into the ground, to make our fort more inaccessible on the river side. We employed the whole month of November about that work, which was very hard, though we had no other food but the bear's flesh our savage killed. These beasts are very common in that place because of the great quantity of grapes they find there; but their flesh being too fat and luscious, our men began to be weary of it and desired leave to go a hunting to kill some wild goats. M. LaSalle denied them that liberty, which caused some murmurs among them; and it was but unwillingly that they continued their work. This, together with the approach of winter and the apprehension that M. LaSalle had that his vessel (the Griffin) was lost, made him very melancholy, though he concealed it as much as he could. We made a cabin wherein we performed divine service every Sunday, and Father Gabriel and I, who preached alternately, took care to take such texts as were suitable to our present circumstances and fit to inspire us with courage, concord and brotherly love. * * * The fort was at last perfected, and called Fort Miamis."

In the year 1711 the missionary Chardon, who was said to be very zealous and apt in the acquisition of languages, had a station on the St. Joseph about 60 miles above the mouth. Charlevoix, another distinguished missionary from France, visited a post on this river in 1721. In a letter dated at the place, Aug. 16, he says: "There is a commandant here, with a small garrison. His house, which is but a very sorry one, is called the fort, from its being surrounded with an indifferent palisado, which is pretty near the case in all the rest. We have here two villages of Indians, one of the Miamis and the other of the Pottawatomies, both of them mostly Christians; but as they have been for a long time without any pastors, the missionary who has been lately sent to them will have no small difficulty in bringing them back to the exercise of their religion." He speaks also of the main commodity for which the Indians would part with their goods, namely, spirituous liquors, which they drink and keep drunk upon as long as a supply lasted.

More than a century and a half has now passed since Charlevoix penned the above, without any change whatever in this trait of Indian character.

In 1765 the Miami nation, or confederacy, was composed of four tribes, whose total number of warriors was estimated at only 1,050 men. Of these about 250 were Twightwees, or Miamis proper, 300 Weas, or Ouiatenons, 300 Piankeshaws and 200 Shockeys; and at this time the principal villages of the Twightwees were situated about the head of the Maumee river at and near the place where Fort Wayne now is. The larger Wea villages were near the banks of the Wabash river, in the vicinity of the Post Ouiatenon; and the Shockeys and Piankeshaws dwelt on the banks of the Vermillion and on the borders of the Wabash between Vincennes and Ouiatenon. Branches of the Pottawatomie, Shawnee, Delaware and Kickapoo tribes were permitted at different times to enter within the boundaries of the Miamis and reside for a while.

The wars in which France and England were engaged, from 1688 to 1697, retarded the growth of the colonies of those nations in North America, and the efforts made by France to connect Canada and the Gulf of Mexico by a chain of trading posts and colonies naturally excited the jealousy of England and gradually laid the foundation for a struggle at arms. After several stations were established elsewhere in the West, trading posts were started at the Miami villages, which stood at the head of the Maumee, at the Wea villages about Ouiatenon on the Wabash, and at the Piankeshaw villages about the present sight of Vincennes. It is probable that before the close of the year 1719, temporary trading posts were erected at the sites of Fort Wayne, Ouiatenon and Vincennes. These points were probably often visited by French fur traders prior to 1700. In the meanwhile the English people in this country commenced also to establish military posts west of the Alleghanies, and thus matters went on until they naturally culminated in a general war, which, being waged by the French and Indians combined on one side, was called "the French and Indian war." This war was terminated in 1763 by a treaty at Paris, by which France ceded to Great Britain all of North America east of the Mississippi except New Orleans and the island on which it is situated; and indeed, France had the preceding autumn, by a secret convention, ceded to Spain all the country west of that river.

PONTIAC'S WAR.

In 1762, after Canada and its dependencies had been surrendered to the English, Pontiac and his partisans secretly organized a powerful confederacy in order to crush at one blow all English power in the West. This great scheme was skillfully projected and cautiously matured.

The principal act in the programme was to gain admittance into the fort at Detroit, on pretense of a friendly visit, with shortened muskets concealed under their blankets, and on a given signal suddenly break forth upon the garrison; but an inadvertent remark of an Indian woman led to a discovery of the plot, which was consequently averted. Pontiac and his warriors afterward made many attacks upon the English, some of which were successful, but the Indians were finally defeated in the general war.

BRITISH POLICY.

In 1765 the total number of French families within the limits of the Northwestern Territory did not probably exceed 600. These were in settlements about Detroit, along the river Wabash and the neighborhood of Fort Chartres on the Mississippi. Of these families, about 80 or 90 resided at Post Vincennes, 14 at Fort Ouiatenon, on the Wabash, and nine or ten at the confluence of the St. Mary and St. Joseph rivers.

The colonial policy of the British government opposed any measures which might strengthen settlements in the interior of this country, lest they become self-supporting and independent of the mother country; hence the early and rapid settlement of the Northwestern territory was still further retarded by the short-sighted selfishness of England. That fatal policy consisted mainly in holding the land in the hands of the government and not allowing it to be subdivided and sold to settlers. But in spite of all her efforts in this direction, she constantly made just such efforts as provoked the American people to rebel, and to rebel successfully, which was within 15 years after the perfect close of the French and Indian war.

AMERICAN POLICY.

Thomas Jefferson, the shrewd statesman and wise Governor of Virginia, saw from the first that actual occupation of Western lands was the only way to keep them out of the hands of foreigners and

Indians. Therefore, directly after the conquest of Vincennes by Clark, he engaged a scientific corps to proceed under an escort to the Mississippi, and ascertain by celestial observations the point on that river intersected by latitude 36° 30', the southern limit of the State, and to measure its distance to the Ohio. To Gen. Clark was entrusted the conduct of the military operations in that quarter. He was instructed to select a strong position near that point and establish there a fort and garrison; thence to extend his conquests northward to the lakes, erecting forts at different points, which might serve as monuments of actual possession, besides affording protection to that portion of the country. Fort "Jefferson" was erected and garrisoned on the Mississippi a few miles above the southern limit.

The result of these operations was the addition, to the chartered limits of Virginia, of that immense region known as the "Northwestern Territory." The simple fact that such and such forts were established by the Americans in this vast region convinced the British Commissioners that we had entitled ourselves to the land. But where are those "monuments" of our power now?

INDIAN SAVAGERY.

As a striking example of the inhuman treatment which the early Indians were capable of giving white people, we quote the following blood-curdling story from Mr. Cox' "Recollections of the Wabash Valley":

On the 11th of February, 1781, a wagoner named Irvin Hinton was sent from the block-house at Louisville, Ky., to Harrodsburg for a load of provisions for the fort. Two young men, Richard Rue and George Holman, aged respectively 19 and 16 years, were sent as guards to protect the wagon from the depredations of any hostile Indians who might be lurking in the cane-brakes or ravines through which they must pass. Soon after their start a severe snow-storm set in which lasted until afternoon. Lest the melting snow might dampen the powder in their rifles, the guards fired them off, intending to reload them as soon as the storm ceased. Hinton drove the horses while Rue walked a few rods ahead and Holman about the same distance behind. As they ascended a hill about eight miles from Louisville Hinton heard some one say Whoa to the horses. Supposing that something was wrong about the wagon, he stopped and asked Holman why he had called him to halt. Holman said that he had not spoken; Rue also denied it,

but said that he had heard the voice distinctly. At this time a voice
cried out, " I will solve the mystery for you; it was Simon Girty that
cried Whoa, and he meant what he said,"—at the same time emerg-
ing from a sink-hole a few rods from the roadside, followed by 13
Indians, who immediately surrounded the three Kentuckians and
demanded them to surrender or die instantly. The little party,
making a virtue of necessity, surrendered to this renegade white
man and his Indian allies.

Being so near two forts, Girty made all possible speed in making
fast his prisoners, selecting the lines and other parts of the harness,
he prepared for an immediate flight across the Ohio. The pantaloons of the prisoners were cut off about four inches above the
knees, and thus they started through the deep snow as fast as the
horses could trot, leaving the wagon, containing a few empty barrels, standing in the road. They continued their march for several cold days, without fire at night, until they reached Wa-puc-ca-
nat-ta, where they compelled their prisoners to run the gauntlet as
they entered the village. Hinton first ran the gauntlet and reached
the council-house after receiving several severe blows upon the head
and shoulders. Rue next ran between the lines, pursued by an
Indian with an uplifted tomahawk. He far outstripped his pursuer
and dodged most of the blows aimed at him. Holman complaining
that it was too severe a test for a worn-out stripling like himself,
was allowed to run between two lines of squaws and boys, and was
followed by an Indian with a long switch.

The first council of the Indians did not dispose of these young
men; they were waiting for the presence of other chiefs and warriors. Hinton escaped, but on the afternoon of the second day he
was re-captured. Now the Indians were glad that they had an
occasion to indulge in the infernal joy of burning him at once.
Soon after their supper, which they shared with their victim, they
drove the stake into the ground, piled up the fagots in a circle
around it, stripped and blackened the prisoner, tied him to the
stake, and applied the torch. It was a slow fire. The war-whoop
then thrilled through the dark surrounding forest like the chorus
of a band of infernal spirits escaped from pandemonium, and the
scalp dance was struck up by those demons in human shape, who
for hours encircled their victim, brandishing their tomahawks and
war clubs, and venting their execrations upon the helpless sufferer,
who died about midnight from the effects of the slow heat. As
soon as he fell upon the ground, the Indian who first discovered

him in the woods that evening sprang in, sunk his tomahawk into his skull above the ear, and with his knife stripped off the scalp, which he bore back with him to the town as a trophy, and which was tauntingly thrust into the faces of Rue and Holman, with the question, " Can you smell the fire on the scalp of your red-headed friend? We cooked him and left him for the wolves to make a breakfast upon; that is the way we serve runaway prisoners."

After a march of three days more, the prisoners, Rue and Holman, had to run the gauntlets again, and barely got through with their lives. It was decided that they should both be burned at the stake that night, though this decision was far from being unanimous. The necessary preparations were made, dry sticks and brush were gathered and piled around two stakes, the faces and hands of the doomed men were blackened in the customary manner, and as the evening approached the poor wretches sat looking upon the setting sun for the last time. An unusual excitement was manifest in a number of chiefs who still lingered about the council-house. At a pause in the contention, a noble-looking Indian approached the prisoners, and after speaking a few words to the guards, took Holman by the hand, lifted him to his feet, cut the cords that bound him to his fellow prisoners, removed the black from his face and hands, put his hand kindly upon his head and said: " I adopt you as my son, to fill the place of the one I have lately buried; you are now a kinsman of Logan, the white man's friend, as he has been called, but who has lately proven himself to be a terrible avenger of the wrongs inflicted upon him by the bloody Cresap and his men." With evident reluctance, Girty interpreted this to Holman, who was thus unexpectedly freed.

But the preparations for the burning of Rue went on. Holman and Rue embraced each other most affectionately, with a sorrow too deep for description. Rue was then tied to one of the stakes; but the general contention among the Indians had not ceased. Just as the lighted fagots were about to be applied to the dry brush piled around the devoted youth, a tall, active young Shawnee, a son of the victim's captor, sprang into the ring, and cutting the cords which bound him to the stake, led him out amidst the deafening plaudits of a part of the crowd and the execrations of the rest. Regardless of threats, he caused water to be brought and the black to be washed from the face and hands of the prisoner, whose clothes were then returned to him, when the young brave said: " I take this young man to be my brother, in the place of one I lately lost;

I loved that brother well; I will love this one, too; my old mother will be glad when I tell her that I have brought her a son, in place of the dear departed one. We want no more victims. The burning of Red-head [Hinton] ought to satisfy us. These innocent young men do not merit such cruel fate; I would rather die myself than see this adopted brother burned at the stake."

A loud shout of approbation showed that the young Shawnee had triumphed, though dissension was manifest among the various tribes afterward. Some of them abandoned their trip to Detroit, others returded to Wa-puc-ca-nat-ta, a few turned toward the Mississinewa and the Wabash towns, while a portion continued to Detroit. Holman was taken back to Wa-puc-ca-nat ta, where he remained most of the time of his captivity. Rue was taken first to the Mississinewa, then to the Wabash towns. Two years of his eventful captivity were spent in the region of the Wabash and Illinois rivers, but the last few months at Detroit; was in captivity altogether about three years and a half.

Rue effected his escape in the following manner: During one of the drunken revels of the Indians near Detroit one of them lost a purse of $90; various tribes were suspected of feloniously keeping the treasure, and much ugly speculation was indulged in as to who was the thief. At length a prophet of a tribe that was not suspected was called to divine the mystery. He spread sand over a green deer-skin, watched it awhile and performed various manipulations, and professed to see that the money had been stolen and carried away by a tribe entirely different from any that had been suspicioned; but he was shrewd enough not to announce who the thief was or the tribe he belonged to, lest a war might arise. His decision quieted the belligerent uprisings threatened by the excited Indians.

Rue and two other prisoners saw this display of the prophet's skill and concluded to interrogate him soon concerning their families at home. The opportunity occurred in a few days, and the Indian seer actually astonished Rue with the accuracy with which he described his family, and added, "You all intend to make your escape, and you will effect it soon. You will meet with many trials and hardships in passing over so wild a district of country, inhabited by so many hostile nations of Indians. You will almost starve to death; but about the time you have given up all hope of finding game to sustain you in your famished condition, succor will come when you least expect it. The first game you will succeed in taking

will be a male of some kind; after that you will have plenty of
game and return home in safety."

The prophet kept this matter a secret for the prisoners, and the
latter in a few days set off upon their terrible journey, and had
just such experience as the Indian prophet had foretold; they
arrived home with their lives, but were pretty well worn out with the
exposures and privations of a three weeks' journey.

On the return of Holman's party of Indians to Wa-puc-ca-nat-ta,
much dissatisfaction existed in regard to the manner of his release
from the sentence of condemnation pronounced against him by the
council. Many were in favor of recalling the council and trying
him again, and this was finally agreed to. The young man was
again put upon trial for his life, with a strong probability of his
being condemned to the stake. Both parties worked hard for victory in the final vote, which eventually proved to give a majority of
one for the prisoner's acquittal.

While with the Indians, Holman saw them burn at the stake a
Kentuckian named Richard Hogeland, who had been taken prisoner
at the defeat of Col. Crawford. They commenced burning him at
nine o'clock at night, and continued roasting him until ten o'clock
the next day, before he expired. During his excruciating tortures he
begged for some of them to end his life and sufferings with a gun
or tomahawk. Finally his cruel tormentors promised they would,
and cut several deep gashes in his flesh with their tomahawks, and
shoveled up hot ashes and embers and threw them into the gaping
wounds. When he was dead they stripped off his scalp, cut him
to pieces and burnt him to ashes, which they scattered through the
town to expel the evil spirits from it.

After a captivity of about three years and a half, Holman saw an
opportunity of going on a mission for the destitute Indians, namely,
of going to Harrodsburg, Ky., where he had a rich uncle, from
whom they could get what supplies they wanted. They let him go
with a guard, but on arriving at Louisville, where Gen. Clark was
in command, he was ransomed, and he reached home only three
days after the arrival of Rue. Both these men lived to a good old
age, terminating their lives at their home about two miles south of
Richmond, Ind.

EXPEDITIONS OF COL. GEORGE ROGERS CLARK.

In the summer of 1778, Col. George Rogers Clark, a native of Albemarle county, Va., led a memorable expedition against the ancient French settlements about Kaskaskia and Post Vincennes. With respect to the magnitude of its design, the valor and perseverance with which it was carried on, and the memorable results which were produced by it, this expedition stands without a parallel in the early annals of the valley of the Mississippi. That portion of the West called Kentucky was occupied by Henderson & Co., who pretended to own the land and who held it at a high price. Col. Clark wished to test the validity of their claim and adjust the government of the country so as to encourage immigration. He accordingly called a meeting of the citizens at Harrodstown, to assemble June 6, 1776, and consider the claims of the company and consult with reference to the interest of the country. He did not at first publish the exact aim of this movement, lest parties would be formed in advance and block the enterprise; also, if the object of the meeting were not announced beforehand, the curiosity of the people to know what was to be proposed would bring out a much greater attendance.

The meeting was held on the day appointed, and delegates were elected to treat with the government of Virginia, to see whether it would be best to become a county in that State and be protected by it, etc. Various delays on account of the remoteness of the white settlers from the older communities of Virginia and the hostility of Indians in every direction, prevented a consummation of this object until some time in 1778. The government of Virginia was friendly to Clark's enterprise to a certain extent, but claimed that they had not authority to do much more than to lend a little assistance for which payment should be made at some future time, as it was not certain whether Kentucky would become a part of Virginia or not. Gov. Henry and a few gentlemen were individually so hearty in favor of Clark's benevolent undertaking that they assisted him all they could. Accordingly Mr. Clark organized his expedition, keeping every particular secret lest powerful parties would form in the West against him. He took in stores at Pitts-

burg and Wheeling, proceeded down the Ohio to the "Falls," where he took possession of an island of a about seven acres, and divided it among a small number of families, for whose protection he constructed some light fortifications. At this time Post Vincennes comprised about 400 militia, and it was a daring undertaking for Col. Clark, with his small force, to go up against it and Kaskaskia, as he had planned. Indeed, some of his men, on hearing of his plan, deserted him. He conducted himself so as to gain the sympathy of the French, and through them also that of the Indians to some extent, as both these people were very bitter against the British, who had possession of the Lake Region.

From the nature of the situation Clark concluded it was best to take Kaskaskia first. The fact that the people regarded him as a savage rebel, he regarded as really a good thing in his favor; for after the first victory he would show them so much unexpected lenity that they would rally to his standard. In this policy he was indeed successful. He arrested a few men and put them in irons. The priest of the village, accompanied by five or six aged citizens, waited on Clark and said that the inhabitants expected to be separated, perhaps never to meet again, and they begged to be permitted to assemble in their church to take leave of each other. Clark mildly replied that he had nothing against their religion, that they might continue to assemble in their church, but not venture out of town, etc. Thus, by what has since been termed the "Rarey" method of taming horses, Clark showed them he had power over them but designed them no harm, and they readily took the oath of allegiance to Virginia.

After Clark's arrival at Kaskaskia it was difficult to induce the French settlers to accept the "Continental paper" introduced by him and his troops. Nor until Col. Vigo arrived there and guaranteed its redemption would they receive it. Peltries and piastres formed the only currency, and Vigo found great difficulty in explaining Clark's financial arrangements. "Their commandants never made money," was the reply to Vigo's explanation of the policy of the old Dominion. But notwithstanding the guarantees, the Continental paper fell very low in the market. Vigo had a trading establishment at Kaskaskia, where he sold coffee at one dollar a pound, and all the other necessaries of life at an equally reasonable price. The unsophisticated Frenchmen were generally asked in what kind of money they would pay their little bills.

"Douleur," was the general reply; and as an authority on the subject says, "It took about twenty Continental dollars to purchase a
silver dollar's worth of coffee; and as the French word "douleur" sig-
nifies grief or pain, perhaps no word either in the French or English languages expressed the idea more correctly than the *douleur*
for a Continental dollar. At any rate it was truly *douleur* to the
Colonel, for he never received a single dollar in exchange for the
large amount taken from him in order to sustain Clark's credit.

Now, the post at Vincennes, defended by Fort Sackville, came
next. The priest just mentioned, Mr. Gibault, was really friendly
to "the American interest;" he had spiritual charge of the church
at Vincennes, and he with several others were deputed to assemble
the people there and authorize them to garrison their own fort like
a free and independent people, etc. This plan had its desired effect,
and the people took the oath of allegiance to the State of Virginia
and became citizens of the United States. Their style of language
and conduct changed to a better hue, and they surprised the numerous Indians in the vicinity by displaying a new flag and informing
them that their old father, the King of France, was come to life
again, and was mad at them for fighting the English; and they ad-
vised them to make peace with the Americans as soon as they
could, otherwise they might expect to make the land very bloody,
etc. The Indians concluded they would have to fall in line, and
they offered no resistance. Capt. Leonard Helm, an American,
was left in charge of this post, and Clark began to turn his attention to other points. But before leaving this section of the country he made treaties of peace with the Indians; this he did, however, by a different method from what had always before been
followed. By indirect methods he caused them to come to him,
instead of going to them. He was convinced that inviting them to
treaties was considered by them in a different manner from what
the whites expected, and imputed them to fear, and that giving
them great presents confirmed it. He accordingly established
treaties with the Piankeshaws, Ouiatenons, Kickapoos, Illinois,
Kaskaskias, Peorias and branches of some other tribes that inhabited the country between Lake Michigan and the Mississippi.
Upon this the General Assembly of the State of Virginia declared
all the citizens settled west of the Ohio organized into a county of
that State, to be known as "Illinois" county; but before the provisions of the law could be carried into effect, Henry Hamilton, the
British Lieutenant-Governor of Detroit, collected an army of about

30 regulars, 50 French volunteers and 400 Indians, went down and re-took the post Vincennes in December, 1778. No attempt was made by the population to defend the town. Capt. Helm and a man named Henry were the only Americans at the fort, the only members of the garrison. Capt. Helm was taken prisoner and a number of the French inhabitants disarmed.

Col. Clark, hearing of the situation, determined to re-capture the place. He accordingly gathered together what force he could in this distant land, 170 men, and on the 5th of February, started from Kaskaskia and crossed the river of that name. The weather was very wet, and the low lands were pretty well covered with water. The march was difficult, and the Colonel had to work hard to keep his men in spirits. He suffered them to shoot game whenever they wished and eat it like Indian war-dancers, each company by turns inviting the others to their feasts, which was the case every night. Clark waded through water as much as any of them, and thus stimulated the men by his example. They reached the Little Wabash on the 13th, after suffering many and great hardships. Here a camp was formed, and without waiting to discuss plans for crossing the river, Clark ordered the men to construct a vessel, and pretended that crossing the stream would be only a piece of amusement, although inwardly he held a different opinion.

The second day afterward a reconnoitering party was sent across the river, who returned and made an encouraging report. A scaffolding was built on the opposite shore, upon which the baggage was placed as it was tediously ferried over, and the new camping ground was a nice half acre of dry land. There were many amusements, indeed, in getting across the river, which put all the men in high spirits. The succeeding two or three days they had to march through a great deal of water, having on the night of the 17th to encamp in the water, near the Big Wabash.

At daybreak on the 18th they heard the signal gun at Vincennes, and at once commenced their march. Reaching the Wabash about two o'clock, they constructed rafts to cross the river on a boat-stealing expedition, but labored all day and night to no purpose. On the 19th they began to make a canoe, in which a second attempt to steal boats was made, but this expedition returned, reporting that there were two "large fires" within a mile of them. Clark sent a canoe down the river to meet the vessel that was supposed to be on her way up with the supplies, with orders to hasten forward day and night. This was their last hope, as their provisions were entirely gone, and starvation seemed to be hovering about them. The next day they commenced to make more canoes, when about noon the sentinel on the river brought a boat with five Frenchmen from the fort. From this party they learned that they were not as yet discovered. All the army crossed the river in two canoes the next day, and as Clark had determined to reach the town that night, he ordered his men to move forward. They plunged into the water sometimes to the neck, for over three miles.

Without food, benumbed with cold, up to their waists in water, covered with broken ice, the men at one time mutinied and refused to march. All the persuasions of Clark had no effect upon the half-starved and half-frozen soldiers. In one company was a small drummer boy, and also a sergeant who stood six feet two inches in socks, and stout and athletic. He was devoted to Clark. The General mounted the little drummer on the shoulders of the stalwart sergeant and ordered him to plunge into the water, half-frozen as it was. He did so, the little boy beating the charge from his lofty perch, while Clark, sword in hand, followed them, giving the command as he threw aside the floating ice, "Forward." Elated and amused with the scene, the men promptly obeyed, holding their rifles above their heads, and in spite of all the obstacles they reached the high land in perfect safety. But for this and the ensuing days of this campaign we quote from Clark's account:

"This last day's march through the water was far superior to anything the Frenchmen had any idea of. They were backward in speaking; said that the nearest land to us was a small league, a sugar camp on the bank of the river. A canoe was sent off and returned without finding that we could pass. I went in her myself and sounded the water and found it as deep as to my neck. I returned with a design to have the men transported on board the canoes to the sugar camp, which I knew would expend the whole day and ensuing night, as the vessels would pass slowly through the bushes. The loss of so much time to men half starved was a matter of consequence. I would have given now a great deal for a day's provision, or for one of our horses. I returned but slowly to the troops, giving myself time to think. On our arrival all ran to hear what was the report; every eye was fixed on me; I unfortunately spoke in a serious manner to one of the officers. The whole were alarmed without knowing what I said. I viewed their confusion for about one minute; I whispered to those near me to do as I did, immediately put some water in my hand, poured on powder, blackened my face, gave the war-whoop, and marched into the water without saying a word. The party gazed and fell in, one after another without saying a word, like a flock of sheep. I ordered those near me to begin a favorite song of theirs; it soon passed through the line, and the whole went on cheerfully.

"I now intended to have them transported across the deepest part of the water; but when about waist-deep, one of the men informed me that he thought he felt a path; we examined and found it so, and concluded that it kept on the highest ground, which it did, and by taking pains to follow it, we got to the sugar camp, with no difficulty, where there was about half an acre of dry ground,—at least ground not under water, and there we took up our lodging.

*   *   *   *   *   *

"The night had been colder than any we had had, and the ice in the morning was one-half or three-quarters of an inch thick in still water; the morning was the finest. A little after sunrise I lectured the whole; what I said to them I forget, but I concluded by informing them that passing the plain then in full view, and reaching the opposite woods would put an end to their fatigue; that in a few hours they would have a sight of their long wished-for object; and immediately stepped into the water without waiting for any reply. A huzza took place. As we generally marched through the water in a line, before the third man entered, I called to Major Bowman, ordering him to fall in the rear of the 25 men, and put to death any man who refused to march. This met with a cry of approbation, and on we went. Getting about the middle of the plain, the water about mid-deep, I found myself sensibly failing; and as there were no trees nor bushes for the men to support themselves by, I feared that many of the weak would be drowned. I ordered the canoes to make the land, discharge their loading, and play backward and forward with all diligence and pick up the men; and to encourage the party, sent some of the strongest men forward, with orders when they got to a certain distance, to pass the word back that the water was getting shallow, and when getting near the woods, to cry out land. This stratagem had its desired effect; the men exerted themselves almost beyond their abilities, the weak holding by the stronger. The water, however, did not become shallower, but continued deepening. Getting to the woods where the men expected land, the water was up to my shoulders; but gaining the woods was of great consequence; all the low men and weakly hung to the trees and floated on the old logs until they were taken off by the canoes; the strong and tall got ashore and built fires. Many would reach the shore and fall with their bodies half in the water, not being able to support themselves without it.

"This was a dry and delightful spot of ground of about ten acres. Fortunately, as if designed by Providence, a canoe of Indian squaws and children was coming up to town, and took through this part of the plain as a nigh way; it was discovered by our canoe-men as they were out after the other men. They gave chase and took the Indian canoe, on board of which was nearly half a quarter of buffalo, some corn, tallow, kettles, etc. This was an invaluable prize. Broth was immediately made and served out, especially to the weakly; nearly all of us got a little; but a great many gave their part to the weakly, saying something cheering to their comrades. By the afternoon, this refreshment and fine weather had greatly invigorated the whole party.

" Crossing a narrow and deep lake in the canoes, and marching some distance, we came to a copse of timber called ' Warrior's Island.' We were now in full view of the fort and town; it was about two miles distant, with not a shrub intervening. Every man now feasted his eyes and forgot that he had suffered anything, saying that all which had passed was owing to good policy, and nothing but what a man could bear, and that a soldier had no right to think, passing from one extreme to the other,—which is common in such cases. And now stratagem was necessary. The plain between us and the town was not a perfect level; the sunken grounds were covered with water full of ducks. We observed several men within a half a mile of us shooting ducks, and sent out some of our active young Frenchmen to take one of these men prisoners without alarming the rest, which they did. The information we got from this person was similar to that which we got from those taken on the river, except that of the British having that evening completed the wall of the fort, and that there were a great many Indians in town.

"Our situation was now critical. No possibility of retreat in case of defeat, and in full view of a town containing at this time more than 600 men, troops, inhabitants and Indians. The crew of the galley, though not 50 men, would have been now a re-enforcement of immense magnitude to our little army, if I may so call it, but we would not think of them. We were now in the situation that I had labored to get ourselves in. The idea of being made prisoner was foreign to almost every man, as they expected nothing but torture from the savages if they fell into their hands. Our fate was now to be determined, probably in a few hours; we knew that nothing but the most daring conduct would insure success; I know also that a number of the inhabitants wished us well. This was a favorable circumstance; and as there was but little proability of our remaining until dark undiscovered, I determined to begin operations immediately, and therefore wrote the following placard to the inhabitants:

To the Inhabitants of Post Vincennes:

Gentlemen:—Being now within two miles of your village with my army, determined to take your fort this night, and not being willing to surprise you, I take this method to request such of you as are true citizens and willing to enjoy the liberty I bring you, to remain still in your houses; and those, if any there be, that are friends to the king, will instantly repair to the fort and join the hair-buyer general and fight like men; and if any such as do not go to the fort shall be discovered afterward, they may depend on severe punishment. On the contrary, those who are true friends to liberty may depend on being well treated; and I once more request them to keep out of the streets; for every one I find in arms on my arrival I shall treat as an enemy.

[Signed]   G. R. CLARK.

"I had various ideas on the results of this letter. I knew it could do us no damage, but that it would cause the lukewarm to be decided, and encourage our friends and astonish our enemies. We anxiously viewed this messenger until he entered the town, and in a few minutes we discovered by our glasses some stir in every street we could penetrate, and great numbers running or riding out into the commons, we supposed to view us, which was the case. But what surprised us was that nothing had yet happened that had the appearance of the garrison being alarmed,—neither gun nor drum. We began to suppose that the information we got from our prisoners was false, and that the enemy had already knew of us and were prepared. A little before sunset we displayed ourselves in full view of the town,—crowds gazing at us. We were plunging ourselves into certain destruction or success; there was no midway thought of. We had but little to say to our men, except inculcating an idea of the necessity of obedience, etc. We moved on slowly in full view of the town; but as it was a point of some consequence to us to make ourselves appear formidable, we, in leaving the covert we were in, marched and counter-marched in such a manner that we appeared numerous. Our colors were displayed to the best advantage; and as the low plain we marched through was not a perfect level, but had frequent risings in it, of 7 or 8 higher than the common level, which was covered with water; and as these risings generally run in an oblique direction to the town, we took the advantage of one of them, marching through the water by it, which completely prevented our being numbered. We gained the heights back of the town. As there were as yet no hostile appearance, we were impatient to have the cause unriddled. Lieut. Bayley was ordered with 14 men to march and fire on the fort; the main body moved in a different direction and took possession of the strongest part of the town."

Clark then sent a written order to Hamilton commanding him to surrender immediately or he would be treated as a murderer; Hamilton replied that he and his garrison were not disposed to be awed into any action unworthy of British subjects. After one hour more of fighting, Hamilton proposed a truce of three days for conference, on condition that each side cease all defensive work; Clark rejoined that he would "not agree to any terms other than Mr. Hamilton surrendering himself and garrison prisoners at discretion," and added that if he, Hamilton, wished to talk with him he could meet him immediately at the church with Capt. Helm. In less than an hour Clark dictated the terms of surrender, Feb. 24, 1779. Hamilton agreed to the total surrender because, as he there claimed in writing, he was too far from aid from his own government, and because of the "unanimity" of his officers in the surrender, and his "confidence in a generous enemy."

"Of this expedition, of its results, of its importance, of the merits of those engaged in it, of their bravery, their skill, of their prudence, of their success, a volume would not more than suffice for the details. Suffice it to say that in my opinion, and I have accurately and critically weighed and examined all the results produced by the contests in which we were engaged during the Revolutionary war, that for bravery, for hardships endured, for skill and consummate tact and prudence on the part of the commander, obedience, discipline and love of country on the part of his followers, for the immense benefits acquired, and signal advantages obtained by it for the whole union, it was second to no enterprise undertaken during that struggle. I might add, second to no undertaking in ancient or modern warfare. The whole credit of this conquest belongs to two men; Gen. George Rogers Clark and Col. Francis Vigo. And when we consider that by it the whole territory now covered by the three great states of Indiana, Illinois and Michigan was added to the union, and so admitted to be by the British commissioners at the preliminaries to the treaty of peace in 1783; (and but for this very conquest, the boundaries of our territories west would have been the Ohio instead of the Mississippi, and so acknowledged by both our commissioners and the British at that conference;) a territory embracing upward of 2,000,000 people, the human mind is lost in the contemplation of its effects; and we can but wonder that a force of 170 men, the whole number of Clark's troops, should by this single action have produced such important results." [John Law.

The next day Clark sent a detachment of 60 men up the river Wabash to intercept some boats which were laden with provisions and goods from Detroit. This force was placed under command of Capt. Helm, Major Bosseron and Major Legras, and they proceeded up the river, in three armed boats, about 120 miles, when the British boats, about seven in number, were surprised and captured without firing a gun. These boats, which had on board about $50,000 worth of goods and provisions, were manned by about 40 men, among whom was Philip Dejean, a magistrate of Detroit. The provisions were taken for the public, and distributed among the soldiery.

Having organized a military government at Vincennes and appointed Capt. Helm commandant of the town, Col. Clark returned in the vessel to Kaskaskia, where he was joined by reinforcements from Kentucky under Capt. George. Meanwhile, a party of traders who were going to the falls, were killed and plundered by the Delawares of White River; the news of this disaster having reached Clark, he sent a dispatch to Capt. Helm ordering him to make war on the Delawares and use every means in his power to destroy them; to show no mercy to the men, but to save the women and children. This order was executed without delay. Their camps were attacked in every quarter where they could be found. Many fell, and others were carried to Post Vincennes and put to death. The surviving Delawares at once pleaded for mercy and appeared anxious to make some atonement for their bad conduct. To these overtures Capt. Helm replied that Col. Clark, the "Big Knife," had ordered the war, and that he had no power to lay down the hatchet, but that he would suspend hostilities until a messenger could be sent to Kaskaskia. This was done, and the crafty Colonel, well understanding the Indian character, sent a message to the Delawares, telling them that he would not accept their friendship or treat with them for peace; but that if they could get some of the neighboring tribes to become responsible for their future conduct, he would discontinue the war and spare their lives; otherwise they must all perish.

Accordingly a council was called of all the Indians in the neighborhood, and Clark's answer was read to the assembly. After due deliberation the Piankeshaws took on themselves to answer for the future good conduct of the Delawares, and the "Grand Door" in a long speech denounced their base conduct. , This ended the war with the Delawares and secured the respect of the neighboring tribes

Clark's attention was next turned to the British post at Detroit, but being unable to obtain sufficient troops he abandoned the enterprise.

CLARK'S INGENIOUS RUSE AGAINST THE INDIANS.

Tradition says that when Clark captured Hamilton and his garrison at Fort Sackville, he took possession of the fort and kept the British flag flying, dressed his sentinels with the uniform of the British soldiery, and let everything about the premises remain as they were, so that when the Indians sympathizing with the British arrived they would walk right into the citadel, into the jaws of death. His success was perfect. Sullen and silent, with the scalp-lock of his victims hanging at his girdle, and in full expectation of his reward from Hamilton, the unwary savage, unconscious of danger and wholly ignorant of the change that had just been effected in his absence, passed the supposed British sentry at the gate of the fort unmolested and unchallenged; but as soon as in, a volley from the rifles of a platoon of Clark's men, drawn up and awaiting his coming, pierced their hearts and sent the unconscious savage, reeking with murder, to that tribunal to which he had so frequently, by order of the hair-buyer general, sent his American captives, from the infant in the cradle to the grandfather of the family, tottering with age and infirmity. It was a just retribution, and few men but Clark would have planned such a ruse or carried it out successfully. It is reported that fifty Indians met this fate within the fort; and probably Hamilton, a prisoner there, witnessed it all

SUBSEQUENT CAREER OF HAMILTON.

Henry Hamilton, who had acted as Lieutenant and Governor of the British possessions under Sir George Carleton, was sent forward, with two other prisoners of war, Dejean and LaMothe, to Williamsburg, Va., early in June following, 1779. Proclamations, in his own handwriting, were found, in which he had offered a specific sum for every American scalp brought into the camp, either by his own troops or his allies, the Indians; and from this he was denominated the "hair-buyer General." This and much other testimony of living witnesses at the time, all showed what a savage he was. Thomas Jefferson, then Governor of Virginia, being made aware of the inhumanity of this wretch, concluded to resort to a little retaliation by way of closer confinement. Accordingly he ordered that these three prisoners be put in irons, confined in a dungeon, deprived of the use of pen, ink and paper, and be excluded from all conversation except with their keeper. Major General Phillips, a British officer out on parole in the vicinity of Charlottesville, where the prisoners now were, in closer confinement, remonstrated, and President Washington, while approving of Jefferson's course, requested a mitigation of the severe order, lest the British be goaded to desperate measures.

Soon afterward Hamilton was released on parole, and he subsequently appeared in Canada, still acting as if he had jurisdiction in the United States.

GIBAULT.

The faithful, self-sacrificing and patriotic services of Father Pierre Gibault in behalf of the Americans require a special notice of him in this connection. He was the parish priest at Vincennes, as well as at Kaskaskia. He was, at an early period, a Jesuit missionary to the Illinois. Had it not been for the influence of this man, Clark could not have obtained the influence of the citizens at either place. He gave all his property, to the value of 1,500 Spanish milled dollars, to the support of Col. Clark's troops, and never received a single dollar in return. So far as the records inform us, he was given 1,500 Continental paper dollars, which proved in the end entirely valueless. He modestly petitioned from the Government a small allowance of land at Cahokia, but we find no account of his ever receiving it. He was dependent upon the public in his older days, and in 1790 Winthrop Sargent "conceded" to him a lot of about "14 toises, one side to Mr. Millet, another to Mr. Vaudrey, and to two streets,"—a vague description of land.

Col. Francis Vigo was born in Mondovi, in the kingdom of Sardinia, in 1747. He left his parents and guardians at a very early age, and enlisted in a Spanish regiment as a soldier. The regiment was ordered to Havana, and a detachment of it subsequently to New Orleans, then a Spanish post; Col. Vigo accompanied this detachment. But he left the army and engaged in trading with the Indians on the Arkansas and its tributaries. Next he settled at St. Louis, also a Spanish post, where he became closely connected, both in friendship and business, with the Governor of Upper Louisiana, then residing at the same place. This friendship he enjoyed, though he could only write his name; and we have many circumstantial evidences that he was a man of high intelligence, honor, purity of heart, and ability. Here he was living when Clark captured Kaskaskia, and was extensively engaged in trading up the Missouri.

A Spaniard by birth and allegiance, he was under no obligation to assist the Americans. Spain was at peace with Great Britain, and any interference by her citizens was a breach of neutrality, and subjected an individual, especially one of the high character and standing of Col. Vigo, to all the contumely, loss and vengeance which British power could inflict. But Col. Vigo did not falter. With an innate love of liberty, an attachment to Republican principles, and an ardent sympathy for an oppressed people struggling for their rights, he overlooked all personal consequences, and as soon as he learned of Clark's arrival at Kaskaskia, he crossed the line and went to Clark and tendered him his means and influence, both of which were joyfully accepted.

Knowing Col. Vigo's influence with the ancient inhabitants of the country, and desirous of obtaining some information from Vincennes, from which he had not heard for several months, Col. Clark proposed to him that he might go to that place and learn the actual state of affairs. Vigo went without hesitation, but on the Embarrass river he was seized by a party of Indians, plundered of all he possessed, and brought a prisoner before Hamilton, then in possession of the post, which he had a short time previously captured, holding Capt. Helm a prisoner of war. Being a Spanish subject, and consequently a non-combatant, Gov. Hamilton, although he strongly suspected the motives of the visit, dared not confine him, but admitted him to parole, on the single condition that he should daily report himself at the fort. But Hamilton was embarrassed by his detention, being besieged by the inhabitants of the town, who loved Vigo and threatened to withdraw their support from the garrison if he would not release him. Father Gibault was the chief pleader for Vigo's release. Hamilton finally yielded, on condition that he, Vigo, would do no injury to the British interests on his way to St. Louis. He went to St. Louis, sure enough, doing no injury to British interests, but immediately returned to Kaskaskia and reported to Clark in detail all he had learned at Vincennes, without which knowledge Clark would have been unable to accomplish his famous expedition to that post with final triumph. The redemption of this country from the British is due as much, probably, to Col. Vigo as Col. Clark.

GOVERNMENT OF THE NORTHWEST.

Col. John Todd, Lieutenant for the county of Illinois, in the spring of 1779 visited the old settlements at Vincennes and Kaskaskia, and organized temporary civil governments in nearly all the settlements west of the Ohio. Previous to this, however, Clark had established a military government at Kaskaskia and Vincennes, appointed commandants in both places and taken up his headquarters at the falls of the Ohio, where he could watch the operations of the enemy and save the frontier settlements from the depredations of Indian warfare. On reaching the settlements, Col. Todd issued a proclamation regulating the settlement of unoccupied lands and requiring the presentation of all claims to the lands settled, as the number of adventurers who would shortly overrun the country would be serious. He also organized a Court of civil and criminal jurisdiction at Vincennes, in the month of June, 1779. This Court was composed of several magistrates and presided over by Col. J. M. P. Legras, who had been appointed commandant at Vincennes. Acting from the precedents established by the early French commandants in the West, this Court began to grant tracts of land to the French and American inhabitants; and to the year 1783, it had granted to different parties about 26,000 acres of land; 22,000 more was granted in this manner by 1787, when the practice was prohibited by Gen. Harmer. These tracts varied in size from a house lot to 500 acres. Besides this loose business, the Court entered into a stupendous speculation, one not altogether creditable to its honor and dignity. The commandant and the magistrates. under him suddenly adopted the opinion that they were invested with the authority to dispose of the whole of that large region which in 1842 had been granted by the Piankeshaws to the French inhabitants of Vincennes. Accordingly a very convenient arrangement was entered into by which the whole tract of country mentioned was to be divided between the members of the honorable Court. A record was made to that effect, and in order to gloss over the steal, each member took pains to be absent from Court on the day that the order was made in his favor.

In the fall of 1780 La Balme, a Frenchman, made an attempt to capture the British garrison of Detroit by leading an expedition against it from Kaskaskia. At the head of 30 men he marched to Vincennes, where his force was slightly increased. From this place he proceeded to the British trading post at the head of the Maumee, where Fort Wayne now stands, plundered the British traders and Indians and then retired. While encamped on the bank of a small stream on his retreat, he was attacked by a band of Miamis, a number of his men were killed, and his expedition against Detroit was ruined.

In this manner border war continued between Americans and their enemies, with varying victory, until 1783, when the treaty of Paris was concluded, resulting in the establishment of the independence of the United States. Up to this time the territory now included in Indiana belonged by conquest to the State of Virginia; but in January, 1783, the General Assembly of that State resolved to cede to the Congress of the United States all the territory northwest of the Ohio. The conditions offered by Virginia were accepted by Congress Dec. 20, that year, and early in 1784 the transfer was completed. In 1783 Virginia had platted the town of Clarksville, at the falls of the Ohio. The deed of cession provided that the territory should be laid out into States, containing a suitable extent of territory not less than 100 nor more than 150 miles square, or as near thereto as circumstances would permit; and that the States so formed shall be distinct Republican States and admitted members of the Federal Union, having the same rights of sovereignty, freedom and independence as the other States. The other conditions of the deed were as follows: That the necessary and reasonable expenses incurred by Virginia in subduing any British posts, or in maintaining forts and garrisons within and for the defense, or in acquiring any part of the territory so ceded or relinquished, shall be fully reimbursed by the United States; that the French and Canadian inhabitants and other settlers of the Kas-

kaskia, Post Vincennes and the neighboring villages who have pro-
fessed themselves citizens of Virginia, shall have their titles and
possessions confirmed to them, and be protected in the enjoyment
of their rights and privileges; that a quantity not exceeding 150,-
000 acres of land, promised by Virginia, shall be allowed and
granted to the then Colonel, now General, George Rogers Clark,
and to the officers and soldiers of his regiment, who marched with
him when the posts and of Kaskaskia and Vincennes were reduced,
and to the officers and soldiers that have been since incorporated
into the said regiment, to be laid off in one tract, the length of
which not to exceed double the breadth, in such a place on the
northwest side of the Ohio as a majority of the officers shall
choose, and to be afterward divided among the officers and soldiers
in due proportion according to the laws of Virginia; that in case
the quantity of good lands on the southeast side of the Ohio, upon
the waters of Cumberland river, and between Green river and Ten.
nessee river, which have been reserved by law for the Virginia
troops upon Continental establishment, should, from the North
Carolina line, bearing in further upon the Cumberland lands than
was expected, prove insufficient for their legal bounties, the deficiency shall be made up to the said troops in good lands to be laid
off between the rivers Scioto and Little Miami, on the northwest
side of the river Ohio, in such proportions as have been engaged
to them by the laws of Virginia; that all the lands within the territory so ceded to the United States, and not reserved for or appropriated to any of the before-mentioned purposes, or disposed of in
bounties to the officers and soldiers of the American army, shall be
considered as a common fund for the use and benefit of such of the
United States as have become, or shall become, members of the
confederation or federal alliance of the said States, Virginia included,
according to their usual respective proportions in the general
charge and expenditure, and shall be faithfully and *bona fide* disposed of for that purpose and for no other use or purpose whatever.

After the above deed of cession had been accepted by Congress,
in the spring of 1784, the matter of the future government of the
territory was referred to a committee consisting of Messrs. Jefferson of Virginia, Chase of Maryland and Howell of Rhode Island,
which committee reported an ordinance for its government, providing, among other things, that slavery should not exist in said territory after 1800, except as punishment of criminals; but this article
of the ordinance was rejected. and an ordinance for the temporary

government of the county was adopted. In 1785 laws were passed by Congress for the disposition of lands in the territory and prohibiting the settlement of unappropriated lands by reckless speculators. But human passion is ever strong enough to evade the law to some extent, and large associations, representing considerable means, were formed for the purpose of monopolizing the land business. Millions of acres were sold at one time by Congress to associations on the installment plan, and so far as the Indian titles could be extinguished, the work of settling and improving the lands was pushed rapidly forward.

ORDINANCE OF 1787.

This ordinance has a marvelous and interesting history. Considerable controversy has been indulged in as to who is entitled to the credit for framing it. This belongs, undoubtedly, to Nathan Dane; and to Rufus King and Timothy Pickering belong the credit for suggesting the proviso contained in it against slavery, and also for aids to religion and knowledge, and for assuring forever the common use, without charge, of the great national highways of the Mississippi, the St. Lawrence and their tributaries to all the citizens of the United States. To Thomas Jefferson is also due much credit, as some features of this ordinance were embraced in his ordinance of 1784. But the part taken by each in the long, laborious and eventful struggle which had so glorious a consummation in the ordinance, consecrating forever, by one imprescriptible and unchangeable monument, the very heart of our country to Freedom, Knowledge, and Union, will forever honor the names of those illustrious statesmen.

Mr. Jefferson had vainly tried to secure a system of government for the Northwestern territory. He was an emancipationist and favored the exclusion of slavery from the territory, but the South voted him down every time he proposed a measure of this nature. In 1787, as late as July 10, an organizing act without the anti-slavery clause was pending. This concession to the South was expected to carry it. Congress was in session in New York. On July 5, Rev. Manasseh Cutler, of Massachusetts, came into New York to lobby on the Northwestern territory. Everything seemed to fall into his hands. Events were ripe. The state of the public credit, the growing of Southern prejudice, the basis of his mission, his personal character, all combined to complete one of those sudden and marvelous revolutions of public sentiment that once in five or ten centuries are seen to sweep over a country like the breath of the Almighty.

Cutler was a graduate of Yale. He had studied and taken degrees in the three learned professions, medicine, law, and divinity. He had published a scientific examination of the plants of New England. As a scientist in America his name stood second only to that of Franklin. He was a courtly gentleman of the old style, a man of commanding presence and of inviting face. The Southern members said they had never seen such a gentleman in the North. He came representing a Massachusetts company that desired to purchase a tract of land, now included in Ohio, for the purpose of planting a colony. It was a speculation. Government money was worth eighteen cents on the dollar. This company had collected enough to purchase 1,500,000 acres of land. Other speculators in New York made Dr. Cutler their agent, which enabled him to represent a demand for 5,500,000 acres. As this would reduce the national debt, and Jefferson's policy was to provide for the public credit, it presented a good opportunity to do something.

Massachusetts then owned the territory of Maine, which she was crowding on the market. She was opposed to opening the Northwestern region. This fired the zeal of Virginia. The South caught the inspiration, and all exalted Dr. Cutler. The entire South rallied around him. Massachusetts could not vote against him, because many of the constituents of her members were interested personally in the Western speculation. Thus Cutler, making friends in the South, and doubtless using all the arts of the lobby, was enabled to command the situation. True to deeper convictions, he dictated one of the most compact and finished documents of wise statesmanship that has ever adorned any human law book. He borrowed from Jefferson the term "Articles of Compact," which, preceding the federal constitution, rose into the most sacred character. He then followed very closely the constitution of Massachusetts, adopted three years before. Its most prominent points were:

1. The exclusion of slavery from the territory forever.

2. Provision for public schools, giving one township for a seminary and every section numbered 16 in each township; that is, one thirty-sixth of all the land for public schools.

3. A provision prohibiting the adoption of any constitution or the enactment of any law that should nullify pre-existing contracts.

Be it forever remembered that this compact declared that "religion, morality, and knowledge being necessary to good government and the happiness of mankind, schools and the means of education shall always be encouraged." Dr. Cutler planted himself on this platform and would not yield. Giving his unqualified declaration that it was that or nothing,—that unless they could make the land desirable they did not want it,—he took his horse and buggy and started for the constitutional convention at Philadelphia. On July 13, 1787, the bill was put upon its passage, and was unanimously adopted. Thus the great States of Ohio, Indiana, Illinois, Michigan and Wisconsin, a vast empire, were consecrated to freedom, intelligence, and morality. Thus the great heart of the nation was prepared to save the union of States, for it was this act that was the salvation of the republic and the destruction of slavery. Soon the South saw their great blunder and tried to have the compact repealed. In 1803 Congress referred it to a committee, of which John Randolph was chairman. He reported that this ordinance was a compact and opposed repeal. Thus it stood, a rock in the way of the on-rushing sea of slavery.

The "Northwestern Territory" included of course what is now the State of Indiana; and Oct 5, 1787, Maj. Gen. Arthur St. Clair was elected by Congress Governor of this territory. Upon commencing the duties of his office he was instructed to ascertain the real temper of the Indians and do all in his power to remove the causes for controversy between them and the United States, and to effect the extinguishment of Indian titles to all the land possible. The Governor took up quarters in the new settlement of Marietta, Ohio, where he immediately began the organization of the government of the territory. The first session of the General Court of the new territory was held at that place in 1788, the Judges being Samuel H. Parsons, James M. Varnum and John C. Symmes, but under the ordinance Gov. St. Clair was President of the Court. After the first session, and after the necessary laws for government were adopted, Gov. St. Clair, accompanied by the Judges, visited Kaskaskia for the purpose of organizing a civil government there. Full instructions had been sent to Maj. Hamtramck, commandant at Vincennes, to ascertain the exact feeling and temper of the Indian tribes of the Wabash. These instructions were accompanied by speeches to each of the tribes. A Frenchman named Antoine Gamelin was dispatched with these messages April 5, 1790, who visited nearly all the tribes on the Wabash, St. Joseph and St.

Mary's rivers, but was coldly received; most of the chiefs being dissatisfied with the policy of the Americans toward them, and prejudiced through English misrepresentation. Full accounts of his adventures among the tribes reached Gov. St. Clair at Kaskaskia in June, 1790. Being satisfied that there was no prospect of effecting a general peace with the Indians of Indiana, he resolved to visit Gen. Harmar at his headquarters at Fort Washington and consult with him on the means of carrying an expedition against the hostile Indians; but before leaving he intrusted Winthrop Sargent, the Secretary of the Territory, with the execution of the resolutions of Congress regarding the lands and settlers on the Wabash. He directed that officer to proceed to Vincennes, lay out a county there, establish the militia and appoint the necessary civil and military officers. Accordingly Mr. Sargent went to Vincennes and organized Camp Knox, appointed the officers, and notified the inhabitants to present their claims to lands. In establishing these claims the settlers found great difficulty, and concerning this matter the Secretary in his report to the President wrote as follows:

"Although the lands and lots which were awarded to the inhabitants appeared from very good oral testimony to belong to those persons to whom they were awarded, either by original grants, purchase or inheritance, yet there was scarcely one case in twenty where the title was complete, owing to the desultory manner in which public business had been transacted and some other unfortunate causes. The original concessions by the French and British commandants were generally made upon a small scrap of paper, which it has been customary to lodge in the notary's office, who has seldom kept any book of record, but committed the most important land concerns to loose sheets, which in process of time have come into possession of persons that have fraudulently destroyed them; or, unacquainted with their consequence, innocently lost or trifled them away. By French usage they are considered family inheritances, and often descend to women and children. In one instance, and during the government of St. Ange here, a royal notary ran off with all the public papers in his possession, as by a certificate produced to me. And I am very sorry further to observe that in the office of Mr. Le Grand, which continued from 1777 to 1787, and where should have been the vouchers for important land transactions, the records have been so falsified, and there is such gross fraud and forgery, as to invalidate all evidence and information which I might have otherwise acquired from his papers."

Mr. Sargent says there were about 150 French families at Vincennes in 1790. The heads of all these families had been at some time vested with certain titles to a portion of the soil; and while the Secretary was busy in straightening out these claims, he received a petition signed by 80 Americans, asking for the confirmation of grants of land ceded by the Court organized by Col. John Todd under the authority of Virginia. With reference to this cause, Congress, March 3, 1791, empowered the Territorial Governor, in cases where land had been actually improved and cultivated under a supposed grant for the same, to confirm to the persons who made such improvements the lands supposed to have been granted, not, however, exceeding the quantity of 400 acres to any one person.

LIQUOR AND GAMING LAWS.

The General Court in the summer of 1790, Acting Governor Sargent presiding, passed the following laws with reference to vending liquor among the Indians and others, and with reference to games of chance:

1. An act to prohibit the giving or selling intoxicating liquors to Indians residing in or coming into the Territory of the United States northwest of the river Ohio, and for preventing foreigners from trading with Indians therein.

2. An act prohibiting the sale of spirituous or other intoxicating liquors to soldiers in the service of the United States, being within ten miles of any military post in the territory; and to prevent the selling or pawning of arms, ammunition, clothing or accoutrements.

3. An act prohibiting every species of gaming for money or property, and for making void contracts and payments made in consequence thereof, and for restraining the disorderly practice of discharging arms at certain hours and places.

Winthrop Sargent's administration was highly eulogized by the citizens at Vincennes, in a testimonial drawn up and signed by a committee of officers. He had conducted the investigation and settlement of land claims to the entire satisfaction of the residents, had upheld the principles of free government in keeping with the animus of the American Revolution, and had established in good order the machinery of a good and wise government. In the same address Major Hamtramck also received a fair share of praise for his judicious management of affairs.

EXPEDITIONS OF HARMAR, SCOTT AND WILKINSON.

Gov. St. Clair, on his arrival at Fort Washington from Kas-kaskia, had a long conversation with Gen. Harmar, and concluded to send a powerful force to chastise the savages about the head-waters of the Wabash. He had been empowered by the President to call on Virginia for 1,000 troops and on Pennsylvania for 500, and he immediately availed himself of this resource, ordering 300 of the Virginia militia to muster at Fort Steuben and march with the garrison of that fort to Vincennes, and join Maj. Hamtramck, who had orders to call for aid from the militia of Vincennes, march up the Wabash, and attack any of the Indian villages which he might think he could overcome. The remaining 1,200 of the mi-litia were ordered to rendezvous at Fort Washington, and to join the regular troops at that post under command of Gen. Harmar. At this time the United States troops in the West were estimated by Gen. Harmar at 400 effective men. These, with the militia, gave him a force of 1,450 men. With this army Gen. Harmar marched from Fort Washington Sept. 30, and arrived at the Mau-mee Oct. 17. They commenced the work of punishing the Indians, but were not very successful. The savages, it is true, received a severe scourging, but the militia behaved so badly as to be of little or no service. A detachment of 340 militia and 60 regulars, under the command of Col. Hardin, were sorely defeated on the Maumee Oct. 22. The next day the army took up the line of march for Fort Washington, which place they reached Nov. 4, having lost in the expedition 183 killed and 31 wounded; the Indians lost about as many. During the progress of this expedition Maj. Hamtramck marched up the Wabash from Vincennes, as far as the Vermillion river, and destroyed several deserted villages, but without finding an enemy to oppose him.

Although the savages seem to have been severely punished by these expeditions, yet they refused to sue for peace, and continued their hostilities. Thereupon the inhabitants of the frontier settle-ments of Virginia took alarm, and the delegates of Ohio, Monon-

gahela, Harrison, Randolph, Greenbrier, Kanawha and Montgomery counties sent a joint memorial to the Governor of Virginia, saying that the defenseless condition of the counties, forming a line of nearly 400 miles along the Ohio river, exposed to the
hostile invasion of their Indian enemies, destitute of every kind of
support, was truly alarming; for, notwithstanding all the regulations of the General Government in that country, they have reason
to lament that they have been up to that time ineffectual for their
protection; nor indeed could it be otherwise, for the garrisons kept
by the Continental troops on the Ohio river, if of any use at all,
must protect only the Kentucky settlements, as they immediately
covered that country. They further stated in their memorial: "We
beg leave to observe that we have reason to fear that the consequences of the defeat of our army by the Indians in the late expedition will be severely felt on our frontiers, as there is no doubt
that the Indians will, in their turn, being flushed with victory, invade our settlements and exercise all their horrid murder upon the
inhabitants thereof whenever the weather will permit them to
travel.   Then is it not better to support us where we are, be the expense what it may, than to oblige such a number of your brave
citizens, who have so long supported, and still continue to support,
a dangerous frontier (although thousands of their relatives in the
flesh have in the prosecution thereof fallen a sacrifice to savage inventions) to quit the country, after all they have done and suffered,
when you know that a frontier must be supported somewhere?"

This memorial caused the Legislature of Virginia to authorize
the Governor of that State to make any defensive operations necessary for the temporary defense of the frontiers, until the general
Government could adopt and carry out measures to suppress the
hostile Indians.   The Governor at once called upon the military
commanding officers in the western counties of Virginia to raise by
the first of March, 1791, several small companies of rangers for this
purpose.   At the same time Charles Scott was appointed Brigadier-
General of the Kentucky militia, with authority to raise 226 volunteers, to protect the most exposed portions of that district.   A
full report of the proceedings of the Virginia Legislature being
transmitted to Congress, that body constituted a local Board of
War for the district of Kentucky, consisting of five men.   March 9,
1791, Gen. Henry Knox, Secretary of War, sent a letter of instructions to Gen. Scott, recommending an expedition of mounted men
not exceeding 750, against the Wea towns on the Wabash.   With

this force Gen. Scott accordingly crossed the Ohio, May 23, 1791, and reached the Wabash in about ten days. Many of the Indians, having discovered his approach, fled, but he succeeded in destroying all the villages around Ouiatenon, together with several Kickapoo towns, killing 32 warriors and taking 58 prisoners. He released a few of the most infirm prisoners, giving them a "talk," which they carried to the towns farther up the Wabash, and which the wretched condition of his horses prevented him from reaching.

March 3, 1791, Congress provided for raising and equipping a regiment for the protection of the frontiers, and Gov. St. Clair was invested with the chief command of about 3,000 troops, to be raised and employed against the hostile Indians in the territory over which his jurisdiction extended. He was instructed by the Secretary of War to march to the Miami village and establish a strong and permanent military post there; also such posts elsewhere along the Ohio as would be in communication with Fort Washington. The post at Miami village was intended to keep the savages in that vicinity in check, and was ordered to be strong enough in its garrison to afford a detachment of 500 or 600 men in case of emergency, either to chastise any of the Wabash or other hostile Indians or capture convoys of the enemy's provisions. The Secretary of War also urged Gov. St. Clair to establish that post as the first and most important part of the campaign. In case of a previous treaty the Indians were to be conciliated upon this point if possible; and he presumed good arguments might be offered to induce their acquiescence. Said he: "Having commenced your march upon the main expedition, and the Indians continuing hostile, you will use every possible exertion to make them feel the effects of your superiority; and, after having arrived at the Miami village and put your works in a defensible state, you will seek the enemy with the whole of your remaining force, and endeavor by all possible means to strike them with great severity.   *   *   *   *
In order to avoid future wars, it might be proper to make the Wabash and thence over to the Maumee, and down the same to its mouth, at Lake Erie, the boundary between the people of the United States and the Indians (excepting so far as the same should relate to the Wyandots and Delawares), on the supposition of their continuing faithful to the treaties; but if they should join in the war against the United States, and your army be victorious, the said tribes ought to be removed without the boundary mentioned."

Previous to marching a strong force to the Miami town, Gov. St.

Clair, June 25, 1791, authorized Gen Wilkinson to conduct a second expedition, not exceeding 500 mounted men, against the Indian villages on the Wabash. Accordingly Gen. Wilkinson mustered his forces and was ready July 20, to march with 525 mounted volunteers, well armed, and provided with 30 days' provisions, and with this force he reached the Ke-na-pa-com-a-qua village on the north bank of Eel river about six miles above its mouth, Aug. 7, where he killed six warriors and took 34 prisoners. This town, which was scattered along the river for three miles, was totally destroyed. Wilkinson encamped on the ruins of the town that night, and the next day he commenced his march for the Kickapoo town on the prairie, which he was unable to reach owing to the impassable condition of the route which he adopted and the failing condition of his horses. He reported the estimated results of the expedition as follows: "I have destroyed the chief town of the Ouiatenon nation, and have made prisoners of the sons and sisters of the king. I have burned a respectable Kickapoo village, and cut down at least 400 acres of corn, chiefly in the milk."

EXPEDITIONS OF ST. CLAIR AND WAYNE.

The Indians were greatly damaged by the expeditions of Harmar, Scott and Wilkinson, but were far from being subdued. They regarded the policy of the United States as calculated to exterminate them from the land; and, goaded on by the English of Detroit, enemies of the Americans, they were excited to desperation. At this time the British Government still supported garrisons at Niagara, Detroit and Michilimackinac, although it was declared by the second article of the definitive treaty of peace of 1783, that the king of Great Britain would, " with all convenient speed, and without causing any destruction or carrying away any negroes or property of the American inhabitants, withdraw all his forces, garrisons and fleets from the United States, and from every post, place and harbor within the same." That treaty also provided that the creditors on either side should meet with no lawful impediments to the recovery of the full value, in sterling money, of all bona fide debts previously contracted. The British Government claimed that the United States had broken faith in this particular understanding of the treaty, and in consequence refused to withdraw its forces from the territory. The British garrisons in the Lake Region were a source of much annoyance to the Americans, as they afforded succor to hostile Indians, encouraging them to make raids among the Americans. This state of affairs in the Territory Northwest of the Ohio continued from the commencement of the Revolutionary war to 1796, when under a second treaty all British soldiers were withdrawn from the country.

In September, 1791, St. Clair moved from Fort Washington with about 2,000 men, and November 3, the main army, consisting of about 1,400 effective troops, moved forward to the head-waters of the Wabash, where Fort Recovery was afterward erected, and here the army encamped. About 1,200 Indians were secreted a few miles distant, awaiting a favorable opportunity to begin an attack, which they improved on the morning of Nov. 4, about half an hour before sunrise. The attack was first made upon the militia, which immediately gave way. St. Clair was defeated and he returned to Fort Washington with a broken and dispirited army, having lost 39 officers killed, and 539 men killed and missing; 22 officers and 232 men were wounded. Several pieces of artillery, and all the baggage, ammunition and provisions were left on the field of battle and fell into the hands of the victorious Indians. The stores and other public property lost in the action were valued at $32,800. There were also 100 or more American women with the army of the whites, very few of whom escaped the cruel carnage of the savage Indians. The latter, characteristic of their brutal nature, proceeded in the flush of victory to perpetrate the most horrible acts of cruelty and brutality upon the bodies of the living and the dead Americans who fell into their hands. Believing that the whites had made war for many years merely to acquire land, the Indians crammed clay and sand into the eyes and down the throats of the dying and the dead!

GEN. WAYNE'S GREAT VICTORY.

Although no particular blame was attached to Gov. St. Clair for the loss in this expedition, yet he resigned the office of Major-General, and was succeeded by Anthony Wayne, a distinguished officer of the Revolutionary war. Early in 1792 provisions were made by the general Government for re-organizing the army, so that it should consist of an efficient degree of strength. Wayne arrived at Pittsburg in June, where the army was to rendezvous. Here he continued actively engaged in organizing and training his forces until October, 1793, when with an army of about 3,600 men he moved westward to Fort Washington.

While Wayne was preparing for an offensive campaign, every

possible means was employed to induce the hostile tribes of the Northwest to enter into a general treaty of peace with the American Government; speeches were sent among them, and agents to make treaties were also sent, but little was accomplished. Major Hamtramck, who still remained at Vincennes, succeeded in concluding a general peace with the Wabash and Illinois Indians; but the tribes more immediately under the influence of the British refused to hear the sentiments of friendship that were sent among them, and tomahawked several of the messengers. Their courage had been aroused by St. Clair's defeat, as well as by the unsuccessful expeditions which had preceded it, and they now felt quite prepared to meet a superior force under Gen. Wayne. The Indians insisted on the Ohio river as the boundary line between their lands and the lands of the United States, and felt certain that they could maintain that boundary.

Maj. Gen. Scott, with about 1,600 mounted volunteers from Kentucky, joined the regular troops under Gen. Wayne July 26, 1794, and on the 28th the united forces began their march for the Indian towns on the Maumee river. Arriving at the mouth of the Auglaize, they erected Fort Defiance, and Aug. 15 the army advanced toward the British fort at the foot of the rapids of the Maumee, where, on the 20th, almost within reach of the British, the American army gained a decisive victory over the combined forces of the hostile Indians and a considerable number of the Detroit militia. The number of the enemy was estimated at 2,000, against about 900 American troops actually engaged. This horde of savages, as soon as the action began, abandoned themselves to flight and dispersed with terror and dismay, leaving Wayne's victorious army in full and quiet possession of the field. The Americans lost 33 killed and 100 wounded; loss of the enemy more than double this number.

The army remained three days and nights on the banks of the Maumee, in front of the field of battle, during which time all the houses and cornfields were consumed and destroyed for a considerable distance both above and below Fort Miami, as well as within pistol shot of the British garrison, who were compelled to remain idle spectators to this general devastation and conflagration, among which were the houses, stores and property of Col. McKee, the British Indian agent and "principal stimulator of the war then existing between the United States and savages." On the return march to Fort Defiance the villages and cornfields for about 50 miles on each side of the Maumee were destroyed, as well as those for a considerable distance around that post.

Sept. 14, 1794, the army under Gen. Wayne commenced its march toward the deserted Miami villages at the confluence of St. Joseph's and St. Mary's rivers, arriving Oct. 17, and on the following day the site of Fort Wayne was selected. The fort was completed Nov. 22, and garrisoned by a strong detachment of infantry and artillery, under the command of Col. John F. Hamtramck, who gave to the new fort the name of Fort Wayne. In 1814 a new fort was built on the site of this structure. The Kentucky volunteers returned to Fort Washington and were mustered out of service. Gen. Wayne, with the Federal troops, marched to Greenville and took up his headquarters during the winter. Here, in August, 1795, after several months of active negotiation, this gallant officer succeeded in concluding a general treaty of peace with all the hostile tribes of the Northwestern Territory. This treaty opened the way for the flood of immigration for many years, and ultimately made the States and territories now constituting the mighty Northwest.

Up to the organization of the Indiana Territory there is but little history to record aside from those events connected with military affairs. In July, 1796, as before stated, after a treaty was concluded between the United States and Spain, the British garrisons, with their arms, artillery and stores, were withdrawn from the posts within the boundaries of the United States northwest of the Ohio river, and a detachment of American troops, consisting of 65 men, under the command of Capt. Moses Porter, took possession of the evacuated post of Detroit in the same month.

In the latter part of 1796 Winthrop Sargent went to Detroit and organized the county of Wayne, forming a part of the Indiana Territory until its division in 1805, when the Territory of Michigan was organized.

TERRITORIAL HISTORY.

On the final success of American arms and diplomacy in 1796, the principal town within the Territory, now the State, of Indiana was Vincennes, which at this time comprised about 50 houses, all presenting a thrifty and tidy appearance. Each house was surrounded by a garden fenced with poles, and peach and apple-trees grew in most of the enclosures. Garden vegetables of all kinds were cultivated with success, and corn, tobacco, wheat, barley and cotton grew in the fields around the village in abundance. During the last few years of the 18th century the condition of society at Vincennes improved wonderfully.

Besides Vincennes there was a small settlement near where the town of Lawrenceburg now stands, in Dearborn county, and in the course of that year a small settlement was formed at "Armstrong's Station," on the Ohio, within the present limits of Clark county. There were of course several other smaller settlements and trading posts in the present limits of Indiana, and the number of civilized inhabitants comprised within the territory was estimated at 4,875.

The Territory of Indiana was organized by Act of Congress May 7, 1800, the material parts of the ordinance of 1787 remaining in force; and the inhabitants were invested with all the rights, privileges and advantages granted and secured to the people by that ordinance. The seat of government was fixed at Vincennes. May 13, 1800, Wm. Henry Harrison, a native of Virginia, was appointed Governor of this new territory, and on the next day John Gibson, a native of Pennsylvania and a distinguished Western pioneer, (to whom the Indian chief Logan delivered his celebrated speech in 1774), was appointed Secretary of the Territory. Soon afterward Wm. Clark, Henry Vanderburgh and John Griffin were appointed territorial Judges.

Secretary Gibson arrived at Vincennes in July, and commenced, in the absence of Gov. Harrison, the administration of government. Gov. Harrison did not arrive until Jan. 10, 1801, when he immediately called together the Judges of the Territory, who proceeded to pass such laws as they deemed necessary for the present government of the Territory. This session began March 3, 1801.

From this time to 1810 the principal subjects which attracted the attention of the people of Indiana were land speculations, the adjustment of land titles, the question of negro slavery, the purchase of Indian lands by treaties, the organization of Territorial legislatures, the extension of the right of suffrage, the division of Indiana Territory, the movements of Aaron Burr, and the hostile views and proceedings of the Shawanee chief, Tecumseh, and his brother, the Prophet.

Up to this time the sixth article of the celebrated ordinance of 1787, prohibiting slavery in the Northwestern Territory, had been somewhat neglected in the execution of the law, and many French settlers still held slaves in a manner. In some instances, according to rules prescribed by Territorial legislation, slaves agreed by indentures to remain in servitude under their masters for a certain number of years; but many slaves, with whom no such contracts were made, were removed from the Indiana Territory either to the west of the Mississippi or to some of the slaveholding States. Gov. Harrison convoked a session of delegates of the Territory, elected by a popular vote, who petitioned Congress to declare the sixth article of the ordinance of 1787, prohibiting slavery, suspended; but Congress never consented to grant that petition, and many other petitions of a similar import. Soon afterward some of the citizens began to take colored persons out of the Territory for the purpose of selling them, and Gov. Harrison, by a proclamation April 6, 1804, forbade it, and called upon the authorities of the Territory to assist him in preventing such removal of persons of color.

During the year 1804 all the country west of the Mississippi and north of 33° was attached to Indiana Territory by Congress, but in a few months was again detached and organized into a separate territory.

When it appeared from the result of a popular vote in the Territory that a majority of 138 freeholders were in favor of organizing a General Assembly, Gov. Harrison, Sept. 11, 1804, issued a proclamation declaring that the Territory had passed into the second grade of government, as contemplated by the ordinance of 1787, and fixed Thursday, Jan. 3, 1805, as the time for holding an election in the several counties of the Territory, to choose members of a House of Representatives, who should meet at Vincennes Feb. 1 and adopt measures for the organization of a Territorial Council. These delegates were elected, and met according to the proclamation, and selected ten men from whom the President of the United States, Mr. Jefferson, should appoint five to be and constitute the Legislative Council of the Territory, but he declining, requested Mr. Harrison to make the selection, which was accordingly done. Before the first session of this Council, however, was held, Michigan Territory was set off, its south line being one drawn from the southern end of Lake Michigan directly east to Lake Erie.

FIRST TERRITORIAL LEGISLATURE.

The first General Assembly, or Legislature, of Indiana Territory met at Vincennes July 29, 1805, in pursuance of a gubernatorial proclamation. The members of the House of Representatives were Jesse B. Thomas, of Dearborn county; Davis Floyd, of Clark county; Benjamin Parke and John Johnson, of Knox county; Shadrach Bond and William Biggs, of St. Clair county, and George Fisher, of Randolph county. July 30 the Governor delivered his first message to "the Legislative Council and House of Representatives of the Indiana Territory." Benjamin Parke was the first delegate elected to Congress. He had emigrated from New Jersey to Indiana in 1801.

THE "WESTERN SUN"

was the first newspaper published in the Indiana Territory, now comprising the four great States of Indiana, Illinois, Michigan and Wisconsin, and the second in all that country once known as the "Northwestern Territory." It was commenced at Vincennes in 1803, by Elihu Stout, of Kentucky, and first called the *Indiana Gazette*, and July, 4, 1804, was changed to the *Western Sun*. Mr. Stout continued the paper until 1845, amid many discouragements, when he was appointed postmaster at the place, and he sold out the office.

INDIANA IN 1810.

The events which we have just been describing really constitute the initiatory steps to the great military campaign of Gen. Harrison which ended in the "battle of Tippecanoe;" but before proceeding to an account of that brilliant affair, let us take a glance at the resources and strength of Indiana Territory at this time, 1810:

Total population, 24,520; 33 grist mills; 14 saw mills; 3 horse mills; 18 tanneries; 28 distilleries; 3 powder mills; 1,256 looms;

1,350 spinning wheels; value of manufactures—woolen, cotton
hempen and flaxen cloths, $159,052; of cotton and wool spun in
mills, $150,000; of nails, 30,000 pounds, $4,000; of leather tanned,
$9,300; of distillery products, 35,950 gallons, $16,230; of gun-
powder, 3,600 pounds, $1,800; of wine from grapes, 96 barrels,
$6,000, and 5 0,000 pounds of maple sugar.

During the year 1810 a Board of Commissioners was established
to straighten out the confused condition into which the land-title
controversy had been carried by the various and conflicting admin-
istrations that had previously exercised jurisdiction in this regard.
This work was attended with much labor on the part of the Commissioners and great dissatisfaction on the part of a few designing speculators, who thought no extreme of perjury too hazardous in their
mad attempts to obtain lands fraudulently. In closing their report
the Commissioners used the following expressive language: "We
close this melancholy picture of human depravity by rendering our
devout acknowledgment that, in the awful alternative in which we
have been placed, of either admitting perjured testimony in support of the claims before us, or having it turned against our characters and lives, it has as yet pleased that divine providence which
rules over the affairs of men, to preserve us, both from legal murder and private assassination."

The question of dividing the Territory of Indiana was agitated
from 1806 to 1809, when Congress erected the Territory of Illinois,
to comprise all that part of Indiana Territory lying west of the
Wabash river and a direct line drawn from that river and Post
Vincennes due north to the territorial line between the United
States and Canada. This occasioned some confusion in the government of Indiana, but in due time the new elections were confirmed,
and the new territory started off on a journey of prosperity which
this section of the United States has ever since enjoyed.

From the first settlement of Vincennes for nearly half a century
there occurred nothing of importance to relate, at least so far as
the records inform us. The place was too isolated to grow very
fast, and we suppose there was a succession of priests and commandants, who governed the little world around them with almost
infinite power and authority, from whose decisions there was no
appeal, if indeed any was ever desired. The character of society
in such a place would of course grow gradually different from the
parent society, assimilating more or less with that of neighboring
tribes. The whites lived in peace with the Indians, each under-

standing the other's peculiarities, which remained fixed long enough for both parties to study out and understand them. The government was a mixture of the military and the civil. There was little to incite to enterprise. Speculations in money and property, and their counterpart, beggary, were both unknown; the necessaries of life were easily procured, and beyond these there were but few wants to be supplied; hospitality was exercised by all, as there were no taverns; there seemed to be no use for law, judges or prisons; each district had its commandant, and the proceedings of a trial were singular. The complaining party obtained a notification from the commandant to his adversary, accompanied by a command to render justice. If this had no effect he was notified to appear before the commandant on a particular day and answer; and if the last notice was neglected, a sergeant and file of men were sent to bring him,—no sheriff and no costs. The convicted party would be fined and kept in prison until he rendered justice according to the decree; when extremely refractory the cat-o'-nine-tails brought him to a sense of justice. In such a state of society there was no demand for learning and science. Few could read, and still fewer write. Their disposition was nearly always to deal honestly, at least simply. Peltries were their standard of value. A brotherly love generally prevailed. But they were devoid of public spirit, enterprise or ingenuity.

GOV. HARRISON AND THE INDIANS.

Immediately after the organization of Indiana Territory Governor Harrison's attention was directed, by necessity as well as by instructions from Congress, to settling affairs with those Indians who still held claims to lands. He entered into several treaties, by which at the close of 1805 the United States Government had obtained about 46,000 square miles of territory, including all the lands lying on the borders of the Ohio river between the mouth of the Wabash river and the State of Ohio.

The levying of a tax, especially a poll tax, by the General Assembly, created considerable dissatisfaction among many of the inhabitants. At a meeting held Sunday, August 16, 1807, a number of Frenchmen resolved to "withdraw their confidence and support forever from those men who advocated or in any manner promoted the second grade of government."

In 1807 the territorial statutes were revised and under the new code, treason, murder, arson and horse-stealing were each punishable by death. The crime of manslaughter was punishable by the common law. Burglary and robbery were punishable by whipping, fine and in some cases by imprisonment not exceeding forty years. Hog stealing was punishable by fine and whipping. Bigamy was punishable by fine, whipping and disfranchisement, etc.

In 1804 Congress established three land offices for the sale of lands in Indiana territory; one was located at Detroit, one at Vincennes and one at Kaskaskia. In 1807 a fourth one was opened at Jeffersonville, Clark county; this town was first laid out in 1802, agreeably to plans suggested by Mr. Jefferson then President of the United States.

Governor Harrison, according to his message to the Legislature in 1806, seemed to think that the peace then existing between the whites and the Indians was permanent; but in the same document he referred to a matter that might be a source of trouble, which indeed it proved to be, namely, the execution of white laws among the Indians—laws to which the latter had not been a party in their enactment. The trouble was aggravated by the partiality with which the laws seem always to have been executed; the Indian was nearly always the sufferer. All along from 1805 to 1810 the Indians complained bitterly against the encroachments of the white people upon the lands that belonged to them. The invasion of their hunting grounds and the unjustifiable killing of many of their people were the sources of their discontent. An old chief, in laying the trouble of his people before Governor Harrison, said: "You call us children; why do you not make us as happy as our fathers, the French, did? They never took from us our lands; indeed, they were common between us. They planted where they pleased, and they cut wood where they pleased; and so did we; but now if a poor Indian attempts to take a little bark from a tree to cover him from the rain, up comes a white man and threatens to shoot him, claiming the tree as his own."

The Indian truly had grounds for his complaint, and the state of feeling existing among the tribes at this time was well calculated to develop a patriotic leader who should carry them all forward to victory at arms, if certain concessions were not made to them by the whites. But this golden opportunity was seized by an unworthy warrior. A brother of Tecumseh, a "prophet" named Law-le-was-i-kaw, but who assumed the name of Pems-quat-a-wah (Open Door), was the crafty Shawanee warrior who was enabled to work upon both the superstitions and the rational judgment of his fellow Indians. He was a good orator, somewhat peculiar in his appearance and well calculated to win the attention and respect of the savages. He began by denouncing witchcraft, the use of intoxicating liquors, the custom of Indian women marrying white men, the dress of the whites and the practice of selling Indian lands to the United States. He also told the Indians that the commands of the Great Spirit required them to punish with death those who practiced the arts of witchcraft and magic; that the Great Spirit had given him power to find out and expose such persons; that he had power to cure all diseases, to confound his enemies and to stay the arm of death in sickness and on the battle-field. His harangues aroused among some bands of Indians a high degree of superstitious excitement. An old Delaware chief named Ta-te-bock-o-she, through whose influence a treaty had been made with the Delawares in 1804, was accused of witchcraft, tried, condemned and tomahawked, and his body consumed by fire. The old chief's wife, nephew ("Billy Patterson") and an aged Indian named Joshua were next accused of witchcraft and condemned to death. The two men were burned at the stake, but the wife of Ta-te-bock-o-she was saved from

death by her brother, who suddenly approached her, took her by the hand, and, without meeting any opposition from the Indians present, led her out of the council-house. He then immediately returned and checked the growing influence of the Prophet by exclaiming in a strong, earnest voice, " The Evil Spirit has come among us and we are killing each other."—[*Dillon's History of Indiana.*

When Gov. Harrison was made acquainted with these events he sent a special messenger to the Indians, strongly entreating them to renounce the Prophet and his works. This really destroyed to some extent the Prophet's influence; but in the spring of 1808, having aroused nearly all the tribes of the Lake Region, the Prophet with a large number of followers settled near the mouth of the Tippecanoe river, at a place which afterward had the name of "Prophet's-Town." Taking advantage of his brother's influence, Tecumseh actively engaged himself in forming the various tribes into a confederacy. He announced publicly to all the Indians that the treaties by which the United States had acquired lands northwest of the Ohio were not made in fairness, and should be considered void. He also said that no single tribe was invested with power to sell lands without the consent of all the other tribes, and that he and his brother, the Prophet, would oppose and resist all future attempts which the white people might make to extend their settlements in the lands that belonged to the Indians.

Early in 1808, Gov. Harrison sent a speech to the Shawanees, in which was this sentence: " My children, this business must be stopped; I will no longer suffer it. You have called a number of men from the most distant tribes to listen to a fool, who speaks not the words of the Great Spirit but those of the devil and the British agents. My children, your conduct has much alarmed the white settlers near you. They desire that you will send away those people; and if they wish to have the impostor with them they can carry him along with them. Let him go to the lakes; he can hear the British more distinctly." This message wounded the pride of the Prophet, and he prevailed on the messenger to inform Gov. Harrison that he was not in league with the British, but was speaking truly the words of the Great Spirit.

In the latter part of the summer of 1808, the Prophet spent several weeks at Vincennes, for the purpose of holding interviews with Gov. Harrison. At one time he told the Governor that he was a Christian and endeavored to persuade his people also to become Christians, abandon the use of liquor, be united in brotherly love, etc., making Mr. Harrison believe at least, that he was honest; but before long it was demonstrated that the "Prophet" was designing, cunning and unreliable; that both he and Tecumseh were enemies of the United States, and friends of the English; and that in case of a war between the Americans and English, they would join the latter. The next year the Prophet again visited Vincennes, with assurances that he was not in sympathy with the English, but the Governor was not disposed to believe him; and in a letter to the Secretary of War, in July, 1809, he said that he regarded the bands of Indians at Prophet's Town as a combination which had been produced by British intrigue and influence, in anticipation of a war between them and the United States.

In direct opposition to Tecumseh and the prophet and in spite of all these difficulties, Gov. Harrison continued the work of extinguishing Indian titles to lands, with very good success. By the close of 1809, the total amount of land ceded to the United States, under treaties which had been effected by Mr. Harrison, exceeded 30,000,000 acres.

From 1805 to 1807, the movements of Aaron Burr in the Ohio valley created considerable excitement in Indiana. It seemed that he intended to collect a force of men, invade Mexico and found a republic there, comprising all the country west of the Alleghany mountains. He gathered, however, but a few men, started south, and was soon arrested by the Federal authorities. But before his arrest he had abandoned his expedition and his followers had dispersed.

HARRISON'S CAMPAIGN.

While the Indians were combining to prevent any further transfer of land to the whites, the British were using the advantage as a groundwork for a successful war upon the Americans. In the spring of 1810 the followers of the Prophet refused to receive their annuity of salt, and the officials who offered it were denounced as "American dogs," and otherwise treated in a disrespectful manner. Gov. Harrison, in July, attempted to gain the friendship of the Prophet by sending him a letter,offering to treat with him personally in the matter of his grievances, or to furnish means to send him, with three of his principal chiefs, to the President at Washington; but the messenger was coldly received, and they returned word that they would visit Vincennes in a few days and interview the Governor. Accordingly, Aug. 12, 1810, the Shawanee chief with 70 of his principal warriors, marched up to the door of the

Governor's house, and from that day until the 22d held daily interviews with His Excellency. In all of his speeches Tecumseh was haughty, and sometimes arrogant. On the 20th he delivered that celebrated speech in which he gave the Governor the alternative of returning their lands or meeting them in battle.

While the Governor was replying to this speech Tecumseh interrupted him with an angry exclamation, declaring that the United States, through Gov. Harrison, had "cheated and imposed on the Indians." When Tecumseh first rose, a number of his party also sprung to their feet, armed with clubs, tomahawks and spears, and made some threatening demonstrations. The Governor's guards, who stood a little way off, were marched up in haste, and the Indians, awed by the presence of this small armed force, abandoned what seemed to be an intention to make an open attack on the Governor and his attendants. As soon as Tecumseh's remarks were interpreted, the Governor reproached him for his conduct, and commanded him to depart instantly to his camp.

On the following day Tecumseh repented of his rash act and requested the Governor to grant him another interview, and protested against any intention of offense. The Governor consented, and the council was re-opened on the 21st, when the Shawanee chief addressed him in a respectful and dignified manner, but remained immovable in his policy. The Governor then requested Tecumseh to state plainly whether or not the surveyors who might be sent to survey the lands purchased at the treaty of Fort Wayne in 1809, would be molested by Indians. Tecumseh replied: "Brother, when you speak of annuities to me, I look at the land and pity the women and children. I am authorized to say that they will not receive them. Brother, we want to save that piece of land. We do not wish you to take it. It is small enough for our purpose. If you do take it, you must blame yourself as the cause of the trouble between us and the tribes who sold it to you. I want the present boundary line to continue. Should you cross it, I assure you it will be productive of bad consequences."

The next day the Governor, attended only by his interpreter, visited the camp of the great Shawanee, and in the course of a long interview told him that the President of the United States would not acknowledge his claims. "Well," replied the brave warrior, "as the great chief is to determine the matter, I hope the Great Spirit will put sense enough into his head to induce him to direct you to give up this land. It is true, he is so far off he will not be

injured by the war.   He may sit still in his town and drink his
wine, while you and I will have to fight it out."

In his message to the new territorial Legislature in 1810 Gov.
Harrison called attention to the dangerous views held by Tecumseh
and the Prophet, to the pernicious influence of alien enemies
among the Indians, to the unsettled condition of the Indian trade
and to the policy of extinguishing Indian titles to lands.   The
eastern settlements were separated from the western by a considerable extent of Indian lands, and the most fertile tracts within the
territory were still in the hands of the Indians.   Almost entirely
divested of the game from which they had drawn their subsistence,
it had become of little use to them; and it was the intention of
the Government to substitute for the precarious and scanty supplies of the chase the more certain and plentiful support of agriculture and stock-raising.   The old habit of the Indians to hunt
so long as a deer could be found was so inveterate that they would
not break it and resort to intelligent agriculture unless they were
compelled to, and to this they would not be compelled unless they
were confined to a limited extent of territory.   The earnest language of the Governor's appeal was like this: " Are then those
extinguishments of native title which are at once so beneficial to
the Indian and the territory of the United States, to be suspended on
account of the intrigues of a few individuals?   Is one of the fair-
est portions of the globe to remain in a state of nature, the haunt
of a few wretched savages, when it seems destined by the Creator
to give support to a large population, and to be the seat of civilization, of science and true religion?"

In the same message the Governor also urged the establishment
of a system of popular education.

Among the acts passed by this session of the Legislature, one
authorized the President and Directors of the Vincennes Public
Library to raise $1,000 by lottery.   Also, a petition was sent to
Congress for a permanent seat of government for the Territory, and
commissioners were appointed to select the site.

With the beginning of the year 1811 the British agent for
Indian affairs adopted measures calculated to secure the support of
the savages in the war which at this time seemed almost inevitable.
Meanwhile Gov. Harrison did all in his power to destroy the influence of Tecumseh and his brother and break up the Indian confederacy which was being organized in the interests of Great Britain.
Pioneer settlers and the Indians naturally grew more and more

aggressive and intolerant, committing depredations and murders, until the Governor felt compelled to send the following speech, substantially, to the two leaders of the Indian tribes: "This is the third year that all the white people in this country have been alarmed at your proceedings; you threaten us with war; you invite all the tribes north and west of you to join against us, while your warriors who have lately been here deny this. The tribes on the Mississippi have sent me word that you intended to murder me and then commence a war upon my people, and your seizing the salt I recently sent up the Wabash is also sufficient evidence of such intentions on your part. My warriors are preparing themselves, not to strike you, but to defend themselves and their women and children. You shall not surprise us, as you expect to do. Your intended act is a rash one: consider well of it. What can induce you to undertake such a thing when there is so little prospect of success? Do you really think that the handful of men you have about you are able to contend with the seventeen 'fires?' or even that the whole of the tribes united could contend against the Kentucky 'fire' alone? I am myself of the Long 'Knife fire.' As soon as they hear my voice you will see them pouring forth their swarms of hunting-shirt men as numerous as the musquitoes on the shores of the Wabash. Take care of their stings. It is not our wish to hurt you; if we did, we certainly have power to do it.

" You have also insulted the Government of the United States, by seizing the salt that was intended for other tribes. Satisfaction must be given for that also. You talk of coming to see me, attended by all of your young men; but this must not be. If your intentions are good, you have no need to bring but a few of your young men with you. I must be plain with you. I will not suffer you to come into our settlements with such a force. My advice is that you visit the President of the United States and lay your grievances before him.

" With respect to the lands that were purchased last fall I can enter into no negotiations with you; the affair is with the President. If you wish to go and see him, I will supply you with the means.

" The person who delivers this is one of my war officers, and is a man in whom I have entire confidence; whatever he says to you, although it may not be contained in this paper, you may believe comes from me. My friend Tecumseh, the bearer is a good man and a brave warrior; I hope you will treat him well. You are yourself a warrior, and all such should have esteem for each other."

The bearer of this speech was politely received by Tecumseh, who replied to the Governor briefly that he should visit Vincennes in a few days. Accordingly he arrived July 27, 1811, bringing with him a considerable force of Indians, which created much alarm among the inhabitants. In view of an emergency Gov. Harrison reviewed his militia—about 750 armed men—and stationed two companies and a detachment of dragoons on the borders of the town. At this interview Tecumseh held forth that he intended no war against the United States; that he would send messengers among the Indians to prevent murders and depredations on the white settlements; that the Indians, as well as the whites, who had committed murders, ought to be forgiven; that he had set the white people an example of forgiveness, which they ought to follow; that it was his wish to establish a union among all the Indian tribes; that the northern tribes were united; that he was going to visit the southern Indians, and then return to the Prophet's town. He said also that he would visit the President the next spring and settle all difficulties with him, and that he hoped no attempts would be made to make settlements on the lands which had been sold to the United States, at the treaty of Fort Wayne, because the Indians wanted to keep those grounds for hunting.

Tecumseh then, with about 20 of his followers, left for the South, to induce the tribes in that direction to join his confederacy.

By the way, a lawsuit was instituted by Gov. Harrison against a certain Wm. McIntosh, for asserting that the plaintiff had cheated the Indians out of their lands, and that by so doing he had made them enemies to the United States. The defendant was a wealthy Scotch resident of Vincennes, well educated, and a man of influence among the people opposed to Gov. Harrison's land policy. The jury rendered a verdict in favor of Harrison, assessing the damages at $4,000. In execution of the decree of Court a large quantity of the defendant's land was sold in the absence of Gov. Harrison; but some time afterward Harrison caused about two-thirds of the land to be restored to Mr. McIntosh, and the remainder was given to some orphan children.

Harrison's first movement was to erect a new fort on the Wabash river and to break up the assemblage of hostile Indians at the Prophet's town. For this purpose he ordered Col. Boyd's regiment of infantry to move from the falls of Ohio to Vincennes. When the military expedition organized by Gov. Harrison was nearly ready to march to the Prophet's town,several Indian chiefs arrived at Vincennes Sept. 25, 1811, and declared that the Indians would comply with the demands of the Governor and disperse; but this did not check the military proceedings. The army under command of Harrison moved from Vincennes Sept. 26, and Oct. 3, encountering no opposition from the enemy, encamped at the place where Fort Harrison was afterward built, and near where the city of Terre Haute now stands. On the night of the 11th a few hostile Indians approached the encampment and wounded one of the sentinels, which caused considerable excitement. The army was immediately drawn up in line of battle, and small detachments were sent in all directions; but the enemy could not be found. Then the Governor sent a message to Prophet's Town, requiring the Shawanees, Winnebagoes, Pottawatomies and Kickapoos at that place to return to their respective tribes; he also required the Prophet to restore all the stolen horses in his possession, or to give satisfactory proof that such persons were not there, nor had lately been, under his control. To this message the Governor received no answer, unless that answer was delivered in the battle of Tippecanoe.

The new fort on the Wabash was finished Oct. 28, and at the request of all the subordinate officers it was called "Fort Harrison," near what is now Terre Haute. This fort was garrisoned with a small number of men under Lieutenant-Colonel Miller. On the 29th the remainder of the army, consisting of 910 men, moved toward the Prophet's town; about 270 of the troops were mounted. The regular troops, 250 in number, were under the command of Col. Boyd. With this army the Governor marched to within a half mile of the Prophet's town, when a conference was opened with a distinguished chief, in high esteem with the Prophet, and he informed Harrison that the Indians were much surprised at the approach of the army, and had already dispatched a message to him by another route. Harrison replied that he would not attack them until he had satisfied himself that they would not comply with his demands; that he would continue his encampment on the Wabash, and on the following morning would have an interview with the prophet. Harrison then resumed his march, and, after some difficulty, selected a place to encamp—a spot not very desirable. It was a piece of dry oak land rising about ten feet above the marshy prairie in front toward the Indian town, and nearly twice that height above a similar prairie in the rear, through which and near this bank ran a small stream clothed with willow and brush wood. Toward the left flank this highland widened considerably, but became gradually narrower in the opposite direction, and at the distance of 150 yards terminated in an abrupt point. The two columns of infantry occupied the front and rear of this ground, about 150 yards from each other on the left, and a little more than half that distance on the right, flank. One flank was filled by two companies of mounted riflemen, 120 men, under command of Major-General Wells, of the Kentucky militia, and one by Spencer's company of mounted riflemen, numbering 80 men. The front line was composed of one battalion of United States infantry, under command of Major Floyd, flanked on the right by two companies of militia, and on the left by one company. The rear line was composed of a battalion of United States troops, under command of Capt. Bean, acting as Major, and four companies of militia infantry under Lieutenant-Colonel Decker. The regular troops of this line joined the mounted riflemen under Gen. Wells, on the left flank, and Col. Decker's battalion formed an angle with Spencer's company on the left. Two troops of dragoons, about 60 men in all, were encamped in the rear of the left flank, and Capt. Parke's troop, which was larger than the other two, in rear of the right line. For a night attack the order of encampment was the order of battle, and each man slept opposite his post in the line. In the formation of the troops single file was adopted, in order to get as great an extension of the lines as possible.

BATTLE OF TIPPECANOE.

No attack was made by the enemy until about 4 o'clock on the morning of Nov. 7, just after the Governor had arisen. The attack was made on the left flank. Only a single gun was fired by the sentinels or by the guard in that direction, which made no resistance, abandoning their posts and fleeing into camp; and the first notice which the troops of that line had of the danger was the yell of the savages within a short distance of them. But the men were courageous and preserved good discipline. Such of them as were awake, or easily awakened, seized arms and took their stations; others, who were more tardy, had to contend with the enemy in the doors of their tents. The storm first fell upon Capt. Barton's company of the Fourth United States Regiment, and Capt. Geiger's company of mounted riflemen, which formed the left angle of the rear line. The fire from the Indians was exceedingly severe, and men in these companies suffered considerably before relief could be brought to them. Some few Indians passed into the encampment near the angle, and one or two penetrated to some distance before they were killed. All the companies formed for action before they were fired on. The morning was dark and cloudy, and the fires of the Americans afforded only a partial light, which gave greater advantage to the enemy than to the troops, and they were therefore extinguished.

As soon as the Governor could mount his horse he rode to the angle which was attacked, where he found that Barton's company had suffered severely, and the left of Geiger's entirely broken. He immediately ordered Cook's and Wentworth's companies to march up to the center of the rear line, where were stationed a small company of U. S. riflemen and the companies of Bean, Snelling and Prescott. As the General rode up he found Maj. Daviess forming the dragoons in the rear of these companies, and having ascertained that the heaviest fire proceeded from some trees 15 or 20 paces in front of these companies, he directed the Major to dislodge them with a part of the dragoons; but unfortunately the Major's gallantry caused him to undertake the execution of the order with a smaller force than was required, which enabled the enemy to avoid him in front and attack his flanks. He was mortally wounded and his men driven back. Capt. Snelling, however, with his company immediately dislodged those Indians. Capt. Spencer and his 1st and 2nd Lieutenants were killed, and Capt. Warwick mortally wounded. The soldiery remained brave. Spencer had too much ground originally, and Harrison re-enforced him with a company of riflemen which had been driven from their position on the left flank.

Gen. Harrison's aim was to keep the lines entire, to prevent the enemy from breaking into the camp until daylight, which would enable him to make a general and effectual charge. With this view he had re-enforced every part of the line that had suffered much, and with the approach of morning he withdrew several companies from the front and rear lines and re-enforced the right and left flanks, foreseeing that at these points the enemy would make their last effort. Maj. Wells, who had commanded the left flank, charged upon the enemy and drove them at the point of the bayonet into the marsh, where they could not be followed. Meanwhile Capt. Cook and Lieut. Larrabee marched their companies to the right flank and formed under fire of the enemy, and being there joined by the riflemen of that flank, charged upon the enemy, killing a number and putting the rest to a precipitate flight.

Thus ended the famous battle of Tippecanoe, victoriously to the whites and honorably to Gen. Harrison.

In this battle Mr. Harrison had about 700 efficient men, while the Indians had probably more than that. The loss of the Americans was 37 killed and 25 mortally wounded, and 126 wounded; the Indians lost 38 killed on the field of battle, and the number of the wounded was never known. Among the whites killed were Daviess, Spencer, Owen, Warwick, Randolph, Bean and White. Standing on an eminence near by, the Prophet encouraged his warriors to battle by singing a favorite war-song. He told them that they would gain an easy victory, and that the bullets of their enemies would be made harmless by the Great Spirit. Being informed during the engagement that some of the Indians were killed, he said that his warriors must fight on and they would soon be victorious. Immediately after their defeat the surviving Indians lost faith in their great (?) Prophet, returned to their respective tribes, and thus the confederacy was destroyed. The Prophet, with a very few followers, then took up his residence among a small band of Wyandots encamped on Wild-Cat creek. His famous town, with all its possessions, was destroyed the next day, Nov. 8.

On the 18th the American army returned to Vincennes, where most of the troops were discharged. The Territorial Legislature, being in session, adopted resolutions complimentary to Gov. Harrison and the officers and men under him, and made preparations for a reception and celebration.

Capt. Logan, the eloquent Shawanee chief who assisted our forces so materially, died in the latter part of November, 1812, from the effects of a wound received in a skirmish with a reconnoitering party of hostile Indians accompanied by a white man in the British service, Nov. 22. In that skirmish the white man was killed, and Winamac, a Pottawatomie chief of some distinction, fell by the rifle of Logan. The latter was mortally wounded, when he retreated with two warriors of his tribe, Capt. Johnny and Bright-Horn, to the camp of Gen. Winchester, where he soon afterward died. He was buried with the honors of war.

WAR OF 1812 WITH GREAT BRITAIN.

The victory recently gained by the Americans at the battle of Tippecanoe insured perfect peace for a time, but only a short time as the more extensive schemes of the British had so far ripened as to compel the United States again to declare war against them. Tecumseh had fled to Malden, Canada, where, counseled by the English, he continued to excite the tribes against the Americans. As soon as this war with Great Britain was declared (June 18, 1812), the Indians, as was expected, commenced again to commit depredations. During the summer of 1812 several points along the Lake Region succumbed to theBritish, as Detroit, under Gen. Hull, Fort Dearborn (now Chicago), commanded by Capt. Heald under Gen. Hull, the post at Mackinac, etc.

In the early part of September, 1812, parties of hostile Indians began to assemble in considerable numbers in the vicinity of Forts Wayne and Harrison, with a view to reducing them. Capt. Rhea, at this time, had command of Fort Wayne, but his drinking propensities rather disqualified him for emergencies. For two weeks the fort was in great jeopardy. An express had been sent to Gen. Harrison for reinforcements, but many days passed without any tidings of expected assistance. At length, one day, Maj. Wm. Oliver and four friendly Indians arrived at the fort on horseback. One of the Indians was the celebrated Logan. They had come in defiance of "500 Indians," had "broken their ranks" and reached the fort in safety. Oliver reported that Harrison was aware of the situation and was raising men for a re-enforcement. Ohio was also raising volunteers; 800 were then assembled at St. Mary's, Ohio, 60 miles south of Fort Wayne, and would march to the relief of the fort in three or four days, or as soon as they were joined by re-enforcements from Kentucky.

Oliver prepared a letter, announcing to Gen. Harrison his safe arrival at the besieged fort, and giving an account of its beleaguered situation, which he dispatched by his friendly Shawanees, while he concluded to take his chances at the fort. Brave Logan and his companions started with the message, but had scarcely left the fort when they were discovered and pursued by the hostile Indians, yet passing the Indian lines in safety, they were soon out of reach. The Indians now began a furious attack upon the fort; but the little garrison, with Oliver to cheer them on, bravely met the assault, repelling the attack day after day, until the army approached to their relief. During this siege the commanding officer, whose habits of intemperance rendered him unfit for the command, was confined in the "black hole," while the junior officer assumed charge. This course was approved by the General, on his arrival, but Capt. Rhea received very little censure, probably on account of his valuable services in the Revolutionary war.

Sept. 6, 1812, Harrison moved forward with his army to the relief of Fort Wayne; the next day he reached a point within three miles of St. Mary's river; the next day he reached the river and was joined at evening by 200 mounted volunteers, under Col. Richard M. Johnson; the next day at "Shane's Crossing" on the St. Mary's they were joined by 800 men from Ohio, under Cols. Adams and Hawkins. At this place Chief Logan and four other Indians offered their services as spies to Gen. Harrison, and were accepted. Logan was immediately disguised and sent forward. Passing through the lines of the hostile Indians, he ascertained their number to be about 1,500, and entering the fort, he encouraged the soldiers to hold out, as relief was at hand. Gen. Harrison's force at this time was about 3,500.

After an early breakfast Friday morning they were under marching orders; it had rained and the guns were damp; they were discharged and reloaded; but that day only one Indian was encountered; preparations were made at night for an expected attack by the Indians, but no attack came; the next day, Sept. 10, they expected to fight their way to Fort Wayne, but in that they were happily disappointed; and "At the first grey of the morning," as Bryce eloquently observes, "the distant halloos of the disappointed savages revealed to the anxious inmates of the fort the glorious news of the approach of the army. Great clouds of dust could be seen from the fort, rolling up in the distance, as the valiant soldiery under Gen. Harrison moved forward to the rescue of the garrison and the brave boys of Kentucky and Ohio."

This siege of Fort Wayne of course occasioned great loss to the few settlers who had gathered around the fort. At the time of its commencement quite a little village had clustered around the military works, but during the siege most of their improvements and crops were destroyed by the savages. Every building out of the reach of the guns of the fort was leveled to the ground, and thus the infant settlement was destroyed.

During this siege the garrison lost but three men, while the Indians lost 25. Gen. Harrison had all the Indian villages for 25 miles around destroyed. Fort Wayne was nothing but a military post until about 1819.

Simultaneously with the attack on Fort Wayne the Indians also besieged Fort Harrison, which was commanded by Zachary Taylor. The Indians commenced firing upon the fort about 11 o'clock one night, when the garrison was in a rather poor plight for receiving them. The enemy succeeded in firing one of the block-houses, which contained whisky, and the whites had great difficulty in preventing the burning of all the barracks. The word "fire" seemed to have thrown all the men into confusion; soldiers' and citizens' wives, who had taken shelter within the fort, were crying; Indians were yelling; many of the garrison were sick and unable to be on duty; the men despaired and gave themselves up as lost; two of the strongest and apparently most reliable men jumped the pickets in the very midst of the emergency, etc., so that Capt. Taylor was at his wit's end what to do; but he gave directions as to the many details, rallied the men by a new scheme, and after about seven hours succeeded in saving themselves. The Indians drove up the horses belonging to the citizens, and as they could not catch them very readily, shot the whole of them in the sight of their owners, and also killed a number of the hogs belonging to the whites. They drove off all of the cattle, 65 in number, as well as the public oxen.

Among many other depredations committed by the savages during this period, was the massacre of the Pigeon Roost settlement, consisting of one man, five women and 16 children; a few escaped. An unsuccessful effort was made to capture these Indians, but when the news of this massacre and the attack on Fort Harrison reached Vincennes, about 1,200 men, under the command of Col. Wm. Russell, of the 7th U. S. Infantry, marched forth for the relief of the fort and to punish the Indians. On reaching the fort the Indians had retired from the vicinity; but on the 15th of September a small detachment composed of 11 men, under Lieut. Richardson, and acting as escort of provisions sent from Vincennes to Fort Harrison, was attacked by a party of Indians within the present limits of Sullivan county. It was reported that seven of these men were killed and one wounded. The provisions of course fell into the hands of the Indians.

EXPEDITIONS AGAINST THE INDIANS.

By the middle of August, through the disgraceful surrender of Gen. Hull, at Detroit, and the evacuation of Fort Dearborn and massacre of its garrison, the British and Indians were in possession of the whole Northwest. The savages, emboldened by their successes, penetrated deeper into the settlements, committing great depredations. The activity and success of the enemy aroused the people to a realization of the great danger their homes and families were in. Gov. Edwards collected a force of 350 men at Camp Russell, and Capt. Russell came from Vincennes with about 50 more. Being officered and equipped, they proceeded about the middle of October on horseback, carrying with them 20 day's rations, to Peoria. Capt. Craig was sent with two boats up the Illinois, with provisions and tools to build a fort. The little army proceeded to Peoria Lake, where was located a Pottawatomie village. They arrived late at night, within a few miles of the village, without their presence being known to the Indians. Four men were sent out that night to reconnoiter the position of the village. The four brave men who volunteered for this perilous service were Thomas Carlin (afterward Governor), and Robert, Stephen and Davis Whiteside. They proceeded to the village, and explored it and the approaches to it thoroughly, without starting an Indian or provoking the bark of a dog. The low lands between the Indian village and the troops were covered with a rank growth of tall grass, so high and dense as to readily conceal an Indian on horseback, until within a few feet of him. The ground had become still more yielding by recent rains, rendering it almost impassable by mounted men. To prevent detection the soldiers had camped without lighting the usual camp-fires. The men lay down in their cold and cheerless camp, with many misgivings. They well remembered how the skulking savages fell upon Harrison's men at Tippecanoe during the night. To add to their fears, a gun in the hands of a soldier was carelessly discharged, raising great consternation in the camp.

Through a dense fog which prevailed the following morning, the army took up its line of march for the Indian town, Capt. Judy with his corps of spies in advance. In the tall grass they came up with an Indian and his squaw, both mounted. The Indian wanted to surrender, but Judy observed that he "did not leave home to take prisoners," and instantly shot one of them. With the blood streaming from his mouth and nose, and in his agony "singing the death song," the dying Indian raised his gun, shot and mortally wounded a Mr. Wright, and in a few minutes expired! Many guns were immediately discharged at the other Indian, not then known to be a squaw, all of which missed her. Badly scared, and her husband killed by her side, the agonizing wails of the squaw were heart-rending. She was taken prisoner, and afterward restored to her nation.

On nearing the town a general charge was made, the Indians fleeing to the interior wilderness. Some of their warriors made a stand, when a sharp engagement occurred, but the Indians were routed. In their flight they left behind all their winter's store of provisions, which was taken, and their town burned. Some Indian children were found who had been left in the hurried flight, also some disabled adults, one of whom was in a starving condition, and with a voracious appetite partook of the bread given him. He is said to have been killed by a cowardly trooper straggling behind, after the main army had resumed its retrograde march, who wanted to be able to boast that he had killed an Indian.

September 19, 1812, Gen. Harrison was put in command of the Northwestern army, then estimated at 10,000 men, with these orders: "Having provided for the protection of the western frontier, you will retake Detroit; and, with a view to the conquest of upper Canada, you will penetrate that country as far as the force under your command will in your judgment justify."

Although surrounded by many difficulties, the General began immediately to execute these instructions. In calling for volunteers from Kentucky, however, more men offered than could be received. At this time there were about 2,000 mounted volunteers at Vincennes, under the command of Gen. Samuel Hopkins, of the Revolutionary war, who was under instructions to operate against the enemy along the Wabash and Illinois rivers. Accordingly, early in October, Gen. Hopkins moved from Vincennes towards the Kickapoo villages in the Illinois territory, with about 2,000 troops; but after four or five days' march the men and officers raised a mutiny which gradually succeeded in carrying all back to Vincennes. The cause of their discontent is not apparent.

About the same time Col. Russell, with two small companies of U. S. rangers, commanded by Capts. Perry and Modrell, marched from the neighborhood of Vincennes to unite with a small force of mounted militia under the command of Gov. Edwards, of Illinois, and afterward to march with the united troops from Cahokia toward Lake Peoria, for the purpose of co operating with Gen. Hopkins against the Indian towns in that vicinity; but not finding the latter on the ground, was compelled to retire.

Immediately after the discharge of the mutinous volunteers, Gen. Hopkins began to organize another force, mainly of infantry, to reduce the Indians up the Wabash as far as the Prophet's town. These troops consisted of three regiments of Kentucky militia, commanded by Cols. Barbour, Miller and Wilcox; a small company of regulars commanded by Capt. Zachary Taylor; a company of rangers commanded by Capt. Beckes; and a company of scouts or spies under the command of Capt. Washburn. The main body of this army arrived at Fort Harrison Nov. 5; on the 11th it proceeded up the east side of the Wabash into the heart of the Indian country, but found the villages generally deserted. Winter setting in severely, and the troops poorly clad, they had to return to Vincennes as rapidly as possible. With one exception the men behaved nobly, and did much damage to the enemy. That exception was the precipitate chase after an Indian by a detachment of men somewhat in liquor, until they found themselves surrounded by an overwhelming force of the enemy, and they had to retreat in disorder.

At the close of this campaign Gen. Hopkins resigned his command.

In the fall of 1812 Gen. Harrison assigned to Lieut. Col. John B. Campbell, of the 19th U. S. Inf., the duty of destroying the Miami villages on the Mississinewa river, with a detachment of about 600 men. Nov. 25, Lieut. Col. Campbell marched from Franklinton, according to orders, toward the scene of action, cautiously avoiding falling in with the Delawares, who had been ordered by Gen. Harrison to retire to the Shawanee establishment on the Auglaize river, and arriving on the Mississinewa Dec. 17, when they discovered an Indian town inhabited by Delawares and Miamis This and three other villages were destroyed. Soon after this, the supplies growing short and the troops in a suffering condition, Campbell began to consider the propriety of returning to Ohio; but just as he was calling together his officers early one morning to deliberate on the proposition, an army of Indians rushed upon them with fury. The engagement lasted an hour, with a loss of eight killed and 42 wounded, besides about 150 horses killed. The whites, however, succeeded in defending themselves and taking a number of Indians prisoners, who proved to be Munsies, of Silver Heel's band. Campbell, hearing that a large force of Indians were assembled at Mississinewa village, under Tecumseh, determined to return to Greenville. The privations of his troops and the severity of the cold compelled him to send to that place for re-enforcements and supplies. Seventeen of the men had to be carried on litters. They were met by the re-enforcement about 40 miles from Greenville.

Lieut. Col. Campbell sent two messages to the Delawares, who lived on White river and who had been previously directed and requested to abandon their towns on that river and remove into Ohio. In these messages he expressed his regret at unfortunately killing some of their men, and urged them to move to the Shawanee settlement on the Auglaize river. He assured them that their people, in his power, would be compensated by the Government for their losses, if not found to be hostile; and the friends of those killed satisfied by presents, if such satisfaction would be received. This advice was heeded by the main body of the Delawares and a few Miamis. The Shawanee Prophet, and some of the principal chiefs of the Miamis, retired from the country of the Wabash, and, with their destitute and suffering bands, moved to Detroit, where they were received as the friends and allies of Great Britain.

On the approach of Gen. Harrison with his army in September, 1813, the British evacuated Detroit, and the Ottawas, Chippewas, Pottawatomies, Miamis and Kickapoos sued for peace with the United States, which was granted temporarily by Brig. Gen. McArthur, on condition of their becoming allies of the United States in case of war.

In June, 1813, an expedition composed of 137 men, under command of Col. Joseph Bartholomew, moved from Valonia toward the Delaware towns on the west fork of White river, to surprise and punish some hostile Indians who were supposed to be lurking about those villages. Most of these places they found deserted; some of them burnt. They had been but temporarily occupied for the purpose of collecting and carrying away corn. Col. Bartholomew's forces succeeded in killing one or two Indians and destroying considerable corn, and they returned to Valonia on the 21st of this month.

July 1, 1813, Col. William Russell, of the 7th U. S., organized a force of 573 effective men at Valonia and marched to the Indian villages about the mouth of the Mississinewa. His experience was much like that of Col. Bartholomew, who had just preceded him. He had rainy weather, suffered many losses, found the villages deserted, destroyed stores of corn, etc. The Colonel reported that he went to every place where he expected to find the enemy, but they nearly always seemed to have fled the country. The march from Valonia to the mouth of the Mississinewa and return was about 250 miles.

Several smaller expeditions helped to "checker" the surrounding

country, and find that the Indians were very careful to keep themselves out of sight, and thus closed this series of campaigns.

CLOSE OF THE WAR.

The war with England closed on the 24th of December, 1814,
when a treaty of peace was signed at Ghent. The 9th article of
the treaty required the United States to put an end to hostilities
with all tribes or nations of Indians with whom they had been at
war; to restore to such tribes or nations respectively all the rights
and possessions to which they were entitled in 1811, before the
war, on condition that such Indians should agree to desist from all
hostilities against the United States. But in February, just before
the treaty was sanctioned by our Government, there were signs of
Indians accumulating arms and ammunition, and a cautionary
order was therefore issued to have all the white forces in readiness
for an attack by the Indians; but the attack was not made. During
the ensuing summer and fall the United States Government acquainted the Indians with the provisions of the treaty, and entered
into subordinate treaties of peace with the principal tribes.

Just before the treaty of Spring Wells (near Detroit) was signed,
the Shawanee Prophet retired to Canada, but declaring his resolution to abide by any treaty which the chiefs might sign. Some
time afterward he returned to the Shawanee settlement in Ohio, and
lastly to the west of the Mississippi, where he died, in 1834. The
British Government allowed him a pension from 1813 until his
death. His brother Tecumseh was killed at the battle of the
Thames, Oct. 5, 1813, by a Mr. Wheatty, as we are positively informed by Mr. A. J. James, now a resident of La Harpe township,
Hancock county, Ill., whose father-in-law, John Pigman, of Co-
shocton county, Ohio, was an eye witness. Gen. Johnson has generally had the credit of killing Tecumseh.

If one should inquire who has been the greatest Indian, the most noted, the "principal Indian" in North America since its discovery by Columbus, we would be obliged to answer, Tecumseh. For all those qualities which elevate a man far above his race; for talent, tact, skill and bravery as a warrior; for high-minded, honorable and chivalrous bearing as a man; in a word, for all those elements of greatness which place him a long way above his fellows in savage life, the name and fame of Tecumseh will go down to posterity in the West as one of the most celebrated of the aborigines of this continent,—as one who had no equal among the tribes that dwelt in the country drained by the Mississippi. Born to command himself, he used all the appliances that would stimulate the courage and nerve the valor of his followers. Always in the front rank of battle, his followers blindly followed his lead, and as his war-cry rang clear above the din and noise of the battle-field, the Shawnee warriors, as they rushed on to victory or the grave, rallied around him, foemen worthy of the steel of the most gallant commander that ever entered the lists in defense of his altar or his home.

The tribe to which Tecumseh, or Tecumtha, as some write it, belonged, was the Shawnee, or Shawanee. The tradition of the nation held that they originally came from the Gulf of Mexico; that they wended their way up the Mississippi and the Ohio, and settled at or near the present site of Shawneetown, Ill., whence they removed to the upper Wabash. In the latter place, at any rate, they were found early in the 18th century, and were known as the "bravest of the brave." This tribe has uniformly been the bitter enemy of the white man, and in every contest with our people has exhibited a degree of skill and strategy that should characterize the most dangerous foe.

Tecumseh's notoriety and that of his brother, the Prophet, mutually served to establish and strengthen each other. While the Prophet had unlimited power, spiritual and temporal, he distributed his greatness in all the departments of Indian life with a kind of fanaticism that magnetically aroused the religious and superstitious passions, not only of his own followers, but also of all the tribes in this part of the country; but Tecumseh concentrated his greatness upon the more practical and business affairs of military conquest. It is doubted whether he was really a sincere believer in the pretensions of his fanatic brother; if he did not believe in the pretentious feature of them he had the shrewdness to keep his unbelief to himself, knowing that religious fanaticism was one of the strongest impulses to reckless bravery.

During his sojourn in the Northwestern Territory, it was Tecumseh's uppermost desire of life to confederate all the Indian tribes of the country together against the whites, to maintain their choice hunting-grounds. All his public policy converged toward this single end. In his vast scheme he comprised even all the Indians in the Gulf country,—all in America west of the Alleghany mountains. He held, as a subordinate principle, that the Great Spirit had given the Indian race all these hunting-grounds to keep in common, and that no Indian or tribe could cede any portion of the land to the whites without the consent of all the tribes. Hence, in all his councils with the whites he ever maintained that the treaties were null and void.

When he met Harrison at Vincennes in council the last time, and, as he was invited by that General to take a seat with him on the platform, he hesitated; Harrison insisted, saying that it was the "wish of their Great Father, the President of the United States, that he should do so." The chief paused a moment, raised his tall and commanding form to its greatest height, surveyed the troops and crowd around him, fixed his keen eyes upon Gov. Harrison, and then turning them to the sky above, and pointing toward heaven with his sinewy arm in a manner indicative of supreme contempt for the paternity assigned him, said in clarion tones: " My father? The sun is my father, the earth is my mother, and on her bosom I will recline." He then stretched himself, with his warriors, on the green sward. The effect was electrical, and for some moments there was perfect silence.

The Governor, then, through an interpreter, told him that he understood he had some complaints to make and redress to ask, etc., and that he wished to investigate the matter and make restitution wherever it might be decided it should be done. As soon as the Governor was through with this introductory speech, the stately warrior arose, tall, athletic, manly, dignified and graceful, and with a voice at first low, but distinct and musical, commenced a reply. As he warmed up with his subject his clear tones might be heard, as if " trumpet-tongued," to the utmost limits of the assembly. The most perfect silence prevailed, except when his warriors gave their guttural assent to some eloquent recital of the red man's wrong and the white man's injustice. Tecumseh recited the wrongs which his race had suffered from the time of the massacre of the Moravian Indians to the present; said he did not know how he could ever again be the friend of the white man; that the Great Spirit had given to the Indian all the land from the Miami to the Mississippi, and from the lakes to the Ohio, as a common property to all the tribes in these borders, and that the land could not and should not be sold without the consent of all; that all the tribes on the continent formed but one nation; that if the United States would not give up the lands they had bought of the Miamis and the other tribes, those united with him were determined to annihilate those tribes; that they were determined to have no more chiefs, but in future to be governed by their warriors; that unless the whites ceased their encroachments upon Indian lands, the fate of the Indians was sealed; they had been driven from the banks of the Delaware across the Alleghanies, and their possessions on the Wabash and the Illinois were now to be taken from them; that in a few years they would not have ground enough to bury their warriors on this side of the "Father of Waters;" that all would perish, all their possessions taken from them by fraud or force, unless they stopped the progress of the white man westward; that it must be a war of races in which one or the other must perish; that their tribes had been driven toward the setting sun like a galloping horse (ne-kat a-kush-e ka-top-o-lin-to).

The Shawnee language, in which this most eminent Indian statesman spoke, excelled all other aboriginal tongues in its musical articulation; and the effect of Tecumseh's oratory on this occasion can be more easily imagined than described. Gov. Harrison, although as brave a soldier and General as any American, was overcome by this speech. He well knew Tecumseh's power and influence among all the tribes, know his bravery, courage and determination, and knew that he meant what he said. When Tecumseh was done speaking there was a stillness throughout the assembly which was really painful; not a whisper was heard, and all eyes were turned from the speaker toward Gov. Harrison, who after a few moments came to himself, and recollecting many of the absurd statements of the great Indian orator, began a reply which was more logical, if not so eloquent. The Shawnees were attentive until Harrison's interpreter began to translate his speech to the Miamis and Pottawatomies, when Tecumseh and his warriors sprang to their feet, brandishing their war-clubs and tomahawks. "Tell him," said Tecumseh, addressing the interpreter in Shawnee, "he lies." The interpreter undertook to convey this message to the Governor in smoother language, but Tecumseh noticed the effort and remonstrated, "No, no; tell him he lies." The warriors began to grow more excited, when Secretary Gibson ordered the American troops in arms to advance. This allayed the rising storm, and as soon as Tecumseh's "He lies" was literally interpreted to the Governor, the latter told Tecumseh through the interpreter to tell Tecumseh he would hold no further council with him.

Thus the assembly was broken up, and one can hardly imagine a more exciting scene. It would constitute the finest subject for a historical painting to adorn the rotunda of the capitol. The next day Tecumseh requested another interview with the Governor, which was granted on condition that he should make an apology to the Governor for his language the day before. This he made through the interpreter. Measures for defense and protection were taken, however, lest there should be another outbreak. Two companies of militia were ordered from the country, and the one in town added to them, while the Governor and his friends went into council fully armed and prepared for any contingency. On this occasion the conduct of Tecumseh was entirely different from that of the day before. Firm and intrepid, showing not the slightest fear or alarm, surrounded with a military force four times his own, he preserved the utmost composure and equanimity. No one would have supposed that he could have been the principal actor in the thrilling scene of the previous day. He claimed that half the Americans were in sympathy with him. He also said that whites had informed him that Gov. Harrison had purchased land from the Indians without any authority from the Government; that he, Harrison, had but two years more to remain in office, and that if he, Tecumseh, could prevail upon the Indians who sold the lands not to receive their annuities for that time, and the present Governor displaced by a good man as his successor, the latter would restore to the Indians all the lands purchased from them.

The Wyandots, Kickapoos, Pottawatomies, Ottawas and the Winnebagoes, through their respective spokesmen, declared their adherence to the great Shawnee warrior and statesman. Gov. Harrison then told them that he would send Tecumseh's speech to the Presi-

dent of the United States and return the answer to the Indians as soon
as it was received. Tecumseh then declared that he and his allies were
determined that the old boundary line should continue; and that
if the whites crossed it, it would be at their peril. Gov. Harrison replied that he would be equally plain with him and state that the
President would never allow that the lands on the Wabash were the
property of any other tribes than those who had occupied them
since the white people first came to America; and as the title to
the lands lately purchased was derived from those tribes by a fair
purchase, he might rest assured that the right of the United States
would be supported by the sword. "So be it," was the stern and
haughty reply of the Shawnee chieftan, as he and his braves took
leave of the Governor and wended their way in Indian file to their
camping ground.

Thus ended the last conference on earth between the chivalrous
Tecumseh and the hero of the battle of Tippecanoe. The bones of
the first lie bleaching on the battle-field of the Thames, and those
of the last in a mausoleum on the banks of the Ohio; each struggled for the mastery of his race, and each no doubt was equally
honest and patriotic in his purposes. The weak yielded to the
strong, the defenseless to the powerful, and the hunting-ground of
the Shawnee is all occupied by his enemy.

Tecumseh, with four of his braves, immediately embarked in a
birch canoe, descended the Wabash, and went on to the South to
unite the tribes of that country in a general system of self-defense
against the encroachment of the whites. His emblem was a dis-
jointed snake, with the motto, "Join or die!" In union alone was
strength.

Before Tecumseh left the Prophet's town at the mouth of the
Tippecanoe river, on his excursion to the South, he had a definite
understanding with his brother and the chieftains of the other tribes
in the Wabash country, that they should preserve perfect peace
with the whites until his arrangements were completed for a confederacy of the tribes on both sides of the Ohio and on the Mississippi river; but it seems that while he was in the South engaged
in his work of uniting the tribes of that country some of the Northern tribes showed signs of fight and precipitated Harrison into that
campaign which ended in the battle of Tippecanoe and the total
route of the Indians. Tecumseh, on his return from the South,
learning what had happened, was overcome with chagrin, disappoint-
ment and anger, and accused his brother of duplicity and coward-

ice; indeed, it is said that he never forgave him to the day of his death. A short time afterward, on the breaking out of the war of Great Britain, he joined Proctor, at Malden, with a party of his warriors, and finally suffered the fate mentioned on page 108.

CIVIL MATTERS 1812--'5.

Owing to the absence of Gov. Harrison on military duty, John Gibson, the Secretary of the Territory, acted in the administration of civil affairs. In his message to the Legislature convening on the 1st of February, 1813, he said, substantially:

"Did I possess the abilities of Cicero or Demosthenes, I could not portray in more glowing colors our foreign and domestic political situation than it is already experienced within our own breasts. The United States have been compelled, by frequent acts of injustice, to declare war against England. For a detail of the causes of this war I would refer to the message of President Madison; it does honor to his head and heart. Although not an admirer of war, I am glad to see our little but inimitable navy riding triumphant on the seas, but chagrined to find that our armies by land are so little successful. The spirit of '76 appears to have fled from our continent, or, if not fled, is at least asleep, for it appears not to pervade our armies generally. At your last assemblage our political horizon seemed clear, and our infant Territory bid fair for rapid and rising grandeur; but, alas, the scene has changed; and whether this change, as respects our Territory, has been owing to an over anxiety in us to extend our dominions, or to a wish for retaliation by our foes, or to a foreign influence, I shall not say. The Indians, our former neighbors and friends, have become our most inveterate foes. Our former frontiers are now our wilds, and our inner settlements have become frontiers. Some of our best citizens, and old men worn down with age, and helpless women and innocent babes, have fallen victims to savage cruelty. I have done my duty as well as I can, and hope that the interposition of Providence will protect us."

The many complaints made about the Territorial Government Mr. Gibson said, were caused more by default of officers than of the law. Said he: "It is an old and, I believe, correct adage, that 'good officers make good soldiers.' This evil having taken root, I do not know how it can be eradicated; but it may be remedied. In place of men searching after and accepting commissions before they are even tolerably qualified, thereby subjecting themselves to ridicule and their country to ruin, barely for the name of the thing, I think may be remedied by a previous examination."

During this session of the Legislature the seat of the Territorial Government was declared to be at Corydon, and immediately acting Governor Gibson prorogued the Legislature to meet at that place, the first Monday of December, 1813. During this year the Territory was almost defenseless; Indian outrages were of common occurrence, but no general outbreak was made. The militia-men were armed with rifles and long knives, and many of the rangers carried tomahawks.

In 1813 Thomas Posey, who was at that time a Senator in Congress from Tennessee, and who had been officer of the army of the Revolution, was appointed Governor of Indiana Territory, to succeed Gen. Harrison. He arrived in Vincennes and entered upon the discharge of his duties May 25, 1813. During this year several expeditions against the Indian settlements were set on foot.

In his first message to the Legislature the following December, at Corydon, Gov. Posey said: "The present crisis is awful, and big with great events. Our land and nation is involved in the common calamity of war; but we are under the protecting care of the beneficent Being, who has on a former occasion brought us safely through an arduous struggle and placed us on a foundation of independence, freedom and happiness. He will not suffer to be taken from us what He, in His great wisdom has thought proper to confer and bless us with, if we make a wise and virtuous use of His good gifts. * * * Although our affairs, at the commencement of the war, wore a gloomy aspect, they have brightened, and promise a certainty of success, if properly directed and conducted, of which I have no doubt, as the President and heads of departments of the general Government are men of undoubted patriotism, talents and experience, and who have grown old in the service of their country. * * * It must be obvious to every thinking man that we were forced into the war. Every measure consistent with honor, both before and since the declaration of war, has tried to be on amicable terms with our enemy. * * * You who reside in various parts of the Territory have it in your power to understand what will tend to its local and general advantage. The judiciary system would require a revisal and amendment. The militia law is very defective and requires your immediate attention. It is necessary to have good roads and highways in as many directions through the Territory as the circumstances and situation of the inhabitants will admit; it would contribute very much to promote the settlement and improvement of the Territory. Attention to education is highly necessary. There is an appropriation made by Congress, in lands, for the purpose of establishing public schools. It comes now within your province to carry into operation the design of the appropriation."

This Legislature passed several very necessary laws for the welfare of the settlements, and the following year, as Gen. Harrison was generally successful in his military campaigns in the Northwest, the settlements in Indiana began to increase and improve. The fear of danger from Indians had in a great measure subsided, and the tide of immigration began again to flow. In January, 1814, about a thousand Miamis assembled at Fort Wayne for the purpose of obtaining food to prevent starvation. They met with ample hospitality, and their example was speedily followed by others. These, with other acts of kindness, won the lasting friendship of the Indians, many of whom had fought in the interests of Great Britain. General treaties between the United States and the Northwestern tribes were subsequently concluded, and the way was fully opened for the improvement and settlement of the lands.

POPULATION IN 1815.

The population of the Territory of Indiana, as given in the official returns to the Legislature of 1815, was as follows, by counties:

COUNTIES.	White males of 21 and over.	TOTAL.
Wayne	1,225	6,407
Franklin	1,430	7,370
Dearborn	902	4,424
Switzerland	377	1,832
Jefferson	874	4,270
Clark	1,387	7,150
Washington	1,420	7,317
Harrison	1,056	6,975
Knox	1,391	8,068
Gibson	1,100	5,340
Posey	320	1,619
Warrick	280	1,415
Perry	350	1,720
Grand Totals	12,112	63,897

GENERAL VIEW.

The well-known ordinance of 1787 conferred many "rights and privileges" upon the inhabitants of the Northwestern Territory, and consequently upon the people of Indiana Territory, but after all it came far short of conferring as many privileges as are enjoyed at the present day by our Territories. They did not have a full form of Republican government. A freehold estate in 500 acres of land was one of the necessary qualifications of each member of the legislative council of the Territory; every member of the Territorial House of Representatives was required to hold, in his own right, 200 acres of land; and the privilege of voting for members of the House of Representatives was restricted to those inhabitants who, in addition to other qualifications, owned severally at least 50 acres of land. The Governor of the the Territory was invested with the power of appointing officers of the Territorial militia, Judges of the inferior Courts, Clerks of the Courts, Justices of the Peace, Sheriffs, Coroners, County Treasurers and County Surveyors. He was also authorized to divide the Territory into districts; to apportion among the several counties the members of the House of Representatives; to prevent the passage of any Territorial law; and to convene and dissolve the General Assembly whenever he thought best. None of the Governors, however, ever exercised these extraordinary powers arbitrarily. Nevertheless, the people were constantly agitating the question of extending the right of suffrage. Five years after the organization of the Territory, the Legislative Council, in reply to the Governor's Message, said: "Although we are not as completely independent in our legislative capacity as we would wish to be, yet we are sensible that we must wait with patience for that period of time when our population will burst the trammels of a Territorial government, and we shall assume the character more consonant to Republicanism. * * * The confidence which our fellow citizens have uniformly had in your administration has been such that they have hitherto had no reason to be jealous of the unlimited power which you possess over our legislative proceedings. We, however, cannot help regretting that such powers have been lodged in the hands of any one, especially when it is recollected to what dangerous lengths the exercise of those powers may be extended."

After repeated petitions the people of Indiana were empowered by Congress to elect the members of the Legislative Council by popular vote. This act was passed in 1809, and defined what was known as the property qualification of voters. These qualifications were abolished by Congress in 1811, which extended the right of voting for members of the General Assembly and for a Territorial delegate to Congress to every free white male person who had attained the age of twenty-one years, and who, having paid a county or Territorial tax, was a resident of the Territory and had resided in it for a year. In 1814 the voting qualification in Indiana was defined by Congress, "to every free white male person having a freehold in the Territory, and being a resident of the same." The House of Representatives was authorized by Congress to lay off the Territory into five districts, in each of which the qualified voters were empowered to elect a member of the Legislative Council. The division was made, one to two counties in each district.

At the session in August, 1814, the Territory was also divided into three judicial circuits, and provisions were made for holding courts in the same. The Governor was empowered to appoint a presiding Judge in each circuit, and two Associate Judges of the circuit court in each county. Their compensation was fixed at $700 per annum.

The same year the General Assembly granted charters to two banking institutions, the Farmers' and Mechanics' Bank of Madison and the Bank of Vincennes. The first was authorized to raise a capital of $750,000, and the other $500,000. On the organization of the State these banks were merged into the State Bank and its branches.

Here we close the history of the Territory of Indiana.

The last regular session of the Territorial Legislature was held at Corydon, convening in December, 1815. The message of Governor Posey congratulated the people of the Territory upon the general success of the settlements and the great increase of immigration, recommended light taxes and a careful attention to the promotion of education and the improvement of the State roads and highways. He also recommended a revision of the territorial laws and an amendment of the militia system. Several laws were passed preparatory to a State Government, and December 14, 1815, a memorial to Congress was adopted praying for the authority to adopt a constitution and State Government. Mr. Jennings, the Territorial delegate, laid this memorial before Congress on the 28th, and April 19, 1816, the President approved the bill creating the State of Indiana. Accordingly, May 30 following, a general election was held for a constitutional convention, which met at Corydon June 10 to 29, Johathan Jennings presiding and Wm. Hendricks acting as Secretary.

"The convention that formed the first constitution of the State of Indiana was composed mainly of clear-minded, unpretending men of common sense, whose patriotism was unquestionable and whose morals were fair. Their familiarity with the theories of the Declaration of American Independence, their Territorial experience under the provisions of the ordinance of 1787, and their knowledge of the principles of the constitution of the United States were sufficient, when combined, to lighten materially their labors in the great work of forming a constitution for a new State. With such landmarks in view, the labors of similar conventions in other States and Territories have been rendered comparatively light. In the clearness and conciseness of its style, in the comprehensive and just provisions which it made for the maintainance of civil and religious liberty, in its mandates, which were designed to protect the rights of the people collectively and individually, and to provide for the public welfare, the constitution that was formed for Indiana in 1816 was not inferior to any of the State constitutions which were in existence at that time."—*Dillon's History of Indiana.*

The first State election took place on the first Monday of August, 1816, and Jonathan Jennings was elected Governor, and Christopher Harrison, Lieut. Governor. Wm. Hendricks was elected to represent the new State in the House of Representatives of the United States.

The first General Assembly elected under the new constitution began its session at Corydon, Nov. 4, 1816. John Paul was called to the chair of the Senate pro tem., and Isaac Blackford was elected Speaker of the House of Representatives.

Among other things in the new Governor's message were the following remarks: "The result of your deliberation will be considered as indicative of its future character as well as of the future happiness and prosperity of its citizens. In the commencement of the State government the shackles of the colonial should be forgotten in our exertions to prove, by happy experience, that a uniform adherence to the first principles of our Government and a virtuous exercise of its powers will best secure efficiency to its measures and stability to its character. Without a frequent recurrence to those principles, the administration of the Government will imperceptibly become more and more arducus, until the simplicity of our Republican institutions may eventually be lost in dangerous expedients and political design. Under every free government the happiness of the citizens must be identified with their morals; and while a constitutional exercise of their rights shall continue to have its due weight in discharge of the duties required of the constituted authorities of the State, too much attention cannot be bestowed to the encouragement and promotion of every moral virtue, and to the enactment of laws calculated to restrain the vicious, and prescribe punishment for every crime commensurate with its enormity. In measuring, however, to each crime its adequate punishment, it will be well to recollect that the certainty of punishment has generally the surest effect to prevent crime; while punishments unnecessarily severe too often produce the acquittal of the guilty and disappoint one of the greatest objects of legislation and good government. * * * The dissemination of useful knowledge will be indispensably necessary as a support to morals and as a restraint to vice; and on this subject it will only be necessary to direct your attention to the plan of education as prescribed by the constitution. * * * I recommend to your consideration the propriety of providing by law, to prevent more effectually any unlawful attempts to seize and carry into bondage

persons of color legally entitled to their freedom; and at the same time, as far as practicable, to prevent those who rightfully owe service to the citizens of any other State or Territory from seeking within the limits of this State a refuge from the possession of their lawful owners. Such a measure will tend to secure those who are free from any unlawful attempts (to enslave them) and secures the rights of the citizens of the other States and Territories as far as ought reasonably to be expected."

This session of the Legislature elected James Noble and Waller Taylor to the Senate of the United States; Robert A. New was elected Secretary of State; W. H. Lilley, Auditor of State; and Daniel C. Lane, Treasurer of State. The session adjourned January 3, 1817.

As the history of the State of Indiana from this time forward is best given by topics, we will proceed to give them in the chronological order of their origin.

The happy close of the war with Great Britain in 1814 was followed by a great rush of immigrants to the great Territory of the Northwest, including the new States, all now recently cleared of the enemy; and by 1820 the State of Indiana had more than doubled her population, having at this time 147,178, and by 1825 nearly doubled this again, that is to say, a round quarter of a million,—a growth more rapid probably than that of any other section in this country since the days of Columbus.

The period 1825-'30 was a prosperous time for the young State. Immigration continued to be rapid, the crops were generally good and the hopes of the people raised higher than they had ever been before. Accompanying this immigration, however, were paupers and indolent people, who threatened to be so numerous as to become a serious burden. On this subject Governor Ray called for legislative action, but the Legislature scarcely knew what to do and they deferred action.

BLACK HAWK WAR.

In 1830 there still lingered within the bounds of the State two tribes of Indians, whose growing indolence, intemperate habits, dependence upon their neighbors for the bread of life, diminished prospects of living by the chase, continued perpetration of murders and other outrages of dangerous precedent, primitive ignorance and unrestrained exhibitions of savage customs before the children of the settlers, combined to make them subjects for a more rigid government. The removal of the Indians west of the Mississippi was a melancholy but necessary duty. The time having arrived for the emigration of the Pottawatomies, according to the stipulations contained in their treaty with the United States, they evinced that reluctance common among aboriginal tribes on leaving the homes of their childhood and the graves of their ancestors. Love of country is a principle planted in the bosoms of all mankind. The Laplander and the Esquimaux of the frozen north, who feed on seals, moose and the meat of the polar bear, would not exchange their country for the sunny clime of "Araby the blest." Color and shades of complexion have nothing to do with the heart's best, warmest emotions. Then we should not wonder that the Pottawatomie, on leaving his home on the Wabash, felt as sad as Æschines did when ostracised from his native land, laved by the waters of the classic Scamander; and the noble and eloquent Naswaw-kay, on leaving the encampment on Crooked creek, felt his banishment as keenly as Cicero when thrust from the bosom of his beloved Rome, for which he had spent the best efforts of his life, and for which he died.

On Sunday morning, May 18, 1832, the people on the west side of the Wabash were thrown into a state of great consternation, on account of a report that a large body of hostile Indians had approached within 15 miles of Lafayette and killed two men. The alarm soon spread throughout Tippecanoe, Warren, Vermillion, Fountain, Montgomery, and adjoining counties. Several brave commandants of companies on the west side of the Wabash in Tippecanoe county, raised troops to go and meet the enemy, and dispatched an express to Gen. Walker with a request that he should

(126)

make a call upon the militia of the county to equip themselves instantly and march to the aid of their bleeding countrymen. Thereupon Gen. Walker, Col. Davis, Lieut-Col. Jenners, Capt. Brown, of the artillery, and various other gallant spirits mounted their war steeds and proceeded to the army, and thence upon a scout to the Grand Prairie to discover, if possible, the number, intention and situation of the Indians. Over 300 old men, women and children flocked precipitately to Lafayette and the surrounding country east of the Wabash. A remarkable event occurred in this stampede, as follows:

A man, wife and seven children resided on the edge of the Grand Prairie, west of Lafayette, in a locality considered particularly dangerous. On hearing of this alarm he made hurried preparations to fly with his family to Lafayette for safety. Imagine his surprise and chagrin when his wife told him she would not go one step; that she did not believe in being scared at trifles, and in her opinion there was not an Indian within 100 miles of them. Importunity proved unavailing, and the disconsolate and frightened husband and father took all the children except the youngest, bade his wife and babe a long and solemn farewell, never expecting to see them again, unless perhaps he might find their mangled remains, minus their scalps. On arriving at Lafayette, his acquaintances rallied and berated him for abandoning his wife and child in that way, but he met their jibes with a stoical indifference, avowing that he should not be held responsible for their obstinacy.

As the shades of the first evening drew on, the wife felt lonely; and the chirping of the frogs and the notes of the whippoorwill only intensified her loneliness, until she half wished she had accompanied the rest of the family in their flight. She remained in the house a few hours without striking a light, and then concluded that " discretion was the better part of valor," took her babe and some bed-clothes, fastened the cabin door, and hastened to a sink-hole in the woods, in which she afterward said that she and her babe slept soundly until sunrise next morning.

Lafayette literally boiled over with people and patriotism. A meeting was held at the court-house, speeches were made by patriotic individuals, and to allay the fears of the women an armed police was immediately ordered, to be called the " Lafayette Guards." Thos. T. Benbridge was elected Captain, and John Cox, Lieutenant. Capt. Benbridge yielded the active drill of his guards to the Lieutenant, who had served two years in the war of 1812. After the meeting adjourned, the guards were paraded on the green where Purdue's block now stands, and put through sundry evolutions by Lieut. Cox, who proved to be an expert drill officer, and whose clear, shrill voice rung out on the night air as he marched and counter-marched the troops from where the paper-mill stands to Main street ferry, and over the suburbs, generally. Every old gun and sword that could be found was brought into requisition, with a new shine on them.

Gen. Walker, Colonels Davis and Jenners, and other officers joined in a call of the people of Tippecanoe county for volunteers to march to the frontier settlements. A large meeting of the citizens assembled in the public square in the town, and over 300 volunteers mostly mounted men, left for the scene of action, with an alacrity that would have done credit to veterans.

The first night they camped nine miles west of Lafayette, near Grand Prairie. They placed sentinels for the night and retired to rest. A few of the subaltern officers very injudiciously concluded to try what effect a false alarm would have upon the sleeping soldiers, and a few of them withdrew to a neighboring thicket, and thence made a charge upon the picket guards, who, after hailing them and receiving no countersign, fired off their guns and ran for the Colonel's marquee in the center of the encampment. The aroused Colonels and staff sprang to their feet, shouting "To arms! to arms!" and the obedient, though panic-stricken soldiers seized their guns and demanded to be led against the invading foe. A wild scene of disorder ensued, and amid the din of arms and loud commands of the officers the raw militia felt that they had already got into the red jaws of battle. One of the alarm sentinels, in running to the center of the encampment, leaped over a blazing camp fire, and alighted full upon the breast and stomach of a sleeping lawyer, who was, no doubt, at that moment dreaming of vested and contingent remainders, rich clients and good fees, which in legal parlance was suddenly estopped by the hob-nails in the stogas of the scared sentinel. As soon as the counselor's vitality and consciousness sufficiently returned, he put in some strong demurrers to the conduct of the affrighted picket men, averring that he would greatly prefer being wounded by the enemy to being run over by a cowardly booby. Next morning the organizers of the ruse were severely reprimanded.

May 28, 1832, Governor Noble ordered General Walker to call out his whole command, if necessary, and supply arms, horses and provisions, even though it be necessary to seize them. The next day four baggage wagons, loaded with camp equipments, stores, provisions and other articles, were sent to the little army, who were thus provided for a campaign of five or six weeks. The following Thursday a squad of cavalry, under Colonel Sigler, passed through Lafayette on the way to the hostile region; and on the 13th of June Colonel Russell, commandant of the 40th Regiment, Indiana Militia, passed through Lafayette with 340 mounted volunteers from the counties of Marion, Hendricks and Johnson. Also, several companies of volunteers from Montgomery, Fountain and Warren counties, hastened to the relief of the frontier settlers. The troops from Lafayette marched to Sugar creek, and after a short time, there being no probability of finding any of the enemy, were ordered to return. They all did so except about 45 horsemen, who volunteered to cross Hickory creek, where the Indians had committed their depredations. They organized a company by electing Samuel McGeorge, a soldier of the war of 1812, Captain, and Amos Allen and Andrew W. Ingraham, Lieutenants.

Crossing Hickory creek, they marched as far as O'Plein river without meeting with opposition. Finding no enemy here they concluded to return. On the first night of their march home they encamped on the open prairie, posting sentinels, as usual. About ten o'clock it began to rain, and it was with difficulty that the sentinels kept their guns dry. Capt. I. H. Cox and a man named Fox had been posted as sentinels within 15 or 20 paces of each other. Cox drew the skirt of his overcoat over his gun-lock to keep it dry; Fox, perceiving this motion, and in the darkness taking him for an Indian, fired upon him and fractured his thigh-bone. Several soldiers immediately ran toward the place where the flash of the gun had been seen; but when they cocked and leveled their guns on the figure which had fired at Cox, the wounded man caused them to desist by crying, " Don't shoot him, it was a sentinel who shot me." The next day the wounded man was left behind the company in care of four men, who, as soon as possible, removed him on a litter to Col. Moore's company of Illinois militia, then encamped on the O'Plein, where Joliet now stands.

Although the main body returned to Lafayette in eight or nine days, yet the alarm among the people was so great that they could not be induced to return to their farms for some time. The presence of the hostiles was hourly expected by the frontier settlements of Indiana, from Vincennes to La Porte. In Clinton county the inhabitants gathered within the forts and prepared for a regular siege, while our neighbors at Crawfordsville were suddenly astounded by the arrival of a courier at full speed with the announcement that the Indians, more than a thousand in number, were then crossing the Nine-Mile prairie about twelve miles north of town, killing and scalping all. The strongest houses were immediately put in a condition of defense, and sentinels were placed at the principal points in the direction of the enemy. Scouts were sent out to reconnoitre, and messengers were dispatched in different directions to announce the danger to the farmers, and to urge them to hasten with their families into town, and to assist in fighting the momentarily expected savages. At night-fall the scouts brought in the news that the Indians had not crossed the Wabash, but were hourly expected at Lafayette. The citizens of Warren, Fountain and Vermillion counties were alike terrified by exaggerated stories of Indian massacres, and immediately prepared for defense. It turned out that the Indians were not within 100 miles of these temporary forts; but this by no means proved a want of courage in the citizens.

After some time had elapsed, a portion of the troops were marched back into Tippecanoe county and honorably discharged; but the settlers were still loth for a long time to return to their farms. Assured by published reports that the Miamis and Pottawatomies did not intend to join the hostiles, the people by degrees recovered from the panic and began to attend to their neglected crops.

During this time there was actual war in Illinois. Black Hawk and his warriors, well nigh surrounded by a well-disciplined foe, attempted to cross to the west bank of the Mississippi, but after being chased up into Wisconsin and to the Mississippi again, he was in a final battle taken captive. A few years after his liberation, about 1837 or 1838, he died, on the banks of the Des Moines river, in Iowa, in what is now the county of Davis, where his remains were deposited above ground, in the usual Indian style. His remains were afterward stolen and carried away, but they were recovered by the Governor of Iowa and placed in the museum of the Historical Society at Burlington, where they were finally destroyed by fire.

In July, 1837, Col. Abel C. Pepper convened the Pottawatomie nation of Indians at Lake Ke-waw-nay for the purpose of removing them west of the Mississippi. That fall a small party of some 80 or 90 Pottawatomies was conducted west of the Mississippi river by George Proffit, Esq. Among the number were Ke-waw-nay, Nebash, Nas-waw-kay, Pash-po-ho and many other leading men of the nation. The regular emigration of these poor Indians, about 1,000 in number, took place under Col. Pepper and Gen. Tipton in the summer of 1838.

It was a sad and mournful spectacle to witness these children of the forest slowly retiring from the home of their childhood, that contained not only the graves of their revered ancestors, but also many endearing scenes to which their memories would ever recur as sunny spots along their pathway through the wilderness. They felt that they were bidding farewell to the hills, valleys and streams of their infancy; the more exciting hunting-grounds of their advanced youth, as well as the stern and bloody battle-fields where they had contended in riper manhood, on which they had received wounds, and where many of their friends and loved relatives had fallen covered with gore and with glory. All these they were leaving behind them, to be desecrated by the plowshare of the white man. As they cast mournful glances back toward these loved scenes that were rapidly fading in the distance, tears fell from the cheek of the downcast warrior, old men trembled, matrons wept, the swarthy maiden's cheek turned pale, and sighs and half-suppressed sobs escaped from the motley groups as they passed along, some on foot, some on horseback, and others in wagons,—sad as a funeral procession. Several of the aged warriors were seen to cast glances toward the sky, as if they were imploring aid from the spirits of their departed heroes, who were looking down upon them from the clouds, or from the Great Spirit, who would ultimately redress the wrongs of the red man, whose broken bow had fallen from his hand, and whose sad heart was bleeding within him. Ever and anon one of the party would start out into the brush and break back to their old encampments on Eel river and on the Tippecanoe, declaring that they would rather die than be banished from their country. Thus, scores of discontented emigrants returned from different points on their journey; and it was several years before they could be induced to join their countrymen west of the Mississippi.

Several years after the removal of the Pottawatomies the Miami nation was removed to their Western home, by coercive means, under an escort of United States troops. They were a proud and once powerful nation, but at the time of their removal were far inferior, in point of numbers, to the Pottawatomie guests whom they had permitted to settle and hunt upon their lands, and fish in their lakes and rivers after they had been driven southward by powerful and warlike tribes who inhabited the shores of the Northern lakes.

INDIAN TITLES.

In 1831 a joint resolution of the Legislature of Indiana, requesting an appropriation by Congress for the extinguishment of the Indian title to lands within the State, was forwarded to that body, which granted the request. The Secretary of War, by authority, appointed a committee of three citizens to carry into effect the provisions of the recent law. The Miamis were surrounded on all sides by American settlers, and were situated almost in the heart of the State on the line of the canal then being made. The chiefs were called to a council for the purpose of making a treaty; they promptly came, but peremptorily refused to go westward or sell the remainder of their land. The Pottawatomies sold about 6,000,000 acres in Indiana, Illinois and Michigan, including all their claim in this State.

In 1838 a treaty was concluded with the Miami Indians through the good offices of Col. A. C. Pepper, the Indian agent, by which a considerable of the most desirable portion of their reserve was ceded to the United States.

LAND SALES.

As an example of the manner in which land speculators were treated by the early Indianians, we cite the following instances from Cox's "Recollections of the Wabash Valley."

At Crawfordsville, Dec. 24, 1824, many parties were present from the eastern and southern portions of the State, as well as from Ohio, Kentucky, Tennessee and even Pennsylvania, to attend a land sale. There was but little bidding against each other. The settlers, or "squatters," as they were called by the speculators, had arranged matters among themselves to their general satisfaction. If, upon comparing numbers, it appeared that two were after the same tract of land, one would ask the other what he would take not to bid against him; if neither would consent to be bought off they would retire and cast lots, and the lucky one would enter the tract at Congress price, $1.25 an acre, and the other would enter the second choice on his list. If a speculator made a bid, or showed a disposition to take a settler's claim from him, he soon saw the white of a score of eyes glaring at him, and he would "crawfish" out of the crowd at the first opportunity.

The settlers made it definitely known to foreign capitalists that they would enter the tracts of land they had settled upon before allowing the latter to come in with their speculations. The land was sold in tiers of townships, beginning at the southern part of the district and continuing north until all had been offered at public sale. This plan was persisted in, although it kept many on the ground for several days waiting, who desired to purchase land in the northern part of the district.

In 1827 a regular Indian scare was gotten up to keep speculators away for a short time. A man who owned a claim on Tippecanoe river, near Pretty prairie, fearing that some one of the numerous land hunters constantly scouring the country might enter the land he had settled upon before he could raise the money to buy it, and seeing one day a cavalcade of land hunters riding toward where his land lay, mounted his horse and darted off at full speed to meet them, swinging his hat and shouting at the top of his voice, "Indians! Indians! the woods are full of Indians, murdering and scalping all before them!" They paused a moment, but as the terrified horseman still urged his jaded animal and cried, "Help! Longlois, Cicots, help!" they turned and fled like a troop of retreating cavalry, hastening to the thickest settlements and giving the alarm, which spread like fire among stubble until the whole frontier region was shocked with the startling cry. The squatter who fabricated the story and started this false alarm took a circuitous route home that evening, and while others were busy building temporary block-houses and rubbing up their guns to meet the Indians, he was quietly gathering up money and slipped down to Crawfordsville and entered his land, chuckling to himself, "There's a Yankee trick for you, done up by a Hoosier."

HARMONY COMMUNITY.

In 1814 a society of Germans under Frederick Rappe, who had originally come from Wirtemberg, Germany, and more recently from Pennsylvania, founded a settlement on the Wabash about 50 miles above its mouth. They were industrious, frugal and honest Lutherans. They purchased a large quantity of land and laid off a town, to which they gave the name of "Harmony," afterward called "New Harmony." They erected a church and a public school-house, opened farms, planted orchards and vineyards, built flouring mills, established a house of public entertainment, a public store, and carried on all the arts of peace with skill and regularity. Their property was "in common," according to the custom of ancient Christians at Jerusalem, but the governing power, both temporal and spiritual, was vested in Frederick Rappe, the elder, who was regarded as the founder of the society. By the year 1821 the society numbered about 900. Every individual of proper age contributed his proper share of labor. There were neither spendthrifts, idlers nor drunkards, and during the whole 17 years of their sojourn in America there was not a single lawsuit among them. Every controversy arising among them was settled by arbitration, explanation and compromise before sunset of the day, literally according to the injunction of the apostle of the New Testament.

About 1825 the town of Harmony and a considerable quantity of land adjoining was sold to Robert Owen, father of David Dale Owen, the State Geologist, and of Robert Dale Owen, of later notoriety. He was a radical philosopher from Scotland, who had become distinguished for his philanthropy and opposition to

Christianity. He charged the latter with teaching false notions regarding human responsibility—notions which have since been clothed in the language of physiology, mental philosophy, etc. Said he:

"That which has hitherto been called wickedness in our fellow men has proceeded from one of two distinct causes, or from some combination of those causes. They are what are termed bad or wicked,

"1. Because they are born with faculties or propensities which render them more liable, under the same circumstances, than other men, to commit such actions as are usually denominated wicked; or,

"2. Because they have been placed by birth or other events in particular countries,—have been influenced from infancy by parents, playmates and others, and have been surrounded by those circumstances which gradually and necessarily trained them in the habits and sentiments called wicked; or,

"3. They have become wicked in consequence of some particular combination of these causes.

"If it should be asked, Whence then has wickedness proceeded? I reply, Solely from the ignorance of our forefathers.

"Every society which exists at present, as well as every society which history records, has been formed and governed on a belief in the following notions, assumed as first principles:

"1. That it is in the power of every individual to form his own character. Hence the various systems called by the name of religion, codes of law, and punishments; hence, also, the angry passions entertained by individuals and nations toward each other.

"2. That the affections are at the command of the individual. Hence insincerity and degradation of character; hence the miseries of domestic life, and more than one-half of all the crimes of mankind.

"3. That it is necessary a large portion of mankind should exist in ignorance and poverty in order to secure to the remaining part such a degree of happiness as they now enjoy. Hence a system of counteraction in the pursuits of men, a general opposition among individuals to the interests of each other, and the necessary effects of such a system,—ignorance, poverty and vice.

During the administration of Gov. Whitcomb the war with Mexico occurred, which resulted in annexing to the United States vast tracts of land in the south and west. Indiana contributed her full ratio to the troops in that war, and with a remarkable spirit of promptness and patriotism adopted all measures to sustain the general Government. These new acquisitions of territory re-opened the discussion of the slavery question, and Governor Whitcomb expressed his opposition to a further extension of the "national sin."

The causes which led to a declaration of war against Mexico in 1846, must be sought for as far back as the year 1830, when the present State of Texas formed a province of New and Independent Mexico. During the years immediately preceding 1830, Moses Austin, of Connecticut, obtained a liberal grant of lands from the established Government, and on his death his son was treated in an equally liberal manner. The glowing accounts rendered by Austin, and the vivid picture of Elysian fields drawn by visiting journalists, soon resulted in the influx of a large tide of immigrants, nor did the movement to the Southwest cease until 1830. The Mexican province held a prosperous population, comprising 10,000 American citizens. The rapacious Government of the Mexicans looked with greed and jealousy upon their eastern province, and, under the presidency of Gen. Santa Anna, enacted such measures, both unjust and oppressive, as would meet their design of goading the people of Texas on to revolution, and thus afford an opportunity for the infliction of punishment upon subjects whose only crime was industry and its accompaniment, prosperity. Precisely in keeping with the course pursued by the British toward the colonists of the Eastern States in the last century, Santa Anna's Government met the remonstrances of the colonists of Texas with threats; and they, secure in their consciousness of right quietly issued their declaration of independence, and proved its literal meaning on the field of Gonzales in 1835, having with a force of

500 men forced the Mexican army of 1,000 to fly for refuge to their strongholds. Battle after battle followed, bringing victory always to the Colonists, and ultimately resulting in the total rout of the Mexican army and the evacuation of Texas. The routed army after a short term of rest reorganized, and reappeared in the Territory, 8,000 strong. On April 21, a division of this large force under Santa Anna encountered the Texans under General Samuel Houston on the banks of the San Jacinto, and though Houston could only oppose 800 men to the Mexican legions, the latter were driven from the field, nor could they reform their scattered ranks until their General was captured next day and forced to sign the declaration of 1835. The signature of Santa Anna, though ignored by the Congress of the Mexican Republic, and consequently left unratified on the part of Mexico, was effected in so much, that after the second defeat of the army of that Republic all the hostilities of an important nature ceased, the Republic of Texas was recognized by the powers, and subsequently became an integral part of the United States, July 4, 1846. At this period General Herrera was president of Mexico. He was a man of peace, of common sense, and very patriotic; and he thus entertained, or pretended to entertain, the great neighboring Republic in high esteem. For this reason he grew unpopular with his people, and General Paredes was called to the presidential chair, which he continued to occupy until the breaking out of actual hostilities with the United States, when Gen. Santa Anna was elected thereto.

President Polk, aware of the state of feeling in Mexico, ordered Gen. Zachary Taylor, in command of the troops in the Southwest, to proceed to Texas, and post himself as near to the Mexican border as he deemed prudent. At the same time an American squadron was dispatched to the vicinity, in the Gulf of Mexico. In November, General Taylor had taken his position at Corpus Christi, a Texan settlement on a bay of the same name, with about 4,000 men. On the 13th of January, 1846, the President ordered him to advance with his forces to the Rio Grande; accordingly he proceeded, and in March stationed himself on the north bank of that river, within cannon-shot of the Mexican town of Matamoras. Here he hastily erected a fortress, called Fort Brown. The territory lying between the river Nueces and the Rio Grande river, about 120 miles in width, was claimed both by Texas and Mexico; according to the latter, therefore, General Taylor had actually invaded her Territory, and had thus committed an open act of war. On the 26th of April, the Mexican General, Ampudia, gave notice to this effect to General Taylor, and on the same day a party of American dragoons, sixty-three in number, being on the north side of the Rio Grande, were attacked, and, after the loss of sixteen men killed and wounded, were forced to surrender. Their commander, Captain Thornton, only escaped. The Mexican forces had now crossed the river above Matamoras and were supposed to meditate an attack on Point Isabel, where Taylor had established a depot of supplies for his army. On the 1st of May, this officer left a small number of troops at Fort Brown, and marched with his chief forces, twenty-three hundred men, to the defense of Point Isabel. Having garrisoned this place, he set out on his return. On the 8th of May, about noon, he met the Mexican army, six thousand strong, drawn up in battle array, on the prairie near Palo Alto. The Americans at once advanced to the attack, and, after an action of five hours, in which their artillery was very effective, drove the enemy before them, and encamped upon the field. The Mexican loss was about one hundred killed; that of the Americans, four killed and forty wounded. Major Ringgold, of the artillery, an officer of great merit, was mortally wounded. The next day, as the Americans advanced, they again met the enemy in a strong position near Resaca de la Palma, three miles from Fort Brown. An action commenced, and was fiercely contested, the artillery on both sides being served with great vigor. At last the Mexicans gave way, and fled in confusion, General de la Vega having fallen into the hands of the Americans. They also abandoned their guns and a large quantity of ammunition to the victors. The remaining Mexican soldiers speedily crossed the Rio Grande, and the next day the Americans took up their position at Fort Brown. This little fort, in the absence of General Taylor, had gallantly sustained an almost uninterrupted attack of several days from the Mexican batteries of Matamoras.

When the news of the capture of Captain Thornton's party was spread over the United States, it produced great excitement. The President addressed a message to Congress, then in session, declaring " that war with Mexico existed by her own act;" and that body, May, 1846, placed ten millions of dollars at the President's disposal, and authorized him to accept the services of fifty thousand volunteers. A great part of the summer of 1846 was spent in preparation for the war, it being resolved to invade Mexico at several points. In pursuance of this plan, General Taylor, who had taken possession of Matamoras, abandoned by the enemy in May, marched northward in the enemy's country in August, and on the 19th of September he appeared before Monterey, capital of the Mexican State of New Leon. His army, after having garrisoned several places along his route, amounted to six thousand men. The attack began on the 21st, and after a succession of assaults, during the period of four days, the Mexicans capitulated, leaving the town in possession of the Americans. In October, General Taylor terminated an armistice into which he had entered with the Mexican General, and again commenced offensive operations. Various towns and fortresses of the enemy now rapidly fell into our possession. In November, Saltillo, the capital of the State of Coahuila was occupied by the division of General Worth; in December, General Patterson took possession of Victoria, the capital of Tamaulipas, and nearly at the same period, Commodore Perry captured the fort of Tampico. Santa Fe, the capital of New Mexico, with the whole territory of the State had been subjugated by General Harney, after a march of one thousand miles through the wilderness. Events of a startling character had taken place at still earlier dates along the Pacific coast. On the 4th of July, Captain Fremont, having repeatedly defeated superior Mexican forces with the small band under his command, declared California independent of Mexico. Other important places in this region had yielded to the American naval force, and in August, 1846, the whole of California was in the undisputed occupation of the Americans.

The year 1847 opened with still more brilliant victories on the part of our armies. By the drawing off of a large part of General Taylor's troops for a meditated attack on Vera Cruz, he was left with a comparatively small force to meet the great body of Mexican troops, now marching upon him, under command of the celebrated Santa Anna, who had again become President of Mexico.

Ascertaining the advance of this powerful army, twenty thousand strong, and consisting of the best of the Mexican soldiers, General Taylor took up his position at Buena Vista, a valley a few miles from Saltillo. His whole troops numbered only four thousand seven hundred and fifty-nine, and here, on the 23d of February, he was vigorously attacked by the Mexicans. The battle was very severe, and continued nearly the whole day, when the Mexicans fled from the field in disorder, with a loss of nearly two thousand men. Santa Anna speedily withdrew, and thus abandoned the region of the Rio Grande to the complete occupation of our troops. This left our forces at liberty to prosecute the grand enterprise of the campaign, the capture of the strong town of Vera Cruz, with its renowned castle of San Juan d'Ulloa. On the 9th of March, 1847, General Scott landed near the city with an army of twelve thousand men, and on the 18th commenced an attack. For four days and nights an almost incessant shower of shot and shells was poured upon the devoted town, while the batteries of the castle and the city replied with terrible energy. At last, as the Americans were preparing for an assault, the Governor of the city offered to surrender, and on the 26th the American flag floated triumphantly from the walls of the castle and the city. General Scott now prepared to march upon the city of Mexico, the capital of the country, situated two hundred miles in the interior, and approached only through a series of rugged passes and mountain fastnesses, rendered still more formidable by several strong fortresses. On the 8th of April the army commenced their march. At Cerro Gordo, Santa Anna had posted himself with fifteen thousand men. On the 18th the Americans began the daring attack, and by midday every intrenchment of the enemy had been carried. The loss of the Mexicans in this remarkable battle, besides one thousand killed and wounded, was three thousand prisoners, forty-three pieces of cannon, five thousand stand of arms, and all their ammunitions and materials of war. The loss of the Americans was four hundred and thirty-one in killed and wounded. The next day our forces advanced, and, capturing fortress after fortress, came on the 18th of August within ten miles of Mexico, a city of two hundred thousand inhabitants, and situated in one of the most beautiful valleys in the world. On the 20th they attacked and carried the strong batteries of Contreras, garrisoned by 7,000 men, in an impetuous assault, which lasted but seventeen minutes. On the same day an attack was made by the Americans on the fortified post of Churubusco, four miles northeast of Contreras. Here nearly the entire Mexican army—more than 20,000 in number—were posted; but they were defeated at every point, and obliged to seek a retreat in the city, or the still remaining fortress of Chapultepec. While preparations were being made on the 21st by General Scott, to level his batteries against the city, prior to summoning it to surrender, he received propositions from the enemy, which terminated in an armistice. This ceased on the 7th of September. On the 8th the outer defense of Chapultepec was successfully stormed by General Worth, though he lost one-fourth of his men in the desperate struggle. The castle of Chapultepec, situated on an abrupt and rocky eminence, 150 feet above the surrounding country, presented a most formidable object of attack. On the 12th, however, the batteries were opened against it, and on the next day the citadel was carried by storm. The Mexicans still struggled along the great causeway leading to the city, as the Americans advanced, but before nightfal a part of our army was within the gates of the city. Santa Anna and the officers of the Government fled, and the next morning, at seven o'clock, the flag of the Americans floated from the national palace of Mexico. This conquest of the capital was the great and final achievement of the war. The Mexican republic was in fact prostrate, her sea-coast and chief cities being in the occupation of our troops. On the 2d of February, 1848, terms of peace were agreed upon by the American commissioner and the Mexican Government, this treaty being ratified by the Mexican Congress on the 30th of May following, and by the United States soon after. President Polk proclaimed peace on the 4th of July, 1848. In the preceding sketch we have given only a mere outline of the war with Mexico. We have necessarily passed over many interesting events, and have not even named many of our soldiers who performed gallant and important services. General Taylor's successful operations in the region of the Rio Grande were duly honored by the people of the United States, by bestowing upon him the Presidency. General Scott's campaign, from the attack on Vera Cruz, to the surrender of the city of Mexico, was far more remarkable, and, in a military point of view, must be considered as one of the most brilliant of modern times. It is true the Mexicans are not to be ranked with the great nations of the earth; with a population of seven or eight millions, they have little more than a million of the white race, the rest being half-civilized Indians and mestizos, that is, those of mixed blood. Their government is inefficient, and the people divided among themselves. Their soldiers often fought bravely, but they were badly officered. While, therefore, we may consider the conquest of so extensive and populous a country, in so short a time, and attended with such constant superiority even to the greater numbers of the enemy, as highly gratifying evidence of the courage and capacity of our army, still we must not, in judging of our achievements, fail to consider the real weakness of the nation whom we vanquished.

One thing we may certainly dwell upon with satisfaction—the admirable example, not only as a soldier, but as a man, set by our commander, Gen. Scott, who seems, in the midst of war and the ordinary license of the camp, always to have preserved the virtue, kindness, and humanity belonging to a state of peace. These qualities secured to him the respect, confidence and good-will even of the enemy he had conquered. Among the Generals who effectually aided General Scott in this remarkable campaign, we must not omit to mention the names of Generals Wool, Twiggs, Shields, Worth, Smith, and Quitman, who generally added to the high qualities of soldiers the still more estimable characteristics of good men. The treaty of Guadalupe-Hidalgo stipulated that the disputed territory between the Nueces and the Rio Grande should belong to the United States, and it now forms a part of Texas, as has been already stated; that the United States should assume and pay the debts due from Mexico to American citizens, to the amount of $3,500,000; and that, in consideration of the sum of $15,000,000 to be paid by the United States to Mexico, the latter should relinquish to the former the whole of New Mexico and Upper California.

The soldiers of Indiana who served in this war were formed into five regiments of volunteers, numbered respectively, 1st, 2d, 3rd, 4th and 5th. The fact that companies of the three first-named regiments served at times with the men of Illinois, the New York volunteers, the Palmettos of South Carolina, and United States marines, under Gen. James Shields, makes for them a history; because the campaigns of the Rio Grande and Chihuahua, the siege of Vera Cruz, the desperate encounter at Cerro Gordo, the tragic contests in the valley, at Contreras and Churubusco, the storming of Chapultepec, and the planting of the stars and stripes upon every turret and spire within the conquered city of Mexico, were all carried out by the gallant troops under the favorite old General, and consequently each of them shared with him in the glories attached to such exploits. The other regiments under Cols. Gorman and Lane participated in the contests of the period under other commanders. The 4th Regiment of Indiana Volunteers, comprising ten companies, was formally organized at Jeffersonville, Indiana, by Capt. R. C. Gatlin, June 15, 1847, and on the 16th elected Major Willis A. Gorman, of the 3rd Regiment, to the Colonelcy; Ebenezer Dumont, Lieutenant-Colonel, and W. McCoy, Major. On the 27th of June the regiment left Jeffersonville for the front, and subsequently was assigned to Brigadier-General Lane's command, which then comprised a battery of five pieces from the 3rd Regiment U. S. Artillery; a battery of two pieces from the 2nd Regiment U. S. Rrtillery, the 4th Regiment of Indiana Volunteers and the 4th Regiment of Ohio, with a squadron of mounted Louisianians and detachments of recruits for the U. S. army. The troops of this brigade won signal honors at Passo de Ovegas, August 10, 1847; National Bridge, on the 12th; Cerro Gordo, on the 15th; Las Animas, on the 19th, under Maj. F. T. Lally, of General Lane's staff, and afterward under Lane, directly, took a very prominent part in the siege of Puebla, which began on the 15th of September and terminated on the 12th of October. At Atlixco, October 19th; Tlascala, November 10th; Matamoras and Pass Galajara, November 23rd and 24th; Guerrilla Ranche, December 5th; Napaloncan, December 10th, the Indiana volunteers of the 4th Regiment performed gallant service, and carried the campaign into the following year, representing their State at St. Martin's, February 27, 1848; Cholula, March 26th; Matacordera, February 19th; Sequalteplan, February 25th; and on the cessation of hostilities reported at Madison, Indiana, for discharge, July 11, 1848; while the 5th Indiana Regiment, under Col. J. H. Lane, underwent a similar round of duty during its service with other brigades, and gained some celebrity at Vera Cruz, Churubusco and with the troops of Illinois under Gen. Shields at Chapultepec.

This war cost the people of the United States sixty-six millions of dollars. This very large amount was not paid away for the attainment of mere glory; there was something else at stake, and this something proved to be a country larger and more fertile than the France of the Napoleons, and more steady and sensible than the France of the Republic. It was the defense of the great Lone Star State, the humiliatioi and chastisement of a quarrelsome neighbor.

SLAVERY.

We have already referred to the prohibition of slavery in the Northwestern Territory, and Indiana Territory by the ordinance of 1787; to the imperfection in the execution of this ordinance and the troubles which the authorities encountered; and the complete establishment of the principles of freedom on the organization of the State. The next item of significance in this connection is the following language in the message of Gov. Ray to the Legislature of 1828: "Since our last separation, while we have witnessed with anxious solicitude the belligerent operations of another hemisphere, the cross contending against the crescent, and the prospect of a general rupture among the legitimates of other quarters of the globe, our attention has been arrested by proceedings in our own country truly dangerous to liberty, seriously premeditated, and disgraceful to its authors if agitated only to tamper with the American people. If such experiments as we see attempted in certain deluded quarters do not fall with a burst of thunder upon the heads of their seditious projectors, then indeed the Republic has begun to experience the days of its degeneracy. The union of these States is the people's only sure charter for their liberties and independence. Dissolve it and each State will soon be in a condition as deplorable as Alexander's conquered countries after they were divided amongst his victorious military captains."

In pursuance of a joint resolution of the Legislature of 1850, a block of native marble was procured and forwarded to Washington, to be placed in the monument then in the course of erection at the National Capital in memory of George Washington. In the absence of any legislative instruction concerning the inscription upon this emblem of Indiana's loyalty, Gov. Wright ordered the following words to be inscribed upon it: INDIANA KNOWS NO NORTH, NO SOUTH, NOTHING BUT THE UNION. Within a dozen years thereafter this noble State demonstrated to the world her loyalty to the Union and the principles of freedom by the sacrifice of blood and treasure which she made. In keeping with this sentiment Gov. Wright indorsed the compromise measures of Congress on the slavery question, remarking in his message that "Indiana takes her stand in the ranks, not of Southern destiny, nor yet of

(144)

Northern destiny: she plants herself on the basis of the Constitution and takes her stand in the ranks of American destiny."

FIFTEENTH AMENDMENT.

At the session of the Legislature in January, 1869, the subject of ratifying the fifteenth amendment to the Federal Constitution, allowing negro suffrage, came up with such persistency that neither party dared to undertake any other business lest it be checkmated in some way, and being at a dead lock on this matter, they adjourned in March without having done much important business. The Democrats, as well as a portion of the conservative Republicans, opposed its consideration strongly on the ground that it would be unfair to vote on the question until the people of the State had had an opportunity of expressing their views at the polls; but most of the Republicans resolved to push the measure through, while the Democrats resolved to resign in a body and leave the Legislature without a quorum. Accordingly, on March 4, 17 Senators and 36 Representatives resigned, leaving both houses without a quorum.

As the early adjournment of the Legislature left the benevolent institutions of the State unprovided for, the Governor convened that body in extra session as soon as possible, and after the necessary appropriations were made, on the 19th of May the fifteenth amendment came up; but in anticipation of this the Democratic members had all resigned and claimed that there was no quorum present. There was a quorum, however, of Senators in office, though some of them refused to vote, declaring that they were no longer Senators; but the president of that body decided that as he had not been informed of their resignation by the Governor, they were still members. A vote was taken and the ratifying resolution was adopted. When the resolution came up in the House, the chair decided that, although the Democratic members had resigned, there was a quorum of the *de facto* members present, and the House proceeded to pass the resolution. This decision of the chair was afterward sustained by the Supreme Court.

At the next regular session of the Legislature, in 1871, the Democrats undertook to repeal the ratification, and the Republican members resigned to prevent it. The Democrats, as the Republicans did on the previous occasion, proceeded to pass their resolution of repeal; but while the process was under way, before the House Committee had time to report on the matter, 34 Republican members resigned, thereby preventing its passage and putting a stop to further legislation.

The events of the earlier years of this State have been reviewed down to that period in the nation's history when the Republic demanded a first sacrifice from the newly erected States; to the time when the very safety of the glorious heritage, bequeathed by the fathers as a rich legacy, was threatened with a fate worse than death —a life under laws that harbored the slave—a civil defiance of the first principles of the Constitution.

Indiana was among the first to respond to the summons of patriotism, and register itself on the national roll of honor, even as she was among the first to join in that song of joy which greeted a Republic made doubly glorious within a century by the dual victory which won liberty for itself, and next bestowed the precious boon upon the colored slave.

The fall of Fort Sumter was a signal for the uprising of the State. The news of the calamity was flashed to Indianapolis on the 14th of April, 1861, and early the next morning the electric wire brought the welcome message to Washington:—

EXECUTIVE DEPARTMENT OF INDIANA,
INDIANAPOLIS, April 15, 1861.

To ABRAHAM LINCOLN, *President of the United States*:—On behalf of the State of Indiana, I tender to you for the defense of the Nation, and to uphold the authority of the Government, ten thousand men.

OLIVER P. MORTON,
Governor of Indiana.

This may be considered the first official act of Governor Morton, who had just entered on the duties of his exalted position. The State was in an almost helpless condition, and yet the faith of the "War Governor" was prophetic, when, after a short consultation with the members of the Executive Council, he relied on the fidelity of ten thousand men and promised their services to the Protectorate at Washington. This will be more apparent when the military condition of the State at the beginning of 1861 is considered. At that time the armories contained less than five hundred stand of serviceable small arms, eight pieces of cannon which might be useful in a museum of antiquities, with sundry weapons which would merely do credit to the aborigines of one hundred years ago. The financial condition of the State was even worse than the military.

The sum of $10,368.58 in trust funds was the amount of cash in the hands of the Treasurer, and this was, to all intents and purposes unavailable to meet the emergency, since it could not be devoted to the military requirements of the day. This state of affairs was dispiriting in the extreme, and would doubtless have militated against the ultimate success of any other man than Morton; yet he overleaped every difficulty, nor did the fearful realization of Floyd's treason, discovered during his visit to Washington, damp his indomitable courage and energy, but with rare persistence he urged the claims of his State, and for his exertions was requited with an order for five thousand muskets. The order was not executed until hostilities were actually entered upon, and consequently for some days succeeding the publication of the President's proclamation the people labored under a feeling of terrible anxiety mingled with uncertainty, amid the confusion which followed the criminal negligence that permitted the disbandment of the magnificent *corps d' armee* (51,000 men) of 1832 two years later in 1834. Great numbers of the people maintained their equanamity with the result of beholding within a brief space of time every square mile of their State represented by soldiers prepared to fight to the bitter end in defense of cherished institutions, and for the extension of the principle of human liberty to all States and classes within the limits of the threatened Union. This, their zeal, was not animated by hostility to the slave holders of the Southern States, but rather by a fraternal spirit, akin to that which urges the eldest brother to correct the persistent follies of his juniors, and thus lead them from crime to the maintenance of family honor; in this correction, to draw them away from all that was cruel, diabolical and inhuman in the Republic, to all that is gentle, holy and sublime therein. Many of the raw troops were not only animated by a patriotic feeling, but also by that beautiful idealization of the poet, who in his unconscious Republicanism, said:

> "I would not have a slave to till my ground,
> To carry me, to fan me while I sleep,
> And tremble when I wake, for all the wealth
> That sinews bought and sold have ever earned
> No: dear as freedom is—and, in my heart's
> Just estimation, prized above all price—
> I had much rather be myself the slave,
> And wear the bonds, than fasten them on him."

Thus animated, it is not a matter for surprise to find the first call to arms issued by the President, and calling for 75,000 men,

answered nobly by the people of Indiana.   The quota of troops to
be furnished by the State on the first call was 4,683 men for three
years' service from April 15, 1860.   On the 16th of April, Governor Morton issued his proclamation calling on all citizens of the
State, who had the welfare of the Republic at heart, to organize
themselves into six regiments in defense of their rights, and in
opposition to the varied acts of rebellion, charged by him against
the Southern Confederates.   To this end, the Hon. Lewis Wallace,
a soldier of the Mexican campaign was appointed Adjutant-General,
Col. Thomas A. Morris of the United States Military Academy,
Quartermaster-General, and Isaiah Mansur, a merchant of Indianapolis, Commissary-General.   These general officers converted the
grounds and buildings of the State Board of Agriculture into a
military headquarters, and designated the position Camp Morton,
as the beginning of the many honors which were to follow the popular Governor throughout his future career.   Now the people, im-
bued with confidence in their Government and leaders, rose to the
grandeur of American freemen, and with an enthusiasm never
equaled hitherto, flocked to the standard of the nation; so that
within a few days (19th April) 2,400 men were ranked beneath
their regimental banners, until as the official report testifies, the
anxious question, passing from mouth to mouth, was, "Which of
us will be allowed to go?"   It seemed as if Indiana was about to
monopolize the honors of the period, and place the 75,000 men
demanded of the Union by the President, at his disposition.   Even
now under the genial sway of guaranteed peace, the features of
Indiana's veterans flush with righteous pride when these days—re-
membrances of heroic sacrifice—are named, and freemen, still unborn, will read their history only to be blessed and glorified in the
possession of such truly, noble progenitors.   Nor were the ladies
of the State unmindful of their duties.   Everywhere they partook
of the general enthusiasm, and made it practical so far as in their
power, by embroidering and presenting standards and regimental
colors, organizing aid and relief societies, and by many other acts
of patriotism and humanity inherent in the high nature of woman.

During the days set apart by the military authorities for the organization of the regiments, the financiers of the State were engaged in the reception of munificent grants of money from private citizens, while the money merchants within and without the
State offered large loans to the recognized Legislature without even
imposing a condition of payment.   This most practical generosity

strengthened the hands of the Executive, and within a very few days Indiana had passed the crucial test, recovered some of her military prestige lost in 1834, and so was prepared to vie with the other and wealthier States in making sacrifices for the public welfare.

On the 20th of April, Messrs. I. S. Dobbs and Alvis D. Gall received their appointments as Medical Inspectors of the Division, while Major T. J. Wood arrived at headquarters from Washington to receive the newly organized regiments into the service of the Union. At the moment this formal proceeding took place, Morton, unable to restrain the patriotic ardor of the people, telegraphed to the capitol that he could place six regiments of infantry at the disposal of the General Government within six days, if such a proceeding were acceptable; but in consequence of the wires being cut between the State and Federal capitols, no answer came. Taking advantage of the little doubt which may have had existence in regard to future action in the matter and in the absence of general orders, he gave expression to an intention of placing the volunteers in camp, and in his message to the Legislature, who assembled three days later, he clearly laid down the principle of immediate action and strong measures, recommending a note of $1,000,000 for the reorganization of the volunteers, for the purchase of arms and supplies, and for the punishment of treason. The message was received most enthusiastically. The assembly recognized the great points made by the Governor, and not only yielded to them *in toto*, but also made the following grand appropriations:

General military purposes...$1,000,000
Purchase of arms...500,000
Contingent military expenses...100,000
Organization and support of militia for two years..........................140,000

These appropriations, together with the laws enacted during the session of the Assembly, speak for the men of Indiana. The celerity with which these laws were put in force, the diligence and economy exercised by the officers, entrusted with their administration, and that systematic genius, under which all the machinery of Government seemed to work in harmony,—all, all, tended to make for the State a spring-time of noble deeds, when seeds might be cast along her fertile fields and in the streets of her villages of industry to grow up at once and blossom in the ray of fame, and after to bloom throughout the ages. Within three days after the opening of the extra session of the Legislature (27th April) six new regiments were organized, and commissioned for three months' service. These regiments, notwithstanding the fact that the first six regiments were already mustered into the general service, were known as "The First Brigade, Indiana Volunteers," and with the simple object of making the way of the future student of a brilliant history clear, were numbered respectively

Sixth Regiment, commanded by Col. T. T. Crittenden.
Seventh   "   "   " " Ebenezer Dumont.
Eighth   "   "   " " W. P. Benton.
Ninth   "   "   " " R. H. Milroy.
Tenth   "   "   " " T. T. Reynolds.
Eleventh   "   "   " " Lewis Wallace.

The idea of these numbers was suggested by the fact that the military representation of Indiana in the Mexican Campaign was one brigade of five regiments, and to observe consecutiveness the regiments comprised in the first division of volunteers were thus numbered, and the entire force placed under Brigadier General T. A. Morris, with the following staff: John Love, Major; Cyrus C. Hines, Aid-de-camp; and J. A. Stein, Assistant Adjutant General. To follow the fortunes of these volunteers through all the vicissitudes of war would prove a special work; yet their valor and endurance during their first term of service deserved a notice of even more value than that of the historian, since a commander's opinion has to be taken as the basis upon which the chronicler may expatiate. Therefore the following dispatch, dated from the headquarters of the Army of Occupation, Beverly Camp, W. Virginia, July 21, 1861, must be taken as one of the first evidences of their utility and valor:—

"GOVERNOR O. P. MORTON, *Indianapolis, Indiana*

GOVERNOR:—I have directed the three months' regiments from Indiana to move to Indianapolis, there to be mustered out and reorganized for three years' service.

I cannot permit them to return to you without again expressing my high appreciation of the distinguished valor and endurance of the Indiana troops, and my hope that but a short time will elapse before I have the pleasure of knowing that they are again ready for the field.   *   *   *   *   *   *   *

I am, very respectfully, your obedient servant,
GEORGE B. McCLELLAN,
Major-General, U. S. A.

On the return of the troops to Indianapolis, July 29, Brigadier Morris issued a lengthy, logical and well-deserved congratulatory address, from which one paragraph may be extracted to characterize the whole. After passing a glowing eulogium on their military qualities and on that unexcelled gallantry displayed at Laurel Hill, Phillipi and Carrick's Ford, he says:—

"Soldiers! You have now returned to the friends whose prayers went with you to the field of strife. They welcome you with pride and exultation. Your State and country acknowledge the value of your labors. May your future career be as your past has been,—honorable to yourselves and serviceable to your country."

The six regiments forming Morris' brigade, together with one composed of the surplus volunteers, for whom there was no regiment in April, now formed a division of seven regiments, all reorganized for three years' service, between the 20th August and 20th September, with the exception of the new or 12th, which was accepted for one year's service from May 11th, under command of Colonel John M. Wallace, and reorganized May 17, 1862, for three years' service under Col. W. H. Link, who, with 172 officers and men, received their mortal wounds during the Richmond (Kentucky) engagement, three months after its reorganization.

The 13TH REGIMENT, under Col. Jeremiah Sullivan, was mustered into the United States in 1861 and joined Gen. McClellan's command at Rich Mountain on the 10th July. The day following it was present under Gen. Rosencrans and lost eight men killed; three successive days it was engaged under Gen. I. I. Reynolds, and won its laurels at Cheat Mountain summit, where it participated in the decisive victory over Gen. Lee.

The 14TH REGIMENT, organized in 1861 for one year's service, and reorganized on the 7th of June at Terre Haute for three years' service. Commanded by Col. Kimball and showing a muster roll of 1,134 men, it was one of the finest, as it was the first, three years' regiment organized in the State, with varying fortunes attached to its never ending round of duty from Cheat Mountain, September, 1861, to Morton's Ford in 1864, and during the movement South in May of that year to the last of its labors, the battle of Cold Harbor.

The 15TH REGIMENT, reorganized at La Fayette 14th June, 1861, under Col. G. D. Wagner, moved on Rich Mountain on the 11th of July in time to participate in the complete rout of the enemy. On the promotion of Col. Wagner, Lieutenant-Col. G. A. Wood became Colonel of the regiment, November, 1862, and during the first days of January, 1863, took a distinguished part in the severe action of Stone River. From this period down to the battle of Mission Ridge it was in a series of destructive engagements, and was, after enduring terrible hardships, ordered to Chattanooga, and thence to Indianapolis, where it was mustered out the 18th June, 1864,—four days after the expiration of its term of service.

The 16TH REGIMENT, organized under Col. P. A. Hackleman at Richmond for one year's service, after participating in many minor military events, was mustered out at Washington, D.C., on the 14th of May, 1862. Col. Hackleman was killed at the battle of Iuka, and Lieutenant-Col. Thomas I. Lucas succeeded to the command. It was reorganized at Indianapolis for three years' service, May 27, 1862, and took a conspicuous part in all the brilliant engagements of the war down to June, 1865, when it was mustered out at New Orleans. The survivors, numbering 365 rank and file, returned to Indianapolis the 10th of July amid the rejoicing of the populace.

The 17TH REGIMENT was mustered into service at Indianapolis the 12th of June, 1861, for three years, under Col. Hascall, who on being promoted Brigadier General in March, 1862, left the Colonelcy to devolve on Lieutenant Colonel John T. Wilder. This regiment participated in the many exploits of Gen. Reynold's army from Green Brier in 1862, to Macon in 1865, under Gen. Wilson. Returning to Indianapolis the 16th of August, in possession of a brilliant record, the regiment was disbanded.

The 18TH REGIMENT, under Colonel Thomas Pattison, was organized at Indianapolis, and mustered into service on the 16th of August, 1861. Under Gen. Pope it gained some distinction at Blackwater, and succeeded in retaining a reputation made there, by its gallantry at Pea Ridge, February, 1862, down to the moment when it planted the regimental flag on the arsenal of Augusta, Georgia, where it was disbanded August 28, 1865.

The 19TH REGIMENT, mustered into three years' service at the State capital July 29, 1861, was ordered to join the army of the Potomac, and reported its arrival at Washington, August 9. Two days later it took part in the battle of Lewinsville, under Colonel Solomon Meredith. Occupying Falls Church in September, 1861, it continued to maintain a most enviable place of honor on the military roll until its consolidation with the 20th Regiment, October, 1864, under Colonel William Orr, formerly its Lieutenant Colonel.

The 20TH REGIMENT of La Fayette was organized in July, 1861, mustered into three years' service at Indianapolis on the 22d of the same month, and reached the front at Cockeysville, Maryland, twelve days later. Throughout all its brilliant actions from Hatteras Bank, on the 4th of October, to Clover Hill, 9th of April, 1865, including the saving of the United States ship *Congress*, at Newport News, it added daily some new name to its escutcheon. This regiment was mustered out at Louisville in July, 1865, and returning to Indianapolis was welcomed by the great war Governor of their State.

The 21st REGIMENT was mustered into service under Colonel I. W. McMillan, July 24, 1861, and reported at the front the third day of August. It was the first regiment to enter New Orleans. The fortunes of this regiment were as varied as its services, so that its name and fame, grown from the blood shed by its members, are destined to live and flourish. In December, 1863, the regiment was reorganized, and on the 19th February, 1864, many of its veterans returned to their State, where Morton received them with that spirit of proud gratitude which he was capable of showing to those who deserve honor for honors won.

The 22D REGIMENT, under Colonel Jeff. C. Davis, left Indianapolis the 15th of August, and was attached to Fremont's Corps at St. Louis on the 17th. From the day it moved to the support of Colonel Mulligan at Lexington, to the last victory, won under General Sherman at Bentonville, on the 19th of March, 1865, it gained a high military reputation. After the fall of Johnston's southern army, this regiment was mustered out, and arrived at Indianapolis on the 16th June.

The 23D BATTALION, commanded by Colonel W. L. Sanderson, was mustered in at New Albany, the 29th July, 1861, and moved to the front early in August. From its unfortunate marine experiences before Fort Henry to Bentonville it won unusual honors, and after its disbandment at Louisville, returned to Indianapolis July 24, 1865, where Governor Morton and General Sherman reviewed and complimented the gallant survivors.

The 24th BATTALION, under Colonel Alvin P. Hovey, was mustered at Vincennes the 31st of July, 1861. Proceeding immediately to the front it joined Fremont's command, and participated under many Generals in important affairs during the war. Three hundred and ten men and officers returned to their State in August, 1865, and were received with marked honors by the people and Executive.

The 25th REGIMENT, of Evansville mustered into service there for three years under Col. J. C. Veatch, arrived at St. Louis on the 26th of August, 1861. During the war this regiment was present at 18 battles and skirmishes, sustaining therein a loss of 352 men and officers. Mustered out at Louisville, July 17, 1865, it returned to Indianapolis on the 21st amid universal rejoicing.

The 26TH BATTALION, under W. M. Wheatley, left Indianapolis for the front the 7th of September, 1861, and after a brilliant campaign under Fremont, Grant, Heron and Smith, may be said to disband the 18th of September, 1865, when the non-veterans and recruits were reviewed by Morton at the State capital.

The 27th REGIMENT, under Col. Silas Colgrove, moved from Indianapolis to Washington City, September 15th, 1861, and in October was allied to Gen. Banks' army. From Winchester Heights, the 9th of March 1862, through all the affairs of General Sherman's campaign, it acted a gallant and faithful part, and was disbanded immediately after returning to their State.

The 28TH or 1ST CAVALRY was mustered into service at Evansville on the 20th of August, 1861, under Col. Conrad Baker. From the skirmish at Ironton, on the 12th of September, wherein three companies under Col. Gavin captured a position held by a few rebels, to the battle of the Wilderness, the First Cavalry performed prodigies of valor. In June and July, 1865, the troops were mustered out at Indianapolis.

The 29TH BATTALION of La Porte, under Col. J. F. Miller, left on the 5th of October, 1861, and reaching Camp Nevin, Kentucky, on the 9th, was allied to Rosseau's Brigade, serving with McCook's division at Shiloh, with Buell's army in Alabama, Tennessee and Kentucky, with Rosencrans at Murfreesboro, at Decatur, Alabama, and at Dalton, Georgia. The Twenty-ninth won many laurels, and had its Colonel promoted to the rank of Brigadier General. This officer was succeeded in the command by Lieutenant-Col. D. M. Dunn.

The 30TH REGIMENT of Fort Wayne, under Col. Sion S. Bass, proceeded to the front via Indianapolis, and joined General Rosseau at Camp Nevin on the 9th of October, 1861. At Shiloh, Col. Bass received a mortal wound, and died a few days later at Paducah, leaving the Colonelcy to devolve upon Lieutenant-Col. J. B. Dodge. In October 1865, it formed a battalion of General Sheridan's army of observation in Texas.

The 31st REGIMENT, organized at Terre Haute, under Col. Charles Cruft, in September 1861, was mustered in, and left in a few days for Kentucky. Present at the reduction of Fort Donelson on the 13th, 14th, and 15th of February, 1862, its list of killed and wounded proves its desperate fighting qualities. The organization was subjected to many changes, but in all its phases maintained a fair fame won on many battle fields. Like the former regiment, it passed into Gen. Sheridan's Army of Observation, and held the district of Green Lake, Texas.

The 32D REGIMENT OF GERMAN INFANTRY, under Col. August Willich, organized at Indianapolis, mustered on the 24th of August, 1861, served with distinction throughout the campaign Col. Willich was promoted to the rank of Brigadier-General, and Lieut.-Col. Henry Von Trebra commissioned to act, under whose command the regiment passed into General Sheridan's Army, holding the post of Salado Creek, until the withdrawal of the corps of observation in Texas.

The 33D REGIMENT of Indianapolis possesses a military history of no small proportions. The mere facts that it was mustered in under Col. John Coburn, the 16th of September, won a series of distinctions throughout the war district and was mustered out at Louisville, July 21, 1865, taken with its name as one of the most powerful regiments engaged in the war, are sufficient here.

The 34TH BATTALION, organized at Anderson on the 16th September, 1861, under Col. Ashbury Steele, appeared among the investing battalions before New Madrid on the 30th of March, 1862. From the distinguished part it took in that siege, down to the 13th of May, 1865, when at Palmetto Ranche, near Palo Alto, it fought for hours against fearful odds the last battle of the war for the Union. Afterwards it marched 250 miles up the Rio Grande, and was the first regiment to reoccupy the position, so long in Southern hands, of Ringold barracks. In 1865 it garrisoned Beaconsville as part of the Army of Observation.

The 35TH OR FIRST IRISH REGIMENT, was organized at Indianapolis, and mustered into service on the 11th of December, 1861, under Col. John C. Walker. At Nashville, on the 22d of May, 1862, it was joined by the organized portion of the Sixty-first or Second Irish Regiment, and unassigned recruits. Col. Mullen now became Lieut.-Colonel of the 35th, and shortly after, its Colonel. From the pursuit of Gen. Bragg through Kentucky and the affair at Perryville on the 8th of October, 1862, to the terrible hand to hand combat at Kenesaw mountain, on the night of the 20th of June, 1864, and again from the conclusion of the Atlanta campaign to September, 1865, with Gen. Sheridan's army, when it was mustered out, it won for itself a name of reckless daring and unsurpassed gallantry.

The 36TH REGIMENT, of Richmond, Ind., under Col. William Grose, mustered into service for three years on the 16th of September, 1861, went immediately to the front, and shared the fortunes of the Army of the Ohio until the 27th of February, 1862, when a forward movement led to its presence on the battle-field of Shiloh. Following up the honors won at Shiloh, it participated in some of the most important actions of the war, and was, in October, 1865, transferred to Gen. Sheridan's army. Col. Grose was promoted in 1864 to the position of Brigadier-General, and the Colonelcy devolved on Oliver H. P. Carey, formerly Lieut.-Colonel of the regiment.

The 37TH BATTALION, of Lawrenceburg, commanded by Col. Geo. W. Hazzard, organized the 18th of September, 1861, left for the seat of war early in October. From the eventful battle of Stone river, in December, 1862, to its participation in Sherman's march through Georgia, it gained for itself a splendid reputation. This regiment returned to, and was present at, Indianapolis, on the 30th of July, 1865, where a public reception was tendered to men and officers on the grounds of the Capitol.

The 38TH REGIMENT, under Col. Benjamin F. Scribner, was mustered in at New Albany, on the 18th of September, 1861, and in a few days were en route for the front. To follow its continual round of duty, is without the limits of this sketch; therefore, it will suffice to say, that on every well-fought field, at least from February, 1862, until its dissolution, on the 15th of July, 1865, it earned an enviable renown, and drew from Gov. Morton, on returning to Indianapolis the 18th of the same month, a congratulatory address couched in the highest terms of praise.

The 39TH REGIMENT, OR EIGHTH CAVALRY, was mustered in as an infantry regiment, under Col. T. J. Harrison, on the 28th of August, 1861, at the State capital. Leaving immediately for the front it took a conspicuous part in all the engagements up to April, 1863, when it was reorganized as a cavalry regiment. The record of this organization sparkles with great deeds which men will extol while language lives; its services to the Union cannot be over estimated, or the memory of its daring deeds be forgotten by the unhappy people who raised the tumult, which culminated in their second shame.

The 40TH REGIMENT, of Lafayette, under Col. W. C. Wilson, subsequently commanded by Col. J. W. Blake, and again by Col. Henry Leaming, was organized on the 30th of December, 1861, and at once proceeded to the front, where some time was necessarily spent in the Camp of Instruction at Bardstown, Kentucky. In February, 1862, it joined in Buell's forward movement. During the war the regiment shared in all its hardships, participated in all its honors, and like many other brave commands took service under Gen. Sheridan in his Army of Occupation, holding the post of Port Lavaca, Texas, until peace brooded over the land.

THE 41ST REGIMENT OR SECOND CAVALRY, the first complete regiment of horse ever raised in the State, was organized on the 3d of September, 1861, at Indianapolis, under Col. John A. Bridgland, and December 16 moved to the front. Its first war experience was gained *en route* to Corinth on the 9th of April, 1862, and at Pea Ridge on the 15th. Gallatin, Vinegar Hill, and Perryville, and Talbot Station followed in succession, each battle bringing to the cavalry untold honors. In May, 1864, it entered upon a glorious career under Gen. Sherman in his Atlanta campaign, and again under Gen. Wilson in the raid through Alabama during April, 1865. On the 22d of July, after a brilliant career, the regiment was mustered out at Nashville, and returned at once to Indianapolis for discharge.

THE 42D, under Col J. G. Jones, mustered into service at Evansville, October 9, 1861, and having participated in the principal military affairs of the period, Wartrace, Mission Ridge, Altoona, Kenesaw, Savannah, Charlestown and Bentonville, was discharged at Indianapolis on the 25th of July, 1865.

THE 43D BATTALION was mustered in on the 27th of September, 1861, under Col. George K. Steele, and left Terre Haute *en route* to the front within a few days. Later it was allied to Gen. Pope's corps, and afterwards served with Commodore Foote's marines in the reduction of Fort Pillow. It was the first Union regiment to enter Memphis. From that period until the close of the war it was distinguished for its unexcelled qualifications as a military body, and fully deserved the encomiums passed upon it on its return to Indianapolis in March, 1865.

THE 44TH OR THE REGIMENT OF THE 10TH CONGRESSIONAL DISTRICT was organized at Fort Wayne on the 24th of October, 1861, under Col. Hugh B. Reed. Two months later it was ordered to the front, and arriving in Kentucky, was attached to Gen. Cruft's Brigade, then quartered at Calhoun. After years of faithful service it was mustered out at Chattanooga, the 14th of September, 1865.

THE 45TH, OR THIRD CAVALRY, comprised ten companies

organized at different periods and for varied services in 1861-
'62, under Colonel Scott Carter and George H. Chapman. The
distinguished name won by the Third Cavalry is established in
every village within the State.   Let it suffice to add that after its
brilliant participation in Gen. Sheridan's raid down the James'
river canal, it was mustered out at Indianapolis on the 7th of August, 1865.

   THE 46TH REGIMENT, organized at Logansport under Colonel
Graham N. Fitch, arrived in Kentucky the 16th of February, 1862,
and a little later became attached to Gen. Pope's army, then quartered at Commerce.   The capture of Fort Pillow, and its career
under Generals Curtis, Palmer, Hovey, Gorman, Grant, Sherman,
Banks and Burbridge are as truly worthy of applause as ever fell to
the lot of a regiment.   The command was mustered out at Louisville on the 4th of September, 1865.

   THE 47TH was organized at Anderson, under Col. I. R. Slack, early
in October, 1862.   Arriving at Bardstown, Kentucky, on the 21st
of December, it was attached to Gen. Buell's army; but within two
months was assigned to Gen. Pope, under whom it proved the first
regiment to enter Fort Thompson near New Madrid.   In 1864 the
command visited Indianapolis on veteran furlough and was enthusiastically received by Governor Morton and the people.   Returning to the front it engaged heartily in Gen. Banks' company.   In
December, Col. Slack received his commission as Brigadier-General,
and was succeeded on the regimental command by Col. J. A. Mc-
Laughton; at Shreveport under General Heron it received the submission of General Price and his army, and there also was it mustered out of service on the 23d of October, 1865.

   The 48TH REGIMENT, organized at Goshen the 6th of December,
1861, under Col. Norman Eddy, entered on its duties during the
siege of Corinth in May, and again in October, 1862.   The record
of this battalion may be said to be unsurpassed in its every feature,
so that the grand ovation extended to the returned soldiers in
1865 at Indianapolis, is not a matter for surprise.

   The 49TH REGIMENT, organized at Jeffersonville, under Col. J. W.
Ray, and mustered in on the 21st of November, 1861, for service,
left en route for the camp at Bardstown.   A month later it arrived
at the unfortunate camp-ground of Cumberland Ford, where disease carried off a number of gallant soldiers.   The regiment, however, survived the dreadful scourge and won its laurels on many

a well-fought field until September, 1865, when it was mustered out at Louisville.

The 50TH REGIMENT, under Col. Cyrus L. Dunham, organized during the month of September, 1861, at Seymour, left *en route* to Bardstown for a course of military instruction. On the 20th of August, 1862, a detachment of the 50th, under Capt. Atkinson, was attacked by Morgan's Cavalry near Edgefield Junction; but the gallant few repulsed their oft-repeated onsets and finally drove them from the field. The regiment underwent many changes in organization, and may be said to muster out on the 10th of September, 1865.

The 51ST REGIMENT, under Col. Abel. D. Streight, left Indianapolis on the 14th of December, 1861, for the South. After a short course of instruction at Bardstown, the regiment joined General Buell's and acted with great effect during the campaign in Kentucky and Tennessee. Ultimately it became a participator in the work of the Fourth Corps, or Army of Occupation, and held the post of San Antonio until peace was doubly assured.

The 52D REGIMENT was partially raised at Rushville, and the organization completed at Indianapolis, where it was consolidated with the Railway Brigade, or 56th Regiment, on the 2d of February, 1862. Going to the front immediately after, it served with marked distinction throughout the war, and was mustered out at Montgomery on the 10th of September, 1865. Returning to Indianapolis six days later, it was welcomed by Gov. Morton and a most enthusiastic reception accorded to it.

The 53RD BATTALION was raised at New Albany, and with the addition of recruits raised at Rockport formed a standard regiment, under command of Col. W. Q. Gresham. Its first duty was that of guarding the rebels confined on Camp Morton, but on going to the front it made for itself an endurable name. It was mustered out in July, 1865, and returned to Indiananoplis on the 25th of the same month.

The 54TH REGIMENT was raised at Indianapolis on the 10th of June, 1862, for three months' service under Col. D. G. Rose. The succeeding two months saw it in charge of the prisoners at Camp Morton, and in August it was pushed forward to aid in the defense of Kentucky against the Confederate General, Kirby Smith. The remainder of its short term of service was given to the cause. On the muster out of the three months' service regiment it was reorganized for one year's service and gained some distinction, after which it was mustered out in 1863 at New Orleans.

The 55TH REGIMENT, organized for three months' service, retains the brief history applicable to the first organization of the 54th. It was mustered in on the 16th of June, 1862, under Col. J. R. Mahon, disbanded on the expiration of its term and was not reorganized.

The 56TH REGIMENT, referred to in the sketch of the 52nd, was designed to be composed of railroad men, marshalled under J. M. Smith as Colonel, but owing to the fact that many railroaders had already volunteered into other regiments, Col. Smith's volunteers were incorporated with the 52nd, and this number left blank in the army list.

The 57TH BATTALION, actually organized by two ministers of the gospel,—the Rev. I. W. T. McMullen and Rev. F. A. Hardin, of Richmond, Ind., mustered into service on the 18th of November, 1861, under the former named reverend gentleman as Colonel, who was, however, succeeded by Col. Cyrus C. Haynes, and he in turn by G. W. Leonard, Willis Blanch and John S. McGrath, the latter holding command until the conclusion of the war. The history of this battalion is extensive, and if participation in a number of battles with the display of rare gallantry wins fame, the 57th may rest assured of its possession of this fragile yet coveted prize. Like many other regiments it concluded its military labors in the service of General Sheridan, and held the post of Port Lavaca in conjunction with another regiment until peace dwelt in the land.

The 58TH REGIMENT, of Princeton, was organized there early in October, 1861, and was mustered into service under the Colonelcy of Henry M. Carr. In December it was ordered to join General Buell's army, after which it took a share in the various actions of the war, and was mustered out on the 25th of July, 1865, at Louisville, having gained a place on the roll of honor.

The 59TH BATTALION was raised under a commission issued by Gov. Morton to Jesse I. Alexander, creating him Colonel. Owing to the peculiarities hampering its organization, Col. Alexander could not succeed in having his regiment prepared to muster in before the 17th of February, 1862. However, on that day the equipment was complete, and on the 18th it left *en route* to Commerce, where on its arrival, it was incorporated under General Pope's command. The list of its casualties speaks a history,—no less than 793 men were lost during the campaign. The regiment, after a term characterized by distinguished service, was mustered out at Louisville on the 17th of July, 1865.

The 60TH REGIMENT was partially organized under Lieut.-Col. Richard Owen at Evansville during November 1861, and perfected at Camp Morton during March, 1862. Its first experience was its gallant resistance to Bragg's army investing Munfordsville, which culminated in the unconditional surrender of its first seven companies on the 14th of September. An exchange of prisoners took place in November, which enabled it to join the remaining companies in the field. The subsequent record is excellent, and forms, as it were, a monument to their fidelity and heroism. The main portion of this battalion was mustered out at Indianapolis, on the 21st of March, 1865.

The 61ST was partially organized in December, 1861, under Col. B. F. Mullen. The failure of thorough organization on the 22d of May, 1862, led the men and officers to agree to incorporation with the 35th Regiment of Volunteers.

The 62D BATTALION, raised under a commission issued to William Jones, of Rockport, authorizing him to organize this regiment in the First Congressional District was so unsuccessful that consolidation with the 53d Regiment was resolved upon.

The 63D REGIMENT, of Covington, under James McManomy, Commandant of Camp, and J. S. Williams, Adjutant, was partially organized on the 31st of December, 1861, and may be considered on duty from its very formation. After guarding prisoners at Camp Morton and Lafayette, and engaging in battle on Manassas Plains on the 30th of August following, the few companies sent out in February, 1862, returned to Indianapolis to find six new companies raised under the call of July, 1862, ready to embrace the fortunes of the 63d. So strengthened, the regiment went forth to battle, and continued to lead in the paths of honor and fidelity until mustered out in May and June, 1865.

The 64TH REGIMENT failed in organization as an artillery corps; but orders received from the War Department prohibiting the consolidation of independent batteries, put a stop to any further move in the matter. However, an infantry regiment bearing the same number was afterward organized.

The 65TH was mustered in at Princeton and Evansville, in July and August, 1862, under Col. J. W. Foster, and left at once *en route* for the front. The record of this battalion is creditable, not only to its members, but also to the State which claimed it. Its last action during the war was on the 18th and 20th of February, 1865, at Fort Anderson and Town creek, after which, on the 22d June, it was disbanded at Greensboro.

The 66th REGIMENT partially organized at New Albany, under Commandant Roger Martin, was ordered to leave for Kentucky on the 19th of August, 1862, for the defense of that State against the incursions of Kirby Smith. After a brilliant career it was mustered out at Washington on the 3d of June, 1865, after which it returned to Indianapolis to receive the thanks of a grateful people.

The 67th REGIMENT was organized within the Third Congressional District under Col. Frank Emerson, and was ordered to Louisville on the 20th of August, 1862, whence it marched to Munfordville, only to share the same fate with the other gallant regiments engaged against Gen. Bragg's advance. Its roll of honor extends down the years of civil disturbance,— always adding garlands, until Peace called a truce in the fascinating race after fame, and insured a term of rest, wherein its members could think on comrades forever vanished, and temper the sad thought with the sublime memories born of that chivalrous fight for the maintenance and integrity of a great Republic. At Galveston on the 19th of July, 1865, the gallant 67th Regiment was mustered out, and returning within a few days to its State received the enthusiastic ovations of her citizens.

The 68th REGIMENT, organized at Greensburg under Major Benjamin C. Shaw, was accepted for general service the 19th of August, 1862, under Col. Edward A. King, with Major Shaw as Lieutenant Colonel; on the 25th its arrival at Lebanon was reported and within a few days it appeared at the defense of Munfordville; but sharing in the fate of all the defenders, it surrendered unconditionally to Gen. Bragg and did not participate further in the actions of that year, nor until after the exchange of prisoners in 1863. From this period it may lay claim to an enviable history extending to the end of the war, when it was disembodied.

The 69th REGIMENT, of Richmond, Ind., under Col. A. Bickle, left for the front on the 20th of August, 1862, and ten days later made a very brilliant stand at Richmond, Kentucky, against the advance of Gen. Kirby Smith, losing in the engagement two hundred and eighteen men and officers together with its liberty. After an exchange of prisoners the regiment was reorganized under Col. T. W. Bennett and took the field in December, 1862, under

Generals Sheldon, Morgan and Sherman of Grant's army. Chickasaw, Vicksburg, Blakely and many other names testify to the valor of the 69th. The remnant of the regiment was in January, 1865, formed into a battalion under Oran Perry, and was mustered out in July following.

The 70TH REGIMENT was organized at Indianapolis on the 12th of August, 1862, under Col. B. Harrison, and leaving for Louisville on the 13th, shared in the honors of Bruce's division at Franklin and Russellville. The record of the regiment is brimful of honor. It was mustered out at Washington, June 8, 1865, and received at Indianapolis with public honors.

The 71ST OR SIXTH CAVALRY was organized as an infantry regiment, at Terre Haute, and mustered into general service at Indianapolis on the 18th of August, 1862, under Lieut.-Col. Melville D. Topping. Twelve days later it was engaged outside Richmond, Kentucky, losing two hundred and fifteen officers and men, including Col. Topping and Major Conklin, together with three hundred and forty-seven prisoners, only 225 escaping death and capture. After an exchange of prisoners the regiment was re-formed under Col. I. Bittle, but on the 28th of December it surrendered to Gen. J. H. Morgan, who attacked its position at Muldraugh's Hill with a force of 1,000 Confederates. During September and October, 1863, it was organized as a cavalry regiment, won distinction throughout its career, and was mustered out the 15th of September, 1865, at Murfreesboro.

The 77TH REGIMENT was organized at Lafayette, and left en route to Lebanon, Kentucky, on the 17th of August, 1862. Under Col. Miller it won a series of honors, and mustered out at Nashville on the 26th of June, 1865.

The 73RD REGIMENT, under Col. Gilbert Hathaway, was mustered in at South Bend on the 16th of August, 1862, and proceeded immediately to the front. Day's Gap, Crooked Creek, and the high eulogies of Generals Rosencrans and Granger speak its long and brilliant history, nor were the welcoming shouts of a great people and the congratulations of Gov. Morton, tendered to the regiment on its return home, in July, 1865, necessary to sustain its well won reputation.

The 74TH REGIMENT, partially organized at Fort Wayne and made almost complete at Indianapolis, left for the seat of war on the 22d of August, 1862, under Col. Charles W. Chapman. The desperate opposition to Gen. Bragg, and the magnificent defeat of Morgan, together with the battles of Dallas, Chattahoochie river, Kenesaw and Atlanta, where Lieut. Col. Myron Baker was killed, all bear evidence of its never surpassed gallantry. It was mustered out of service on the 9th of June, 1865, at Washington. On the return of the regiment to Indianapolis, the war Governor and people tendered it special honors, and gave expression to the admiration and regard in which it was held.

The 75TH REGIMENT was organized within the Eleventh Congressional District, and left Wabash, on the 21st of August, 1862, for the front, under Col. I. W. Petit. It was the first regiment to enter Tullahoma, and one of the last engaged in the battles of the Republic. After the submission of Gen. Johnson's army, it was mustered out at Washington, on the 8th of June 1865.

The 76TH BATTALION was solely organized for thirty days' service under Colonel James Gavin, for the purpose of pursuing the rebel guerrilas, who plundered Newburg on the 13th July, 1862. It was organized and equipped within forty-eight hours, and during its term of service gained the name, " The Avengers of Newburg."

The 77TH, OR FOURTH CAVALRY, was organized at the State capital in August, 1862, under Colonel Isaac P. Gray. It carved its way to fame over twenty battlefields, and retired from service at Edgefield, on the 29th June, 1865.

The 79TH REGIMENT was mustered in at Indianapolis on the 2nd September, 1862, under Colonel Fred Knefler. Its history may be termed a record of battles, as the great numbers of battles, from 1862 to the conclusion of hostilities, were participated in by it. The regiment received its discharge on the 11th June, 1865, at Indianapolis. During its continued round of field duty it captured eighteen guns and over one thousand prisoners.

The 80TH REGIMENT was organized within the First Congressional District under Col. C. Denby, and equipped at Indianapolis, when, on the 8th of September, 1862, it left for the front. During its term it lost only two prisoners; but its list of casualties sums up 325 men and officers killed and wounded. The regiment may be said to muster out on the 22nd of June, 1865, at Saulsbury.

The 81ST REGIMENT, of New Albany, under Colonel W. W. Caldwell, was organized on the 29th August, 1862, and proceeded at once to join Buell's headquarters, and join in the pursuit of General Bragg. Throughout the terrific actions of the war its influence was felt, nor did its labors cease until it aided in driving the rebels across the Tennessee. It was disembodied at Nashville on the 13th June, 1865, and returned to Indianapolis on the 15th, to receive the well-merited congratulations of Governor Morton and the people.

The 82ND REGIMENT, under Colonel Morton C. Hunter, was mustered in at Madison, Ind., on the 30th August, 1862, and leaving immediately for the seat of war, participated in many of the great battles down to the return of peace. It was mustered out at Washington on the 9th June, 1865, and soon returned to its State to receive a grand recognition of its faithful service.

The 83RD REGIMENT, of Lawrenceburg, under Colonel Ben. J. Spooner, was organized in September, 1862, and soon left en route to the Mississippi. Its subsequent history, the fact of its being under fire for a total term of 4,800 hours, and its wanderings over 6,285 miles, leave nothing to be said in its defense. Master of a thousand honors, it was mustered out at Louisville, on the 15th July, 1865, and returned home to enjoy a well-merited repose.

The 84TH REGIMENT was mustered in at Richmond, Ind., on the 8th September, 1862, under Colonel Nelson Trusler. Its first military duty was on the defenses of Covington, in Kentucky, and Cincinnati; but after a short time its labors became more congenial, and tended to the great disadvantage of the slaveholding enemy on many well-contested fields. This, like the other State regiments, won many distinctions, and retired from the service on the 14th of June, 1865, at Nashville.

The 85TH REGIMENT was mustered at Terre Haute, under Colonel John P. Bayard, on the 2d September, 1862. On the 4th March, 1863, it shared in the unfortunate affair at Thompson's Station, when in common with the other regiments forming Coburn's Brigade, it surrendered to the overpowering forces of the rebel General, Forrest. In June, 1863, after an exchange, it again took the field, and won a large portion of that renown accorded to Indiana. It was mustered out on the 12th of June, 1865.

The 86TH REGIMENT, of La Fayette, left for Kentucky on the 26th August, 1862, under Colonel Orville S. Hamilton, and shared in the duties assigned to the 84th. Its record is very creditable, particularly that portion dealing with the battles of Nashville on the 15th and 16th December, 1864. It was mustered out on the 6th of June, 1865, and reported within a few days at Indianapolis for discharge.

The 87TH REGIMENT, organized at South Bend, under Colonels Kline G. Sherlock and N. Gleason, was accepted at Indianapolis on the 31st of August, 1862, and left on the same day en route to the front. From Springfield and Perryville on the 6th and 8th of October, 1862, to Mission Ridge, on the 25th of November, 1863, thence through the Atlanta campaign to the surrender of the Southern armies, it upheld a gallant name, and met with a true and enthusiastic welcome home on the 21st of June, 1865, with a list of absent comrades aggregating 451.

The 88TH REGIMENT, organized within the Fourth Congressional District, under Col. Geo. Humphrey, entered the service on the 29th of August, 1862, and presently was found among the front ranks in war. It passed through the campaign in brilliant form down to the time of Gen. Johnson's surrender to Gen. Grant, after which, on the 7th of June, 1865, it was mustered out at Washington.

The 89TH REGIMENT, formed from the material of the Eleventh Congressional District, was mustered in at Indianapolis, on the 28th of August, 1862, under Col. Chas. D. Murray, and after an exceedingly brilliant campaign was discharged by Gov. Morton on the 4th of August, 1865.

The 90TH REGIMENT, OR FIFTH CAVALRY, was organized at Indianapolis under the Colonelcy of Felix W. Graham, between August and November, 1862. The different companies, joining headquarters at Louisville on the 11th of March, 1863, engaged in observing the movements of the enemy in the vicinity of Cumberland river until the 19th of April, when a first and successful brush was had with the rebels. The regiment had been in 22 engagements during the term of service, captured 640 prisoners, and claimed a list of casualties mounting up to the number of 829. It was mustered out on the 16th of June, 1865, at Pulaski.

The 91ST BATTALION, of seven companies, was mustered into service at Evansville, the 1st of October, 1862, under Lieut.-Colonel John Mehringer, and in ten days later left for the front. In 1863 the regiment was completed, and thenceforth took a very prominent position in the prosecution of the war. During its service it lost 81 men, and retired from the field on the 26th of June, 1865.

The 92D REGIMENT failed in organizing.

The 93D REGIMENT was mustered in at Madison, Ind., on the 20th of October, 1862, under Col. De Witt C. Thomas and Lieut.-Col. Geo. W. Carr. On the 9th of November it began a movement south, and ultimately allied itself to Buckland's Brigade of

Gen. Sherman's. On the 14th of May it was among the first regiments to enter Jackson, the capital of Mississippi; was next present at the assault on Vicksburg, and made a stirring campaign down to the storming of Fort Blakely on the 9th of April, 1865. It was discharged on the 11th of August, that year, at Indianapolis, after receiving a public ovation.

The 94TH AND 95TH REGIMENTS, authorized to be formed within the Fourth and Fifth Congressional Districts, respectively, were only partially organized, and so the few companies that could be mustered were incorporated with other regiments.

The 96TH REGIMENT could only bring together three companies, in the Sixth Congressional District, and these becoming incorporated with the 99th then in process of formation at South Bend, the number was left blank.

The 97TH REGIMENT, raised in the Seventh Congressional District, was mustered into service at Terre Haute, on the 20th of September, 1861, under Col. Robert F. Catterson. Reaching the front within a few days, it was assigned a position near Memphis, and subsequently joined in Gen. Grant's movement on Vicksburg, by overland route. After a succession of great exploits with the several armies to which it was attached, it completed its list of battles at Bentonville, on the 21st of March, 1865, and was disembodied at Washington on the 9th of June following. During its term of service the regiment lost 341 men, including the three Ensigns killed during the assaults on rebel positions along the Augusta Railway, from the 15th to the 27th of June, 1864.

The 98TH REGIMENT, authorized to be raised within the Eighth Congressional District, failed in its organization, and the number was left blank in the army list. The two companies answering to the call of July, 1862, were consolidated with the 100th Regiment then being organized at Fort Wayne.

The 99TH BATTALION, recruited within the Ninth Congressional District, completed its muster on the 21st of October, 1862, under Col. Alex. Fawler, and reported for service a few days later at Memphis, where it was assigned to the 16th Army Corps. The varied vicissitudes through which this regiment passed and its remarkable gallantry upon all occasions, have gained for it a fair fame. It was disembodied on the 5th of June, 1865, at Washington, and returned to Indianapolis on the 11th of the same month.

The 100TH REGIMENT, recruited from the Eighth and Tenth Congressional Districts, under Col. Sandford J. Stoughton, mustered into the service on the 10th of September, left for the front on the 11th of November, and became attached to the Army of Tennessee on the 26th of that month, 1862. The regiment participated in twenty-five battles, together with skirmishing during fully one-third of its term of service, and claimed a list of casualties mounting up to four hundred and sixty-four. It was mustered out of the service at Washington on the 9th of June, and reported at Indianapolis for discharge on the 14th of June, 1865.

The 101st REGIMENT was mustered into service at Wabash on the 7th of September, 1862, under Col. William Garver, and proceeded immediately to Covington, Kentucky. Its early experiences were gained in the pursuit of Bragg's army and John Morgan's cavalry, and these experiences tendered to render the regiment one of the most valuable in the war for the Republic. From the defeat of John Morgan at Milton on the 18th of March, 1863, to the fall of Savannah on the 23rd of September, 1863, the regiment won many honors. and retired from the service on the 25th of June, 1865, at Indianapolis.

THE MORGAN RAID REGIMENTS—MINUTE MEN.

The 102D REGIMENT, organized under Col. Benjamin M. Gregory from companies of the Indiana Legion, and numbering six hundred and twenty-three men and officers, left Indianapolis for the front early in July, and reported at North Vernon on the 12th of July, 1863, and having completed a round of duty, returned to Indianapolis on the 17th to be discharged.

The 103D, comprising seven companies from Hendricks county, two from Marion and one from Wayne counties, numbering 681 men and officers, under Col. Lawrence S. Shuler, was contemporary with the 102d Regiment, varying only in its service by being mustered out one day before, or on the 16th of July, 1863.

The 104TH REGIMENT OF MINUTE MEN was recruited from members of the Legion of Decatur, La Fayette, Madison, Marion and Rush counties. It comprised 714 men and officers under the command of Col. James Gavin, and was organized within forty hours after the issue of Governor Morton's call for minute men to protect Indiana and Kentucky against the raids of Gen. John H Morgan's rebel forces. After Morgan's escape into Ohio the command returned and was mustered out on the 18th of July, 1863.

The 105th REGIMENT consisted of seven companies of the Legion and three of Minute Men, furnished by Hancock, Union, Randolph,

Putnam, Wayne, Clinton and Madison counties. The command numbered seven hundred and thirteen men and officers, under Col. Sherlock, and took a leading part in the pursuit of Morgan. Returning on the 18th of July to Indianapolis it was mustered out.

The 106TH REGIMENT, under Col. Isaac P. Gray, consisted of one company of the Legion and nine companies of Minute Men, aggregating seven hundred and ninety-two men and officers. The counties of Wayne, Randolph, Hancock, Howard, and Marion were represented in its rank and file. Like the other regiments organized to repel Morgan, it was disembodied in July, 1863.

The 107TH REGIMENT, under Col. De Witt C. Rugg, was organized in the city of Indianapolis from the companies' Legion, or Ward Guards. The successes of this promptly organized regiment were unquestioned.

The 108TH REGIMENT comprised five companies of Minute Men, from Tippecanoe county, two from Hancock, and one from each of the counties known as Carroll, Montgomery and Wayne, aggregating 710 men and officers, and all under the command of Col. W. C. Wilson. After performing the only duties presented, it returned from Cincinnati on the 18th of July, and was mustered out.

The 109TH REGIMENT, composed of Minute Men from Coles county, Ill., La Porte, Hamilton, Miami and Randolph counties, Ind., showed a roster of 709 officers and men, under Col. J. R. Mahon. Morgan having escaped from Ohio, its duties were at an end, and returning to Indianapolis was mustered out on the 17th of July, 1863, after seven days' service.

The 110TH REGIMENT of Minute Men comprised volunteers from Henry, Madison, Delaware, Cass, and Monroe counties. The men were ready and willing, if not really anxious to go to the front. But happily the swift-winged Morgan was driven away, and consequently the regiment was not called to the field.

The 111TH REGIMENT, furnished by Montgomery, Lafayette, Rush, Miami, Monroe, Delaware and Hamilton counties, numbering 733 men and officers, under Col. Robert Canover, was not requisitioned.

The 112TH REGIMENT was formed from nine companies of Minute Men, and the Mitchell Light Infantry Company of the Legion. Its strength was 703 men and officers, under Col. Hiram F. Braxton. Lawrence, Washington, Monroe and Orange counties were represented on its roster, and the historic names of North Vernon and Sunman's Station on its banner. Returning from the South after seven days' service, it was mustered out on the 17th of July, 1863.

The 113TH REGIMENT, furnished by Daviess, Martin, Washington, and Monroe counties, comprised 526 rank and file under Col. Geo. W. Burge. Like the 112th, it was assigned to Gen. Hughes' Brigade, and defended North Vernon against the repeated attacks of John H. Morgan's forces.

The 114TH REGIMENT was wholly organized in Johnson county, under Col. Lambertson, and participated in the affair of North Vernon. Returning on the 21st of July, 1863, with its brief but faithful record, it was disembodied at Indianapolis, 11 days after its organization.

All these regiments were brought into existence to meet an emergency, and it must be confessed, that had not a sense of duty, military instinct and love of country animated these regiments. the rebel General, John H. Morton, and his 6,000 cavalry, would doubtless have carried destruction as far as the very capital of their State.

SIX-MONTHS' REGIMENTS.

The 115TH REGIMENT, organized at Indianapolis in answer to the call of the President in June, 1863, was mustered into service on the 17th of August, under Col. J. R. Mahon. Its service was short but brilliant, and received its discharge at Indianapolis the 10th of February, 1864.

The 116TH REGIMENT, mustered in on the 17th of August, 1863, moved to Detroit, Michigan, on the 30th, under Col. Charles Wise. During October it was ordered to Nicholasville, Kentucky, where it was assigned to Col. Mahon's Brigade, and with Gen. Willcox's entire command, joined in the forward movement to Cumberland Gap. After a term on severe duty it returned to Lafayette and there was disembodied on the 24th of February, 1864, whither Gov. Morton hastened, to share in the ceremonies of welcome.

The 117TH REGIMENT of Indianapolis was mustered into service on the 17th of September, 1863, under Col. Thomas. J. Brady. After surmounting every obstacle opposed to it, it returned on the 6th of February, 1864, and was treated to a public reception on the 9th.

The 118TH REGIMENT, whose organization was completed on the 3d of September, 1863, under Col. Geo. W. Jackson, joined the 116th at Nicholasville, and sharing in its fortunes, returned to the

State capital on the 14th of February, 1864. Its casualties were comprised in a list of 15 killed and wounded.

The 119TH, or SEVENTH CAVALRY, was recruited under Col. John P. C. Shanks, and its organization completed on the 1st of October, 1863. The rank and file numbered 1,213, divided into twelve companies. On the 7th of December its arrival at Louisville was reported, and on the 14th it entered on active service. After the well-fought battle of Guntown, Mississippi, on the 10th of June, 1864, although it only brought defeat to our arms, General Grierson addressed the Seventh Cavalry, saying: " Your General congratulates you upon your noble conduct during the late expedition. Fighting against overwhelming numbers, under adverse circumstances, your prompt obedience to orders and unflinching courage commanding the admiration of all, made even defeat almost a victory. For hours on foot you repulsed the charges of the enemies' infantry, and again in the saddle you met his cavalry and turned his assaults into confusion. Your heroic perseverance saved hundreds of your fellow-soldiers from capture. You have been faithful to your honorable reputation, and have fully justified the confidence, and merited the high esteem of your commander."

Early in 1865, a number of these troops, returning from imprisonment in Southern bastiles, were lost on the steamer " Sultana." The survivors of the campaign continued in the service for a long period after the restoration of peace, and finally mustered out.

The 120TH REGIMENT. In September, 1863, Gov. Morton received authority from the War Department to organize eleven regiments within the State for three years' service. By April, 1864, this organization was complete, and being transferred to the command of Brigadier General Alvin P. Hovey, were formed by him into a division for service with the Army of Tennessee. Of those regiments, the 120th occupied a very prominent place, both on account of its numbers, its perfect discipline and high reputation. It was mustered in at Columbus, and was in all the great battles of the latter years of the war. It won high praise from friend and foe, and retired with its bright roll of honor, after the success of Right and Justice was accomplished.

The 121ST, OR NINTH CAVALRY, was mustered in March 1, 1864, under Col. George W. Jackson, at Indianapolis, and though not numerically strong, was so well equipped and possessed such excellent material that on the 3rd of May it was ordered to the front. The record of the 121st, though extending over a brief period, is pregnant with deeds of war of a high character. On the 26th of April, 1865, these troops, while returning from their labors in the South, lost 55 men, owing to the explosion of the engines of the steamer "Sultana." The return of the 386 survivors, on the 5th of September, 1865, was hailed with joy, and proved how well and dearly the citizens of Indiana loved their soldiers.

The 122D REGIMENT ordered to be raised in the Third Congressional District, owing to very few men being then at home, failed in organization, and the regimental number became a blank.

The 123D REGIMENT was furnished by the Fourth and Seventh Congressional Districts during the winter of 1863–'64, and mustered, March 9, 1864, at Greensburg, under Col. John C. McQuiston. The command left for the front the same day, and after winning rare distinction during the last years of the campaign, particularly in its gallantry at Atlanta, and its daring movement to escape Forrest's 15,000 rebel horsemen near Franklin, this regiment was discharged on the 30th of August, 1865, at Indianapolis, being mustered out on the 25th, at Raleigh, North Carolina.

The 124TH REGIMENT completed its organization by assuming three companies raised for the 125th Regiment (which was intended to be cavalry), and was mustered in at Richmond, on the 10th of March, 1864, under Colonel James Burgess, and reported at Louisville within nine days. From Buzzard's Roost, on the 8th of May, 1864, under General Schofield, Lost Mountain in June, and the capture of Decatur, on the 15th July, to the 21st March, 1865, in its grand advance under General Sherman from Atlanta to the coast, the regiment won many laurel wreaths, and after a brilliant campaign, was mustered out at Greensboro on the 31st August, 1865.

The 125TH, OR TENTH CAVALRY, was partially organized during November and December, 1862, at Vincennes, and in February, 1863, completed its numbers and equipment at Columbus, under Colonel T. M. Pace. Early in May its arrival in Nashville was reported, and presently assigned active service. During September and October it engaged rebel contingents under Forrest and Hood, and later in the battles of Nashville, Reynold's Hill and Sugar Creek, and in 1865 Flint River, Courtland and Mount Hope. The explosion of the *Sultana* occasioned the loss of thirty-five men with Captain Gaffney and Lieutenants Twigg and Reeves, and in a collision on the Nashville & Louisville railroad, May, 1864, lost five men killed and several wounded. After a term of service unsurpassed for its utility and character it was disembodied at Vicksburg, Mississippi, on the 31st August, 1863, and returning to Indianapolis early in September, was welcomed by the Executive and people.

The 126TH, OR ELEVENTH CAVALRY, was organized at Indianapolis under Colonel Robert R. Stewart, on the 1st of March, 1864, and left in May for Tennessee. It took a very conspicuous part in the defeat of Hood near Nashville, joining in the pursuit as far as Gravelly Springs, Alabama, where it was dismounted and assigned infantry duty. In June, 1865, it was remounted at St. Louis, and moved to Fort Riley, Kansas, and thence to Leavenworth, where it was mustered out on the 19th September, 1865.

The 127TH, OR TWELFTH CAVALRY, was partially organized at Kendallville, in December, 1863, and perfected at the same place, under Colonel Edward Anderson, in April, 1864. Reaching the front in May, it went into active service, took a prominent part in the march through Alabama and Georgia, and after a service brilliant in all its parts, retired from the field, after discharge, on the 22d of November, 1865.

The 128TH REGIMENT was raised in the Tenth Congressional District of the period, and mustered at Michigan City, under Colonel R. P. De Hart, on the 18th March, 1864. On the 25th it was reported at the front, and assigned at once to Schofield's Division. The battles of Resaca, Dallas, New Hope Church, Lost Mountain, Kenesaw, Atlanta, Jonesboro, Dalton, Brentwood Hills, Nashville. and the six days' skirmish of Columbia, were all participated in by the 128th, and it continued in service long after the termination of hostilities, holding the post of Raleigh, North Carolina.

The 129TH REGIMENT was, like the former, mustered in at Michigan City about the same time, under Colonel Charles Case, and moving to the front on the 7th April, 1864, shared in the fortunes of the 128th until August 29, 1865, when it was disembodied at Charlotte, Notrh Carolina.

The 130TH REGIMENT, mustered at Kokomo on the 12th March, 1864, under Colonel C. S. Parrish, left *en route* to the seat of war on the 16th, and was assigned to the Second Brigade, First Division, Twenty-third Army Corps, at Nashville, on the 19th. During the war it made for itself a brilliant history, and returned to Indianapolis with its well-won honors on the 13th December, 1865.

The 131ST, OR THIRTEENTH CAVALRY, under Colonel G. M L. Johnson, was the last mounted regiment recruited within the State.

It left Indianapolis on the 30th of April, 1864, in infantry trim, and gained its first honors on the 1st of October in its magnificent defense of Huntsville, Alabama, against the rebel division of General Buford, following a line of first-rate military conduct to the end. In January, 1865, the regiment was remounted, won some distinction in its modern form, and was mustered out at Vicksburg on the 18th of November, 1865. The *morale* and services of the regiment were such that its Colonel was promoted Brevet Brigadier-General in consideration of its merited honors.

THE ONE HUNDRED-DAYS VOLUNTEERS.

Governor Morton, in obedience to the offer made under his auspices to the general Government to raise volunteer regiments for one hundred days' service, issued his call on the 23rd of April, 1864. This movement suggested itself to the inventive genius of the war Governor as a most important step toward the subjection or annihilation of the military supporters of slavery within a year, and thus conclude a war, which, notwithstanding its holy claims to the name of Battles for Freedom, was becoming too protracted, and proving too detrimental to the best interests of the Union. In answer to the esteemed Governor's call eight regiments came forward, and formed The Grand Division of the Volunteers.

The 132d REGIMENT, under Col. S. C. Vance, was furnished by Indianapolis, Shelbyville, Franklin and Danville, and leaving on the 18th of May, 1864, reached the front where it joined the forces acting in Tennessee.

The 133D REGIMENT, raised at Richmond on the 17th of May, 1864, under Col. R. N. Hudson, comprised nine companies, and followed the 132d.

The 134TH REGIMENT, comprising seven companies, was organized at Indianapolis on the 25th of May, 1864, under Col. James Gavin, and proceeded immediately to the front.

The 135TH REGIMENT was raised from the volunteers of Bedford, Noblesville and Goshen, with seven companies from the First Congressional District, under Col. W. C. Wilson, on the 25th of May, 1864, and left at once *en route* to the South.

The 136TH REGIMENT comprised ten companies, raised in the same districts as those contributing to the 135th, under Col. J. W. Foster, and left for Tennessee on the 24th of May, 1864.

The 137TH REGIMENT, under Col. E. J. Robinson, comprising volunteers from Kokomo, Zanesville, Medora, Sullivan, Rockville, and Owen and Lawrence counties, left *en route* to Tennessee on the 28th of May, 1864, having completed organization the day previous.

The 138TH REGIMENT was formed of seven companies from the Ninth, with three from the Eleventh Congressional District (unreformed), and mustered in at Indianapolis on the 27th of May, 1864, under Col. J. H. Shannon. This fine regiment was reported at the front within a few days.

The 139TH REGIMENT, under Col. Geo. Humphrey, was raised from volunteers furnished by Kendallville, Lawrenceburg, Elizaville, Knightstown, Connersville, Newcastle, Portland, Vevay, New Albany, Metamora, Columbia City, New Haven and New Philadelphia. It was constituted a regiment on the 8th of June, 1864, and appeared among the defenders in Tennessee during that month.

All these regiments gained distinction, and won an enviable position in the glorious history of the war and the no less glorious one of their own State in its relation thereto.

THE PRESIDENT'S CALL OF JULY, 1864.

The 140th REGIMENT was organized with many others, in response to the call of the nation. Under its Colonel, Thomas J. Brady, it proceeded to the South on the 15th of November, 1864. Having taken a most prominent part in all the desperate struggles, round Nashville and Murfreesboro in 1864, to Town Creek Bridge on the 20th of February, 1865, and completed a continuous round of severe duty to the end, arrived at Indianapolis for discharge on the 21st of July, where Governor Morton received it with marked honors.

The 141ST REGIMENT was only partially raised, and its few companies were incorporated with Col Brady's command.

The 142D REGIMENT was recruited at Fort Wayne, under Col. I. M. Comparet, and was mustered into service at Indianapolis on the d of November, 1864. After a steady and exceedingly effective service, it returned to Indianapolis on the 16th of July, 1865.

THE PRESIDENT'S CALL OF DECEMBER, 1864,

Was answered by Indiana in the most material terms. No less than fourteen serviceable regiments were placed at the disposal of the General Government.

The 143D REGIMENT was mustered in, under Col J. T. Grill, on the 21st February, 1865, reported at Nashville on the 24th, and after a brief but brilliant service returned to the State on the 21st October, 1865.

The 144TH REGIMENT, under Col. G. W. Riddle, was mustered in on the 6th March, 1865, left on the 9th for Harper's Ferry, took an effective part in the close of the campaign and reported at Indianapolis for discharge on the 9th August, 1865.

The 145TH REGIMENT, under Col. W. A. Adams, left Indianapolis on the 18th of February, 1865, and joining Gen. Steadman's division at Chattanooga on the 23d was sent on active service. Its duties were discharged with rare fidelity until mustered out in January, 1866.

The 146TH REGIMENT, under Col. M. C. Welsh, left Indianapolis on the 11th of March en route to Harper's Ferry, where it was assigned to the army of the Shenandoah. The duties of this regiment were severe and continuous, to the period of its muster out at Baltimore on the 31st of August, 1865.

The 147TH REGIMENT, comprised among other volunteers from Benton, Lafayette and Henry counties, organized under Col. Milton Peden on the 13th of March, 1865, at Indianapolis. It shared a fortune similar to that of the 146th, and returned for discharge on the 9th of August, 1865.

The 148TH REGIMENT, under Col. N. R. Ruckle, left the State capital on the 28th of February, 1865, and reporting at Nashville, was sent on guard and garrison duty into the heart of Tennessee. Returning to Indianapolis on the 8th of September, it received a final discharge.

The 149TH REGIMENT was organized at Indianapolis by Col. W. H. Fairbanks, and left on the 3d of March, 1865, for Tennessee, where it had the honor of receiving the surrender of the rebel forces, and military stores of Generals Roddy and Polk. The regiment was welcomed home by Morton on the 29th of September.

The 150TH REGIMENT, under Col. M. B. Taylor, mustered in on the 9th of March, 1865, left for the South on the 13th and reported at Harper's Ferry on the 17th. This regiment did guard duty at Charleston, Winchester, Stevenson Station, Gordon's Springs, and after a service characterized by utility, returned on the 9th of August to Indianapolis for discharge.

The 151ST REGIMENT, under Col. J. Healy, arrived at Nashville on the 9th of March, 1865. On the 14th a movement on Tullahoma was undertaken, and three months later returned to Nashville for garrison duty to the close of the war. It was mustered out on the 22d of September, 1865.

The 152D REGIMENT was organized at Indianapolis, under Col.

W. W Griswold, and left for Harper's Ferry on the 18th of March, 1865. It was attached to the provisional divisions of Shenandoah Army, and engaged until the 1st of September, when it was discharged at Indianapolis.

The 153D REGIMENT was organized at Indianapolis on the 1st of March, 1865, under Col. O. H. P. Carey. It reported at Louisville, and by order of Gen. Palmer, was held on service in Kentucky, where it was occupied in the exciting but very dangerous pastime of fighting Southern guerrillas. Later it was posted at Louisville, until mustered out on the 4th of September, 1865.

The 154TH REGIMENT, organized under Col. Frank Wilcox, left Indianapolis under Major Simpson, for Parkersburg, W. Virginia, on the 28th of April, 1865. It was assigned to guard and garrison duty until its discharge on the 4th of August, 1865.

The 155TH REGIMENT, recruited throughout the State, left on the 26th of April for Washington, and was afterward assigned to a provisional Brigade of the Ninth Army Corps at Alexandria. The companies of this regiment were scattered over the country,—at Dover, Centreville, Wilmington, and Salisbury, but becoming reunited on the 4th of August, 1865, it was mustered out at Dover, Delaware.

The 156TH BATTALION, under Lieut.-Colonel Charles M. Smith, left en route to the Shenandoah Valley on the 27th of April, 1865, where it continued doing guard duty to the period of its muster out the 4th of August, 1865, at Winchester, Virginia.

On the return of these regiments to Indianapolis, Gov. Morton and the people received them with all that characteristic cordiality and enthusiasm peculiarly their own.

INDEPENDENT CAVALRY COMPANY OF INDIANA VOLUNTEERS.

The people of Crawford county, animated with that inspiriting patriotism which the war drew forth, organized this mounted company on the 25th of July, 1863, and placed it at the disposal of the Government, and it was mustered into service by order of the War Secretary, on the 13th of August, 1863, under Captain L. Lamb. To the close of the year it engaged in the laudable pursuit of arresting deserters and enforcing the draft; however, on the 18th of January, 1864, it was reconstituted and incorporated with the Thirteenth Cavalry, with which it continued to serve until the treason of Americans against America was conquered.

OUR COLORED TROOPS.

The 28TH REGIMENT OF COLORED TROOPS was recruited through-out the State of Indiana, and under Lieut.-Colonel Charles S. Russell, left Indianapolis for the front on the 24th of April, 1864. The regiment acted very well in its first, engagement with the rebels at White House, Virginia, and again with Gen. Sheridan's Cavalry, in the swamps of the Chickahominy. In the battle of the "Crater," it lost half its roster; but their place was soon filled by other colored recruits from the State, and Russell promoted to the Colonelcy, and afterward to Brevet Brigadier-General, when he was succeeded in the command by Major Thomas H. Logan. During the few months of its active service it accumulated quite a history, and was ultimately discharged, on the 8th of January, 1866, at Indianapolis.

BATTERIES OF LIGHT ARTILLERY.

FIRST BATTERY, organized at Evansville, under Captain Martin Klauss, and mustered in on the 16th of August, 1861, joined Gen. Fremont's army immediately, and entering readily upon its salu-tary course, aided in the capture of 950 rebels and their position at Blackwater creek. On March the 6th, 1862 at Elkhorn Tavern, and on the 8th at Pea Ridge, the battery performed good service. Port Gibson, Champion Hill, Jackson, the Teche country, Sabine Cross Roads, Grand Encore, all tell of its efficacy. In 1864 it was subjected to reorganization, when Lawrence Jacoby was raised to the Captiancy, vice Klauss resigned. After a long term of useful service, it was mustered out at Indianapolis on the 18th of August, 1865.

SECOND BATTERY was organized, under Captain D. G. Rabb, at Indianapolis on the 9th of August, 1861, and one month later pro-ceeded to the front. It participated in the campaign against Col. Coffee's irregular troops and the rebellious Indians of the Cherokee nation. From Lone Jack, Missouri, to Jenkin's Ferry and Fort Smith it won signal honors until its reorganization in 1864, and even after, to June, 1865, it maintained a very fair reputation.

The THIRD BATTERY, under Capt. W. W. Frybarger, was organ-ized and mustered in at Connersville on the 24th of August, 1861, and proceeded immediately to join Fremont's Army of the Mis-souri. Moon's Mill, Kirksville, Meridian, Fort de Russy, Alex-andria, Round Lake, Tupelo, Clinton and Tallahatchie are names which may be engraven on its guns. It participated in the affairs before Nashville on the 15th and 16th of December, 1864, when General Hood's Army was put to route, and at Fort Blakely, outside Mobile, after which it returned home to report for discharge, August 21, 1865.

The FOURTH BATTERY, recruited in La Porte, Porter and Lake counties, reported at the front early in October, 1861, and at once assumed a prominent place in the army of Gen. Buell. Again under Rosencrans and McCook and under General Sheridan at Stone River, the services of this battery were much praised, and it retained its well-earned reputation to the very day of its muster out —the 1st of August, 1865. Its first organization was completed under Capt. A. K. Bush, and reorganized in Oct., 1864, under Capt B. F. Johnson.

The FIFTH BATTERY was furnished by La Porte, Allen, Whitley and Noble counties, organized under Capt. Peter Simonson, and mustered into service on the 22d of November, 1861. It comprised four six pounders, two being rifled cannon, and two twelve-pounder Howitzers with a force of 153 men. Reporting at Camp Gilbert, Louisville, on the 29th, it was shortly after assigned to the division of Gen. Mitchell, at Bacon Creek. During its term, it served in twenty battles and numerous petty actions, losing its Captain at Pine Mountain. The total loss accruing to the battery was 84 men and officers and four guns It was mustered out on the 20th of July, 1864.

The SIXTH BATTERY was recruited at Evansville, under Captain Frederick Behr, and left, on the 2d of Oct., 1861, for the front, reporting at Henderson, Kentucky, a few days after. Early in 1862 it joined Gen. Sherman's army at Paducah, and participated in the battle of Shiloh, on the 6th of April. Its history grew in brilliancy until the era of peace insured a cessation of its great labors.

The SEVENTH BATTERY comprised volunteers from Terre Haute, Arcadia, Evansville, Salem, Lawrenceburg, Columbus, Vincennes and Indianapolis, under Samuel J. Harris as its first Captain, who was succeeded by G. R. Shallow and O. H. Morgan after its reorganization. From the siege of Corinth to the capture of Atlanta it performed vast services, and returned to Indianapolis on the 11th of July, 1865, to be received by the people and hear its history from the lips of the veteran patriot and Governor of the State.

The EIGHTH BATTERY, under Captain G. T. Cochran, arrived at the front on the 26th of February, 1862, and subsequently entered upon its real duties at the siege of Corinth. It served with distinction throughout, and concluded a well-made campaign under Will Stokes, who was appointed Captain of the companies with which it was consolidated in March, 1865.

The NINTH BATTERY. The organization of this battery was perfected at Indianapolis, on the 1st of January, 1862, under Capt. N. S. Thompson. Moving to the front it participated in the affairs of Shiloh, Corinth, Queen's Hill, Meridian, Fort Dick Taylor, Fort de Russy, Henderson's Hill, Pleasant Hill, Cotile Landing, Bayou Rapids, Mansura, Chicot, and many others, winning a name in each engagement. The explosion of the steamer Eclipse at Johnson-ville, above Paducah, on Jan. 27, 1865, resulted in the destruction of 58 men, leaving only ten to represent the battery. The survivors reached Indianapolis on the 6th of March, and were mustered out.

The TENTH BATTERY was recruited at Lafayette, and mustered in under Capt. Jerome B. Cox, in January, 1861. Having passed through the Kentucky campaign against Gen. Bragg, it participated in many of the great engagements, and finally returned to report for discharge on the 6th of July, 1864, having, in the meantime, won a very fair fame.

The ELEVENTH BATTERY was organized at Lafayette, and mustered in at Indianapolis under Capt. Arnold Sutermeister, on the 17th of December, 1861. On most of the principal battle-fields, from Shiloh, in 1862, to the capture of Atlanta, it maintained a high reputation for military excellence, and after consolidation with the Eighteenth, mustered out on the 7th of June, 1865.

The TWELFTH BATTERY was recruited at Jeffersonville and subsequently mustered in at Indianapolis. On the 6th of March, 1862, it reached Nashville, having been previously assigned to Buell's Army. In April its Captain, G. W. Sterling, resigned, and the position devolved on Capt. James E. White, who, in turn, was succeeded by James A. Dunwoody. The record of the battery holds a first place in the history of the period, and enabled both men and officers to look back with pride upon the battle-fields of the land. It was ordered home in June, 1865, and on reaching Indianapolis, on the 1st of July, was mustered out on the 7th of that month.

The THIRTEENTH BATTERY was organized under Captain Sewell Coulson, during the winter of 1861, at Indianapolis, and proceeded to the front in February, 1862. During the subsequent months it was occupied in the pursuit of John H. Morgan's raiders, and aided effectively in driving them from Kentucky. This artillery company returned from the South on the 4th of July, 1865, and were discharged the day following.

The FOURTEENTH BATTERY, recruited in Wabash, Miami, Lafayette, and Huntington counties, under Captain M. H. Kidd, and Lieutenant J. W. H. McGuire, left Indianapolis on the 11th of April, 1862, and within a few months one portion of it was captured at Lexington by Gen. Forrest's great cavalry command. The main battery lost two guns and two men at Guntown, on the Mississippi, but proved more successful at Nashville and Mobile. It arrived home on the 29th of August, 1865, received a public welcome, and its final discharge.

The FIFTEENTH BATTERY, under Captain I. C. H. Von Sehlin, was retained on duty from the date of its organization, at Indianapolis, until the 5th of July, 1862, when it was moved to Harper's Ferry. Two months later the gallant defense of Maryland Heights was set at naught by the rebel Stonewall Jackson, and the entire garrison surrendered. Being paroled, it was reorganized at Indianapolis, and appeared again in the field in March, 1863, where it won a splendid renown on every well-fought field to the close of the war. It was mustered out on the 24th of June, 1865.

The SIXTEENTH BATTERY was organized at Lafayette, under Capt. Charles A. Naylor, and on the 1st of June, 1862, left for Washington. Moving to the front with Gen. Pope's command, it participated in the battle of Slaughter Mountain, on the 9th of August, and South Mountain, and Antietam, under Gen. McClellan. This battery was engaged in a large number of general engagements and flying column affairs, won a very favorable record, and returned on the 5th of July, 1865.

The SEVENTEENTH BATTERY, under Capt. Milton L. Miner, was mustered in at Indianapolis, on the 20th of May, 1862, left for the front on the 5th of July, and subsequently engaged in the Gettysburg expedition, was present at Harper's Ferry, July 6, 1863, and at Opequan on the 19th of September. Fisher's Hill, New Market, and Cedar Creek brought it additional honors, and won from Gen. Sheridan a tribute of praise for its service on these battle grounds. Ordered from Winchester to Indianapolis it was mustered out there on the 3d of July, 1865.

The EIGHTEENTH BATTERY, under Capt. Eli Lilly, left for the

front in August, 1862, but did not take a leading part in the campaign until 1863, when, under Gen. Rosencrans, it appeared prominent at Hoover's Gap. From this period to the affairs of West Point and Macon, it performed first-class service, and returned to its State on the 25th of June, 1865.

The NINETEENTH BATTERY was mustered into service at Indianapolis, on the 5th of August, 1862, under Capt. S. J. Harris, and proceeded immediately afterward to the front, where it participated in the campaign against Gen. Bragg. It was present at every post of danger to the end of the war, when, after the surrender of Johnson's army, it returned to Indianapolis. Reaching that city on the 6th of June, 1865, it was treated to a public reception and received the congratulations of Gov. Morton. Four days later it was discharged.

The TWENTIETH BATTERY, organized under Capt. Frank A. Rose, left the State capital on the 17th of December, 1862, for the front, and reported immediately at Henderson, Kentucky. Subsequently Captain Rose resigned, and, in 1863, under Capt. Osborn, turned over its guns to the 11th Indiana Battery, and was assigned to the charge of siege guns at Nashville. Gov. Morton had the battery supplied with new field pieces, and by the 5th of October, 1863, it was again in the field, where it won many honors under Sherman, and continued to exercise a great influence until its return on the 23d of June, 1865.

The TWENTY-FIRST BATTERY recruited at Indianapolis, under the direction of Captain W. W. Andrew, left on the 9th of September, 1862, for Covington, Kentucky, to aid in its defense against the advancing forces of Gen. Kirby Smith. It was engaged in numerous military affairs and may be said to acquire many honors, although its record is stained with the names of seven deserters. The battery was discharged on the 21st of June, 1865.

The TWENTY-SECOND BATTERY was mustered in at Indianapolis on the 15th of December, 1862, under Capt. B. F. Denning, and moved at once to the front. It took a very conspicuous part in the pursuit of Morgan's Cavalry, and in many other affairs. It threw the first shot into Atlanta, and lost its Captain, who was killed in the skirmish line, on the 1st of July. While the list of casualties numbers only 35, that of desertions numbers 37. This battery was received with public honors on its return, the 25th of June, 1865, and mustered out on the 7th of the same month.

The TWENTY-THIRD BATTERY, recruited in October 1862, and mustered in on the 8th of November, under Capt. I. II. Myers, proceeded south, after having rendered very efficient services at home in guarding the camps of rebel prisoners. In July, 1865, the battery took an active part, under General Boyle's command, in routing and capturing the raiders at Brandenburgh, and subsequently to the close of the war performed very brilliant exploits, reaching Indianapolis in June, 1865. It was discharged on the 27th of that month.

The TWENTY-FOURTH BATTERY, under Capt. I. A. Simms, was enrolled for service on the 29th of November, 1862; remained at Indianapolis on duty until the 13th of March, 1863, when it left for the field. From its participation in the Cumberland River campaign, to its last engagement at Columbia, Tennessee, it aided materially in bringing victory to the Union ranks and made for itself a widespread fame. Arriving at Indianapolis on the 28th of July, it was publicly received, and in five days later disembodied.

The TWENTY-FIFTH BATTERY was recruited in September and October, 1864, and mustered into service for one year, under Capt. Frederick C. Sturm. December 13th, it reported at Nashville, and took a prominent part in the defeat of Gen. Hood's army. Its duties until July, 1865, were continuous, when it returned to report for final discharge.

The TWENTY-SIXTH BATTERY, or "WILDER'S BATTERY," was recruited under Capt. I. T. Wilder, of Greensburg, in May, 1861; but was not mustered in as an artillery company. Incorporating itself with a regiment then forming at Indianapolis it was mustered as company "A," of the 17th Infantry, with Wilder as Lieutenant-Colonel of the regiment. Subsequently, at Elk Water, Virginia, it was converted into the "First Independent Battery," and became known as "Rigby's Battery." The record of this battery is as brilliant as any won during the war. On every field it has won a distinct reputation; it was well worthy the enthusiastic reception given to it on its return to Indianapolis on the 11th and 12th of July, 1865. During its term of service it was subject to many transmutations; but in every phase of its brief history, a reputation for gallantry and patriotism was maintained which now forms a living testimonial to its services to the public.

The total number of battles in the "War of the Rebellion" in which the patriotic citizens of the great and noble State of Indiana were more or less engaged, was as follows:

Locality.	No. of Battles.	Locality.	No. of Battles.
Virginia	90	Maryland	7
Tennessee	51	Texas	3
Georgia	41	South Carolina	2
Mississippi	24	Indian Territory	2
Arkansas	19	Pennsylvania	1
Kentucky	16	Ohio	1
Louisiana	15	Indiana	1
Missouri	9		
North Carolina	8	Total	308

The regiments sent forth to the defense of the Republic in the hour of its greatest peril, when a host of her own sons, blinded by some unholy infatuation, leaped to arms that they might trample upon the liberty-giving principles of the nation, have been passed in very brief review. The authorities chosen for the dates, names, and figures are the records of the State, and the main subject is based upon the actions of those 267,000 gallant men of Indiana who rushed to arms in defense of all for which their fathers bled, leaving their wives and children and homes in the guardianship of a truly paternal Government.

The relation of Indiana to the Republic was then established; for when the population of the State, at the time her sons went forth to participate in war for the maintenance of the Union, is brought into comparison with all other States and countries, it will be apparent that the sacrifices made by Indiana from 1861-'65 equal, if not actually exceed, the noblest of those recorded in the history of ancient or modern times.

Unprepared for the terrible inundation of modern wickedness. which threatened to deluge the country in a sea of blood and rob, a people of their richest, their most prized inheritance, the State rose above all precedent, and under the benign influence of patriotism, guided by the well-directed zeal of a wise Governor and Government, sent into the field an army that in numbers was gigantic, and in moral and physical excellence never equaled

It is laid down in the official reports, furnished to the War Department, that over 200,000 troops were specially organized to aid in crushing the legions of the slave-holder; that no less than 50,000 militia were armed to defend the State, and that the large, but absolutely necessary number of commissions issued was 17,114. All this proves the scientific skill and military economy exercised by the Governor, and brought to the aid of the people in a most terrible emergency; for he, with some prophetic sense of the gravity of the situation, saw that unless the greatest powers of the Union were put forth to crush the least justifiable and most pernicious of all rebellions holding a place in the record of nations, the best blood of the country would flow in a vain attempt to avert a catastrophe which, if prolonged for many years, would result in at least the moral and commercial ruin of the country.

The part which Indiana took in the war against the Rebellion is one of which the citizens of the State may well be proud. In the number of troops furnished, and in the amount of voluntary contributions rendered, Indiana, in proportion and wealth, stands equal to any of her sister States. " It is also a subject of gratitude and thankfulness," said Gov. Morton, in his message to the Legislature, " that, while the number of troops furnished by Indiana alone in this great contest would have done credit to a first-class nation, measured by the standard of previous wars, not a single battery or battalion from this State has brought reproach upon the national flag, and no disaster of the war can be traced to any want of fidelity, courage or efficiency on the part of any Indiana officer. The endurance, heroism, intelligence and skill of the officers and soldiers sent forth by Indiana to do battle for the Union, have shed a luster on our beloved State, of which any people might justly be proud. Without claiming superiority over our loyal sister States, it is but justice to the brave men who have represented us on almost every battle-field of the war, to say that their deeds have placed Indiana in the front rank of those heroic States which rushed to the rescue of the imperiled Government of the nation. The total number of troops furnished by the State for all terms of service exceeds 200,000 men, much the greater portion of them being for three years; and in addition thereto not less than 50,000 State militia have from time to time been called into active service to repel rebel raids and defend our southern border from invasion."

AFTER THE WAR.

In 1867 the Legislature comprised 91 Republicans and 59 Democrats. Soon after the commencement of the session, Gov. Morton resigned his office in consequence of having been elected to the U. S. Senate, and Lieut.-Gov. Conrad Baker assumed the Executive chair during the remainder of Morton's term. This Legislature, by a very decisive vote, ratified the 14th amendment to the Federal Constitution, constituting all persons born in the country or subject to its jurisdiction, citizens of the United States and of the State wherein they reside, without regard to race or color; reducing the Congressional representation in any State in which there should be a restriction of the exercise of the elective franchise on account of race or color; disfranchising persons therein named who shall have engaged in insurrection or rebellion against the United States; and declaring that the validity of the public debt of the United States authorized by law, shall not be questioned.

This Legislature also passed an act providing for the registry of votes, the punishment of fraudulent practices at elections, and for the apportionment and compensation of a Board of Registration; this Board to consist, in each township, of two freeholders appointed by the County Commissioners, together with the trustee of such township; in cities the freeholders are to be appointed in each ward by the city council. The measures of this law are very strict, and are faithfully executed. No cries of fraud in elections are heard in connection with Indiana.

This Legislature also divided the State into eleven Congressional Districts and apportioned their representation; enacted a law for the protection and indemnity of all officers and soldiers of the United States and soldiers of the Indiana Legion, for acts done in the military service of the United States, and in the military service of the State, and in enforcing the laws and preserving the peace of the country; made definite appropriations to the several benevolent institutions of the State, and adopted several measures for the encouragement of education, etc.

In 1868, Indiana was the first in the field of national politics, both the principal parties holding State conventions early in the year. The Democrats nominated T. A. Hendricks for Governor, and denounced in their platform the reconstruction policy of the Republicans; recommended that United States treasury notes be substituted for national bank currency; denied that the General Government had a right to interfere with the question of suffrage in any of the States, and opposed negro suffrage, etc.; while the Republicans nominated Conrad Baker for Governor, defended its reconstruction policy, opposed a further contraction of the currency, etc. The campaign was an exciting one, and Mr. Baker was elected Governor by a majority of only 961. In the Presidential election that soon followed the State gave Grant 9,572 more than Seymour.

During 1868 Indiana presented claims to the Government for about three and a half millions dollars for expenses incurred in the war, and $1,958,917.94 was allowed. Also, this year, a legislative commission reported that $413,599.48 were allowed to parties suffering loss by the Morgan raid.

This year Governor Baker obtained a site for the House of Refuge. (See a subsequent page.) The Soldiers' and Seamen's Home, near Knightstown, originally established by private enterprise and benevolence, and adopted by the Legislature of the previous year, was in a good condition. Up to that date the institution had afforded relief and temporary subsistence to 400 men who had been disabled in the war. A substantial brick building had been built for the home, while the old buildings were used for an orphans' department, in which were gathered 86 children of deceased soldiers.

DIVORCE LAWS.

By some mistake or liberal design, the early statute laws of Indiana on the subject of divorce were rather more loose than those of most other States in this Union; and this subject had been a matter of so much jest among the public, that in 1870 the Governor recommended to the Legislature a reform in this direction, which was pretty effectually carried out. Since that time divorces can be granted only for the following causes: 1. Adultery. 2. Impotency existing at the time of marriage. 3. Abandonment for two years. 4. Cruel and inhuman treatment of one party by the other. 5. Habitual drunkenness of either party, or the failure of the husband to make reasonable provision for the family. 6 The failure of the husband to make reasonable provision for the family for a period of two years. 7. The conviction of either party of an infamous crime.

FINANCIAL.

Were it not for political government the pioneers would have got along without money much longer than they did. The pressure of governmental needs was somewhat in advance of the monetary income of the first settlers, and the little taxation required to carry on the government seemed great and even oppressive, especially at certain periods.

In November, 1821, Gov. Jennings convened the Legislature in extra session to provide for the payment of interest on the State debt and a part of the principal, amounting to $20,000. It was thought that a sufficient amount would be realized in the notes of the State bank and its branches, although they were considerably depreciated Said the Governor: "It will be oppressive if the State, after the paper of this institution (State bank) was authorized to be circulated in revenue, should be prevented by any assign. ment of the evidences of existing debt, from discharging at least so much of that debt with the paper of the bank as will absorb the collections of the present year; especially when their notes, after being made receivable by the agents of the State, became greatly depreciated by great mismanagement on the part of the bank itself. It ought not to be expected that a public loss to the State should be avoided by resorting to any measures which would not comport with correct views of public justice; nor should it be anticipated that the treasury of the United States would ultimately adopt measures to secure an uncertain debt which would inter. fere with arrangements calculated to adjust the demand against the State without producing any additional embarrassment."

The state of the public debt was indeed embarrassing, as the bonds which had been executed in its behalf had been assigned. The exciting cause of this proceeding consisted in the machinations of unprincipled speculators. Whatever disposition the principal bank may have made of the funds deposited by the United States, the connection of interest between the steam-mill company and the bank, and the extraordinary accommodations, as well as their amount, effected by arrangements of the steam-mill agency and some of the officers of the bank, were among the principal causes which

(194)

had prostrated the paper circulating medium of the State, so far as it was dependent on the State bank and its branches. An abnormal state of affairs like this very naturally produced a blind disbursement of the fund' to some extent, and this disbursement would be called by almost every one an " unwise administration."

During the first 16 years of this century, the belligerent condition of Europe called for agricultural supplies from America, and the consequent high price of grain justified even the remote pioneers of Indiana in undertaking the tedious transportation of the products of the soil which the times forced upon them. The large disbursements made by the general Government among the people naturally engendered a rage for speculation; numerous banks with fictitious capital were established; immense issues of paper were made; and the circulating medium of the country was increased fourfold in the course of two or three years. This inflation produced the consequences which always follow such a scheme. namely, unfounded visions of wealth and splendor and the wild investments which result in ruin to the many and wealth to the few. The year 1821 was consequently one of great financial panic, and was the first experienced by the early settlers of the West.

In 1822 the new Governor, William Hendricks, took a hopeful view of the situation, referring particularly to the "agricultural and social happiness of the State." The crops were abundant this year, immigration was setting in heavily and everything seemed to have an upward look. But the customs of the white race still compelling them to patronize European industries, combined with the remoteness of the surplus produce of Indiana from European markets, constituted a serious drawback to the accumulation of wealth. Such a state of things naturally changed the habits of the people to some extent, at least for a short time, assimilating them to those of more primitive tribes. This change of custom, however, was not severe and protracted enough to change the intelligent and social nature of the people, and they arose to their normal height on the very first opportunity.

In 1822-'3, before speculation started up again, the surplus money was invested mainly in domestic manufactories instead of other and wilder commercial enterprises. Home manufactories were what the people needed to make them more independent. They not only gave employment to thousands whose services were before that valueless, but also created a market for a great portion of the surplus produce of the farmers. A part of the surplus capital, however, was also sunk in internal improvements, some of which were unsuccessful for a time, but eventually proved remunerative.

Noah Noble occupied the Executive chair of the State from 1831 to 1837, commencing his duties amid peculiar embarrassments. The crops of 1832 were short, Asiatic cholera came sweeping along the Ohio and into the interior of the State, and the Black Hawk war raged in the Northwest,—all these at once, and yet the work of internal improvements was actually begun.

STATE BANK.

The State bank of Indiana was established by law January 28, 1834. The act of the Legislature, by its own terms, ceased to be a law, January 1, 1857. At the time of its organization in 1834, its outstanding circulation was $4,208,725, with a debt due to the institution, principally from citizens of the State, of $6,095,368. During the years 1857-'58 the bank redeemed nearly its entire circulation, providing for the redemption of all outstanding obligations; at this time it had collected from most of its debtors the money which they owed. The amounts of the State's interest in the stock of the bank was $1,390,000, and the money thus invested was procured by the issue of five per cent bonds, the last of which was payable July 1, 1866. The nominal profits of the bank were $2,780,604.36. By the law creating the sinking fund, that fund was appropriated, first, to pay the principal and interest on the bonds; secondly, the expenses of the Commissioners; and lastly the cause of common-school education.

The stock in all the branches authorized was subscribed by individuals, and the installment paid as required by the charter. The loan authorized for the payment on the stock allotted to the State, amounting to $500,000, was obtained at a premium of 1.05 per per cent. on five per cent. stock, making the sum of over $5,000 on the amount borrowed. In 1836 we find that the State bank was doing good service; agricultural products were abundant, and the market was good; consequently the people were in the full enjoyment of all the blessings of a free government.

By the year 1843 the State was experiencing the disasters and embarassment consequent upon a system of over-banking, and its natural progeny, over-trading and deceptive speculation. Such a state of things tends to relax the hand of industry by creating false notions of wealth, and tempt to sudden acquisitions by means as delusive in their results as they are contrary to a primary law of nature. The people began more than ever to see the necessity of falling back upon that branch of industry for which Indiana, especially at that time, was particularly fitted, namely, agriculture, as the true and lasting source of substantial wealth.

Gov. Whitcomb, 1843-'49, succeeded well in maintaining the credit of the State. Measures of compromise between the State and its creditors were adopted by which, ultimately, the public works, although incomplete, were given in payment for the claims against the Government.

At the close of his term, Gov. Whitcomb was elected to the Senate of the United States, and from December, 1848, to December, 1849, Lieut-Gov. Paris C. Dunning was acting Governor.

In 1851 a general banking law was adopted which gave a new impetus to the commerce of the State, and opened the way for a broader volume of general trade; but this law was the source of many abuses; currency was expanded, a delusive idea of wealth again prevailed, and as a consequence, a great deal of damaging speculation was indulged in.

In 1857 the charter of the State bank expired, and the large gains to the State in that institution were directed to the promotion of common-school education.

WEALTH AND PROGRESS.

During the war of the Rebellion the financial condition of the people was of course like that of the other Northern States generally. 1870 found the State in a very prosperous condition. October 31 of this year, the date of the fiscal report, there was a surplus of $373,249 in the treasury. The receipts of the year amounted to $3,605,639, and the disbursements to $2,943,600, leaving a balance of $1,035,288. The total debt of the State in November, 1871, was $3,937,821.

At the present time the principal articles of export from the State are flour and pork. Nearly all the wheat raised within the State is manufactured into flour within its limits, especially in the northern part. The pork business is the leading one in the southern part of the State.

When we take into consideration the vast extent of railroad lines in this State, in connection with the agricultural and mineral resources, both developed and undeveloped, as already noted, we can

see what a substantial foundation exists for the future welfare of
this great commonwealth. Almost every portion of the State is
coming up equally. The disposition to monopolize does not exist
to a greater degree than is desirable or necessary for healthy compe-
tition. Speculators in flour, pork and other commodities appeared
during the war, but generally came to ruin at their own game.
The agricultural community here is an independent one, understanding its rights, and " knowing them will maintain them."

Indiana is more a manufacturing State, also, than many imagine.
It probably has the greatest wagon and carriage manufactory in the
world. In 1875 the total number of manufacturing establishments
in this State was 16.812; number of steam engines, 3,684, with a
total horse-power of 114.961; the total horse-power of water wheels,
38,614; number of hands employed in the manufactories. 86,402;
capital employed, is $117,462,161; wages paid, $35,461,987; cost of
material, $104,321,632; value of products, $301,304,271. These
figures are on an average about twice what they were only five years
previously, at which time they were about double what they were
ten years before that. In manufacturing enterprise, it is said that
Indiana, in proportion to her population, is considerably in advance
of Illinois and Michigan.

In 1870 the assessed valuation of the real estate in Indiana was
$460,120.974; of personal estate, $203,334,070; true valuation of
both, $1.268,180,543. According to the evidences of increase at
that time, the value of taxable property in this State must be double
the foregoing figures. This is utterly astonishing, especially when
we consider what a large matter it is to double the elements of a
large and wealthy State, compared with its increase in infancy.

The taxation for State purposes in 1870 amounted to $2,943,078;
for county purposes, $4,654,476; and for municipal purposes,
$3,193,577. The total county debt of Indiana in 1870 was $1,127,-
269, and the total debt of towns, cities, etc., was $2,523,934.

In the compilation of this statistical matter we have before us the
statistics of every element of progress in Indiana, in the U. S.
Census Reports; but as it would be really improper for us further
to burden these pages with tables or columns of large numbers, we
will conclude by remarking that if any one wishes further details in
these matters, he can readily find them in the Census Reports of
the Government in any city or village in the country. Besides,
almost any one can obtain, free of charge, from his representative in

Congress, all these and other public documents in which he may be interested.

INTERNAL IMPROVEMENTS.

This subject began to be agitated as early as 1818, during the administration of Governor Jennings, who, as well as all the Governors succeeding him to 1843, made it a special point in their messages to the Legislature to urge the adoption of measures for the construction of highways and canals and the improvement of the navigation of rivers. Gov. Hendricks in 1822 specified as the most important improvement the navigation of the Falls of the Ohio, the Wabash and White rivers, and other streams, and the construction of the National and other roads through the State.

In 1826 Governor Ray considered the construction of roads and canals as a necessity to place the State on an equal financial footing with the older States East, and in 1829 he added: "This subject can never grow irksome, since it must be the source of the blessings of civilized life. To secure its benefits is a duty enjoined upon the Legislature by the obligations of the social compact."

In 1830 the people became much excited over the project of connecting the streams of the country by "The National New York & Mississippi railroad." The National road and the Michigan and Ohio turnpike were enterprises in which the people and Legislature of Indiana were interested. The latter had already been the cause of much bitter controversy, and its location was then the subject of contention.

In 1832 the work of internal improvements fairly commenced, despite the partial failure of the crops, the Black Hawk war and the Asiatic cholera. Several war parties invaded the Western settlements, exciting great alarm and some suffering. This year the canal commissioners completed the task assigned them and had negotiated the canal bonds in New York city, to the amount of $100,000, at a premium of 13¼ per cent., on terms honorable to the State and advantageous to the work. Before the close of this year $54,000 were spent for the improvement of the Michigan road, and $52,000 were realized from the sale of lands appropriated for its construction. In 1832, 32 miles of the Wabash and Erie canal was placed under contract and work commenced. A communication was addressed to the Governor of Ohio, requesting him to call the attention of the Legislature of that State to the subject of the extension of the canal from the Indiana line through Ohio to the

Lake. In compliance with this request, Governor Lucas promptly laid the subject before the Legislature of the State, and, in a spirit of courtesy, resolutions were adopted by that body, stipulating that if Ohio should ultimately decline to undertake the completion of that portion of the work within her limits before the time fixed by the act of Congress for the completion of the canal, she would, on just and equitable terms, enable Indiana to avail herself of the benefit of the lands granted, by authorizing her to sell them and invest the proceeds in the stock of a company to be incorporated by Ohio; and that she would give Indiana notice of her final determination on or before January 1, 1838. The Legislature of Ohio also authorized and invited the agent of the State of Indiana to select, survey and set apart the lands lying within that State. In keeping with this policy Governor Noble, in 1834, said: "With a view of engaging in works of internal improvement, the propriety of adopting a general plan or system, having reference to the several portions of the State, and the connection of one with the other, naturally suggests itself. No work should be commenced but such as would be of acknowledged public utility, and when completed would form a branch of some general system. In view of this object, the policy of organizing a Board of Public Works is again respectfully suggested." The Governor also called favorable attention to the Lawrenceburg & Indianapolis railway, for which a charter had been granted.

In 1835 the Wabash & Erie canal was pushed rapidly forward. The middle division, extending from the St. Joseph dam to the forks of the Wabash, about 32 miles, was completed, for about $232,000, including all repairs. Upon this portion of the line navigation was opened on July 4, which day the citizens assembled "to witness the mingling of the waters of the St. Joseph with those of the Wabash, uniting the waters of the northern chain of lakes with those of the Gulf of Mexico in the South." On other parts of the line the work progressed with speed, and the sale of canal lands was unusually active

In 1836 the first meeting of the State Board of Internal Improvement was convened and entered upon the discharge of its numerous and responsible duties. Having assigned to each member the direction and superintendence of a portion of the work, the next duty to be performed preparatory to the various spheres of active service, was that of procuring the requisite number of engineers. A delegation was sent to the Eastern cities, but returned without engaging an Engineer-in-Chief for the roads and railways, and without the desired number for the subordinate station; but after considerable delay the Board was fully organized and put in operation. Under their management work on public improvements was successful; the canal progressed steadily; the navigation of the middle division, from Fort Wayne to Huntington, was uninterrupted; 16 miles of the line between Huntington and La Fontaine creek were filled with water this year and made ready for navigation; and the remaining 20 miles were completed, except a portion of the locks; from La Fontaine creek to Logansport progress was made; the line from Georgetown to Lafayette was placed under contract; about 30 miles of the Whitewater canal, extending from Lawrenceburg through the beautiful valley of the Whitewater to Brookville, were also placed under contract, as also 23 miles of the Central canal, passing through Indianapolis, on which work was commenced; also about 20 miles of the southern division of this work, extending from Evansville into the interior, were also contracted for; and on the line of the Cross-Cut canal, from Terre Haute to the intersection of the Central canal, near the mouth of Eel river, a commencement was also made on all the heavy sections. All this in 1836.

Early in this year a party of engineers was organized, and directed to examine into the practicability of the Michigan & Erie canal line, then proposed. The report of their operations favored its expediency. A party of engineers was also fitted out, who entered upon the field of service of the Madison & Lafayette railroad, and contracts were let for its construction from Madison to Vernon, on which work was vigorously commenced. Also, contracts were let for grading and bridging the New Albany & Vincennes road from the former point to Paoli, about 40 miles. Other roads were also undertaken and surveyed, so that indeed a stupendous system of internal improvement was undertaken, and as Gov. Noble truly remarked, upon the issue of that vast enterprise the State of Indiana staked her fortune. She had gone too far to retreat.

In 1837, when Gov. Wallace took the Executive chair, the reaction consequent upon "over-work" by the State in the internal improvement scheme began to be felt by the people. They feared a State debt was being incurred from which they could never be extricated; but the Governor did all he could throughout the term of his administration to keep up the courage of the citizens. He told them that the astonishing success so far, surpassed even the hopes of the most sanguine, and that the flattering auspices of the future were sufficient to dispel every doubt and quiet every fear. Notwithstanding all his efforts, however, the construction of public works continued to decline, and in his last message he exclaimed: " Never before—I speak it advisedly—never before have you witnessed a period in our local history that more urgently called for the exercise of all the soundest and best attributes of grave and patriotic legislators than the present.   *   *   *   The truth is—and it would be folly to conceal it—we have our hands full—full to overflowing; and therefore, to sustain ourselves, to preserve the credit and character of the State unimpaired, and to continue her hitherto unexampled march to wealth and distinction, we have not an hour of time, nor a dollar of money, nor a hand employed in labor, to squander and dissipate upon mere objects of idleness, or taste, or amusement."

The State had borrowed $3,827,000 for internal improvement purposes, of which $1.327,000 was for the Wabash & Erie canal and the remainder for other works.   The five per cent. interest on debts—about $200,000—which the State had to pay, had become burdensome, as her resources for this purpose were only two, besides direct taxation, and they were small, namely, the interest on the balances due for canal lands, and the proceeds of the third installment of the surplus revenue, both amounting, in 1838, to about $45,000.

In August, 1839, all work ceased on these improvements, with one or two exceptions, and most of the contracts were surrendered to the State.   This was done according to an act of the Legislature providing for the compensation of contractors by the issue of treasury notes.   In addition to this state of affairs, the Legislature of 1839 had made no provision for the payment of interest on the State debt incurred for internal improvements.   Concerning this situation Gov. Bigger, in 1840, said that either to go ahead with the works or to abandon them altogether would be equally ruinous to the State, the implication being that the people should wait a little while for a breathing spell and then take hold again.

Of course much individual indebtedness was created during the progress of the work on internal improvement.   When operations ceased in 1839, and prices fell at the same time, the people were left in a great measure without the means of commanding money to pay their debts.   This condition of private enterprise more than ever rendered direct taxation inexpedient. Hence it became the policy of Gov. Bigger to provide the means of paying the interest on the State debt without increasing the rate of taxation, and to continue that portion of the public works that could be immediately completed, and from which the earliest returns could be expected.

In 1840 the system embraced ten different works, the most important of which was the Wabash & Erie canal. The aggregate length of the lines embraced in the system was 1,160 miles, and of this only 140 miles had been completed. The amount expended had reached the sum of $5,600,000, and it required at least $14,000,-000 to complete them. Although the crops of 1841 were very remunerative, this perquisite alone was not sufficient to raise the State again up to the level of going ahead with her gigantic works.

We should here state in detail the amount of work completed and of money expended on the various works up to this time, 1841, which were as follows:

1. The Wabash & Erie canal, from the State line to Tippecanoe, 129 miles in length, completed and navigable for the whole length, at a cost of $2,041,012. This sum includes the cost of the steamboat lock afterward completed at Delphi.

2. The extension of the Wabash & Erie canal from the mouth of the Tippecanoe to Terre Haute, over 104 miles. The estimated cost of this work was $1,500,000; and the amount expended for the same $408,855. The navigation was at this period opened as far down as Lafayette, and a part of the work done in the neighborhood of Covington.

3. The cross-cut canal from Terre Haute to Central canal, 49 miles in length; estimated cost, $718,672; amount expended, $420,679; and at this time no part of the course was navigable.

4. The White Water canal, from Lawrenceburg to the mouth of Nettle creek, 76½ miles; estimated cost, $1,675,738; amount expended to that date, $1,099,867; and 31 miles of the work was navigable, extending from the Ohio river to Brookville.

5. The Central canal, from the Wabash & Erie canal, to Indianapolis, including the feeder bend at Muncietown, 124 miles in length; total estimated cost, $2,299,853; amount expended, $568,046; eight miles completed at that date, and other portions nearly done.

6. Central canal, from Indianapolis to Evansville on the Ohio river, 194 miles in length; total estimated cost, $3,532,394; amount expended, $831,302, 19 miles of which was completed at that date, at the southern end, and 16 miles, extending south from Indianapolis, were nearly completed.

7. Erie & Michigan canal, 182 miles in length; estimated cost, $2,624,823; amount expended, $156,394. No part of this work finished.

8. The Madison & Indianapolis railroad, over 85 miles in length; total estimated cost, $2,046,600; amount expended, $1,493,-013. Road finished and in operation for about 28 miles; grading nearly finished for 27 miles in addition, extending to Edenburg.

9. Indianapolis & Lafayette turnpike road, 73 miles in length; total estimated cost, $593,737; amount expended, $72,118. The bridging and most of the grading was done on 27 miles, from Crawfordsville to Lafayette.

10. New Albany & Vincennes turnpike road, 105 miles in length; estimated cost, $1,127,295; amount expended, $654,411. Forty-one miles graded and macadamized, extending from New Albany to Paoli, and 27 miles in addition partly graded.

11. Jeffersonville & Crawfordsville road, over 164 miles long; total estimated cost, $1,651,800; amount expended, $372,737. Forty-five miles were partly graded and bridged, extending from Jeffersonville to Salem, and from Greencastle north.

12. Improvement of the Wabash rapids, undertaken jointly by Indiana and Illinois; estimated cost to Indiana, $102,500; amount expended by Indiana, $9,539.

Grand totals: Length of roads and canals, 1,289 miles, only 281 of which have been finished; estimated cost of all the works, $19,914,424; amount expended, $8,164,528. The State debt at this time amounted to $18,469,146. The two principal causes which aggravated the embarrassment of the State at this juncture were, first, paying most of the interest out of the money borrowed, and, secondly, selling bonds on credit. The first error subjected the State to the payment of compound interest, and the people, not feeling the pressure of taxes to discharge the interest, naturally became inattentive to the public policy pursued. Postponement of the payment of interest is demoralizing in every way. During this period the State was held up in an unpleasant manner before the gaze of the world; but be it to the credit of this great and glorious State, she would not repudiate, as many other States and municipalities have done.

By the year 1850, the so-called "internal improvement" system having been abandoned, private capital and ambition pushed forward various "public works." During this year about 400 miles of plank road were completed, at a cost of $1.200 to $1,500 per mile, and about 1,200 miles more were surveyed and in progress. There were in the State at this time 212 miles of railroad in successful operation, of which 124 were completed this year. More than 1,000 miles of railroad were surveyed and in progress.

An attempt was made during the session of the Legislature in 1869 to re-burden the State with the old canal debt, and the matter was considerably agitated in the canvass of 1870. The subject of the Wabash & Erie canal was lightly touched in the Republican platform, occasioning considerable discussion, which probably had some effect on the election in the fall. That election resulted in an average majority in the State of about 2,864 for the Democracy. It being claimed that the Legislature had no authority under the constitution to tax the people for the purpose of aiding in the construction of railroads, the Supreme Court, in April, 1871, decided adversely to such a claim.

GEOLOGY.

In 1869 the development of mineral resources in the State attracted considerable attention. Rich mines of iron and coal were discovered, as also fine quarries of building stone. The Vincennes railroad passed through some of the richest portions of the mineral region, the engineers of which had accurately determined the quality of richness of the ores. Near Brooklyn, about 20 miles from Indianapolis, is a fine formation of sandstone, yielding good material for buildings in the city; indeed, it is considered the best building stone in the State. The limestone formation at Gosport, continuing 12 miles from that point, is of great variety, and includes the finest and most durable building stone in the world. Portions of it are susceptible only to the chisel; other portions are soft and can be worked with the ordinary tools. At the end of this limestone formation there commences a sandstone series of strata which extends seven miles farther, to a point about 60 miles from Indianapolis. Here an extensive coal bed is reached consisting of seven distinct veins. The first is about two feet thick, the next three feet, another four feet, and the others of various thicknesses.

These beds are all easily worked, having a natural drain, and they yield heavy profits. In the whole of the southwestern part of the State and for 300 miles up the Wabash, coal exists in good quality and abundance.

The scholars, statesmen and philanthropists of Indiana worked hard and long for the appointment of a State Geologist, with sufficient support to enable him to make a thorough geological survey of the State. A partial survey was made as early as 1837-'8, by David Dale Owen, State Geologist, but nothing more was done until 1869, when Prof. Edward T. Cox was appointed State Geologist. For 20 years previous to this date the Governors urged and insisted in all their messages that a thorough survey should be made, but almost, if not quite, in vain. In 1852, Dr. Ryland T. Brown delivered an able address on this subject before the Legis-lature, showing how much coal, iron, building stone, etc., there were probably; in the State, but the exact localities and qualities not ascertained, and how millions of money could be saved to the State by the expenditure of a few thousand dollars; but "they answered the Doctor in the negative. It must have been because they hadn't time to pass the bill. They were very busy. They had to pass all sorts of regulations concerning the negro. They had to protect a good many white people from marrying negroes. And as they didn't need any labor in the State, if it was 'colored,' they had to make regulations to shut out all of that kind of labor, and to take steps to put out all that unfortunately got in, and they didn't have time to consider the scheme proposed by the white people "— W. W. Clayton.

In 1853, the State Board of Agriculture employed Dr. Brown to make a partial examination of the geology of the State, at a salary of $500 a year, and to this Board the credit is due for the final success of the philanthropists, who in 1869 had the pleasure of witnessing the passage of a Legislative act " to provide for a Depart-ment of Geology and Natural Science, in connection with the State Board of Agriculture." Under this act Governor Baker immedi-ately appointed Prof. Edward T. Cox the State Geologist, who has made an able and exhaustive report of the agricultural, mineral and manufacturing resources of this State, world-wide in its celeb-rity, and a work of which the people of Indiana may be very proud. We can scarcely give even the substance of his report in a work like this, because it is of necessity deeply scientific and made up entirely of local detail.

COAL.

The coal measures, says Prof. E. T. Cox, cover an area of about 6,500 square miles, in the southwestern part of the State, and extend from Warren county on the north to the Ohio river on the south, a distance of about 150 miles. This area comprises the following counties:Warren, Fountain, Parke, Vermillion, Vigo, Clay, Sullivan, Greene, Knox, Daviess, Martin, Gibson, Pike, Dubois, Vanderburg, Warrick, Spencer, Perry and a small part of Crawford, Monroe, Putnam and Montgomery.

This coal is all bituminous, but is divisible into three well-marked varieties: caking-coal, non-caking-coal or block coal and cannel coal. The total depth of the seams or measures is from 600 to 800 feet, with 12 to 14 distinct seams of coal; but these are not all to be found throughout the area; the seams range from one foot to eleven feet in thickness. The caking coal prevails in the western portion of the area described, and has from three to four workable seams, ranging from three and a half to eleven feet in thickness. At most of the places where these are worked the coal is mined by adits driven in on the face of the ridges, and the deepest shafts in the State are less than 300 feet, the average depth for successful mining not being over 75 feet. This is a bright, black, sometimes glossy, coal, makes good coke and contains a very large percentage of pure illuminating gas. One pound will yield about $4\frac{1}{2}$ cubic feet of gas, with a power equal to 15 standard sperm candles. The average calculated calorific power of the caking coals is 7,745 heat units, pure carbon being 8,080. Both in the northern and southern portions of the field, the caking coals present similar good qualities, and are a great source of private and public wealth.

The block coal prevails in the eastern part of the field and has an area of about 450 square miles. This is excellent, in its raw state, for making pig iron. It is indeed peculiarly fitted for metallurgical purposes. It has a laminated structure with carbonaceous matter, like charcoal, between the lamina, with slaty cleavage, and it rings under the stroke of the hammer. It is " free-burning," makes an open fire, and without caking, swelling, scaffolding in the furnace or changing form, burns like hickory wood until it is consumed to a white ash and leaves no clinkers. It is likewise valuable for generating steam and for household uses. Many of the principal railway lines in the State are using it in preference to any other coal, as it does not burn out the fire-boxes, and gives as little trouble as wood.

There are eight distinct seams of block coal in this zone, three of which are workable, having an average thickness of four feet. In some places this coal is mined by adits, but generally from shafts, 40 to 80 feet deep. The seams are crossed by cleavage lines, and the coal is usually mined without powder, and may be taken out in blocks weighing a ton or more. When entries or rooms are driven angling across the cleavage lines, the walls of the mine present a zigzag, notched appearance resembling a Virginia worm fence.

In 1871 there were about 24 block coal mines in operation, and about 1,500 tons were mined daily. Since that time this industry has vastly increased. This coal consists of $81\frac{1}{2}$ to $83\frac{1}{4}$ per cent. of carbon, and not quite three fourths of one per cent. of sulphur. Calculated calorific power equal to 8,283 heat units. This coal also is equally good both in the northern and southern parts of the field.

The great Indiana coal field is within 150 miles of Chicago or Michigan City, by railroad, from which ports the Lake Superior specular and red hematite ores are landed from vessels that are able to run in a direct course from the ore banks. Considering the proximity of the vast quantities of iron in Michigan and Missouri, one can readily see what a glorious future awaits Indiana in respect to manufactories.

Of the cannel coal, one of the finest seams to be found in the country is in Daviess county, this State. Here it is three and a half feet thick, underlaid by one and a half feet of a beautiful, jet-black caking coal. There is no clay, shale or other foreign matter intervening, and fragments of the caking coal are often found adhering to the cannel. There is no gradual change from one to the other, and the character of each is homogeneous throughout.

The cannel coal makes a delightful fire in open grates, and does not pop and throw off scales into the room, as is usual with this kind of coal. This coal is well adapted to the manufacture of illuminating gas, in respect to both quantity and high illuminating power. One ton of 2,000 pounds of this coal yields 10,400 feet of gas, while the best Pennsylvania coal yields but 8,680 cubic feet. This gas has an illuminating power of 25 candles, while the best Pennsylvania coal gas has that of only 17 candles.

Cannel coal is also found in great abundance in Perry, Greene, Parke and Fountain counties, where its commercial value has already been demonstrated.

Numerous deposits of bog iron ore are found in the northern part of the State, and clay iron-stones and impure carbonates and brown oxides are found scattered in the vicinity of the coal field. In some places the beds are quite thick and of considerable commercial value.

An abundance of excellent lime is also found in Indiana, especially in Huntington county, where many large kilns are kept in profitable operation.

AGRICULTURAL.

In 1852 the Legislature passed an act authorizing the organization of county and district agricultural societies, and also establishing a State Board, the provisions of which act are substantially as follows:

1. Thirty or more persons in any one or two counties organizing into a society for the improvement of agriculture, adopting a constitution and by-laws agreeable to the regulations prescribed by the State Board, and appointing the proper officers and raising a sum of $50 for its own treasury, shall be entitled to the same amount from the fund arising from show licenses in their respective counties.

2. These societies shall offer annual premiums for improvement of soils, tillage, crops, manures, productions, stock, articles of domestic industry, and such other articles, productions and improvements as they may deem proper; they shall encourage, by grant of rewards, agricultural and household manufacturing interests, and so regulate the premiums that small farmers will have equal opportunity with the large; and they shall pay special attention to cost and profit of the inventions and improvements, requiring an exact, detailed statement of the processes competing for rewards.

3. They shall publish in a newspaper annually their list of awards and an abstract of their treasurers' accounts, and they shall report in full to the State Board their proceedings. Failing to do the latter they shall receive no payment from their county funds.

STATE BOARD OF AGRICULTURE.

The act of Feb. 17, 1852, also established a State Board of Agriculture, with perpetual succession; its annual meetings to be held at Indianapolis on the first Thursday after the first Monday in January, when the reports of the county societies are to be received and agricultural interests discussed and determined upon; it shall make an annual report to the Legislature of receipts, expenses, proceedings, etc., of its own meeting as well as of those of the local societies; it shall hold State fairs, at such times and places as they may deem proper; may hold two meetings a year, certifying to the State Auditor their expenses, who shall draw his warrant upon the Treasurer for the same.

In 1861 the State Board adopted certain rules, embracing ten sections, for the government of local societies, but in 1868 they were found inexpedient and abandoned. It adopted a resolution admitting delegates from the local societies.

THE EXPOSITION.

As the Board found great difficulty in doing justice to exhibitors without an adequate building, the members went earnestly to work in the fall of 1872 to get up an interest in the matter. They appointed a committee of five to confer with the Council or citizens of Indianapolis as to the best mode to be devised for a more thorough and complete exhibition of the industries of the State. The result of the conference was that the time had arrived for a regular "exposition," like that of the older States. At the January meeting in 1873, Hon. Thomas Dowling, of Terre Haute, reported for the committee that they found a general interest in this enterprise, not only at the capital, but also throughout the State. A sub-committee was appointed who devised plans and specifications for the necessary structure, taking lessons mainly from the Kentucky Exposition building at Louisville. All the members of the State Board were in favor of proceeding with the building except Mr. Poole, who feared that, as the interest of the two enterprises were somewhat conflicting, and the Exposition being the more exciting show, it would swallow up the State and county fairs.

The Exposition was opened Sept. 10, 1873, when Hon. John Sutherland, President of the Board, the Mayor of Indianapolis, Senator Morton and Gov. Hendricks delivered addresses. Senator Morton took the high ground that the money spent for an exposition is spent as strictly for educational purposes as that which goes directly into the common school. The exposition is not a mere show, to be idly gazed upon, but an industrial school where one should study and learn. He thought that Indiana had less untillable land than any other State in the Union; 'twas as rich as any and yielded a greater variety of products; and that Indiana was the most prosperous agricultural community in the United States.

The State had nearly 3,700 miles of railroad, not counting side-track, with 400 miles more under contract for building. In 15 or 18 months one can go from Indianapolis to every county in the State by railroad. Indiana has 6,500 square miles of coal field, 450 of which contain block coal, the best in the United States for manufacturing purposes.

On the subject of cheap transportation, he said: " By the census of 1870, Pennsylvania had, of domestic animals of all kinds, 4,006,-589, and Indiana, 4,511,094. Pennsylvania had grain to the amount of 60,460,000 bushels, while Indiana had 79,350,454. The value of the farm products of Pennsylvania was estimated to be $183,946,-000; those of Indiana, $122,914,000. Thus you see that while Indiana had 505,000 head of live stock more, and 19,000.000 bushels of grain more than Pennsylvania, yet the products of Pennsylvania are estimated at $183,946,000, on account of her greater proximity to market, while those of Indiana are estimated at only $122,914,000. Thus you can understand the importance of cheap transportation to Indiana.

" Let us see how the question of transportation affects us on the other hand, with reference to the manufacturer of Bessemer steel. Of the 174,000 tons of iron ore used in the blast furnaces of Pittsburg last year, 84,000 tons came from Lake Superior, 64,000 tons from Iron Mountain, Missouri, 20,000 tons from Lake Champlain, and less than 5,000 tons from the home mines of Pennsylvania. They cannot manufacture their iron with the coal they have in Pennsylvania without coking it. We have coal in Indiana with which we can, in its raw state, make the best of iron; while we are 250 miles nearer Lake Superior than Pittsburg, and 430 miles nearer to Iron Mountain. So that the question of transportation determines the fact that Indiana must become the great center for the manufacture of Bessemer steel."

" What we want in this country is diversified labor."

The grand hall of the Exposition buildings is on elevated ground at the head of Alabama street, and commands a fine view of the city. The structure is of brick, 308 feet long by 150 in width, and two stories high. Its elevated galleries extend quite around the building, under the roof, thus affording visitors an opportunity to secure the most commanding view to be had in the city. The lower floor of the grand hall is occupied by the mechanical, geological and miscellaneous departments, and by the offices of the Board, which extend along the entire front. The second floor, which is approached by three wide stairways, accommodates the fine art, musical and other departments of light mechanics, and is brilliantly lighted by windows and skylights. But as we are here entering the description of a subject magnificent to behold, we enter a description too vast to complete, and we may as well stop here as anywhere.

The Presidents of the State Fairs have been: Gov. J. A. Wright, 1852-'4; Gen. Jos. Orr, 1855; Dr. A. C. Stevenson, 1856-'8; G. D. Wagner; 1859-60; D. P. Holloway, 1861; Jas. D. Williams, 1862, 1870-'1; A. D. Hamrick, 1863, 1867-'9; Stearns Fisher, 1864-'6; John Sutherland, 1872-'4; Wm. Crim, 1875. Secretaries: John B. Dillon, 1852-'3, 1855, 1858-'9; Ignatius Brown, 1856-'7; W. T. Dennis, 1854, 1860-'1; W. H. Loomis, 1862-'6; A. J. Holmes, 1867-'9; Joseph Poole, 1870-'1; Alex. Heron, 1872-'5. Place of fair, Indianapolis every year except: Lafayette, 1853; Madison, 1854; New Albany, 1859; Fort Wayne, 1865; and Terre Haute, 1867. In 1861 there was no fair. The gate and entry receipts increased from $4,651 in 1852 to $45,330 in 1874.

On the opening of the Exposition, Oct. 7, 1874, addresses were delivered by the President of the Board, Hon. John Sutherland, and by Govs. Hendricks, Bigler and Pollock. Yvon's celebrated painting, the "Great Republic," was unveiled with great ceremony, and many distinguished guests were present to witness it.

The exhibition of 1875 showed that the plate glass from the southern part of the State was equal to the finest French plate; that the force-blowers made in the eastern part of the State was of a world-wide reputation; that the State has within its bounds the largest wagon manufactory in the world; that in other parts of the State there were all sorts and sizes of manufactories, including rolling mills and blast furnaces, and in the western part coal was mined and shipped at the rate of 2,500 tons a day from one vicinity; and many other facts, which "would astonish the citizens of Indiana themselves even more than the rest of the world."

INDIANA HORTICULTURAL SOCIETY.

This society was organized in 1842, thus taking the lead in the West. At this time Henry Ward Beecher was a resident of Indianapolis, engaged not only as a minister but also as editor of the *Indiana Farmer and Gardener*, and his influence was very extensive in the interests of horticulture, floriculture and farming. Prominent among his pioneer co-laborers were Judge Coburn,

Aaron Aldridge, Capt. James Sigarson, D. V. Culley, Reuben Ragan, Stephen Hampton, Cornelius Ratliff, Joshua Lindley, Abner Pope and many others. In the autumn of this year the society held an exhibition, probably the first in the State, if not in the West, in the hall of the new State house. The only premium offered was a set of silver teaspoons for the best seedling apple, which was won by Reuben Ragan, of Putnam county, for an apple christened on this occasion the "Osceola."

The society gave great encouragement to the introduction of new varieties of fruit, especially of the pear, as the soil and climate of Indiana were well adapted to this fruit. But the bright horizon which seemed to be at this time looming up all around the field of the young society's operations was suddenly and thoroughly darkened by the swarm of noxious insects, diseases, blasts of winter and the great distance to market. The prospects of the cause scarcely justified a continuation of the expense of assembling from remote parts of the State, and the meetings of the society therefore soon dwindled away until the organization itself became quite extinct.

But when, in 1852 and afterward, railroads began to traverse the State in all directions, the Legislature provided for the organization of a State Board of Agriculture, whose scope was not only agriculture but also horticulture and the mechanic and household arts. The rapid growth of the State soon necessitated a differentiation of this body, and in the autumn of 1860, at Indianapolis, there was organized the

INDIANA POMOLOGICAL SOCIETY.

October 18, Reuben Ragan was elected President and Wm H. Loomis, of Marion county, Secretary. The constitution adopted provided for biennial meetings in January, at Indianapolis. At the first regular meeting, Jan. 9, 1861, a committee-man for each congressional district was appointed, all of them together to be known as the "State Fruit Committee," and twenty-five members were enrolled during this session. At the regular meeting in 1863 the constitution was so amended as to provide for annual sessions, and the address of the newly elected President, Hon. I. G. D. Nelson, of Allen county, urged the establishment of an agricultural college. He continued in the good cause until his work was crowned with success.

In 1864 there was but little done on account of the exhaust-
ive demands of the great war; and the descent of mercury 60° in
eighteen hours did so much mischief as to increase the discourage-
ment to the verge of despair. The title of the society was at this
meeting, Jan., 1864 changed to that of the Indiana Horticultural
Society.

The first several meetings of the society were mostly devoted to
revision of fruit lists; and although the good work, from its vast-
ness and complication, became somewhat monotonous, it has been
no exception in this respect to the law that all the greatest and
most productive labors of mankind require perseverance and toil.

In 1866, George M. Beeler, who had so indefatigably served as
secretary for several years, saw himself hastening to his grave, and
showed his love for the cause of fruit culture by bequeathing to
the society the sum of $1,000. This year also the State Superin-
tendent of Public Instruction was induced to take a copy of the
Society's transactions for each of the township libraries in the State,
and this enabled the Society to bind its volume of proceedings in
a substantial manner.

At the meeting in 1867 many valuable and interesting papers
were presented, the office of corresponding secretary was created,
and the subject of Legislative aid was discussed. The State Board
of Agriculture placed the management of the horticultural department of the State fair in the care of the Society.

The report for 1868 shows for the first time a balance on hand,
after paying expenses, the balance being $61.55. Up to this time
the Society had to take care of itself,—meeting current expenses, doing its own printing and binding, "boarding and clothing itself,"
and diffusing annually an amount of knowledge utterly incalcu-
lable. During the year called meetings were held at Salem, in the
peach and grape season, and evenings during the State fair, which
was held in Terre Haute the previous fall. The State now assumed
the cost of printing and binding, but the volume of transactions
was not quite so valuable as that of the former year.

In 1870 $100 was given to this Society by the State Board of
Agriculture, to be distributed as prizes for essays, which object
was faithfully carried out. The practice has since then been continued.

In 1871 the Horticultural Society brought out the best volume
of papers and proceedings it ever has had published.

In 1872 the office of corresponding secretary was discontinued; the appropriation by the State Board of Agriculture diverted to the payment of premiums on small fruits given at a show held the previous summer; results of the exhibition not entirely satisfactory.

In 1873 the State officials refused to publish the discussions of the members of the Horticultural Society, and the Legislature appropriated $500 for the purpose for each of the ensuing two years.

In 1875 the Legislature enacted a law requiring that one of the trustees of Purdue University shall be selected by the Horticultural Society.

The aggregate annual membership of this society from its organization in 1860 to 1875 was 1,225.

EDUCATION.

The subject of education has been referred to in almost every gubernatorial message from the organization of the Territory to the present time. It is indeed the most favorite enterprise of the Hoosier State. In the first survey of Western lands, Congress set apart a section of land in every township, generally the 16th, for school purposes, the disposition of the land to be in hands of the residents of the respective townships. Besides this, to this State were given two entire townships for the use of a State Seminary, to be under the control of the Legislature. Also, the State constitution provides that all fines for the breach of law and all commutations for militia service be appropriated to the use of county seminaries. In 1825 the common-school lands amounted to 680,207 acres, estimated at $2 an acre, and valued therefore at $1,216,044. At this time the seminary at Bloomington, supported in part by one of these township grants, was very flourishing. The common schools, however, were in rather a poor condition.

PUBLIC SCHOOLS.

In 1852 the free-school system was fully established, which has resulted in placing Indiana in the lead of this great nation. Although this is a pleasant subject, it is a very large one to treat in a condensed notice, as this has to be.

The free-school system of Indiana first became practically operative the first Monday of April, 1853, when the township trustees

for school purposes were elected through the State. The law committed to them the charge of all the educational affairs in their
respective townships. As it was feared by the opponents of the
law that it would not be possible to select men in all the townships capable of executing the school laws satisfactorily, the
people were thereby awakened to the necessity of electing their
very best men; and although, of course, many blunders have been
made by trustees, the operation of the law has tended to elevate the
adult population as well as the youth; and Indiana still adheres to
the policy of appointing its best men to educational positions.
The result is a grand surprise to all old fogies, who indeed scarcely
dare to appear such any longer.

To instruct the people in the new law and set the educational
machinery going, a pamphlet of over 60 pages, embracing the law,
with notes and explanations, was issued from the office of a superintendent of public instruction, and distributed freely throughout
the State. The first duty of the Board of Trustees was to establish
and conveniently locate a sufficient number of schools for the education of all the children of their township. But where were the
school-houses, and what were they? Previously they had been
erected by single districts, but under this law districts were abolished, their lines obliterated, and houses previously built by districts became the property of the township, and all the houses were
to be built at the expense of the township by an appropriation of
township funds by the trustees. In some townships there was not
a single school-house of any kind, and in others there were a few
old, leaky, dilapidated log cabins, wholly unfit for use even in summer, and in " winter worse than nothing." Before the people could
be tolerably accommodated with schools at least 3,500 school-houses
had to be erected in the State.

By a general law, enacted in conformity to the constitution of
1852, each township was made a municipal corporation, and every
voter in the township a member of the corporation; the Board of
Trustees constituted the township legislature as well as the executive body, the whole body of voters, however, exercising direct control through frequent meetings called by the trustees. Special
taxes and every other matter of importance were directly voted
upon.

Some tax-payers, who were opposed to special townships' taxes,
retarded the progress of schools by refusing to pay their assess-
ment. Contracts for building school-houses were given up, houses

half finished were abandoned, and in many townships all school operations were suspended. In some of them, indeed, a rumor was circulated by the enemies of the law that the entire school law from beginning to end had been declared by the Supreme Court unconstitutional and void; and the Trustees, believing this, actually dismissed their schools and considered themselves out of office. Hon. W. C. Larrabee, the (first) Superintendent of Public Instruction, corrected this error as soon as possible.

But while the voting of special taxes was doubted on a constitutional point, it became evident that it was weak in a practical point; for in many townships the opponents of the system voted down every proposition for the erection of school-houses.

Another serious obstacle was the great deficiency in the number of qualified teachers. To meet the newly created want, the law authorized the appointment of deputies in each county to examine and license persons to teach, leaving it in their judgment to lower the standard of qualification sufficiently to enable them to license as many as were needed to supply all the schools. It was therefore found necessary to employ many " unqualified " teachers, especially in the remote rural districts. But the progress of the times enabled the Legislature of 1853 to erect a standard of qualification and give to the county commissioners the authority to license teachers; and in order to supply every school with a teacher, while there might not be a sufficient number of properly qualified teachers, the commissioners were authorized to grant temporary licenses to take charge of particular schools not needing a high grade of teachers.

In 1854 the available common-school fund consisted of the congressional township fund, the surplus revenue fund, the saline fund, the bank tax fund and miscellaneous fund, amounting in all to $2,460,000. This amount, from many sources, was subsequently increased to a very great extent. The common-school fund was intrusted to the several counties of the State, which were held responsible for the preservation thereof and for the payment of the annual interest thereon. The fund was managed by the auditors and treasurers of the several counties, for which these officers were allowed one-tenth of the income. It was loaned out to the citizens of the county in sums not exceeding $300, on real estate security. The common-school fund was thus consolidated and the proceeds equally distributed each year to all the townships, cities and towns of the State, in proportion to the number of children. This phase of the law met with considerable opposition in 1854.

The provisions of the law for the establishment of township libraries was promptly carried into effect, and much time, labor and thought were devoted to the selection of books, special attention being paid to historical works.

The greatest need in 1854 was for qualified teachers; but nevertheless the progress of public education during this and following years was very great. School-houses were erected, many of them being fine structures, well furnished, and the libraries were considerably enlarged.

The city school system of Indiana received a heavy set-back in 1858, by a decision of the Supreme Court of the State, that the law authorizing cities and townships to levy a tax additional to the State tax was not in conformity with that clause in the Constitution which required uniformity in taxation. The schools were stopped for want of adequate funds. For a few weeks in each year thereafter the feeble " uniform " supply from the State fund enabled the people to open the schools, but considering the returns the public realizes for so small an outlay in educational matters, this proved more expensive than ever. Private schools increased, but the attendance was small. Thus the interests of popular education languished for years. But since the revival of the free schools, the State fund has grown to vast proportions, and the schools of this intelligent and enterprising commonwealth compare favorably with those of any other portion of the United States.

There is no occasion to present all the statistics of school progress in this State from the first to the present time, but some interest will be taken in the latest statistics, which we take from the 9th Biennial Report (for 1877-'8) by the State Superintendent of Public Instruction, Hon. James H. Smart. This report, by the way, is a volume of 480 octavo pages, and is free to all who desire a copy.

The rapid, substantial and permanent increase which Indiana enjoys in her school interests is thus set forth in the above report.

Year.	Length of School in Days.	No of Teachers.	Attendance at School.	School Enumeration.	Total Am't Paid Teachers.
1855	61	4,016	206,994	445,791	$ 239,924
1860	65	7,649	303,744	495,019	481,020
1865	66	9,493	402,812	557,092	1,020,440
1870	97	11,826	462,527	619,627	1,810,866
1875	130	13,133	502,362	667,736	2,830,747
1878	129	13,676	512,535	699,153	3,065,968

The increase of school population during the past ten years has been as follows:

Total in 1868, 592,865.

Increase for year ending		Increase for year ending	
Sept. 1, 1869	17,699	May 1, 1874	13,922
" 1, 1870	9,063	" 1, 1875	13,372
" 1, 1871	3,101	" 1, 1876	11,494
" 1, 1872	8,811	" 1, 1877	15,476
May 1, 1873 (8 months)	8,903	" 1, 1878	4,447
		Total, 1878	699,153

No. of white males	354,271;	females	333,033	687,304
" " colored "	5,937;	"	5,912	11,849

699,153

Twenty-nine per cent. of the above are in the 49 cities and 212 incorporated towns, and 71 per cent. in the 1,011 townships.

The number of white males enrolled in the schools in 1878 was 267,315, and of white females, 237,739; total, 505,054; of colored males, 3,794; females, 3,687; total, 7,481; grand total, 512,535.

The average number enrolled in each district varies from 51 to 56, and the average daily attendance from 32 to 35; but many children reported as absent attend parochial or private schools. Seventy-three per cent. of the white children and 63 per cent. of the colored, in the State, are enrolled in the schools.

The number of days taught vary materially in the different townships, and on this point State Superintendent Smart iterates: "As long as the schools of some of our townships are kept open but 60 days and others 220 days, we do not have a uniform system,—such as was contemplated by the constitution. The school law requires the trustee of a township to maintain each of the schools in his corporation an equal length of time. This provision cannot be so easily applied to the various counties of the State, for the reason that there is a variation in the density of the population, in the wealth of the people, and the amount of the township funds. I think, however, there is scarcely a township trustee in the State who cannot, under the present law, if he chooses to do so, bring his schools up to an average of six months. I think it would be wise to require each township trustee to levy a sufficient local tax to maintain the schools at least six months of the year, provided this can be done without increasing the local tax beyond the amount now permitted by law. This would tend to bring the poorer schools up to the standard of the best, and would thus unify the system, and make it indeed a common-school system."

The State, however, averages six and a half months school per year to each district.

The number of school districts in the State in 1878 was 9,380, in all but 34 of which school was taught during that year. There are 396 district and 151 township graded schools. Number of white male teachers, 7,977, and of female, 5,699; colored, male, 62, and female, 43; grand total, 13,781. For the ten years ending with 1878 there was an increase of 409 male teachers and 811 female teachers. All these teachers, except about 200, attend normal institutes,—a showing which probably surpasses that of any other State in this respect.

The average daily compensation of teachers throughout the State in 1878 was as follows: In townships, males, $1.90; females, $1.70: in towns, males, $3.09; females, $1.81; in cities, males, $4.06; females, $2.29.

In 1878 there were 89 stone school-houses, 1,724 brick, 7,608 frame, and 124 log; total, 9,545, valued at $11.536,647.39.

And lastly, and best of all, we are happy to state that Indiana has a larger school fund than any other State in the Union. In 1872, according to the statistics before us, it was larger than that of any other State by $2.000,000! the figures being as follows:

Indiana	$8,437,593.47	Michigan	$2,500,214.91
Ohio	6,614,816.50	Missouri	2,525,252.52
Illinois	6,348,538.32	Minnesota	2,471,199.31
New York	2,880,017.01	Wisconsin	2,237,414.37
Connecticut	2,809,770.70	Massachusetts	2,310,864.09
Iowa	4,274,581.93	Arkansas	2,000,000.00

Nearly all the rest of the States have less than a million dollars in their school fund.

In 1872 the common-school fund of Indiana consisted of the following:

Non-negotiable bonds	$3,591,316.15	Escheated estates	17,866.55
Common-school fund	1,866,·24.50	Sinking fund, last distribution	67,068.72
Sinking fund, at 8 per cent	569,130.94		
Congressional township fund	2,281,076.69	Sinking fund undistributed	100,165.92
Value of unsold Congressional township lands	94,245.00	Swamp land fund	42,418.40
Saline fund	5,727.66		$8,437,593 47
Bank tax fund	1,744.94		

In 1878 the grand total was $8,974,455.55.

The origin of the respective school funds of Indiana is as follows:

1. The "Congressional township" fund is derived from the proceeds of the 16th sections of the townships. Almost all of these

have been sold and the money put out at interest. The amount of this fund in 1877 was $2,452,936.82.

2. The "saline" fund consists of the proceeds of the sale of salt springs, and the land adjoining necessary for working them to the amount of 36 entire sections, authorized by the original act of Congress. By authority of the same act the Legislature has made these proceeds a part of the permanent school fund.

3. The "surplus revenue" fund. Under the administration of President Jackson, the national debt, contracted by the Revolutionary war and the purchase of Louisiana, was entirely discharged, and a large surplus remained in the treasury. In June, 1836, Congress distributed this money among the States in the ratio of their representation in Congress, subject to recall, and Indiana's share was $860,254. The Legislature subsequently set apart $573,502.96 of this amount to be a part of the school fund. It is not probable that the general Government will ever recall this money. ·

4. "Bank tax" fund. The Legislature of 1834 chartered a State Bank, of which a part of the stock was owned by the State and a part by individuals. Section 15 of the charter required an annual deduction from the dividends, equal to 12½ cents on each share not held by the State, to be set apart for common-school education. This tax finally amounted to $80,000, which now bears interest in favor of education.

5. "Sinking" fund. In order to set the State bank under good headway, the State at first borrowed $1,300,000, and out of the unapplied balances a fund was created, increased by unapplied balances also of the principal, interest and dividends of the amount lent to the individual holders of stock, for the purpose of sinking the debt of the bank; hence the name sinking fund. The 114th section of the charter provided that after the full payment of the bank's indebtedness, principal, interest and incidental expenses, the residue of said fund should be a permanent fund, appropriated to the cause of education. As the charter extended through a period of 25 years, this fund ultimately reached the handsome amount of $5,000,000.

The foregoing are all interest-bearing funds; the following are additional school funds, but not productive:

6. "Seminary" fund. By order of the Legislature in 1852, all county seminaries were sold, and the net proceeds placed in the common-school fund.

7.　All fines for the violation of the penal laws of the State are placed to the credit of the common-school fund

8.　All recognizances of witnesses and parties indicted for crime, when forfeited, are collectible by law and made a part of the school fund.　These are reported to the office of the State Superintendent of Public Instruction annually.　For the five years ending with 1872, they averaged about $34,000 a year.

9.　Escheats.　These amount to $17,865.55, which was still in the State treasury in 1872 and unapplied.

10.　The "swamp-land" fund arises from the sale of certain Congressional land grants, not devoted to any particular purpose by the terms of the grant.　In 1872 there was $42,418.40 of this money, subject to call by the school interests.

11.　Taxes on corporations are to some extent devoted by the Constitution to school purposes, but the clause on this subject is somewhat obscure, and no funds as yet have been realized from this source.　It is supposed that several large sums of money are due the common-school fund from the corporations.

Constitutionally, any of the above funds may be increased, but never diminished.

INDIANA STATE UNIVERSITY.

So early as 1802 the U. S. Congress granted lands and a charter to the people of that portion of the Northwestern Territory residing at Vincennes, for the erection and maintenance of a seminary of learning in that early settled district; and five years afterward an act incorporating the Vincennes University asked the Legislature to appoint a Board of Trustees for the institution and order the sale of a single township in Gibson county, granted by Congress in 1802, so that the proceeds might be at once devoted to the objects of education.　On this Board the following gentlemen were appointed to act in the interests of the institution:　William H. Harrison, John Gibson, Thomas H. Davis, Henry Vanderburgh, Waller Taylor, Benjamin Parke, Peter Jones, James Johnson, John Rice Jones, George Wallace, William Bullitt, Elias McNamee, John Badollet, Henry Hurst, Gen. W. Johnston, Francis Vigo, Jacob Kuykendall, Samuel McKee, Nathaniel Ewing, George Leech, Luke Decker, Samuel Gwathmey and John Johnson.

The sale of this land was slow and the proceeds small.　The members of the Board, too, were apathetic, and failing to meet, the institution fell out of existence and out of memory.

In 1816 Congress granted another township in Monroe county, located within its present limits, and the foundation of a university was laid. Four years later, and after Indiana was erected into a State, an act of the local Legislature appointing another Board of Trustees and authorizing them to select a location for a university and to enter into contracts for its construction, was passed. The new Board met at Bloomington and selected a site at that place for the location of the present building, entered into a contract for the erection of the same in 1822, and in 1825 had the satisfaction of being present at the inauguration of the university. The first session was commenced under the Rev. Baynard R. Hall, with 20 students, and when the learned professor could only boast of a salary of $150 a year; yet, on this very limited sum the gentleman worked with energy and soon brought the enterprise through all its elementary stages to the position of an academic institution. Dividing the year into two sessions of five months each. the Board acting under his advice, changed the name to the "Indiana Academy," under which title it was duly chartered. In 1827 Prof. John H. Harney was raised to the chairs of mathematics, natural philosophy and astronomy, at a salary of $300 a year; and the salary of Mr. Hall raised to $400 a year. In 1828 the name was again changed by the Legislature to the "Indiana College," and the following professors appointed over the different departments: Rev. Andrew Wylie, D. D., Prof. of mental and moral philosophy and belles lettres; John H. Harney, Prof. of mathematics and natural philosophy; and Rev. Bayard R. Hall, Prof. of ancient languages. This year, also, dispositions were made for the sale of Gibson county lands and for the erection of a new college building. This action was opposed by some legal difficulties, which after a time were overcome, and the new college building was put under construction, and continued to prosper until 1854, when it was destroyed by fire, and 9,000 volumes, with all the apparatus, were consumed The curriculum was then carried out in a temporary building, while a new struct-ure was going up.

In 1873 the new college, with its additions, was completed, and the routine of studies continued. A museum of natural history, a laboratory and the Owen cabinet added, and the standard of the studies and *morale* generally increased in excellence and in strict-ness.

Bloomington is a fine, healthful locality, on the Louisville, New Albany & Chicago railway. The University buildings are in the collegiate Gothic style, simply and truly carried out. The building, fronting College avenue is 145 feet in front. It consists of a central building 60 feet by 53, with wings each 38 feet by 26, and the whole, three stories high. The new building, fronting the west, is 130 feet by 50. Buildings lighted by gas.

The faculty numbers thirteen. Number of students in the collegiate department in 1879-'80, 183; in preparatory, 169; total, 349, allowing for three counted twice.

The university may now be considered on a fixed foundation, carrying out the intention of the President, who aimed at scholarship rather than numbers, and demands the attention of eleven professors, together with the State Geologist, who is ex-officio member of the faculty, and required to lecture at intervals and look after the geological and mineralogical interests of the institution. The faculty of medicine is represented by eleven leading physicians of the neighborhood. The faculty of law requires two resident professors, and the other chairs remarkably well represented.

The university received from the State annually about $15,000, and promises with the aid of other public grants and private donations to vie with any other State university within the Republic.

PURDUE UNIVERSITY.

This is a " college for the benefit of agricultural and the mechanic arts," as provided for by act of Congress, July 2, 1862, donating lands for this purpose to the extent of 30,000 acres of the public domain to each Senator and Representative in the Federal assembly. Indiana having in Congress at that time thirteen members, became entitled to 390,000 acres; but as there was no Congress land in the State at this time, scrip had to be taken, and it was upon the following condition (we quote the act):

"SECTION 4. That all moneys derived from the sale of land scrip shall be invested in the stocks of the United States, or of some other safe stocks, yielding no less than five per centum upon the par value of said stocks; and that the moneys so invested shall constitute a perpetual fund, the capital of which shall remain undiminished, except so far as may be provided in section 5 of this act, and the interest of which shall be inviolably appropriated by each State, which may take and claim the benefit of this act, to the endowment, support and maintenance of at least one college, where the leading object shall be, without excluding other scientific and classical studies, and including military tactics, to teach such branches of learning as are related to agriculture and the mechanic arts, in such a manner as the Legislatures of the States may respectively prescribe, in order to promote the liberal and practical education of the industrial classes in the several pursuits and professions of life.

" Sec. 5. That the grant of land and land scrip hereby authorized shall be made on the following conditions, to which, as well as the provision hereinbefore contained, the previous assent of the several States shall be signified by Legislative act:

" First. If any portion of the funds invested as provided by the foregoing section, or any portion of the interest thereon, shall by any action or contingency be diminished or lost, it shall be replaced by the State to which it belongs, so that the capital of the fund shall remain forever undiminished, and the annual interest shall be regularly applied, without diminution, to the purposes mentioned in the fourth section of this act, except that a sum not exceeding ten per centum upon the amount received by any State under the provisions of this act may be expended for the purchase of lands for sites or experimental farms, whenever authorized by the respective Legislatures of said States.

" Second. No portion of said fund, nor interest thereon, shall be applied, directly or indirectly, under any pretence whatever, to the purchase, erection, preservation or repair of any building or buildings.

" Third. Any State which may take and claim the benefit of the provisions of this act, shall provide, within five years at least, not less than one college, as provided in the fourth section of this act, or the grant to such State shall cease and said State be bound to pay the United States the amount received of any lands previously sold, and that the title to purchase under the States shall be valid.

" Fourth. An annual report shall be made regarding the progress of each college, recording any improvements and experiments made, with their cost and result, and such other matter, including State industrial and economical statistics, as may be supposed useful, one copy of which shall be transmitted by mail free, by each, to all other colleges which may be endowed under the provisions of this act, and also one copy to the Secretary of the Interior.

"Fifth. When lands shall be selected from those which have been raised to double the minimum price in consequence of railroad grants, that they shall be computed to the States at the maximum price, and the number of acres proportionately diminished.

"Sixth. No State, while in a condition of rebellion or insurrection against the Government of the United States, shall be entitled to the benefits of this act.

"Seventh. No State shall be entitled to the benefits of this act unless it shall express its acceptance thereof by its Legislature within two years from the date of its approval by the President."

The foregoing act was approved by the President, July 2, 1862. It seemed that this law, amid the din of arms with the great Rebellion, was about to pass altogether unnoticed by the next General Assembly, January, 1863, had not Gov. Morton's attention been called to it by a delegation of citizens from Tippecanoe county, who visited him in the interest of Battle Ground. He thereupon sent a special message to the Legislature, upon the subject, and then public attention was excited to it everywhere, and several localities competed for the institution; indeed, the rivalry was so great that this session failed to act in the matter at all, and would have failed to accept of the grant within the two years prescribed in the last clause quoted above, had not Congress, by a supplementary act, extended the time two years longer.

March 6, 1865, the Legislature accepted the conditions of the national gift, and organized the Board of " Trustees of the Indiana Agricultural College." This Board, by authority, sold the scrip April 9, 1867, for $212,238.50, which sum, by compounding, has increased to nearly $400,000, and is invested in U. S. bonds. Not until the special session of May, 1869, was the locality for this college selected, when John Purdue, of Lafayette, offered $150,000 and Tippecanoe county $50,000 more, and the title of the institution changed to " Purdue University." Donations were also made by the Battle Ground Institute and the Battle Ground Institute of the Methodist Episcopal Church.

The building was located on a 100-acre tract near Chauncey, which Purdue gave in addition to his magnificent donation, and to which 86½ acres more have since been added on the north. The boarding-house, dormitory, the laboratory, boiler and gas house, a frame armory and gymnasium, stable with shed and work-shop are all to the north of the gravel road, and form a group of buildings within a circle of 600 feet. The boiler and gas house occupy a rather central position, and supply steam and gas to the boarding-house, dormitory and laboratory. A description of these buildings may be apropos. The boarding-house is a brick structure, in the modern Italian style, planked by a turret at each of the front angles and measuring 120 feet front by 68 feet deep. The dormitory is a quadrangular edifice, in the plain Elizabethan style, four stories high, arranged to accommodate 125 students. Like the other buildings, it is heated by steam and lighted by gas. Bathing accommodations are in each end of all the stories. The laboratory is almost a duplicate of a similar department in Brown University, R. I. It is a much smaller building than the boarding-house, but yet sufficiently large to meet the requirements. A collection of minerals, fossils and antiquities, purchased from Mr. Richard Owen, former President of the institution, occupies the temporary cabinet or museum, pending the construction of a new building. The military hall and gymnasium is 100 feet frontage by 50 feet deep, and only one story high. The uses to which this hall is devoted are exercises in physical and military drill. The boiler and gas house is an establishment replete in itself, possessing every facility for supplying the buildings of the university with adequate heat and light. It is further provided with pumping works. Convenient to this department is the retort and great meters of the gas house, capable of holding 9,000 cubic feet of gas, and arranged upon the principles of modern science. The barn and shed form a single building, both useful, convenient and ornamental.

In connection with the agricultural department of the university, a brick residence and barn were erected and placed at the disposal of the farm superintendent, Maj. L. A. Burke.

The buildings enumerated above have been erected at a cost approximating the following: boarding-house, $37,807.07; laboratory, $15,000; dormitory, $32,000; military hall and gymnasium, $6,410.47; boiler and gas house, $4,814; barn and shed, $1,500; work-shop, $1,000; dwelling and barn, $2,500.

Besides the original donations, Legislative appropriations, varying in amount, have been made from time to time, and Mr. Pierce, the treasurer, has donated his official salary, $600 a year, for the time he served, for decorating the grounds,—if necessary.

The opening of the university was, owing to varied circumstances, postponed from time to time, and not until March, 1874, was a class formed, and this only to comply with the act of Congress in that connection in its relation to the university. However, in September following a curriculum was adopted, and the first regular term of the Purdue University entered upon. This curriculum

comprises the varied subjects generally pertaining to a first-class
university course, namely: in the school of natural science—
physics and industrial mechanics, chemistry and natural history;
in the school of engineering—civil and mining, together with the
principles of architecture; in the school of agriculture—theoret-
ical and practical agriculture, horticulture and veterinary science;
in the military school—the mathematical sciences, German and
French literature, free-hand and mechanical drawing, with all the
studies pertaining to the natural and military sciences. Modern
languages and natural history embrace their respective courses to
the fullest extent.

There are this year (1880) eleven members of the faculty, 86
students in the regular courses, and 117 other students. In respect
to attendance there has been a constant increase from the first.
The first year, 1874-'5, there were but 64 students.

This institution was founded at Terre Haute in 1870, in accord-
ance with the act of the Legislature of that year. The building is
a large brick edifice situated upon a commanding location and
possessing some architectural beauties. From its inauguration
many obstacles opposed its advance toward efficiency and success;
but the Board of Trustees, composed of men experienced in educational matters, exercised their strength of mind and body to
overcome every difficulty, and secure for the State Normal School
every distinction and emolument that lay within their power.
their efforts to this end being very successful; and it is a fact that
the institution has arrived at, if not eclipsed, the standard of their
expectations. Not alone does the course of study embrace the
legal subjects known as reading, writing, spelling, arithmetic,
geography, United States history, English grammar, physiology,
manners and ethics, but it includes also universal history, the
mathematical sciences and many other subjects foreign to older
institutions. The first studies are prescribed by law and must be
inculcated; the second are optional with the professors, and in the
case of Indiana generally hold place in the curriculum of the normal school.

The model, or training school, specially designed for the training
of teachers, forms a most important factor in State educational
matters, and prepares teachers of both sexes for one of the most
important positions in life; viz., that of educating the youth of the

State. The advanced course of studies, together with the higher studies of the normal school, embraces Latin and German, and prepares young men and women for entrance to the State University.

The efficiency of this school may be elicited from the following facts, taken from the official reports: out of 41 persons who had graduated from the elementary course, nine, after teaching successfully in the public schools of this State from two terms to two years, returned to the institution and sought admission to the advanced classes. They were admitted; three of them were gentlemen and six ladies. After spending two years and two terms in the elementary course, and then teaching in the schools during the time already mentioned they returned to spend two and a half or three years more, and for the avowed purpose of qualifying themselves for teaching in the most responsible positions of the public school service. In fact, no student is admitted to the school who does not in good faith declare his intention to qualify himself for teaching in the schools of the State. This the law requires, and the rule is adhered to literally.

The report further says, in speaking of the government of the school, that the fundamental idea is rational freedom, or that freedom which gives exemption from the power of control of one over another, or, in other words, the self-limiting of themselves, in their acts, by a recognition of the rights of others who are equally free. The idea and origin of the school being laid down, and also the means by which scholarship can be realized in the individual, the student is left to form his own conduct, both during session hours and while away from school. The teacher merely stands between this scholastic idea and the student's own partial conception of it, as expositor or interpreter. The teacher is not legislator, executor or police officer; he is expounder of the true idea of school law, so that the only test of the student's conduct is obedience to, or nonconformity with, that law as interpreted by the teacher. This idea once inculcated in the minds of the students, insures industry, punctuality and order.

NORTHERN INDIANA NORMAL SCHOOL AND BUSINESS INSTITUTE, VALPARAISO.

This institution was organized Sept. 16, 1873, with 35 students in attendance. The school occupied the building known as the Valparaiso Male and Female College building. Four teachers were employed.   The attendance, so small at first, increased rapidly and steadily, until at the present writing, the seventh year in the history of the school, the yearly enrollment is more than three thousand.   The number of instructors now employed is 23.

From time to time, additions have been made to the school buildings, and numerous boarding halls have been erected, so that now the value of the buildings and grounds owned by the school is one hundred thousand dollars.

A large library has been collected, and a complete equipment of philosophical and chemical apparatus has been purchased.   The department of physiology is supplied with skeletons, manikins, and everything necessary to the demonstration of each branch of the subject.   A large cabinet is provided for the study of geology. In fact, each department of the school is completely furnished with the apparatus needed for the most approved presentation of every subject.

There are 15 chartered departments in the institution.   These are in charge of thorough, energetic, and scholarly instructors, and send forth each year as graduates, a large number of finely cultured young ladies and gentlemen, living testimonials of the efficiency of the course of study and the methods used.

The Commercial College in connection with the school is in itself a great institution.   It is finely fitted up and furnished, and ranks foremost among the business colleges of the United States.

The expenses for tuition, room and board, have been made so low that an opportunity for obtaining a thorough education is presented to the poor and the rich alike.

All of this work has been accomplished in the short space of seven years.   The school now holds a high place among educational institutions, and is the largest normal school in the United States.

This wonderful growth and development is wholly due to the energy and faithfulness of its teachers, and the unparalleled executive ability of its proprietor and principal.   The school is not endowed.

DENOMINATIONAL AND PRIVATE INSTITUTIONS.

Nor is Indiana behind in literary institutions under denominational auspices.   It is not to be understood, however, at the present day, that sectarian doctrines are insisted upon at the so-called "denominational" colleges, universities and seminaries; the youth at these places are influenced only by Christian example.

Notre Dame University, near South Bend, is a Catholic institution, and is one of the most noted in the United States. It was founded in 1842 by Father Sorin. The first building was erected in 1843, and the university has continued to grow and prosper until the present time, now having 35 professors, 26 instructors, 9 tutors, 213 students and 12,000 volumes in library. At present the main building has a frontage of 224 feet and a depth of 155. Thousands of young people have received their education here, and a large number have been graduated for the priesthood. A chapter was held here in 1872, attended by delegates from all parts of the world. It is worthy of mention that this institution has a bell weighing 13,000 pounds, the largest in the United States and one of the finest in the world.

The *Indiana Asbury University*, at Greencastle, is an old and well-established institution under the auspices of the Methodist Episcopal Church, named after its first bishop, Asbury. It was founded in 1835, and in 1872 it had nine professors and 172 students.

Howard College, not denominational, is located at Kokomo, and was founded in 1869. In 1872 it had five professors, four instructors, and 69 students.

Union Christian College, Christian, at Merom, was organized in 1858, and in 1872 had four resident professors, seven instructors and 156 students.

Moore's Hill College, Methodist Episcopal, is situated at Moore's Hill, was founded in 1854, and in 1872 had five resident professors, five instructors, and 142 students.

Earlham's College, at Richmond, is under the management of the Orthodox Friends, and was founded in 1859. In 1872 they had six resident professors and 167 students, and 3,300 volumes in library.

Wabash College, at Crawfordsville, was organized in 1834, and had in 1872, eight professors and teachers, and 231 students, with about 12,000 volumes in the library. It is under Presbyterian management.

Concordia College, Lutheran, at Fort Wayne, was founded in 1850; in 1872 it had four professors and 148 students: 3,000 volumes in library.

Hanover College, Presbyterian, was organized in 1833, at Hanover, and in 1872 had seven professors and 118 students, and 7,000 volumes in library.

Hartsville University, United Brethren, at Hartsville, was founded in 1854, and in 1872 had seven professors and 117 students.

Northwestern Christian University, Disciples, is located at Irvington, near Indianapolis. It was founded in 1854, and by 1872 it had 15 resident professors, 181 students, and 5,000 volumes in library.

BENEVOLENT AND PENAL INSTITUTIONS.

By the year 1830, the influx of paupers and invalid persons was so great that the Governor called upon the Legislature to take steps toward regulating the matter, and also to provide an asylum for the poor, but that body was very slow to act on the matter. At the present time, however, there is no State in the Union which can boast a better system of benevolent institutions. The Benevolent Society of Indianapolis was organized in 1843. It was a pioneer institution; its field of work was small at first, but it has grown into great usefulness.

INSTITUTE FOR THE EDUCATION OF THE BLIND.

In behalf of the blind, the first effort was made by James M. Ray, about 1846. Through his efforts William H. Churchman came from Kentucky with blind pupils and gave exhibitions in Mr. Beecher's church, in Indianapolis. These entertainments were attended by members of the Legislature, for whom indeed they were especially intended; and the effect upon them was so good, that before they adjourned the session they adopted measures to establish an asylum for the blind. The commission appointed to carry out these measures, consisting of James M. Ray, Geo. W. Mears, and the Secretary, Treasurer and Auditor of State, engaged Mr. Churchman to make a lecturing tour through the State and collect statistics of the blind population.

The "Institute for the Education of the Blind" was founded by the Legislature of 1847, and first opened in a rented building Oct. 1, of that year. The permanent buildings were opened and occupied in February, 1853. The original cost of the buildings and ground was $110,000, and the present valuation of buildings and grounds approximates $300,000. The main building is 90 feet long by 61 deep, and with its right and left wings, each 30 feet in front and 83 in depth, give an entire frontage of 150 feet. The main building is five stories in height, surmounted by a cupola of the Corinthian style, while each wing is similarly overcapped The porticoes, cornices and verandahs are gotten up with exquisite taste, and the former are molded after the principle of Ionic architecture. The building is very favorably situated, and occupies a space of eight acres.

The nucleus of a fund for supplying indigent graduates of the institution with an outfit suitable to their trades, or with money in lieu thereof, promises to meet with many additions. The fund is the out-come of the benevolence of Mrs. Fitzpatrick, a resident of Delaware, in this State, and appears to be suggested by the fact that her daughter, who was smitten with blindness, studied as a pupil in the institute, and became singularly attached to many of its inmates. The following passage from the lady's will bears testimony not only to her own sympathetic nature but also to the efficiency of the establishment which so won her esteem. " I give to each of the following persons, friends and associates of my blind daughter, Margaret Louisa, the sum of $100 to each, to wit, viz: Melissa and Phœbe Garrettson, Frances Cundiff, Dallas Newland, Naomi Unthunk, and a girl whose name before marriage was Rachel Martin, her husband's name not recollected. The balance of my estate, after paying the expenses of administering, I give to the superintendent of the blind asylum and his successor, in trust, for the use and benefit of the indigent blind of Indiana who may attend the Indiana blind asylum, to be given to them on leaving in such sums as the superintendent may deem proper, but not more than $50 to any one person. I direct that the amount above directed be loaned at interest, and the interest and principal be distributed as above, agreeably to the best judgment of the superintendent, so as to do the greatest good to the greatest number of blind persons."

The following rules, regulating the institution, after laying down in preamble that the institute is strictly an educational establishment, having its main object the moral, intellectual and physical training of the young blind of the State, and is not an asylum for the aged and helpless, nor an hospital wherein the diseases of the eye may be treated, proceed as follows:

1. The school year commences the first Wednesday after the 15th day of September, and closes on the last Wednesday in June, showing a session of 40 weeks, and a vacation term of 84 days.

2. Applicants for admission must be from 9 to 21 years of age; but the trustees have power to admit blind students under 9 or

over 21 years of age; but this power is extended only in very extreme cases.

3.   Imbecile or unsound persons, or confirmed immoralists, cannot be admitted knowingly; neither can admitted pupils who prove disobedient or incompetent to receive instruction be retained on the roll.

4.   No charge is made for the instruction and board given to pupils from the State of Indiana; and even those without the State have only to pay $200 for board and education during the 40 weeks' session.

5.   An abundant and good supply of comfortable clothing for both summer and winter wear, is an indispensable adjunct of the pupil.

6.   The owner's name must be distinctly marked on each article of clothing.

7.   In cases of extreme indigence the institution may provide clothing and defray the traveling expenses of such pupil and levy the amount so expended on the county wherein his or her home is situated.

8.   The pupil, or friends of the pupil, must remove him or her from the institute during the annual vacation, and in case of their failure to do so, a legal provision enables the superintendent to forward such pupil to the trustee of the township where he or she resides, and the expense of such transit and board to be charged to the county.

9.   Friends of the pupils accompanying them to the institution, or visiting them thereat, cannot enter as boarders or lodgers.

10.   Letters to the pupils should be addressed to the care of the Superintendent of the Institute for the Education of the Blind, so as the better to insure delivery.

11.   Persons desirous of admission of pupils should apply to the superintendent for a printed copy of instructions, and no pupil should be sent thereto until the instructions have been complied with.

INSTITUTE FOR THE DEAF AND DUMB.

In 1843 the Governor was also instructed to obtain plans and information respecting the care of mutes, and the Legislature also levied a tax to provide for them.   The first one to agitate the subject was William Willard, himself a mute, who visited Indiana in 1843, and opened a school for mutes on his own account, with 16 pupils.

The next year the Legislature adopted this school as a State institution, appointing a Board of Trustees for its management, consisting of the Governor and Secretary of State, ex-officio, and Revs. Henry
Ward Beecher, Phineas D. Gurley, L. H. Jameson, Dr. Dunlap,
Hon. James Morrison and Rev. Matthew Simpson. They rented the
large building on the southeast corner of Illinois and Maryland
streets, and opened the first State asylum there in 1844; but in 1846,
a site for a permanent building just east of Indianapolis was selected,
consisting first of 30 acres, to which 100 more have been added.
On this site the two first structures were commenced in 1849, and
completed in the fall of 1850, at a cost of $30,000. The school
was immediately transferred to the new building, where it is still
flourishing, with enlarged buildings and ample facilities for instruction in agriculture. In 1869-'70, another building was erected,
and the three together now constitute one of the most beneficent and beautiful institutions to be found on this continent, at
an aggregate cost of $220,000. The main building has a façade of
260 feet. Here are the offices, study rooms, the quarters of officers
and teachers, the pupils' dormitories and the library. The center
of this building has a frontage of eighty feet, and is five stories high,
with wings on either side 60 feet in frontage. In this Central
structure are the store rooms, dining-hall, servants' rooms, hospital,
laundry, kitchen, bakery and several school-rooms. Another structure known as the " rear building " contains the chapel and another
set of school-rooms. It is two stories high, the center being 50 feet
square and the wings 40 by 20 feet. In addition to these there are
many detached buildings, containing the shops of the industrial
department, the engine-house and wash-house.

The grounds comprise 105 acres, which in the immediate vicinity
of the buildings partake of the character of ornamental or pleasure
gardens, comprising a space devoted to fruits, flowers and vegetables, while the greater part is devoted to pasture and agriculture.

The first instructor in the institution was Wm. Willard, a deaf
mute, who had up to 1844 conducted a small school for the instruction of the deaf at Indianapolis, and now is employed by the State,
at a salary of $800 per annum, to follow a similar vocation in its
service. In 1853 he was succeeded by J. S. Brown, and subsequently by Thomas McIntire, who continues principal of the
institution.

HOSPITAL FOR THE INSANE.

The Legislature of 1832-'3 adopted measures providing for a State hospital for the insane. This good work would have been done much earlier had it not been for the hard times of 1837, intensified by the results of the gigantic scheme of internal improvement. In order to survey the situation and awaken public sympathy, the county assessors were ordered to make a return of the insane in their respective counties. During the year 1842 the Governor, acting under the direction of the Legislature, procured considerable information in regard to hospitals for the insane in other States; and Dr. John Evans lectured before the Legislature on the subject of insanity and its treatment. As a result of these efforts the authorities determined to take active steps for the establishment of such a hospital. Plans and suggestions from the superintendents and hospitals of other States were submitted to the Legislature in 1844, which body ordered the levy of a tax of one cent on the $100 for the purpose of establishing the hospital. In 1845 a commission was appointed to obtain a site not exceeding 200 acres. Mount Jackson, then the residence of Nathaniel Bolton, was selected, and the Legislature in 1846 ordered the commissioners to proceed with the erection of the building. Accordingly, in 1847, the central building was completed, at a cost of $75,000. It has since been enlarged by the addition of wings, some of which are larger than the old central building, until it has become an immense structure, having cost over half a million dollars.

The wings of the main building are four stories high, and entirely devoted to wards for patients, being capable of accommodating 500.

The grounds of the institution comprise 160 acres, and, like those of the institute for the deaf and dumb, are beautifully laid out.

This hospital was opened for the reception of patients in 1848. The principal structure comprises what is known as the central building and the right and left wings, and like the institute for the deaf and dumb, erected at various times and probably under various adverse circumstances, it certainly does not hold the appearance of any one design, but seems to be a combination of many. Notwithstanding these little defects in arrangement, it presents a very imposing appearance, and shows what may be termed a frontage of 624 feet. The central building is five stories in height and contains the store-rooms, offices, reception parlors, medical dispensing rooms, mess-rooms and the apartments of the superintendent and other officers, with those of the female employes. Immediately in the rear of the central building, and connected with it by a corridor, is the chapel, a building 50 by 60 feet. This chapel occupies the third floor, while the under stories hold the kitchen, bakery, employes' dining-room, steward's office, employes' apartments and sewing rooms. In rear of this again is the engine-house, 60 by 50 feet, containing all the paraphernalia for such an establishment, such as boilers, pumping works, fire plugs, hose, and above, on the second floor, the laundry and apartments of male employes.

THE STATE PRISON SOUTH.

The first penal institution of importance is known as the "State Prison South," located at Jeffersonville, and was the only prison until 1859. It was established in 1821. Before that time it was customary to resort to the old-time punishment of the whipping-post. Later the manual labor system was inaugurated, and the convicts were hired out to employers, among whom were Capt. Westover, afterward killed at Alamo, Texas, with Crockett, James Keigwin, who in an affray was fired at and severely wounded by a convict named Williams, Messrs. Patterson Hensley, and Jos. R. Pratt. During the rule of the latter of these lessees, the attention of the authorities was turned to a more practical method of utilizing convict labor; and instead of the prisoners being permitted to serve private entries, their work was turned in the direction of their own prison, where for the next few years they were employed in erecting the new buildings now known as the "State Prison South." This structure, the result of prison labor, stands on 16 acres of ground, and comprises the cell houses and work-shops, together with the prisoners' garden, or pleasure-ground.

It seems that in the erection of these buildings the aim of the overseers was to create so many petty dungeons and unventilated laboratories, into which disease in every form would be apt to creep. This fact was evident from the high mortality characterizing life within the prison; and in the efforts made by the Government to remedy a state of things which had been permitted to exist far too long, the advance in prison reform has become a reality. From 1857 to 1871 the labor of the prisoners was devoted to the manufacture of wagons and farm implements; and again the old policy of hiring the convicts was resorted to; for in the latter year, 1871, the Southwestern Car Company was organized, and every prisoner capable of taking a part in the work of car-building was leased out. This did very well until the panic of 1873, when the company suffered irretrievable losses; and previous to its final down-fall in 1876 the warden withdrew convict labor a second time, leaving the prisoners to enjoy a luxurious idleness around the prison which themselves helped to raise.

In later years the State Prison South has gained some notoriety from the desperate character of some of its inmates. During the civil war a convict named Harding mutilated in a most horrible manner and ultimately killed one of the jailors named Tesley. In 1874, two prisoners named Kennedy and Applegate, possessing themselves of some arms, and joined by two other convicts named Port and Stanley, made a break for freedom, swept past the guard, Chamberlain, and gained the fields. Chamberlain went in pursuit but had not gone very far when Kennedy turned on his pursuer, fired and killed him instantly. Subsequently three of the prisoners were captured alive and one of them paid the penalty of death, while Kennedy, the murderer of Chamberlain, failing committal for murder, was sent back to his old cell to spend the remainder of his life. Bill Rodifer, better known as "The Hoosier Jack Sheppard," effected his escape in 1875, in the very presence of a large guard, but was recaptured and has since been kept in irons.

This establishment, owing to former mismanagement, has fallen very much behind, financially, and has asked for and received an appropriation of $20,000 to meet its expenses, while the contrary is the case at the Michigan City prison.

THE STATE PRISON NORTH.

In 1859 the first steps toward the erection of a prison in the northern part of the State were taken, and by an act of the Legislature approved March 5, this year, authority was given to construct prison buildings at some point north of the National road. For this purpose $50,000 were appropriated, and a large number of convicts from the Jeffersonville prison were transported northward to Michigan City, which was just selected as the location for the new penitentiary. The work was soon entered upon, and continued to meet with additions and improvements down to a very recent period. So late as 1875 the Legislature appropriated $20,000

toward the construction of new cells, and in other directions also
the work of improvement has been going on. The system of
government and discipline is similar to that enforced at the Jeffersonville prison; and, strange to say, by its economical working has
not only met the expenses of the administration, but very recently
had amassed over $11,000 in excess of current expenses, from its
annual savings. This is due almost entirely to the continual
employment of the convicts in the manufacture of cigars and
chairs, and in their great prison industry, cooperage. It differs
widely from the Southern, insomuch as its sanitary condition has
been above the average of similar institutions. The strictness of its
silent system is better enforced. The petty revolutions of its
inmates have been very few and insignificant, and the number of
punishments inflicted comparatively small. From whatever point
this northern prison may be looked at, it will bear a very favorable
comparison with the largest and best administered of like establishments throughout the world, and cannot fail to bring high credit to
its Board of Directors and its able warden.

FEMALE PRISON AND REFORMATORY.

The prison reform agitation which in this State attained telling
proportions in 1869, caused a Legislative measure to be brought
forward, which would have a tendency to ameliorate the condition
of female convicts. Gov. Baker recommended it to the General
Assembly, and the members of that body showed their appreciation
of the Governor's philanthropic desire by conferring upon the bill
the authority of a statute; and further, appropriated $50,000 to aid
in carrying out the objects of the act. The main provisions contained in the bill may be set forth in the following extracts from
the proclamation of the Governor:

" Whenever said institution shall have been proclaimed to be
open for the reception of girls in the reformatory department
thereof, it shall be lawful for said Board of Managers to receive
them into their care and management, and the said reformatory
department, girls under the age of 15 years who may be committed
to their custody, in either of the following modes, to-wit:

" 1. When committed by any judge of a Circuit or Common
Pleas Court, either in term time or in vacation, on complaint and
due proof by the parent or guardian that by reason of her incorrigible or vicious conduct she has rendered her control beyond the
power of such parent or guardian, and made it manifestly requisite

that from regard to the future welfare of such infant, and for the protection of society, she should be placed under such guardianship.

"2. When such infant has been committed by such judge, as aforesaid, upon complaint by any citizen, and due proof of such complaint that such infant is a proper subject of the guardianship of such institution in consequence of her vagrancy or incorrigible or vicious conduct, and that from the moral depravity or otherwise of her parent or guardian in whose custody she may be, such parent or guardian is incapable or unwilling to exercise the proper care or discipline over such incorrigible or vicious infant.

"3. When such infant has been committed by such judge as aforesaid, on complaint and due proof thereof by the township trustee of the township where such infant resides, that such infant is destitute of a suitable home and of adequate means of obtaining an honest living, or that she is in danger of being brought up to lead an idle and immoral life."

In addition to these articles of the bill, a formal section of instruction to the wardens of State prisons was embodied in the act, causing such wardens to report the number of all the female convicts under their charge and prepare to have them transferred to the female reformatory immediately after it was declared to be ready for their reception. After the passage of the act the Governor appointed a Board of Managers, and these gentlemen, securing the services of Isaac Hodgson, caused him to draft a plan of the proposed institution, and further, on his recommendation, asked the people for an appropriation of another $50,000, which the Legislature granted in February, 1873. The work of construction was then entered upon and carried out so steadily, that on the 6th of September, 1873, the building was declared ready for the reception of its future inmates. Gov. Baker lost no time in proclaiming this fact, and October 4 he caused the wardens of the State prisons to be instructed to transfer all the female convicts in their custody to the new institution which may be said to rest on the advanced intelligence of the age. It is now called the "Indiana Reformatory Institution for Women and Girls."

This building is located immediately north of the deaf and dumb asylum, near the arsenal, at Indianapolis. It is a three-story brick structure in the French style, and shows a frontage of 174 feet, comprising a main building, with lateral and transverse wings. In front of the central portion is the residence of the superintendent and his associate reformatory officers, while in the rear is the engine house, with all the ways and means for heating the buildings. Enlargements, additions and improvements are still in progress. There is also a school and library in the main building, which are sources of vast good.

October 31, 1879, there were 66 convicts in the " penal " department and 147 in the " girls' reformatory " department. The "ticket-of-leave" system has been adopted, with entire satisfaction, and the conduct of the institution appears to be up with the times.

INDIANA HOUSE OF REFUGE.

In 1867 the Legislature appropriated $50,000 to aid in the formation of an institution to be entitled a house for the correction and reformation of juvenile defenders, and vested with full powers in a Board of Control, the members of which were to be appointed by the Governor, and with the advice and consent of the Senate. This Board assembled at the Governor's house at Indianapolis, April 3, 1867, and elected Charles F. Coffin, as president, and visited Chicago, so that a visit to the reform school there might lead to a fuller knowledge and guide their future proceedings. The House of Refuge at Cincinnati, and the Ohio State Reform school were also visited with this design; and after full consideration of the varied governments of these institutions, the Board resolved to adopt the method known as the " family " system, which divides the inmates into fraternal bodies, or small classes, each class having a separate house, house father and family offices, —all under the control of a general superintendent. The system being adopted, the question of a suitable location next presented itself, and proximity to a large city being considered rather detrimental to the welfare of such an institution, Gov. Baker selected the site three-fourths of a mile south of Plainfield, and about fourteen miles from Indianapolis, which, in view of its eligibility and convenience, was fully concurred in by the Board of Control. Therefore, a farm of 225 acres, claiming a fertile soil and a most picturesque situation, and possessing streams of running water, was purchased, and on a plateau in its center a site for the proposed house of refuge was fixed.

The next movement was to decide upon a plan, which ultimately met the approval of the Governor. It favored the erection of one principal building, one house for a reading-room and hospital, two large mechanical shops and eight family houses. January 1, 1868 three family houses and work-shop were completed; in 1869 the main building, and one additional family house were added; but previous to this, in August, 1867, a Mr. Frank P. Ainsworth and his wife were appointed by the Board, superintendent and matron respectively, and temporary quarters placed at their disposal. In 1869 they of course removed to the new building. This is 64 by 128 feet, and three stories high. In its basement are kitchen, laundry and vegetable cellar. The first floor is devoted to offices, visitors' room, house father and family dining-room and store-rooms. The general superintendent's private apartments, private offices and five dormitories for officers occupy the second floor; while the third floor is given up to the assistant superintendent's apartment, library, chapel and hospital.

The family houses are similar in style, forming rectangular build-ings 36 by 58 feet. The basement of each contains a furnace room, a store-room and a large wash-room, which is converted into a play-room during inclement weather. On the first floor of each of these buildings are two rooms for the house father and his family, and a school-room, which is also convertible into a sitting-room for the boys. On the third floor is a family dormitory, a clothes-room and a room for the " elder brother," who ranks next to the house father. And since the reception of the first boy, from Hendricks county, January 23, 1868, the house plan has proved equally convenient, even as the management has proved efficient.

Other buildings have since been erected.

THE LOG CABIN.

After arriving and selecting a suitable location, the next thing to do was to build a log cabin, a description of which may be interesting to many of our younger readers, as in some sections these old-time structures are no more to be seen. Trees of uniform size were chosen and cut into logs of the desired length, generally 12 to 15 feet, and hauled to the spot selected for the future dwelling. On an appointed day the few neighbors who were available would assemble and have a "house-raising." Each end of every log was saddled and notched so that they would lie as close down as possible; the next day the proprietor would proceed to "chink and daub" the cabin, to keep out the rain, wind and cold. The house had to be re-daubed every fall, as the rains of the intervening time would wash out a great part of the mortar. The usual height of the house was seven or eight feet. The gables were formed by shortening the logs gradually at each end of the building near the top. The roof was made by laying very straight small logs or stout poles suitable distances apart, generally about two and a half feet from gable to gable, and on these poles were laid the "clapboards" after the manner of shingling, showing about two and a half feet to the weather. These clapboards were fastened to their place by "weight-poles," corresponding in place with the joists just described, and these again were held in their place by "runs" or "knees," which were chunks of wood about 18 or 20 inches long fitted between them near the ends. Clapboards were made from the nicest oaks in the vicinity, by chopping or sawing them into four-foot blocks and riving these with a frow, which was a simple blade fixed at right angles to its handle. This was driven into the blocks of wood by a mallet. As the frow was wrenched down through the wood, the latter was turned alternately over from side to side, one end being held by a forked piece of timber.

The chimney of the Western pioneer's cabin was made by leaving in the original building a large open place in one wall, or by cutting one after the structure was up, and by building on the outside, from the ground up, a stone column, or a column of sticks and mud, the sticks being laid up cob-house fashion. The fire-place thus made was often large enough to receive fire-wood six to eight feet long. Sometimes this wood, especially the "back-log," would be nearly as large as a saw-log. The more rapidly the pioneer could burn up the wood in his vicinity the sooner he had his little farm cleared and ready for cultivation. For a window, a piece about two feet long was cut out of one of the wall logs, and the hole closed sometimes by glass, but generally with greased paper. Even greased deer-hide was sometimes used. A doorway was cut through one of the walls, if a saw was to be had; otherwise the door would be left by shortened logs in the original building. The door was made by pinning clapboards to two or three wood bars, and was hung upon wooden hinges. A wooden latch, with catch, then finished the door, and the latch was raised by any one on the outside by pulling a leather string. For security at night this latch-string was drawn in; but for friends and neighbors, and even strangers, the "latch-string was always hanging out," as a welcome. In the interior, over the fire-place would be a shelf, called "the mantel," on which stood the candlestick or lamp, some cooking and table-ware, possibly an old clock, and other articles; in the fire-place would be the crane, sometimes of iron, sometimes of wood — on it the pots were hung for cooking; over the door, in forked cleats, hung the ever trustful rifle and powder-horn; in one corner stood the larger bed for the "old folks," and under it the trundle-bed for the children; in another stood the old-fashioned spinning-wheel, with a smaller one by its side; in another the heavy table, the only table, of course, there was in the house; in the remaining corner was a rude cupboard holding the table-ware, which consisted of a few cups and saucers and blue-edged plates, standing singly on their edges against the back, to make the display of table furniture more conspicuous; while around the room were scattered a few splint-bottomed or Windsor chairs and two or three stools.

These simple cabins were inhabited by a kind and true-hearted people. They were strangers to mock modesty, and the traveler, seeking lodgings for the night, or desirous of spending a few days in the community, if willing to accept the rude offering, was always welcome, although how they were disposed of at night the reader might not easily imagine; for, as described, a single room was made to answer for kitchen, dining-room, sitting-room, bed-room and parlor, and many families consisted of six or eight members.

SLEEPING ACCOMMODATIONS.

The bed was very often made by fixing a post in the floor about six feet from one wall and four feet from the adjoining wall, and fastening a stick to this post about two feet above the floor, on each of two sides, so that the other end of each of the two sticks could be fastened in the opposite wall; clapboards were laid across these, and thus the bed was made complete. Guests were given this bed, while the family disposed of themselves in another corner of the room, or in the "loft." When several guests were on hand at once, they were sometimes kept over night in the following manner: when bed-time came the men were requested to step out of doors while the women spread out a broad bed upon the mid-floor, and put themselves to bed in the center; the signal was given and the men came in, and each husband took his place in bed next his own wife, and the single men outside beyond them again. They were generally so crowded that they had to lie "spoon" fashion, and when any one wished to turn over he would say "Spoon," and the whole company of sleepers would turn over at once. This was the only way they could all keep in bed.

COOKING.

To witness the various processes of cooking in those days would alike surprise and amuse those who have grown up since cooking stoves and ranges came into use. Kettles were hung over the large fire, suspended with pot-hooks, iron or wooden, on the crane, or on poles, one end of which would rest upon a chair. The long-handled frying-pan was used for cooking meat. It was either held over the blaze by hand or set down upon coals drawn out upon the hearth. This pan was also used for baking pan-cakes, also called "flap-jacks," "batter-cakes," etc. A better article for this, however, was the cast-iron spider or Dutch skillet. The best thing for baking bread those days, and possibly even yet in these latter days, was the flat-bottomed bake kettle, of greater depth, with closely fitting cast-iron cover, and commonly known as the "Dutch-oven." With coals over and under it, bread and biscuit would quickly and nicely bake. Turkey and spare-ribs were sometimes roasted before the fire, suspended by a string, a dish being placed underneath to catch the drippings.

Hominy and samp were very much used. The hominy, however, was generally hulled corn — boiled corn from which the hull, or bran, had been taken by hot lye; hence sometimes called "lye hominy." True hominy and samp were made of pounded corn. A popular method of making this, as well as real meal for bread, was to cut out or burn a large hole in the top of a huge stump, in the shape of a mortar, and pounding the corn in this by a maul or beetle suspended on the end of a swing pole, like a well-sweep. This and the well-sweep consisted of a pole 20 to 30 feet long, fixed in an upright fork, so that it could be worked "teeter" fashion. It was a rapid and simple way of drawing water. When the samp was sufficiently pounded it was taken out, the bran floated off, and the delicious grain boiled like rice.

The chief articles of diet in early days were corn bread, hominy or samp, venison, pork, honey, beans, pumpkin (dried pumpkin for more than half the year), turkey, prairie chicken, squirrel and some other game, with a few additional vegetables a portion of the year. Wheat bread, tea, coffee and fruit were luxuries not to be indulged in except on special occasions, as when visitors were present.

WOMEN'S WORK.

Besides cooking in the manner described, the women had many other arduous duties to perform, one of the chief of which was spinning. The "big wheel" was used for spinning yarn, and the "little wheel" for spinning flax. These stringed instruments furnished the principal music of the family, and were operated by our mothers and grandmothers with great skill, attained without pecuniary expense and with far less practice than is necessary for the girls of our period to acquire a skillful use of their costly and elegant instruments. But those wheels, indispensable a few years ago, are all now superseded by the mighty factories which overspread the country, furnishing cloth of all kinds at an expense ten times less than would be incurred now by the old system.

The loom was not less necessary than the wheel, though they were not needed in so great numbers. Not every house had a loom —

one loom had a capacity for the needs of several families. Settlers having succeeded, in spite of the wolves, in raising sheep, commenced the manufacture of woolen cloth; wool was carded and made into rolls by hand cards, and the rolls were spun on the "big wheel." We still occasionally find in the houses of old settlers a wheel of this kind, sometimes used for spinning and twisting stocking yarn. They are turned with the hand, and with such velocity that it will run itself while the nimble worker, by her backward step, draws out and twists her thread nearly the whole length of the cabin. A common article woven on the loom was linsey, or linsey-woolsey, the chain being linen and the filling woolen. The cloth was used for dresses for the women and girls. Nearly all the clothes worn by the men were also home-made; rarely was a farmer or his son seen in a coat made of any other. If, occasionally, a young man appeared in a suit of "boughten" clothes, he was suspected of having gotten it for a particular occasion, which occurs in the life of nearly every young man.

DRESS AND MANNERS.

The dress, habits, etc., of a people throw so much light upon their conditions and limitations that, in order better to show the circumstances surrounding the people of the State, we will give a short exposition of the manner of life of our Western people at different epochs. The Indians themselves are credited by Charlevoix with being "very laborious,"—raising poultry, spinning the wool of the buffalo, and manufacturing garments therefrom. These must have been, however, more than usually favorable representatives of their race.

"The working and voyaging dress of the French masses," says Reynolds, "was simple and primitive. The French were like the lilies of the valley [the Old Ranger was not always exact in his quotations],— they neither spun nor wove any of their clothing, but purchased it from the merchants. The white blanket coat, known as the *capot*, was the universal and eternal coat for the winter with the masses. A cape was made of it that could be raised over the head in cold weather.

"In the house, and in good weather, it hung behind, a cape to the blanket coat. The reason that I know these coats so well is that

I have worn many in my youth, and a working man never wore a better garment. Dressed deer-skins and blue cloth were worn commonly in the winter for pantaloons. The blue handkerchief and the deer-skin moccasins covered the head and feet generally of the French Creoles. In 1800 scarcely a man thought himself clothed unless he had a belt tied round his blanket coat, and on one side was hung the dressed skin of a pole-cat, filled with tobacco, pipe, flint and steel. On the other side was fastened, under the belt, the butcher knife. A Creole in this dress felt like Tam O'Shanter filled with usquebaugh — he could face the devil. Checked calico shirts were then common, but in winter flannel was frequently worn. In the summer the laboring men and the *voyageurs* often took their shirts off in hard work and hot weather, and turned out the naked back to the air and sun."

"Among the Americans," he adds, " home-made wool hats were the common wear. Fur hats were not common, and scarcely a boot was seen. The covering of the feet in winter was chiefly moccasins made of deer-skins and shoe-packs of tanned leather. Some wore shoes, but not common in very early times. In the summer the greater portion of the young people, male and female, and many of the old, went barefoot. The substantial and universal outside wear was the blue linsey hunting shirt. This is an excellent garment, and I have never felt so happy and healthy since I laid it off. It is made of wide sleeves, open before, with ample size so as the envelop the body almost twice around. Sometimes it had a large cape, which answers well to save the shoulders from the rain. A belt is mostly used to keep the garment close around the person, and, nevertheless, there is nothing tight about it to hamper the body. It is often fringed, and at times the fringe is composed of red, and other gay colors. The belt, frequently, is sewed to the hunting shirt. The vest was mostly made of striped linsey. The colors were made often with alum, copperas and madder, boiled with the bark of trees, in such a manner and proportions as the old ladies prescribed. The pantaloons of the masses were generally made of deer-skin and linsey. Coarse blue cloth was sometimes made into pantaloons.

"Linsey, neat and fine, manufactured at home, composed generally the outside garments of the females as well as the males.

The ladies had linsey colored and woven to suit their fancy. A bonnet, composed of calico, or some gay goods, was worn on the head when they were in the open air. Jewelry on the pioneer ladies was uncommon; a gold ring was an ornament not often seen."

In 1820 a change of dress began to take place, and before 1830, according to Ford, most of the pioneer costume had disappeared. "The blue linsey hunting-shirt, with red or white fringe, had given place to the cloth coat. [Jeans would be more like the fact.] The raccoon cap, with the tail of the animal dangling down behind, had been thrown aside for hats of wool or fur. Boots and shoes had supplanted the deer-skin moccasins; and leather breeches, strapped tight around the ankle, had disappeared before unmentionables of a more modern material. The female sex had made still greater progress in dress. The old sort of cotton or woolen frocks, spun, woven and made with their own fair hands, and striped and cross-barred with blue dye and Turkey red, had given place to gowns of silk and calico. The feet, before in a state of nudity, now charmed in shoes of calf-skin or slippers of kid; and the head, formerly unbonneted, but covered with a cotton handkerchief, now displayed the charms of the female face under many forms of bonnets of straw, silk and Leghorn. The young ladies, instead of walking a mile or two to church on Sunday, carrying their shoes and stockings in their hands until within a hundred yards of the place of worship, as formerly, now came forth arrayed complete in all the pride of dress, mounted on fine horses and attended by their male admirers."

The last half century has doubtless witnessed changes quite as great as those set forth by our Illinois historian. The chronicler of to-day, looking back to the golden days of 1830 to 1840, and comparing them with the present, must be struck with the tendency of an almost monotonous uniformity in dress and manners that comes from the easy inter-communication afforded by steamer, railway, telegraph and newspaper. Home manufactures have been driven from the houshold by the lower-priced fabrics of distant mills. The Kentucky jeans, and the copperas-colored clothing of home manufacture, so familiar a few years ago, have given place to the cassimeres and cloths of noted factories. The ready-made clothing stores, like a touch of nature, made the whole world kin, and may drape the charcoal man in a dress-coat and a stove-pipe hat. The prints and

silks of England and France give a variety of choice and an assort-
ment of colors and shades such as the pioneer women could hardly
have dreamed of.   Godey and Demorest and Harper's Bazar are
found in our modern farm-houses, and the latest fashions of Paris
are not uncommon.

FAMILY WORSHIP.

The Methodists were generally first on the ground in pioneer
settlements, and at that early day they seemed more demonstrative
in their devotions than at the present time.   In those days, too,
pulpit oratory was generally more eloquent and effective, while
the grammatical dress and other "worldly" accomplishments were
not so assiduously cultivated as at present.   But in the manner
of conducting public worship there has probably not been so much
change as in that of family worship, or "family prayers" as it was
often called.   We had then most emphatically an American edition
of that pious old Scotch practice so eloquently described in Burns'
"Cotter's Saturday Night:"

> The cheerfu' supper done, wi' serious face
>   They round the ingle formed a circle wide;
> The sire turns o'er, wi' patriarchal grace,
>   The big ha' Bible, ance his father's pride;
> His bonnet rev'rently is laid aside,
>   His lyart haffets wearing thin and bare;
> Those strains that once did in sweet Zion glide;
>   He wales a portion with judicious care,
> And "let us worship God," he says with solemn air.
>
> They chant their artless notes in simple guise;
>   They tune their hearts,—by far the noblest aim;
> Perhaps "Dundee's" wild warbling measures rise,
>   Or plaintive "Martyr's" worthy of the name;
> Or noble "Elgin" beats the heavenward flame,—
>   The sweetest far of Scotia's hallowed lays.
> Compared with these, Italian trills are tame;
>   The tickled ear no heart-felt raptures raise:
> Nae unison hae they with our Creator's praise.
>
> The priest-like father reads the sacred page,—
>   How Abraham was the friend of God on high, etc.
>
> Then kneeling down, to heaven's Eternal King
>   The saint, the father and the husband prays;
> Hope "springs exulting on triumphant wing,"
>   That thus they all shall meet in future days;

There ever bask in uncreated rays,
    No more to sigh or shed the bitter tear,
Together hymning their Creator's praise,
    In such society, yet still more dear,
    While circling time moves round in an eternal sphere.

Once or twice a day, in the morning just before breakfast, or in the evening just before retiring to rest, the head of the family would call those around him to order, read a chapter in the Bible, announce the hymn and tune by commencing to sing it, when all would join; then he would deliver a most fervent prayer. If a pious guest were present he would be called on to take the lead in all the exercises of the evening; and if in those days a person who prayed in the family or in public did not pray as if it were his very last on earth, his piety was thought to be defective.

The familiar tunes of that day are remembered by the surviving old settlers as being more spiritual and inspiring than those of the present day, such as Bourbon, Consolation, China, Canaan, Conquering Soldier, Condescension, Devotion, Davis, Fiducia, Funeral Thought, Florida, Golden Hill, Greenfields, Ganges, Idumea, Imandra, Kentucky, Lenox, Leander, Mear, New Orleans, Northfield, New Salem, New Durham, Olney, Primrose, Pisgah, Pleyel's Hymn, Rockbridge, Rockingham, Reflection, Supplication, Salvation, St. Thomas, Salem, Tender Thought, Windham, Greenville, etc., as they are named in the Missouri Harmony.

Members of other orthodox denominations also had their family prayers in which, however, the phraseology of the prayer was somewhat different and the voice not so loud as characterized the real Methodists, United Brethren, etc.

HOSPITALITY.

The traveler always found a welcome at the pioneer's cabin. It was never full. Although there might be already a guest for every puncheon, there was still "room for one more," and a wider circle would be made for the new-comer at the log fire. If the stranger was in search of land he was doubly welcome, and his host would volunteer to show him all the "first-rate claims in this neck of the woods," going with him for days, showing the corners and advantages of every "Congress tract" within a dozen miles of his own cabin.

To his neighbors the pioneer was equally liberal. If a deer was killed, the choicest bits were sent to his nearest neighbor, a half-dozen miles away, perhaps. When a "shoat" was butchered, the same custom prevailed. If a new-comer came in too late for "cropping," the neighbors would supply his table with just the same luxuries they themselves enjoyed, and in as liberal quantity, until a crop could be raised. When a new-comer had located his claim, the neighbors for miles around would assemble at the site of the new-comer's proposed cabin and aid him in "gittin'" it up. One party with axes would cut down the trees and hew the logs; another with teams would haul the logs to the ground; another party would "raise" the cabin; while several of the old men would "rive the clapboards" for the roof. By night the little forest domicile would be up and ready for a "house-warming," which was the dedicatory occupation of the house, when music and dancing and festivity would be enjoyed at full height. The next day the new-comer would be as well situated as his neighbors.

An instance of primitive hospitable manners will be in place here. A traveling Methodist preacher arrived in a distant neighborhood to fill an appointment. The house where services were to be held did not belong to a church member, but no matter for that. Boards were raked up from all quarters with which to make temporary seats, one of the neighbors volunteering to lead off in the work, while the man of the house, with the faithful rifle on his shoulder, sallied forth in quest of meat, for this truly was a "ground-hog" case, the preacher coming and no meat in the house. The host ceased not the chase until he found the meat, in the shape of a deer; returning, he sent a boy out after it, with directions on what "pint" to find it. After services, which had been listened to with rapt attention by all the audience, mine host said to his wife, "Old woman, I reckon this 'ere preacher is pretty hungry and you must git him a bite to eat." "What shall I git him?" asked the wife, who had not seen the deer; "thar's nuthin' in the house to eat." "Why, look thar," returned he; "thar's deer, and thar's plenty of corn in the field; you git some corn and grate it while I skin the deer, and we'll have a good supper for him." It is needless to add that venison and corn bread made a supper fit for any pioneer preacher, and was thankfully eaten.

TRADE.

In pioneer times the transactions of commerce were generally carried on by neighborhood exchanges. Now and then a farmer would load a flat-boat with beeswax, honey, tallow and peltries, with perhaps a few bushels of wheat or corn or a few hundred clapboards, and float down the rivers into the Ohio, and thence to New Orleans, where he would exchange his produce for substantials in the shape of groceries and a little ready money, with which he would return by some one of the two or three steamboats then running. Betimes there appeared at the best steamboat landings a number of "middle men" engaged in the "commission and forwarding" business, buying up the farmers' produce and the trophies of the chase and the trap, and sending them to the various distant markets. Their winter's accumulations would be shipped in the spring, and the manufactured goods of the far East or distant South would come back in return; and in all these transactions scarcely any money was seen or used. Goods were sold on a year's time to the farmers, and payment made from the proceeds of the ensuing crops. When the crops were sold and the merchant satisfied, the surplus was paid out in orders on the store to laboring men and to satisfy other creditors. When a day's work was done by a working man, his employer would ask, "Well, what store do you want your order on?" The answer being given, the order was written and always cheerfully accepted.

MONEY.

Money was an article little known and seldom seen among the earlier settlers. Indeed, they had but little use for it, as they could transact all their business about as well without it, on the "barter" system, wherein great ingenuity was sometimes displayed. When it failed in any instance, long credits contributed to the convenience of the citizens. But for taxes and postage neither the barter nor the credit system would answer, and often letters were suffered to remain a long time in the postoffice for the want of the twenty-five cents demanded by the Government. With all this high price on postage, by the way, the letter had not been brought 500 miles in a day or two, as the case is nowadays, but had probably been weeks on the route, and the mail was delivered at the pioneer's postoffice, several miles distant from his residence, culy once in a week or two. All the mail would be carried by a lone horseman. Instances are related illustrating how misrepresentation would be resorted to in order to elicit the sympathies of some one who was known to have "two bits" (25 cents) of money with him, and procure the required Governmental fee for a letter.

Peltries came nearer being money than anything else, as it came to be custom to estimate the value of everything in peltries. Such an article was worth so many peltries. Even some tax collectors and postmasters were known to take peltries and exchange them for the money required by the Government.

When the first settlers came into the wilderness they generally supposed that their hard struggle would be principally over after the first year; but alas! they often looked for "easier times next year" for many years before realizing them, and then they came in so slily as to be almost imperceptible. The sturdy pioneer thus learned to bear hardships, privation and hard living, as good soldiers do. As the facilities for making money were not great, they lived pretty well satisfied in an atmosphere of good, social, friendly feeling, and thought themselves as good as those they had left behind in the East. But among the early settlers who came to this State were many who, accustomed to the advantages of an older civilization, to churches, schools and society, became speedily homesick and dissatisfied. They would remain perhaps one summer, or at most two, then, selling whatever claim with its improvements they had made, would return to the older States, spreading reports of the hardships endured by the settlers here and the disadvantages which they had found, or imagined they had found, in the country. These weaklings were not an unmitigated curse. The slight improvements they had made were sold to men of sterner stuff, who were the sooner able to surround themselves with the necessities of life, while their unfavorable report deterred other weaklings from coming. The men who stayed, who were willing to endure privations, belonged to a different guild; they were heroes every one,— men to whom hardships were things to be overcome, and present privations things to be endured for the sake of posterity, and they never shrank from this duty. It is to these hardy pioneers who could endure, that we to-day owe the wonderful improvement we have made and the development, almost miraculous, that has brought our State in the past sixty years, from a wilderness, to the front rank among the States of this great nation.

MILLING.

Not the least of the hardships of the pioneers was the procuring of bread. The first settlers must be supplied at least one year from other sources than their own lands; but the first crops, however abundant, gave only partial relief, there being no mills to grind the grain. Hence the necessity of grinding by hand-power, and many families were poorly provided with means for doing this. Another way was to grate the corn. A grater was made from a piece of tin sometimes taken from an old, worn-out tin bucket or other vessel. It was thickly perforated, bent into a semicircular form, and nailed rough side upward, on a board. The corn was taken in the ear, and grated before it got dry and hard. Corn, however, was eaten in various ways.

Soon after the country became more generally settled, enterprising men were ready to embark in the milling business. Sites along the streams were selected for water-power. A person looking for a mill site would follow up and down the stream for a desired location, and when found he would go before the authorities and secure a writ of *ad quod damnum*. This would enable the miller to have the adjoining land officially examined, and the amount of damage by making a dam was named. Mills being so great a public necessity, they were permitted to be located upon any person's land where the miller thought the site desirable.

AGRICULTURAL IMPLEMENTS.

The agricultural implements used by the first farmers in this State would in this age of improvement be great curiosities. The plow used was called the " bar-share " plow; the iron point consisted of a bar of iron about two feet long, and a broad share of iron welded to it. At the extreme point was a coulter that passed through a beam six or seven feet long, to which were attached handles of corresponding length. The mold-board was a wooden one split out of winding timber, or hewed into a winding shape, in order to turn the soil over. Sown seed was brushed in by dragging over the ground a sapling with a bushy top. In harvesting the

change is most striking. Instead of the reapers and mowers of to-
day, the sickle and cradle were used. The grain was threshed with a
flail, or trodden out by horses or oxen.

HOG KILLING.

Hogs were always dressed before they were taken to market. The
farmer, if forehanded, would call in his neighbors some bright fall
or winter morning to help "kill hogs." Immense kettles of water
were heated; a sled or two, covered with loose boards or plank, constituted the platform on which the hog was cleaned, and was placed
near an inclined hogshead in which the scalding was done; a quilt
was thrown over the top of the latter to retain the heat; from a
crotch of some convenient tree a projecting pole was rigged to hold
the animals for disemboweling and thorough cleaning. When
everything was arranged, the best shot of the neighborhood loaded
his rifle, and the work of killing was commenced. It was considered a disgrace to make a hog "squeal" by bad shooting or by a
"shoulder stick," that is running the point of the butcher-knife
into the shoulder instead of the cavity of the breast. As each hog
fell, the "sticker" mounted him and plunged the butcher-knife,
long and well sharpened, into his throat; two persons would then
catch him by the hind legs, draw him up to the scalding tub, which
had just been filled with boiling-hot water with a shovelful of good
green wood ashes thrown in; in this the carcass was plunged
and moved around a minute or so, that is, until the hair would slip
off easily, then placed on the platform where the cleaners would
pitch into him with all their might and clean him as quickly as
possible, with knives and other sharp-edged implements; then two
stout fellows would take him up between them, and a third man to
manage the "gambrel" (which was a stout stick about two feet long,
sharpened at both ends, to be inserted between the muscles of the
hind legs at or near the hock joint), the animal would be elevated to
the pole, where the work of cleaning was finished.

After the slaughter was over and the hogs had had time to cool,
such as were intended for domestic use were cut up, the lard "tried"
out by the women of the household, and the surplus hogs taken
to market, while the weather was cold, if possible. In those
days almost every merchant had, at the rear end of his place of

business or at some convenient building, a "pork-house," and would buy the pork of his customers and of such others as would sell to him, and cut it for the market. This gave employment to a large number of hands in every village, who would cut and pack pork all winter. The hauling of all this to the river would also give employment to a large number of teams, and the manufacture of pork barrels would keep many coopers employed.

Allowing for the difference of currency and manner of marketing, the price of pork was not so high in those days as at present. Now, while calico and muslin are eight cents a yard and pork is five and six cents a pound, then, while calico and muslin were twenty-five cents a yard pork was one to two cents a pound. When, as the country grew older and communications easier between the seaboard and the great West, prices went up to two and a half and three cents a pound, the farmers thought they would always be content to raise pork at such a price; but times have changed, even contrary to the current-cy.

There was one feature in this method of marketing pork that made the country a paradise for the poor man in the winter time. Spare-ribs, tenderloins, pigs' heads and pigs' feet were not considered of any value, and were freely given to all who could use them. If a barrel was taken to any pork-house and salt furnished, the barrel would be filled and salted down with tenderloins and spare-ribs gratuitously. So great in many cases was the quantity of spare-ribs, etc., to be disposed of, that they would be hauled away in wagon-loads and dumped in the woods out of town.

In those early times much wheat was marketed at twenty-five to fifty cents a bushel, oats the same or less, and corn ten cents a bushel. A good young milch-cow could be bought for $5 to $10, and that payable in work.

Those might truly be called "close times," yet the citizens of the country were accommodating, and but very little suffering for the actual necessities of life was ever known to exist.

PRAIRIE FIRES.

Fires, set out by Indians or settlers, sometimes purposely and sometimes permitted through carelessness, would visit the prairies every autumn, and sometimes the forests, either in autumn or spring, and settlers could not always succeed in defending themselves against the destroying element. Many interesting incidents are related. Often a fire was started to bewilder game, or to bare a piece of ground for the early grazing of stock the ensuing spring, and it would get away under a wind, and soon be beyond control. Violent winds would often arise and drive the flames with such rapidity that riders on the fleetest steeds could scarcely escape. On the approach of a prairie fire the farmer would immediately set about "cutting off supplies" for the devouring enemy by a "back fire." Thus, by starting a small fire near the bare ground about his premises, and keeping it under control next his property, he would burn off a strip around him and prevent the attack of the on-coming flames. A few furrows or a ditch around the farm constituted a help in the work of protection.

An original prairie of tall and exuberant grass on fire, especially at night, was a magnificent spectacle, enjoyed only by the pioneer. Here is an instance where the frontiersman, proverbially deprived of the sights and pleasures of an old community, is privileged far beyond the people of the present day in this country. One could scarcely tire of beholding the scene, as its awe-inspiring features seemed constantly to increase, and the whole panorama unceasingly changed like the dissolving views of a magic lantern, or like the aurora borealis. Language cannot convey, words cannot express, the faintest idea of the splendor and grandeur of such a conflagration at night. It was as if the pale queen of night, disdaining to take her accustomed place in the heavens, had dispatched myriads upon myriads of messengers to light their torches at the altar of the setting sun until all had flashed into one long and continuous blaze.

The following graphic description of prairie fires was written by a traveler through this region in 1849:

"Soon the fires began to kindle wider and rise higher from the long grass; the gentle breeze increased to stronger currents, and soon fanned the small, flickering blaze into fierce torrent flames, which curled up and leaped along in resistless splendor; and like quickly raising the dark curtain from the luminous stage, the scenes before me were suddenly changed, as if by the magician's wand, into one boundless amphitheatre, blazing from earth to heaven and sweeping the horizon round,—columns of lurid flames sportively mounting up to the zenith, and dark clouds of crimson smoke curling away and aloft till they nearly obscured stars and moon, while the rushing, crashing sounds, like roaring cataracts mingled with distant thunders, were almost deafening; danger, death, glared all around; it screamed for victims; yet, notwithstanding the imminent peril

of prairie fires, one is loth, irresolute, almost unable to withdraw
or seek refuge."

WILD HOGS.

When the earliest pioneer reached this Western wilderness, game
was his principal food until he had conquered a farm from the
forest or prairie,—rarely, then, from the latter. As the country
settled game grew scarce, and by 1850 he who would live by his
rifle would have had but a precarious subsistence had it not been
for "wild hogs." These animals, left by home-sick immigrants
whom the chills or fever and ague had driven out, had strayed into
the woods, and began to multiply in a wild state. The woods each
fall were full of acorns, walnuts, hazelnuts, and these hogs would
grow fat and multiply at a wonderful rate in the bottoms and along
the bluffs. The second and third immigration to the country found
these wild hogs an unfailing source of meat supply up to that
period when they had in the townships contiguous to the river become so numerous as to be an evil, breaking in herds into the
farmer's corn-fields or toling their domestic swine into their
retreats, where they too became in a season as wild as those in the
woods. In 1838 or '39, in a certain township, a meeting was called
of citizens of the township to take steps to get rid of wild hogs. At
this meeting, which was held in the spring, the people of the township were notified to turn out *en masse* on a certain day and engage
in the work of catching, trimming and branding wild hogs, which
were to be turned loose, and the next winter were to be hunted and
killed by the people of the township, the meat to be divided *pro
rata* among the citizens of the township. This plan was fully
carried into effect, two or three days being spent in the exciting
work in the spring.

In the early part of the ensuing winter the settlers again turned
out, supplied at convenient points in the bottom with large kettles
and barrels for scalding, and while the hunters were engaged in
killing, others with horses dragged the carcasses to the scalding
platforms where they were dressed; and when all that could be
were killed and dressed a division was made, every farmer getting
more meat than enough, for his winter's supply. Like energetic
measures were resorted to in other townships, so that in two or
three years the breed of wild hogs became extinct.

NATIVE ANIMALS.

The principal wild animals found in the State by the early set-
tler were the deer, wolf, bear, wild-cat, fox, otter, raccoon, generally
called "coon," woodchuck, or ground-hog, skunk, mink, weasel,
muskrat, opossum, rabbit and squirrel; and the principal feathered
game were the quail, prairie chicken and wild turkey. Hawks,
turkey buzzards, crows, blackbirds were also very abundant. Several of these animals furnished meat for the settlers; but their
principal meat did not long consist of game; pork and poultry
were raised in abundance. The wolf was the most troublesome
animal, it being the common enemy of the sheep, and sometimes
attacking other domestic animals and even human beings. But
their hideous howlings at night were so constant and terrifying
that they almost seemed to do more mischief by that annoyance
than by direct attack. They would keep everbody and every animal about the farm-house awake and frightened, and set all the dogs
in the neighborhood to barking. As one man described it: "Suppose six boys, having six dogs tied, whipped them all at the same
time, and you would hear such music as two wolves would make."

To effect the destruction of these animals the county authorities
offered a bounty for their scalps; and, besides, big hunts were
common.

WOLF HUNTS.

In early days more mischief was done by wolves than by any
other wild animal, and no small part of their mischief consisted in
their almost constant barking at night, which always seemed so
menacing and frightful to the settlers. Like mosquitoes, the
noise they made appeared to be about as dreadful as the real depredations they committed. The most effectual, as well as the most
exciting, method of ridding the country of these hateful pests, was
that known as the "circular wolf hunt," by which all the men and
boys would turn out on an appointed day, in a kind of circle comprising many square miles of territory, with horses and dogs, and
then close up toward the center of their field of operation, gathering not only wolves, but also deer and many smaller "varmint."
Five, ten, or more wolves by this means would sometimes be killed
in a single day. The men would be organized with as much
system as a little army, every one being well posted in the meaning
of every signal and the application of every rule. Guns were
scarcely ever allowed to be brought on such occasions, as their use

would be unavoidably dangerous. The dogs were depended upon for the final slaughter. The dogs, by the way, had all to be held in check by a cord in the hands of their keepers until the final signal was given to let them loose, when away they would all go to the center of battle, and a more exciting scene would follow than can be easily described.

BEE-HUNTING.

This wild recreation was a peculiar one, and many sturdy back-woodsmen gloried in excelling in this art. He would carefully watch a bee as it filled itself with the sweet product of some flower or leaf-bud, and notice particularly the direction taken by it as it struck a "bee-line" for its home, which when found would be generally high up in the hollow of a tree. The tree would be marked, and in September a party would go and cut down the tree and capture the honey as quickly as they could before it wasted away through the broken walls in which it had been so carefully stowed away by the little busy bee. Several gallons would often be thus taken from a single tree, and by a very little work, and pleasant at that, the early settlers could keep themselves in honey the year round. By the time the honey was a year old, or before, it would turn white and granulate, yet be as good and healthful as when fresh. This was by some called "candid" honey.

In some districts, the resorts of bees would be so plentiful that all the available hollow trees would be occupied and many colonies of bees would be found at work in crevices in the rock and holes in the ground. A considerable quantity of honey has even been taken from such places.

SNAKES.

In pioneer times snakes were numerous, such as the rattlesnake, viper, adder, blood snake and many varieties of large blue and green snakes, milk snake, garter and water snakes, black snakes, etc., etc. If, on meeting one of these, you would retreat, they would chase you very fiercely; but if you would turn and give them battle, they would immediately crawl away with all possible speed, hide in the grass and weeds, and wait for a "greener" customer. These really harmless snakes served to put people on their guard against the more dangerous and venomous kinds.

It was the practice in some sections of the country to turn out in companies, with spades, mattocks and crow-bars, attack the principal snake dens and slay large numbers of them. In early spring the snakes were somewhat torpid and easily captured. Scores of rattlesnakes were sometimes frightened out of a single den, which, as soon as they showed their heads through the crevices of the rocks, were dispatched, and left to be devoured by the numerous wild hogs of that day. Some of the fattest of these snakes were taken to the house and oil extracted from them, and their glittering skins were saved as specifics for rheumatism.

Another method was to so fix a heavy stick over the door of their dens, with a long grape-vine attached, that one at a distance could plug the entrance to the den when the snakes were all out sunning themselves. Then a large company of the citizens, on hand by appointment, could kill scores of the reptiles in a few minutes.

SHAKES.

One of the greatest obstacles to the early settlement and prosperity of this State was the "chills and fever," "fever and ague," or "shakes," as it was variously called. It was a terror to newcomers; in the fall of the year almost everybody was afflicted with it. It was no respecter of persons; everybody looked pale and sallow as though he were frost-bitten. It was not contagious, but derived from impure water and air, which are always developed in the opening up of a new country of rank soil like that of the Northwest. The impurities continue to be absorbed from day to day, and from week to week, until the whole body corporate became saturated with it as with electricity, and then the shock came; and the shock was a regular shake, with a fixed beginning and ending, coming on in some cases each day but generally on alternate days, with a regularity that was surprising. After the shake came the fever, and this "last estate was worse than the first." It was a burning-hot fever, and lasted for hours. When you had the chill you couldn't get warm, and when you had the fever you couldn't get cool. It was exceedingly awkward in this respect; indeed it was. Nor would it stop for any sort of contingency; not even a wedding in the family would stop it. It was imperative and tyrannical. When the appointed time came around, everything else had to be stopped to attend to its demands. It didn't even have any Sundays or holidays; after the fever went down you still didn't feel much better. You felt as though you had gone through some sort of collision, thrashing-machine or jarring-machine, and came out not killed, but next thing to it. You felt weak, as though you had run too far after something, and then didn't catch it. You felt languid, stupid and sore, and was down in the mouth and heel and partially raveled out. Your back was out of fix, your head ached and your appetite crazy. Your eyes had too much white in them, your ears, especially after taking quinine, had too much roar in them, and your whole body and soul were entirely woe-begone, disconsolate, sad, poor and good for nothing. You didn't think much of yourself, and didn't believe that other people did, either; and you didn't care. You didn't quite make up your mind to commit suicide, but sometimes wished some accident would happen to knock either the malady or yourself out of existence. You imagined that even the dogs looked at you with a kind of self-complacency. You thought the sun had a kind of sickly shine about it.

About this time you came to the conclusion that you would not accept the whole Western country as a gift; and if you had the strength and means, you picked up Hannah and the baby, and your traps, and went back "yander" to "Old Virginny," the "Jarseys," Maryland or "Pennsylvany."

> "And to-day the swallows flitting
> Round my cabin see me sitting
> Moodily within the sunshine,
>   Just inside my silent door,
> Waiting for the 'Ager,' seeming
> Like a man forever dreaming;
> And the sunlight on me streaming
>   Throws no shadow on the floor;
> For I am too thin and sallow
> To make shadows on the floor—
>   Nary shadow any more!"

The above is not a mere picture of the imagination. It is simply recounting in quaint phrase what actually occurred in thousands of cases. Whole families would sometimes be sick at one time and not one member scarcely able to wait upon another. Labor or exercise always aggravated the malady, and it took General Laziness a long time to thrash the enemy out. And those were the days for swallowing all sorts of roots and "yarbs," and whisky, etc., with some faint hope of relief. And finally, when the case wore out, the last remedy taken got the credit of the cure.

EDUCATION.

Though struggling through the pressure of poverty and privation, the early settlers planted among them the school-house at the earliest practical period. So important an object as the education of their children they did not defer until they could build more comely and convenient houses. They were for a time content with such as corresponded with their rude dwellings, but soon better buildings and accommodations were provided. As may readily be supposed, the accommodations of the earliest schools were not good. Sometimes school was taught in a room of a large or a double log cabin, but oftener in a log house built for the purpose. Stoves and such heating apparatus as are now in use were then unknown. A mud-and-stick chimney in one end of the building, with earthen hearth and a fire-place wide and deep enough to receive a four to six-foot back-log, and smaller wood to match, served for warming purposes in winter and a kind of conservatory in summer. For windows, part of a log was cut out in two sides of the building, and may be a few lights of eight by ten glass set in, or the aperture might be covered over with greased paper. Writing desks consisted of heavy oak plank or a hewed slab laid upon wooden pins driven into the wall. The four-legged slab benches were in front of these, and the pupils when not writing would sit with their backs against the front, sharp edge of the writing-desks. The floor was also made out of these slabs, or "puncheons," laid upon log sleepers. Everything was rude and plain; but many of America's greatest men have gone out from just such school-houses to grapple with the world and make names for themselves and reflect honor upon their country. Among these we can name Abraham Lincoln, our martyred president, one of the noblest men known to the world's history. Stephen A. Douglas, one of the greatest statesmen of the age, began his career in Illinois teaching in one of these primitive school-houses. Joseph A. Wright, and several other statesmen of the Northwest have also graduated from the log school-house into political eminence. So with many of her most eloquent and efficient preachers.

The chief public evening entertainment for the first 30 or 40 years of Western pioneering was the celebrated "spelling-school." Both young people and old looked forward to the next spelling-school with as much anticipation and anxiety as we nowadays look forward to a general Fourth-of-July celebration; and when the time arrived the whole neighborhood, yea, and sometimes several neighborhoods, would flock together to the scene of academical combat, where the excitement was often more intense than had been expected. It was far better, of course, when there was good sleighing; then the young folks would turn out in high glee and be fairly beside themselves. The jollity is scarcely equaled at the present day by anything in vogue.

When the appointed hour arrived, the usual plan of commencing battle was for two of the young people who might agree to play against each other, or who might be selected to do so by the school-teacher of the neighborhood, to "choose sides," that is, each contestant, or "captain," as he was generally called, would choose the best speller from the assembled crowd. Each one choosing alternately, the ultimate strength of the respective parties would be about equal. When all were chosen who could be made to serve, each side would "number," so as to ascertain whether amid the confusion one captain had more spellers than the other. In case he had, some compromise would be made by the aid of the teacher, the master of ceremonies, and then the plan of conducting the campaign, or counting the misspelled words, would be canvassed for a moment by the captains, sometimes by the aid of the teacher and others. There were many ways of conducting the contest and keeping tally. Every section of the country had several favorite methods, and all or most of these were different from what other communities had. At one time they would commence spelling at the head, at another time at the foot; at one time they would "spell across," that is, the first on one side would spell the first word, then the first on the other side; next the second in the line on each side, alternately, down to the other end of each line. The question who should spell the first word was determined by the captains guessing what page the teacher would have before him in a partially opened book at a distance; the captain guessing the nearest would spell the first word pronounced. When a word was missed, it would be re-pronounced, or passed along without re-pronouncing (as some teachers strictly followed the rule never to re-pronounce a word), until it was spelled correctly. If a speller on the opposite side finally spelled the missed word correctly, it was counted a gain of one to that side; if the word was finally corrected by some speller on the same side on which it was originated as a missed word, it was "saved," and no tally mark was made.

Another popular method was to commence at one end of the line of spellers and go directly around, and the missed words caught up quickly and corrected by "word-catchers," appointed by the captains from among their best spellers. These word-catchers would attempt to correct all the words missed on his opponent's side, and failing to do this, the catcher on the other side would catch him up with a peculiar zest, and then there was fun.

Still another very interesting, though somewhat disorderly, method, was this: Each word-catcher would go to the foot of the adversary's line, and every time he "catched" a word he would go up one, thus "turning them down" in regular spelling-class style. When one catcher in this way turned all down on the opposing side, his own party was victorious by as many as the opposing catcher was behind. This method required no slate or blackboard tally to be kept.

One turn, by either of the foregoing or other methods, would occupy 40 minutes to an hour, and by this time an intermission or recess was had, when the buzzing, cackling and hurrahing that ensued for 10 or 15 minutes were beyond description.

Coming to order again, the next style of battle to be illustrated was to "spell down," by which process it was ascertained who were the best spellers and could continue standing as a soldier the longest But very often good spellers would inadvertently miss a word in an early stage of the contest and would have to sit down humiliated, while a comparatively poor speller would often stand till nearly or quite the last, amid the cheers of the assemblage. Sometimes the two parties first "chosen up" in the evening would re-take their places after recess, so that by the "spelling-down" process there would virtually be another race, in another form; sometimes there would be a new "choosing up" for the "spelling-down" contest; and sometimes the spelling down would be conducted without any party lines being made. It would occasionally happen that two or three very good spellers would retain the floor so long that the exercise would become monotonous, when a few outlandish words like "chevaux-de-frise," "Ompompanoosuc" or "Baughnaugh-claugh-ber," as they used to spell it sometimes, would create a little ripple of excitement to close with. Sometimes these words would decide the contest, but generally when two or three good spellers kept the floor until the exercise became monotonous, the teacher would declare the race closed and the standing spellers acquitted with a " drawn game."

The audience dismissed, the next thing was to " go home," very often by a round-about way, " a-sleighing with the girls," which, of course, was with many the most interesting part of the evening's performances, sometimes, however, too rough to be commended, as the boys were often inclined to be somewhat rowdyish.

SINGING-SCHOOL.

Next to the night spelling-school the singing-school was an occasion of much jollity, wherein it was difficult for the average singing-master to preserve order, as many went more for fun than for music. This species of evening entertainment, in its introduction to the West, was later than the spelling-school, and served, as it were, as the second step toward the more modern civilization. Good sleighing weather was of course almost a necessity for the success of these schools, but how many of them have been prevented by mud and rain! Perhaps a greater part of the time from November to April the roads would be muddy and often half frozen, which would have a very dampening and freezing effect upon the souls, as well as the bodies, of the young people who longed for a good time on such occasions.

The old-time method of conducting singing-school was also somewhat different from that of modern times. It was more plodding and heavy, the attention being kept upon the simplest rudiments, as the names of the notes on the staff, and their pitch, and beating time, while comparatively little attention was given to expression and light, gleeful music. The very earliest scale introduced in the West was from the South, and the notes, from their peculiar shape, were denominated " patent " or " buckwheat " notes. They were four, of which the round one was always called *sol*, the square one *la*, the triangular one *fa*, and the "diamond-shaped " one *mi*, pronounced *me*; and the diatonic scale, or " gamut " as it was called then, ran thus: *fa*, *sol*, *la*, *fa*, *sol*, *la*, *mi*, *fa*. The part of a tune nowadays called " treble," or " soprano," was then called " tenor;" the part now called " tenor " was called " treble," and what is now " alto " was then "counter," and when sung according to the oldest rule, was sung by a female an octave higher than marked, and still on the " chest register." The " old " " Missouri Harmony " and Mason's " Sacred Harp " were the principal books used with this style of musical notation.

About 1850 the " round-note " system began to " come around," being introduced by the Yankee singing-master. The scale was *do, re, mi, fa, sol, la, si, do*; and for many years thereafter there was much more do-re-mi-ing than is practiced at the present day, when a musical instrument is always under the hand. The Carmina Sacra was the pioneer round-note book, in which the tunes partook more of the German or Puritan character, and were generally regarded by the old folks as being far more spiritless than the old " Pisgah," " Fiducia," " Tender Thought," " New Durham," " Windsor," " Mount Sion," " Devotion," etc., of the old Missouri Harmony and tradition.

GUARDING AGAINST INDIANS.

The fashion of carrying fire-arms was made necessary by the presence of roving bands of Indians, most of whom were ostensibly friendly, but like Indians in all times, treacherous and unreliable. An Indian war was at any time probable, and all the old settlers still retain vivid recollections of Indian massacres, murders, plunder, and frightful rumors of intended raids. While target practice was much indulged in as an amusement, it was also necessary at times to carry their guns with them to their daily field work.

As an illustration of the painstaking which characterized pioneer life, we quote the following from Zebulon Collings, who lived about six miles from the scene of massacre near Pigeon Roost, Indiana: " The manner in which I used to work in those perilous times was as follows: On all occasions I carried my rifle, tomahawk and butcher-knife, with a loaded pistol in my belt. When I went to plow I laid my gun on the plowed ground, and stuck up a stick by it for a mark, so that I could get it quick in case it was wanted. I had two good dogs; I took one into the house, leaving the other out. The one outside was expected to give the alarm, which would cause the one inside to bark, by which I would be awakened, having my arms always loaded. I kept my horse in a stable close to the house, having a port-hole so that I could shoot to the stable door. During two years I never went from home with any certainty of returning, not knowing the minute I might receive a ball from an unknown hand."

THE BRIGHT SIDE.

The history of pioneer life generally presents the dark side of the picture; but the toils and privations of the early settlers were not a series of unmitigated sufferings. No; for while the fathers and mothers toiled hard, they were not averse to a little relaxation, and had their seasons of fun and enjoyment. They contrived to do something to break the monotony of their daily life and furnish them a good hearty laugh. Among the more general forms of amusements were the "quilting-bee," "corn-husking," "apple-paring," "log-rolling" and "house-raising." Our young readers will doubtless be interested in a description of these forms of amuse- ment, when labor was made to afford fun and enjoyment to all par- ticipating. The "quilting-bee," as its name implies, was when the industrious qualities of the busy little insect that "improves each shining hour" were exemplified in the manufacture of quilts for the household. In the afternoon ladies for miles around gathered at an appointed place, and while their tongues would not cease to play, the hands were as busily engaged in making the quilt; and desire as always manifested to get it out as quickly as possible, for then the fun would begin. In the evening the gentlemen came, and the hours would then pass swiftly by in playing games or dancing. "Corn-huskings" were when both sexes united in the work. They usually assembled in a large barn, which was arranged for the oc- casion; and when each gentleman had selected a lady partner the husking began. When a lady found a red ear she was entitled to a kiss from every gentleman present; when a gentleman found one he was allowed to kiss every lady present. After the corn was all husked a good supper was served; then the "old folks" would leave, and the remainder of the evening was spent in the dance and in having a general good time. The recreation afforded to the young people on the annual recurrence of these festive occasions was as highly enjoyed, and quite as innocent, as the amusements of the present boasted age of refinement and culture.

The amusements of the pioneers were peculiar to themselves. Saturday afternoon was a holiday in which no man was expected to work. A load of produce might be taken to "town" for sale or traffic without violence to custom, but no more serious labor could be tolerated. When on Saturday afternoon the town was reached, "fun commenced." Had two neighbors business to transact, here it was done. Horses were "swapped." Difficulties settled and free fights indulged in.   Blue and red ribbons were not worn in those days, and whisky was as free as water; twelve and a half cents would buy a quart, and thirty-five or forty cents a gallon, and at such prices enormous quantities were consumed. Go to any town in the county and ask the first pioneer you meet, and he would tell you of notable Saturday-afternoon fights, either of which to-day would fill a column of the *Police News*, with elaborate engravings to match.

Mr. Sandford C. Cox quaintly describes some of the happy feat-tures of frontier life in this manner:

We cleared land, rolled logs, burned brush, blazed out paths from one neighbor's cabin to another and from one settlement to another, made and used hand-mills and hominy mortars, hunted deer, turkey, otter, and raccoons, caught fish, dug ginseng, hunted bees and the like, and—lived on the fat of the land. We read of a land of "corn and wine," and another "flowing with milk and honey;" but I rather think, in a temporal point of view, taking into account the richness of the soil, timber, stone, wild game and other advantages, that the Sugar creek country would come up to any of them, if not surpass them.

I once cut cord-wood, continues Mr. Cox, at 31¼ cents per cord, and walked a mile and a half night and morning, where the first frame college was built northwest of town (Crawfordsville). Prof. Curry, the lawyer, would sometimes come down and help for an hour or two at a time, by way of amusement, as there was little or no law business in the town or country at that time. Reader, what would you think of going six to eight miles to help roll logs, or raise a cabin? or ten to thirteen miles to mill, and wait three or four days and nights for your grist? as many had to do in the first settlement of this country. Such things were of frequent oc-currence then, and there was but little grumbling about it. It was a grand sight to see the log heaps and brush piles burning in the night on a clearing of 10 or 15 acres. A Democratic torchlight procession, or a midnight march of the Sons of Malta with their grand Gyasticutus in the center bearing the grand jewel of the order, would be nowhere in comparison with the log-heaps and brush piles in a blaze.

But it may be asked, Had you any social amusements, or manly pastimes, to recreate and enliven the dwellers in the wilderness? We had. In the social line we had our meetings and our singing-schools, sugar-boilings and weddings, which were as good as ever

what would you think of going six to eight miles to help roll logs,
or raise a cabin? or ten to thirteen miles to mill, and wait three
or four days and nights for your grist? as many had to do in the
first settlement of this country. Such things were of frequent
occurrence then, and there was but little grumbling about it. It
was a grand sight to see the log heaps and brush piles burning
in the night on a clearing of 10 or 15 acres. A Democratic
torchlight procession, or a midnight march of the Sons of Malta
with their grand Gyasticutus in the center bearing the grand
jewel of the order, would be nowhere in comparison with the
log-heaps and brush-piles in a blaze.

But it may be asked, Had you any social amusements, or manly
pastimes, to recreate and enliven the dwellers in the wilderness?
We had. In the social line we had our meetings and our singing-
schools, sugar-boilings and weddings, which were as good as ever
came off in any country, new or old; and if our youngsters did
not "trip the light fantastic toe" under a professor of the Terp-
sichorean art or expert French dancing master, they had many a
good "hoe-down" on puncheon floors, and were not annoyed by bad
whisky. And as for manly sports, requiring mettle and muscle,
there were lots of wild hogs running in the cat-tail swamps on Lye
creek, and Mill creek, and among them many large boars that
Ossian's heroes and Homer's model soldiers, such as Achilles, Hec-
tor and Ajax would have delighted to give chase to. The boys and
men of those days had quite as much sport, and made more money
and health by their hunting excursions than our city gents nowadays playing chess by telegraph where the players are more than
70 miles apart.

WHAT THE PIONEERS HAVE DONE.

There are few of these old pioneers living as connecting
links of the past with the present. What must their thoughts
be as with their dim eyes they view the scenes that surround them?
We often hear people talk about the old-fogy ideas and fogy ways,
and want of enterprise on the part of the old men who have gone
through the experiences of pioneer life. Sometimes, perhaps,
such remarks are just, but, considering the experiences, education
and entire life of such men, such remarks are better unsaid.
They have had their trials, misfortunes, hardships and adventures,

and shall we now, as they are passing far down the western declivity of life, and many of them gone, point to them the finger of derision, and laugh and sneer at the simplicity of their ways? Let us rather cheer them up, revere and respect them, for beneath those rough exteriors beat hearts as noble as ever throbbed in the human breast. These veterans have been compelled to live for weeks upon hominy and, if bread at all, it was bread made from corn ground in hand-mills, or pounded up with mortors. Their children have been destitute of shoes during the winter; their families had no clothes except what was carded, spun, wove and made into garments by their own hands; schools they had none; churches they had none; afflicted with sickness incident to all new countries, sometimes the entire family at once; luxuries of life they had none; the auxiliaries, improvements, inventions and labor-saving machinery of to-day they had not; and what they possessed they obtained by the hardest of labor and individual exertion, yet they bore these hardships and privations without murmuring, hoping for better times to come, and often, too, with but little prospect of realization.

As before mentioned, the changes written on every hand are most wonderful. It has been but three-score years since the white man began to exercise dominion over this region, erst the home of the red men, yet the visitor of to-day, ignorant of the past of the country, could scarcely be made to realize that within these years there has grown up a population of 2,000,000 people, who in all the accomplishments of life are as far advanced as are the inhabitants of the older States. Schools, churches, colleges, palatial dwellings, beautiful grounds, large, well-cultivated and productive farms, as well as cities, towns and busy manufactories, have grown up, and occupy the hunting grounds and camping places of the Indians, and in every direction there are evidences of wealth, comfort and luxury. There is but little left of the old landmarks. Advanced civilization and the progressive demands of revolving years have obliterated all traces of Indian occupancy, until they are only remembered in name.

BIOGRAPHICAL SKETCHES.

ARTHUR ST. CLAIR, one of the most noted public characters of our early colonial days, was a native of Scotland, being born at Edinburg, in 1735. Becoming a surgeon in the British army, he subsequently crossed the Atlantic with his regiment and thenceforward was identified with the history of this country until the day of his death. Serving as a lieutenant with Wolfe in the memorable campaign against Quebec, St. Clair won sufficient reputation to obtain appointment as commander of Fort Ligonier, Pennsylvania, where a large tract of land was granted to him. During the Revolutionary war he espoused the colonial cause, and before its close had risen to the rank of major general. In 1785 he was elected a delegate to the Continental congress, and afterward became its president. After the passage of the ordinance of 1787, St. Clair was appointed first military governor of the Northwest Territory, with headquarters at Fort Washington, now Cincinnati. In 1791 he undertook an expedition against the northwestern Indians, which resulted in the great disaster known in western history as "St. Clair's defeat." On the 4th of November, the Indians surprised and routed his whole force of about 1,400 regulars and militia, in what is now Darke county, Ohio, killing over 900 men and capturing his artillery and camp equipage. General St. Clair held the office of territorial governor until 1802, when he was removed by President Jefferson. He returned to Ligonier, Penn., poor, aged and infirm. The state granted him an annuity which enabled him to pass the last years of life in comfort. He died near Greensburgh, Penn., August 31st, 1818, leaving a family of one son and three daughters.

WILLIAM HENRY HARRISON, first governor of Indiana, and ninth president of the United States, was a native of Virginia, born in the town of Berkeley, Charles City Co., February 9, 1773. His father, Benjamin Harrison, whose signature is affixed to the Declaration of Independence, was a man of note in the early days of Virginia, of which state he was twice elected governor. William Henry Harrison received a classic education at Hampden Sydney college, and subsequently began the study of medicine, which he soon abandoned to join the military force then being raised to repel the Indian aggression on the frontier. He joined his regiment at Fort Washington, Ohio, was soon appointed lieutenant, and afterward joined the new army under Gen. Anthony Wayne. He was made aid-de-camp to the commanding officer, whom he greatly assisted by his advice concerning an expedition to the Miami, and in 1797, was made captain, and given the command of Fort Washington. While in command of this fort he was married to Anna Symmes, daughter of John Cleves Symmes, the original owner of the land occupied by the city of Cincinnati. In 1798 he resigned his commission and retired to his farm near the Ohio river, from which he was almost immediately recalled by President Madison, who tendered him the position of secretary of the Northwest Territory, by virtue of which he became *ex-officio* lieutenant governor. One year later he was elected a delegate to congress, in which body he distinguished himself by the introduction of measures to facilitate the easier acquirement of land by the early settlers. During the session, part of the Northwest Territory was formed into the territory of Indiana, including the present states of Indiana, Illinois, Michigan and Wisconsin, and Harrison was made its governor and superintendent of Indian affairs — a deserved compliment to his energy and ability. Resigning his seat in congress, Mr. Harrison at once removed to Vincennes, the territorial capital, and entered upon the duties of his office which he discharged with such signal ability that he was re-appointed successively by Presidents Jefferson and Monroe. He organized the legislature in 1805, and applied himself especially to improving the condition of the Indians, in his relations with whom his powers were most completely shown. He pursued a conciliatory course, held frequent councils with them, and although his life was frequently endangered, he succeeded in averting many outbreaks. In July, 1810, he held his celebrated council with Tecumseh, at Vincennes, in the progress of which a bloody conflict was averted by the coolness and skillful tactics of the general. In the following spring depredations by the savages were frequent, and the governor sent word to the chief that unless they should cease the Indians would be punished. In July, 1811, a second council was held, the result of which promised much for the peace of the settlers, but subsequently being convinced of Tecumseh's insincerity, Gen. Harrison proceeded to establish a military fort near Tippecanoe, an Indian village on the upper Wabash. In September, 1811, Harrison with a force of 900 men, marched from Vincennes, and after completing Fort Harrison, near the present site of Terre Haute, pressed forward toward the prophet's town, where, on November 7, was fought the murderous battle of Tippecanoe, which resulted in a signal victory for the Americans, and crippled for a time the power of the red men in the territory. In the battle of the Thames, and the defense of Fort Meigs, Harrison, who had been appointed to the command of the northwest army, by President Monroe, distinguished himself, but he resigned before the close of the war in consequence of difference of opinion with the secretary of war. In 1816 he was elected a member of congress, in 1824, United States senator from Ohio, and in 1828, was appointed minister to Columbia, by President Adams. In 1836 he made the race for the presidency in opposition to Martin Van Buren, and was defeated. In 1840 he was triumphantly elected president of the United States, after one of the most animated and exciting campaigns in the history of the country, the effect of which was too much for his strength, and he died within one month after his inauguration, before any distinctive features of his administration could be seen. His death occurred on the 4th day of April, 1841.

THOMAS POSEY, the last governor of Indiana territory, was born near Alexandria, Va., on the 9th of July, 1750. His educational training was limited, being confined to the branches taught in the different schools of those days. In 1774 he took part in the expedition originated by Governor Dunmore, of Virginia, against the Indians, and was present at the battle of Mt. Pleasant. At the close of this war Mr. Posey went back to his home in Virginia, but did not long pursue his peaceful avocations, being called upon the following year, to take the part of the colonies in their struggle for liberty against the mother country. He participated in the battle of Bemis Heights, as captain in Col. Morgan's command, in 1779 was colonel of the Eleventh Virginia regiment, and afterward commanded a battery under Gen. Wayne. He bore a gallant part in the storming of Stony Point, was at the capitulation of Cornwallis at Yorktown, and continued in the service some time after peace was declared. In 1793, he was appointed brigadier general in the army of the Northwest, and being pleased with the appearance of the country, settled in Kentucky not long after. In that state he was a member of the state senate, being president of the body from November 4, 1805, to November 3, 1806, performing the duties of lieutenant governor at the same time. He removed to Louisiana in 1812, and afterward represented the state in the senate of the United States. While a resident of Louisiana he was appointed governor of Indiana territory, by President Madison, and in May, 1813, he moved to Vincennes, and entered upon the discharge of his official duties. When his term as governor expired by reason of the admission of Indiana into the Union, Col. Posey was appointed Indian agent for Illinois Territory, with headquarters at Shawneetown, where his death occurred March 19, 1818.

JONATHAN JENNINGS, the first governor of Indiana, was born in Hunterdon county, N. J., in the year 1784. His father, a Presbyterian clergyman, moved to Pennsylvania shortly after Jonathan's birth, in which state the future governor received his early educational training and grew to manhood. He early began training himself for the legal profession, but before his admission to the bar he left Pennsylvania, and located at Jeffersonville, Ind., where he completed his preparatory study of the law, and became a practitioner in the courts of that and other towns in the territory. He was subsequently made clerk of the Territorial legislature, and while discharging the duties of that position, became a candidate for congress, against Thomas Randolph, attorney general of the territory. The contest between the two was exciting and bitter, the principal question at issue being slavery, which Mr. Randolph opposed, while his competitor was a firm believer in the divine right of the institution. Jennings was elected by a small majority. He was re-elected in 1811, over Walter Taylor, and in 1813 was chosen the third time, his competitor in the last race being Judge Sparks, a very worthy and popular man. Early in 1816, Mr. Jennings reported a bill to congress, enabling the people of the territory to take the necessary steps to convert it into a state. Delegates to a convention to form a state constitution were elected in May, 1816, Mr. Jennings being chosen one from the county of Clark. He was honored by being chosen to preside over this convention, and in the election which followed he was elected governor of the new state by a majority of 1,277 votes over his competitor, Gov. Posey. In this office he served six years, also acting as Indian commissioner in 1818 by appointment of President Monroe. At the close of his term as governor he was elected representative in congress, and was chosen for four terms in succession. He was nearly always in public life and filled his places acceptably. He died near Charleston, July 26, 1834.

RATLIFF BOON, who became governor of Indiana upon the resignation of Jonathan Jennings, September 12, 1822, was born in the state of Georgia, January 18, 1781. While he was young his father emigrated to Kentucky, settling in Warren county. Ratliff Boon learned the gunsmith trade in Danville, Ky., and in 1809 came to Indiana and settled on the present site of Boonville, in what is now Warrick county. In the organization of this county he took a prominent part, was elected its first treasurer, in the session of 1816–17 he was a member of the house of representatives, and in 1818 was elected to the state senate. In 1819 he was elected lieutenant governor on the ticket with Jonathan Jennings, whom he succeeded as stated above. He was re-elected to the office of lieutenant governor in 1822, but resigned that office in 1824, to become a candidate for congress, to which he was elected in August of the same year. He was re-elected in 1829–1831–1833–1835 and in 1837, serving most of the time as chairman of the committee of public lands. In 1836 he was a candidate for United States senator, but was defeated by Oliver H. Smith. His congressional career ended March, 1839, and a few months afterward he removed to Missouri, settling in Pike county. In that state Gov. Boon became active in public affairs, and was one of the leading men of the state. Placing himself in antagonism to Col. Thomas H. Benton, who then controlled the politics of Missouri, he incurred the latter's deadly enmity. He again became a candidate for congress in 1844, but his death on November 20th of that year put an end to his earthly career. Mr. Boon was a pioneer of two states and left the impress of his character upon both.

WILLIAM HENDRICKS, governor of Indiana from 1822 to 1825, was born at Ligonier, Westmoreland Co., Penn., in 1783. His parents were Abraham and Ann (Jamison) Hendricks, descendants from old families of New Jersey. William Hendricks was educated at Cannonsburg, Penn., and shortly after his graduation in 1810, went to Cincinnati, Ohio, where he studied law in the office of Mr. Carry, supporting himself in the meantime by teaching school. In 1814 he removed to Indiana, and located at Madison, which continued to be his home during the rest of his life. He began the practice of law at Madison, where he was also identified with journalism for some time, and shortly after his removal to the state he was made secretary of the Territorial legislature at Vincennes. In June, 1816, he was appointed secretary of the constitutional convention, and in August of the same year was elected as the first and sole representative to congress from the newly created state, serving three successive terms. He discharged the duties of his high position with so much acceptability that at the end of his third term, in 1822, he was elected governor of the state without opposition. Before the expiration of his term as governor, the legislature elected him a senator of the United States, and on February 12, 1825, he filed his resignation as governor. In 1831 he was re-elected, and at the expiration of this term, in 1837, he retired to private life and never afterward took upon himself the cares of public office. In 1840 he was one of the state electors on the Van Buren ticket, and it was during the campaign of that year that he contracted a disease from which he suffered the remainder of his life. Gov. Hendricks was a man of imposing appearance. He was six feet in height, handsome in face and figure, and had a ruddy complexion. He was easy in manner, genial and kind in disposition, and was a man who attracted the attention of all and won the warm friendship of many. He was brought up in the Presbyterian faith, early united with that church, and lived a consistent, earnest, Christian through life. The *Indiana Gazette*, of 1850, has the following mention of him: "Gov. Hendricks was for many years by far the most popular man in the state. He had been its sole representative in congress for six years, elected on each occasion by large majorities, and no member of that body, probably, was more attentive to the interests of the state he represented, or more industrious in arranging all the private or local business intrusted to him. He left no letter unanswered, no public office or document did he fail to visit or examine on request; with personal manners very engaging, he long retained his popularity." He died May 16, 1850.

JAMES BROWN RAY, governor of Indiana, was born in Jefferson county, Ky., February 19, 1794. Early in life he went to Cincinnati, Ohio, and after studying law in that city he was admitted to the bar. He began the practice at Brookville, Ind., where he soon ranked among the ablest and most influential of an able and ambitious bar. In 1822 he was elected to the legislature. On the 30th of

January, 1824, Lieut. Gov. Ratliff Boon resigned his office, and Mr. Ray was elected president *pro tempore* of the senate, and presided during the remainder of the session. He was governor of the state from 1825 to 1831, and during this time was appointed United States commissioner with Lewis Cass and John Tipton, to negotiate a treaty with the Miami and Pottawatomie Indians. The constitution of the state prevented the governor from holding any office under the United States government, in consequence of which he became involved in a controversy. He remembered the difficulty Jonathan Jennings had encountered under like circumstances, and sought to avoid trouble by acting without a regular commission, but his precaution did not save him from trouble. Through his exertions the Indians gave land to aid in building a road from Lake Michigan to the Ohio river. Gov. Ray was active in promoting railroad concentration in Indianapolis, and took an active part in the internal improvement of the state. At the expiration of his term of office he resumed the practice of law, and in 1837 was candidate for congress in the Indianapolis district, but was defeated by a large majority. This want of appreciation by the public soured him, and in later years he became very eccentric. In 1848, while at Cincinnati, he was taken with the cholera, which terminated in his death, August 4, of that year. In person, Gov. Ray in his younger days was very prepossessing. He was tall and straight, with a body well proportioned. He wore his hair long and tied in a queue. His forehead was broad and high, and his features denoted intelligence of a high order. For many years he was a leading man of Indiana, and no full history of the state can be written without a mention of his name.

NOAH NOBLE, fourth governor of Indiana, was born in Clark county, Va., January 15, 1794. When a small boy he was taken by his parents to Kentucky, in which state he grew to manhood. About the time Indiana was admitted into the Union, Mr. Noble came to the state, and located at Brookville, where a few years later he was elected sheriff of Franklin county. In 1824 he was chosen a representative to the state legislature from Franklin county, in which body he soon became quite popular and gained a state reputation. In 1826 he was appointed receiver of public moneys to succeed his brother Lazarus Noble, who died while moving the office from Brookville to Indianapolis, in which capacity he continued with great acceptability until his removal in 1829, by President Jackson.

4

In 1830 he was appointed one of the commissioners to locate and lay out the Michigan road. In 1831 he was a candidate for governor, and although a whig, and the democracy had a large majority in the state, he was elected by a majority of 2,791. This was remarkable, for Milton Stapp, also a whig, was a candidate, and polled 4,422 votes. In 1834 Gov. Noble was a candidate for re-election, when he was also successful, defeating his competitor, James G. Reed, by 7,662 votes. In 1839, after his gubernatorial term had expired, he was elected a member of the board of internal improvements. In 1841 he was chosen a fund commissioner, and the same year was offered by the president of the United States, the office of general land commissioner, which he declined. Gov. Noble died at his home near Indianapolis, February 8, 1844. Governor Noble had a laudable ambition to go to the United States senate, and in 1836 was a candidate to succeed William Hendricks, but was defeated by Oliver H. Smith. In 1839 he was again a candidate to succeed Gen. John Tipton, but was defeated by Albert S. White on the thirty-sixth ballot. Oliver H. Smith says that Gov. Noble " was one of the most popular men with the masses in the state. His person was tall and slim, and his constitution delicate, his smile winning, his voice feeble, and the pressure of his hand irresistible. He spoke plainly and well, but made no pretence to oratory. As governor he was very popular, and his social entertainments will long be remembered."

DAVID WALLACE, governor of Indiana from 1837 to 1840, was a native of Mifflin county, Penn., born April 24, 1799. He removed with his father to Brookville, Ind., when quite young, and in early manhood began the study of law in the office of Miles Eggleston, a distinguished jurist of that day. In 1823 he was admitted to the bar and soon obtained a large practice. He served in the legislature from 1828 to 1830, and in 1831 was elected lieutenant governor of Indiana, and re-elected in 1834. In 1837 he was elected governor over John Dumont, an able and distinguished lawyer, who lived at Vevay, on the southern border of the state. During his periods of service as legislator and lieutenant governor, he was active as an advocate of internal improvements and in establishing a school system, and he was elected governor upon those issues. In 1841 he was elected to congress from the Indianapolis district, defeating Col. Nathan B. Palmer. As a member of the committee on commerce he gave the casting vote in favor of an appropriation to develop

Col. S. T. B. Morse's magnetic telegraph, which vote had great weight in defeating him for re-election in 1843. At the expiration of his term in congress he resumed the practice of law which he continued uninterruptedly until 1850, when he was elected a delegate to the constitutional convention from the county of Marion. In 1856 he was elected judge of the court of common pleas, which position he held until his death on the 4th of September, 1859. Gov. Wallace was twice married. His first wife was a daughter of John Test, and his second a daughter of John H. Sanders. The latter still lives and is prominent in reformatory and religious work. When a young man, Gov. Wallace had a well proportioned body, but in his later years its symmetry was marred by an undue amount of flesh. He had black hair, dark eyes, and a ruddy complexion. He was cultured and well-bred, his address was good and his manners unexceptionable. He was a laborious and impartial jurist, a painstaking executive, and as an orator had few equals in the nation.

SAMUEL BIGGER, who succeeded David Wallace as governor of Indiana, was born in Warren county, Ohio, March 20, 1802, and was the eldest son of John Bigger, a western pioneer, and for many years a member of the Ohio legislature. He was prepared for college in his own neighborhood, graduated with honors from the University of Athens, and afterward began the study of law. In 1829 he removed to Liberty, Ind., where he was duly admitted to the bar, and soon secured a lucrative practice. He remained at Liberty but a short time, removing thence to Rushville, where his public life began in 1834 as representative of Rush county, in the state legislature. He was re-elected in 1835, and shortly after the expiration of his term was chosen judge of the eastern circuit, a position for which he proved himself ably qualified, and which he held in an acceptable manner for many years. In 1840 he was nominated for governor by the whig state convention, and after an exciting race was elected, defeating Gen. Tilghman A. Howard. He was a candidate for re-election in 1843, but was defeated by James Whitcomb. After the expiration of his gubernatorial term Gov. Bigger moved to Fort Wayne. Ind., and resumed the practice of law; which he continued until his death, September 9, 1845. "Gov. Bigger possessed talents of a high order, rather substantial than brilliant. His judgment was remarkably sound, dispassionate and discriminating, and it was this chiefly that made him eminently a leader in every circle in which he moved, whether in political life, at the bar, or society at large." He was a man of fine form and presence. He was six feet two inches in height and weighed 240 pounds. His hair was black, his eyes a blue hazel, and his complexion dark. The expression of his face was kind and benignant, and denoted goodness of heart. He was a patriotic citizen, an incorruptible judge, and an executive officer of very respectable ability.

JAMES WHITCOMB was born near Windsor, Vt., December 1, 1795. His father removed to Ohio, and settled near Cincinnati, when James was quite young, and it was there upon a farm that the youthful years of the future governor and senator were passed. He received a classical education at Transylvania university, subsequently studied law, and in March, 1822, was admitted to the bar in Lexington, Fayette Co., Ky. Two years later he came to Indiana, and located at Bloomington, where he soon became known as an able advocate and successful practitioner. In 1826 he was appointed prosecuting attorney of his circuit, and in the discharge of the duties of this office, traveled over a large scope of country, and became acquainted with many leading men of the state. In 1820 and 1830 he was elected to the state senate, where he did much to stay the progress of the internal improvement fever which was then at its highest point. In October, 1836, President Jackson appointed Mr. Whitcomb commissioner of the general land office, to which he was re-appointed by President Van Buren, and served as such until the expiration of the latter's term of office. Early in 1841, he returned to Indiana and resumed the practice of law in Terre Haute, where he soon acquired a large and lucrative business. He was at that time one of the best known and most popular members of his party, and at the democratic state convention of 1843, he was nominated for governor of the state. His opponent was Samuel Bigger, whom he defeated by a majority of 2,013 votes. Three years afterward he was re-elected, beating Joseph G. Marshall, the whig candidate, by 3,958 votes. When he became governor he found the state loaded down with debt, upon which no interest had been paid for years, but when he left the office the debt was adjusted and the state's credit restored. He also, by his efforts, created a public sentiment that demanded the establishment of benevolent and reformatory institutions, and he awakened the people to the importance of establishing common schools, and providing a fund for their maintenance. During his term of office he raised five regiments of infantry that represented the state in the war with Mexico. The legislature of 1849 elected Gov. Whitcomb to the senate of the United States, for which high position he was well qualified by talent, by education and by experience. Owing to feeble health he was unable to discharge his senatorial duties as he wished, and he died from a painful disease when he had served little more than half his term. In 1843 he wrote a pamphlet entitled, " Facts for the People," the most effective treatise against protective tariff ever known. As a lawyer, Mr. Whitcomb ranked among the ablest in the country, and as governor will always be remembered as one of the ablest of the distinguished men who have occupied that position. Gov. Whitcomb was compactly and strongly built; he was somewhat above the average size of man; he had a dark complexion and black hair. His features were good and expressive, and his manners the most elegant. He was a talented and an honest man, and when the roll of Indiana's great men is made up, among the first in the list will be the name of Whitcomb.

PARIS C. DUNNING was born in Guilford county, N. C., in March, 1806, but emigrated to Indiana with his mother and elder brother, and located at Bloomington in 1823. He studied law and was admitted to practice about 1830. In 1833 he was elected to represent Monroe county, in the state legislature, and was three times re-elected. In 1836 he was elected to the state senate from Monroe and Brown counties, and remained there until 1840, when he voluntarily retired. He was chosen as a democratic presidential elector in 1844, and during the campaign exhibited extraordinary energy and ability as a public speaker. In 1846 he was elected lieutenant governor on the democratic ticket, and when Gov. Whitcomb was elected to the United States senate, Mr. Dunning succeeded him as governor. Alter his retirement in 1850, he practiced his profession for many years, having meantime declined a nomination for congress. In 186) he was a delegate to the Charleston and Baltimore national conventions, where he distinguished himself as an earnest advocate of the nomination of Stephen A. Douglas, and subsequently worked assiduously for that statesman's election to the presidency. At the breaking out of the rebellion in 1861, Mr. Dunning identified himself with the Union cause, and throughout the war rendered valiant aid to the country. In 1861 he was elected to the state senate without distinction of party. Subsequently he was elected twice as president of the senate. Governor Dunning was twice married, first to Miss Sarah Alexander, and the second time to Mrs. Ellen D. Ashford. Ex-Gov. Dunning takes high rank as one of the self-made men of Indiana, and he filled the many positions of honor and trust conferred upon him with great credit to himself and to the entire satisfaction of the citizens of Indiana.

JOSEPH A. WRIGHT, for seven years governor of Indiana, was born in Washington, Penn., April 17, 1810. In 1819 his family moved to Bloomington, Ind., where he and his two brothers assisted their father at work in a brickyard, and in the brick business generally. In 1822 his father died and he, then fourteen years of age, having but little if any aid from others, was left to depend entirely upon his own resources. He attended school, and college about two years, and while at college was janitor, rang the bell and took care of the buildings. It is said that what little pocket money he had was made by gathering walnuts and hickory nuts in the fall and selling them to students in the winter. He subsequently studied law with Craven P. Hester, of Bloomington, and began the practice of his profession in 1829, at Rockville, Park county, where he met with good success from the start. In 1833 he was elected to the state legislature, and in 1840, the year of the Harrison political tornado, was chosen a member of the state senate. He was also elected district attorney for two terms in 1836 and 1837, and later was appointed by President Polk, United States commissioner to Texas. In 1843 he was elected to congress from the Seventh district, over Edward McGaughey, by three majority, and served until Polk was inaugurated March 4, 1845. In 1849 he was elected governor of Indiana, under the old constitution, and in 1852, was re-elected by over 20,000 majority, and served until 1857. In the summer of the latter year he was appointed minister to Prussia, by James Buchanan, and as such served until 1861. In 1862 he was appointed by Gov. Morton United States senator, and sat in the senate until the next January. He was appointed commissioner to the Hamburg exposition in 1863, and in 1865 went again to Prussia as United States minister, and remained there until his death, which occurred at Berlin, March 11, 1867. Gov. Wright will be best remembered as governor of Indiana, his services in the general assembly, senate and congress being too brief for him to make much impression in any of those bodies. As governor he was an important factor in shaping legislation and moulding public opinion. He was an orthodox democrat of the straightest sect, stood high in the councils of his party, and contested with Jesse D. Bright for the leadership, but without success. He was strong with the people but weak with the leaders. In personal appearance Gov. Wright was tall and raw-boned. He had a large head and an unusually high forehead. His hair was light and thin, his eyes blue, and his nose and mouth large and prominent. He was an effective speaker, mainly on account of his earnestness and simplicity. While not the greatest man in the state, he was one of the most influential; and to his honor be it said, his influence was exercised for the public good. Economy and honesty in public life, and morality and religion in private station, had in him an advocate and an exemplar.

ASHBEL PARSONS WILLARD was born October 31, 1820, at Vernon, Oneida Co., N. Y., the son of Col. Erastus Willard, at one time sheriff of Oneida county. He pursued his preparatory studies in the Oneida Liberal Institute, and when eighteen years of age entered Hamilton college in the class of 1842. After graduating from that institution he studied law for some time with Judge Baker, of his native county, and later emigrated to Michigan, locating in the town of Marshall, where he remained for over a year. He then made a trip to Texas on horseback, and on his return stopped at Carrollton, Ky., and there taught school. After this he taught for some time near Louisville, but subsequently left the school room for the political arena. In the contest for the presidency in 1844, between Clay and Polk, young Willard began stumping for the latter, and during the campaign made a speech in New Albany, Ind , which made such a favorable impression that many of the first men of the town solicited him to come and settle among them. He soon afterward located in New Albany, which place remained his home until his death. He at once opened a law office but was compelled to encounter a very able bar, in consequence of which his practice for some time was by no means lucrative. The first office he held was that of common councilman. He took pride in the place and won the good opinion of the people irrespective of party. In 1850 he was elected to the state legislature, and from that time until his death he occupied a conspicuous place in the public mind. Such was his career in the legislature that when the democratic convention of 1852 convened the delegates were met by an overwhelming public sentiment demanding the nomination of Willard for lieutenant governor. The demand was recognized and the nomination made. He filled this office until 1856, when he was elected governor, after a very bitter and exciting political contest. In the summer of 1860, his health gave way, and he went to Minnesota in quest of health, which he did not find, but died there on October 4th of that year. Gov. Willard was the first governor of Indiana to die in office. The people, without respect to party, paid homage to his remains, and a general feeling of the most profound sorrow was felt at his untimely taking off. " In person Gov. Willard was very prepossessing. His head and face were cast in finest moulds, his eyes were blue, his hair auburn, and his complexion florid. A more magnetic and attractive man could nowhere be found, and had he lived to the allotted age of mankind he must have reached still higher honors."

ABRAM ADAMS HAMMOND, who succeeded to the governorship on the death of A. P. Willard, by virtue of his office of lieutenant governor, was a native of Vermont, born in the town of Brattleboro, March 21, 1814. He came to Indiana when six years of age, and was raised near Brookville, where he began the study of law in the office of John Ryman, a lawyer of note in that town. He was admitted to the bar in 1835, moved to Columbus, Bartholomew Co., in 1840, where he was afterward chosen prosecuting attorney, an office which he filled with more than ordinary ability. In 1846 he became a resident of Indianapolis, and the following year removed to Cincinnati, Ohio. He returned to Indianapolis in 1849, and in 1850 was chosen first judge of the common pleas court of Marion county. In 1852 he emigrated to California, and for some time practiced his profession in San Francisco. He soon returned to his adopted state, locating at Terre Haute, where he resided until his election as lieutenant governor in 1852. He made a most excellent presiding officer of the senate, his rulings being so fair and his decisions so just that even his political opponents bestowed encomiums upon him. On the death of Gov. Willard, in 1860, Mr. Hammond became governor, and as such served with dignity until the inauguration of Gov. Lane, January, 1861. Governor Hammond was not a showy man, but he was an able one. He possessed an analytic and logical mind, and was remarkably clear in stating his positions when drawing conclusions. When in his prime he was a fine specimen of physical manhood. He was of medium height, compactly built, and of dark complexion. His head was large and well shaped, while the expression of his countenance was kind and gentle. Frank in manners, honorable in his dealings and dignified in deportment, he commanded the esteem of all with whom he came in contact. Although not one of the most learned governors of Indiana, he was by nature one of the ablest.

CONRAD BAKER, governor of Indiana from 1867 to 1873, was born in Franklin county, Penn., February 12, 1817. He was educated at the Pennsylvania college, Gettysburg. and read law at the office of Stevens and Smyser, and was admitted to the bar in the spring of 1839, at Gettysburg, where he had a lucrative practice for two years. He came to Indiana in 1841, and settled at Evansville, where he practiced his profession until after the commencement of the rebellion. He was elected to the lower house of the general assembly of Indiana in 1845, and served one session, elected judge of the district composed of the counties of Vanderburg and Warrick, in 1852, in which capacity he served about one year, when he resigned. In 1856 he was nominated for lieutenant governor by the republican party without his knowledge, on the ticket with Oliver P. Morton. They were defeated by Willard and Hammond. In 1861 Mr. Baker was commissioned colonel of the First cavalry regiment of Indiana volunteers, which he organized, and with which he served until September, 1864, in which year he was elected lieutenant governor. In 1865 Gov. Morton convened the general assembly in special session, and immediately after delivering his message, started for Europe in quest of health leaving Col. Baker in charge of the executive department of the state government. Gov. Morton was absent five months, during which time the duties of the executive office were performed by Lieut. Gov. Baker. In February, 1867, Gov. Morton was elected to the senate of the United States, in consequence of which the duties of governor devolved upon Mr. Baker. He was unanimously nominated by the republican convention of 1868, for governor, and was elected over Thomas A. Hendricks, by a majority of 961 votes. He served as governor with ability and dignity, until the inauguration of Mr. Hendricks in 1873, since which time he has been engaged in the practice of law in Indianapolis, being a member of one of the strongest and most widely known firms in the state.

OLIVER PERRY MORTON, Indiana's great war governor and United States senator, was born in Saulsbury, Wayne Co., Ind., August 4, 1823. The family name was originally Throckmorton, and was so written by the grandfather, who emigrated from England, about the beginning of the revolutionary war and 'settled in New Jersey. Gov. Morton's father was James T. Morton, a native of New Jersey, who moved in an early day to Wayne county, Ind., where he married the mother of Oliver P., whose maiden name was Sarah Miller. Of the early life of Gov. Morton but little is known. When a boy he attended the academy of Prof. Hoshour, at Centerville, but owing to the poverty of the family, he was taken from school, and at the age of fifteen, with an older brother, began learning the hatter's trade. After working at his trade a few years, he determined to fit himself for the legal profession, and with this object in view he entered the Miami university in 1843, where he pursued his studies vigorously for a period of two years. While in college he earned the reputation of being the best debater at the institution, and it was here that he developed those powers of ready analysis and argument which made him so celebrated in after life. He began his professional reading in the office of Judge Newman, of Centerville, and after his admission to the bar was not long in rising to an eminent place among the successful lawyers of Indiana. In 1852 he was elected circuit judge, but resigned at the end of one year and afterward increased his knowledge of the profession by an attendance at a Cincinnati law school. On resuming the practice the number of his friends and legal cases rapidly increased, and his reputation soon extended beyond the limits of his own state. As a lawyer he possessed the faculty of selecting the salient points of a case and getting at the heart of a legal question. His mind was massive and logical, and he could apply great principles to given cases, discard nonessentials and reach decisive points. Mr. Morton's political career was of such a brilliant character that his great achievements in the arena of statesmanship, his wonderful power as an organizer, won for him a recognition from the strongest opponents, and faith in his powers, and the lasting fealty and admiration of thousands of friends until he reached the highest point among the great American statesmen. Up to his thirty-first year, Mr. Morton was a democrat. The county in which he lived was largely whig, thus virtually precluding him from holding elective offices. He was opposed to the extension of slavery, however, and upon the organization of the republican party, he entered the movement, and in 1856 was one of the three delegates from Indiana, to the Pittsburgh convention. His prominence was such that in 1856 he was unanimously nominated by the new party for governor of Indiana, against Ashbel P. Willard, an able and brilliant speaker, the superior of Mr. Morton as an orator, but his inferior as a logician and debater. These two distinguished men canvassed the state together, and drew immense crowds. The speeches of Willard were florid, eloquent and spirit stirring, while Mr. Morton's style was earnest, convincing and forcible. He never appealed to men's passions, but always to their intellect and reason, and whether in attack or defense, proved himself a ready and powerful debater. Although beaten at the polls, he came out of the contest with his popularity increased, and with the reputation of being one of the ablest public men in the state. In 1860 he was nominated for lieutenant governor on the ticket with Hon. Henry S. Lane, with the understanding that if successful he should go to the senate, and Mr. Morton become governor. He made a vigorous canvass, and the result of the election was a republican success, which placed Mr. Lane in the senate, and Mr. Morton in the gubernatorial chair. From the day of his inauguration Mr. Morton gave evidence of possessing extraordinary executive ability. It was while filling this term as governor that he did his best public work and created for himself a fame as lasting as that of his state. A great civil war was breaking out when he became governor, and few so well comprehended what would be its magnitude as he. He was one of the first to foresee the coming storm of battle, and most active in his preparations to meet it. Perceiving the danger of a dilatory policy, he visited Washington soon after the inauguration of President Lincoln, to advise vigorous action and to give assurance of Indiana's support to such a policy. He commenced preparing for the forthcoming conflict, and when Sumter was fired on, April 12, 1861, h neither surprised nor appalled. Three days after the attack, President Lincoln called for 75,000 men to put down the rebellion, and the same day Gov. Morton sent him the following telegram:

" INDIANAPOLIS, April 15, 1861.

"To ABRAHAM LINCOLN, *President of the United States.* — On behalf of the state of Indiana, I tender to you, for the defense of the nation, and to uphold the authority of the government, ten thousand men.

" OLIVER P. MORTON,

" Governor of Indiana."

In seven days from the date of this offer over three times the number of men required to fill Indiana's quota of the president's call, offered their services to the country. Never in the world's history did the people of a state respond more cheerfully and more enthusiastically to the call of duty, than did the people of Indiana in 1861. · This record of the state, which Mr. Morton was instrumental in planning, reflects imperishable honor on his name, and from that time forth he was known throughout the nation as the " Great War Governor." During the entire period of the war he performed an incredible amount of labor, counseling the president, encouraging the people, organizing regiments, hurrying troops to the field, forwarding stores, and inspiring all with the enthusiasm of his own earnestness. His labors for the relief of the soldiers, and their dependent and needy families, were held up as matters of emulation by the governors of other states, and the result of his efforts seconded by the people was that. during the war over $600,000 of moneys and supplies were collected and conveyed to Indiana soldiers in camp, field, hospital and prison. The limits of a sketch like this forbid a detailed account of Gov. Morton's public acts. He displayed extraordinary industry and ability, and in his efforts in behalf of the soldier justly earned the title of " The Soldiers' Friend." The legislature of 1862 was not in accord with the political views of Gov. Morton, and it refused to receive his message, and in other ways treated him with want of consideration and respect. It was on the point of taking from him the command of the militia, when the republican members withdrew, leaving both houses without a quorum. In order to carry on the state government and pay the state bonds he obtained advances from banks and county boards, and appointed a bureau of finance, which for two years made all disbursements of the state, amounting to more than $1,000,000. During this period he refused to summon the legislature, and the supreme court condemned his arbitrary course, but the people subsequently applauded his action. By assuming great responsibilities he kept the machinery of the state in motion and preserved the financial credit of the commonwealth by securing advances through an eastern banking house to pay the interest on the public debt. In 1864 he was again nominated for governor against Hon. Joseph E. McDonald, whom he defeated by an overwhelming majority. These two distinguished men made a joint canvass of the state, and passed through it with the utmost good feeling. In 1865 Gov. Morton received a partial paralytic stroke, affecting the lower part of his body, so that he never walked afterward without the use of canes. His mind, however, was in no wise affected by the shock, but continued to grow stronger while he lived. In January, 1867, he was elected to the United States senate, and immediately thereafter resigned the governorship to Conrad Baker, who served the remainder of the gubernatorial term. In 1873 he was re-elected to the senate and continued a leading member of that body while he lived. In the senate he ranked among the ablest members, was chairman of the committee on privileges and elections, was the acknowledged leader of the republicans, and for several years exercised a determining influence over the course of the party. He labored zealously to secure the passage of the fifteenth amendment, was active in the impeachment proceedings against Andrew Johnson, and was the trusted adviser of the republicans of the south. In the national republican convention of 1876, he received next to the highest number of ballots for the presidential nomination, and in 1877 was a member of the celebrated electoral commission. In 1870 President Grant offered Senator Morton the English mission, which was declined. After visiting Oregon in the spring of 1877, as chairman of a committee to investigate the election of Senator Grover, of that state, he suffered another stroke of paralysis, which terminated in his death, November 1st, of the same year. The death of no man with the exception of President Lincoln, ever created so much grief in Indiana, as did that of Senator Morton, and he was mourned almost as much throughout the entire nation. On the 17th of the next January, Mr. McDonald offered in the senate a series of resolutions in relation to Senator Morton's death, which were unanimously adopted. In speaking of these resolutions, Mr. McDonald said: "Naturally combative and aggressive, intensely in earnest in his undertakings, and intolerant in regard to those who differed with him. it is not strange that while he held together his friends and followers with hooks of steel, he caused many whose patriotism and love of country were as sincere and unquestioned as his own, to place themselves in political hostility to him. That Oliver P. Morton was a great man is conceded by all. In regard to his qualities as a statesman, men do differ now and always will. But that he was a great partisan leader — the greatest of his day and generation — will hardly be questioned, and his place in that particular field will not, perhaps, be soon supplied." Senator Burnside said: "Morton was a great man. His judgment was good, his power of research was great, his integrity

was high, his patriotism was lofty, his love of family and friends unlimited; his courage indomitable." The following is from Senator
Edmonds: "He was a man of strong passions and great talents, and
as a consequence a devoted partisan. In the field in which his
patriotism was exerted it may be said of him as it was of the Knights
of St. John in the holy wars, ' In the fore front of every battle was
seen his burnished mail and in the gloomy rear of every retreat was
heard his voice of constancy and courage.'" The closing speech
upon the adoption of the resolutions was made by his successor,
D. W. Voorhees who used the following: "Senator Morton was
without doubt a very remarkable man. His force of character cannot be over estimated. His will power was simply tremendous. He
threw himself into all his undertakings with that fixedness of purpose
and disregard of obstacles which are always the best guarantees of
success. This was true of him whether engaged in a lawsuit, organizing troops during the war, conducting a political campaign, or a de-
bate in the senate. The same daring, aggressive policy characterized
his conduct everywhere."

HENRY SMITH LANE, for two days governor of Indiana, was born
February 24, 1811, in Montgomery county, Ky. He secured a good
practical education, and at the age of eighteen, commenced the study
of law. Soon after attaining his majority, he was admitted to the
bar, and in 1835, came to Indiana and located at Crawfordsville where
he soon obtained a good legal practice. His winning manners made
him very popular with the people, and in 1837, he was elected to
represent Montgomery county in the state legislature. In 1840 he
was a candidate for congress against Edward A. Hannegan, whom
he defeated by 1,500 votes. He was re-elected the next year over
John Bryce, and as a national representative, ranked with the ablest
of his colleagues. He took an active part in the presidential campaign of 1844, and made a brilliant canvass throughout Indiana for
his favorite candidate, Henry Clay. On the breaking out of the
Mexican war, Mr. Lane at once organized a company, was chosen
captain, and later, became major and lieutenant colonel of the regiment, and followed its fortunes until mustered out of service. In
1858 Col. Lane was elected to the United States senate, but owing to
opposition on the part of democratic senators, he did not take his
seat. On February 27, 1860, he was nominated by acclamation for

governor, and was elected over Hon. Thomas A. Hendricks by a majority of about 10,000 votes. Two days after the delivery of his first message, Gov. Lane was elected to the senate of the United States. He at once resigned the governorship, the shortest term in that office on record in Indiana. In the senate, Mr. Lane did not attain any great distinction, as it was not the place for the exercise of his peculiar talents as an orator, which were better suited to the hustings than to a dignified legislative body. When Col. Lane's senatorial term expired, he returned to his home in Crawfordsville, and never afterward held public office except the appointment of Indian commissioner, by Pres. Grant. He was chosen president of the first national convention that assembled in 1856, and nominated John C. Fremont. It is worthy of note that every nomination ever conferred upon him was by acclamation and without opposition in his party. In person, Col. Lane was tall, slender and somewhat stoop shouldered. His face was thin and wore a kindly expression. In his later days, the long beard he wore was white as snow. He moved quickly, and his bearing was that of a cultured man. He departed this life at his home in Crawfordsville, on the 18th day of June, 1881.

THOMAS A. HENDRICKS was the son of Major John Hendricks, and the grandson of Abraham Hendricks, a descendant of the Huguenots, who emigrated to New Jersey and thence to Pennsylvania, prior to the revolution. Abraham Hendricks was a man of remarkable force of character. He was elected to the Pennsylvania assembly first in 1792, and served four terms, the last ending in 1798. William Hendricks, second governor of Indiana, preceded his brother John in moving to this state from Ohio, and had gained much notoriety as a talented and public man when Major John finally concluded to risk his fortune in the wilds of the new west. John Hendricks, prior to 1829, resided with his family at Zanesville, Ohio. His wife, whose maiden name was Jane Thompson, and a niece, were the only members of the Thompson family who emigrated west, the others remaining in Pennsylvania and other eastern states, where some of them gained enviable reputations in law, medicine, politics and ministry. Shortly after their marriage John Hendricks and wife moved to Muskingum, Ohio, where they lived for some time in a rude log house, one story, one room, one door and two windows, built of round logs and chinked and daubed after the pioneer fashion. In this little domicile were born two sons, Abraham and Thomas A.

The last named, Thomas A., was born September 7, 1819. The next year, 1820, lured by the brilliant career of William Hendricks, heretofore spoken of, Major John Hendricks with his little family, removed to Madison, Ind., then the metropolis of the state. Two years later the family removed to Shelby county, at that time a wilderness, and settled on the present site of Shelbyville. Here the father commenced to erect a house and carve a career for their hopeful son, then scarcely three years of age. A dwelling was soon constructed, trees felled, and a farm opened, and the Hendricks house early became a favorite stopping place for all who saw fit to accept its hospitalities. The future vice president received his early educational training in the schools of Shelbyville, and among his first teachers was the wife of Rev. Eliphalet Kent, a lady of excellent culture, fine education, graceful, and nobly consecrated to the Master, to whom Mr. Hendricks was largely indebted for much of his training and success. Having completed his course in the common schools, he entered Hanover college in 1836, where he remained for the greater part of the time until 1841. On leaving college he returned to Shelbyville, and commenced the study of law in the office of Stephen Major, then a young lawyer of brilliant attainments, and considerable tact and experience. In 1843 Mr. Hendricks went to Chambersburg, Penn., where he entered the law school, in which Alexander Thompson was instructor, a man of distinguished ability, extensive learning, and much experience as judge of the sixteenth judicial district of that state. After eight months' arduous work in this institution, he returned to Shelbyville, passed an examination, and was the same year admitted to the bar. His first case was before Squire Lee, his opponent being Nathan Powell, a young acquaintance who had opened an office about the same time. The cause was a trivial one, yet the young attorneys worked hard and with the vim of old practitioners for their respective clients. Mr. Hendricks won, and after complimenting Mr. Powell upon his effort, he gracefully served the apples which had been generously furnished by an enthusiastic spectator. Thus started the young advocate who was destined to become one of the nation's greatest and most beloved statesmen. In 1843 he formed the acquaintance of Miss Eliza Morgan, who was the daughter of a widow, living at North Bend, and two years later, September 26, 1845, the two were united in the bonds of wedlock. So soon as Mr. Hendricks emerged from boyhood his success as a lawyer and public man was assured. Having established an office in Shelbyville, he gained in a short time a fair competence, and soon became one of the leading attorneys of the place. As an advocate he had few equals, and as a safe counsellor none surpassed him at the Shelby county bar. In the year 1848 Mr. Hendricks was nominated for the lower house of the general assembly, was elected after a brilliant canvass, and served his term with marked distinction. In 1850 he was chosen a delegate to the state constitutional convention, in the deliberations of which he took an active part, having served on two very important committees, and won distinction by a brilliant speech upon the resolution relative to the abolition of the grand jury system. The following year was the beginning of Mr. Hendricks' career in national politics. He was nominated for congress at Indianapolis, May 16, 1851, over several other candidates, made a vigorous canvass, and was elected by a decided majority over Col. James P. Rush, the whig candidate. In congress he progressed with signal ability, and was called to act on some of the most important committees, and soon won a national reputation. Scarce had congress adjourned when he was required to make another campaign, for the constitution had transferred the congressional elections to even years, and the month to October. The whig candidate, John H. Bradley, of Indianapolis, was a brilliant man and a public speaker of rare attainments, whom Mr. Hendricks defeated by a largely increased majority. In 1854, when the northern whigs were in a chaotic condition, pro-slavery, anti-slavery, free-soilers, abolitionists, know-nothings and democrats commingling in a storm of confusion a "fusion" state and congressional ticket was formed for the occasion. Opposed to Mr. Hendricks was Lucian Barbour, a talented lawyer of Indianapolis, who exerted himself to combine all the opponents of democracy. Mr. Hendricks made a vigorous and manly contest, but was defeated, after which he retired to his profession and his home, at Shelbyville. In 1855 he was appointed by President Pierce, general land commissioner, in which capacity he served nearly four years, and in 1860 was nominated for governor of Indiana, against Henry S. Lane. After a brilliant and able canvass, during which the two competitors spoke together in nearly every county of the state, defeat again came to Mr. Hendricks. In the same year he moved to Indianapolis, where he lived until his death. In January, 1863, he was elected to the United States senate, which position he held for six years. In 1872 he was again nominated for governor, his opponent being Gen. Thomas Brown, a man of ability and enviable reputation. This campaign was peculiar in one particular. The republicans had infused the crusaders with the idea that they were the salvation of their cause, while the democracy opposed all sumptuary laws. Yet Mr. Hendricks went before the people as a temperance man, opposed to prohibition, but willing to sign any constitutional legislation looking toward the amelioration of crime and the advancement of temperance. He was elected and kept his pledges to the letter. He always kept his pledges inviolate, and ever remained true to his friends. He had a high sense of duty, and a spirit of philanthropy pervaded his whole nature. In 1876 he was nominated for the vice presidency on the democratic ticket with Samuel J. Tilden, of New York, and of this election it was claimed they were flagrantly defrauded by returning boards and the electoral commission. In 1880 the name of Thomas A. Hendricks was placed in nomination for the presidency, at Cincinnati, by Indiana, and his nomination was strongly urged in the convention. In 1884 he was a delegate to the Chicago convention, and as chairman of the Indiana delegation, presented in fitting terms and masterly manner, the name of Joseph E. McDonald for the presidency. After the latter had positively refused to accept the second place on the ticket, Mr. Hendricks was almost unanimously chosen, and the successful ticket for 1884, the first in twenty-five years, became Grover Cleveland and Thomas A. Hendricks. But few greater calamities ever befell the people than the death of Vice President Hendricks, which occurred on the 25th day November, 1885, at his home in Indianapolis, of heart disease. Mr. Hendricks was one of the nation's greatest men; deep, broad-minded, diplomatic and above all, a true man. His acts and speeches in congress, both in the house and senate, his defense of what he conceived to be right, his labors for the poor, the oppressed and the wronged of every class in this and other countries, were of great interest to his people and worthy of emulation by all. His devotion to his party, his candor and honesty of purpose, his noble ambition to serve the people faithfully, his philanthropy and universal love of mankind, all combined to make him one of the noblest of men. Strong in his convictions, yet courteous to opponents. Great in intellect, yet approachable by the humblest of men. High in position, he met every man as his equal. Independent in thought, self-reliant in principle, and rich in pleasant greetings to all whom he met. Though dead he yet lives in the hearts of the people, and his noble characteristics stand out in bold relief as beacon lights to guide and direct generations yet to be.

JAMES D. WILLIAMS was born in Pickaway county, Ohio, January 16, 1808, and moved with his parents to Indiana, in 1818, settling near the town of Vincennes, Knox county. He grew to manhood there, and upon the death of his father, in 1828, the support of the family devolved on him. He received a limited education in the pioneer log school-house, but, by mingling with the best people in the neighborhood, he obtained a sound practical knowledge of men and things, which, in a great measure, compensated for his early deficiency in literary studies, so that when on reaching his majority, he was unusually well versed for one in his circumstances. He was reared a farmer, and naturally chose agriculture for his life work, and followed it with much more than ordinary success, until the close of his long and useful life. Gov. Williams entered public life in 1839, as justice of the peace, the duties of which he discharged in an eminently satisfactory manner for a period of four years, resigning in 1843. In the latter year he was elected to the lower house of the state legislature, and from that time until his election to the national congress in 1874, he was almost continuously identified with the legislative service of the state. Few men in Indiana have been so long in the public service, and few have been identified with more popular legislative measures than he. It is to him that the widows of Indiana are indebted for the law which allows them to hold, without administration, the estates of their deceased husbands, when they do not exceed $300 in value. He was the author of the law which distributed the sinking fund among the counties of the state, and to him are the people largely indebted for the establishment of the state board of agriculture, an institution that has done much to foster and develop the agricultural interests of Indiana. He was a delegate to the national democratic convention at Baltimore in 1872, and in 1873 was the democratic nominee for United States senator, against Oliver P. Morton, but the party being in the minority, he was defeated. He served in the national house of representatives from December, 1875, till December, 1876, when he resigned, having been elected governor in the latter year. The campaign of 1876 was a memorable one, during which the opposition, both speakers and press, ridiculed the democratic nominee for governor, making sport of his homespun clothes and plain appearance, but the democracy seized upon his peculiarities' and made them the watchwords of victory. Gov. Williams, or Blue Jeans, as his friends were pleased to call him, was a man of the strictest integrity, and was known as a careful, painstaking executive entering into the minutest details of his office. He was self-willed and self-reliant, and probably consulted fewer persons about his official duties than any of his predecessors. In personal appearance, Gov. Williams was over six feet high, remarkably straight, had large hands and feet, high cheek bones, long sharp nose, gray eyes, and a well formed head, covered profusely with black hair. He was courteous in his intercourse with others, a good conversationalist, and possessed in a very marked degree, shrewdness and force of character. He died in the year 1880.

ISAAC PUSEY GRAY, one of the most prominent party leaders of Indiana, was born in Chester county, Penn., October 18, 1828. In 1836, he was clerk in a dry goods store in New Madison, Ohio, and afterward became its proprietor. In 1855 he removed to Union City, Ind., where he engaged in business for three years. Like nearly every other successful politician in Indiana, the future Gov. Gray eventually adopted the law as the surest stepping stone to fame and fortune. After a few years of practice, however, the civil war came on and, being an ardent unionist, Mr. Gray accepted a captaincy of the Fourth Indiana cavalry, which position he retained until compelled to retire on account of ill health. Subsequently he recruited the One Hundred and Forty-seventh Indiana infantry. Originally a whig, Mr. Gray drifted naturally into the republican party after its formation, and was for a long time one of its influential members. Dissatisfied with the administration of Grant, he joined the Greeley liberal movement in 1872, and from that time on, acted with the democrats. The latter received him with open arms and speedily showered upon him their highest honors. He was elected lieutenant governor on the democratic ticket in 1876, and was renominated for the same position in 1880, but was defeated. In 1884 he reached the goal of his ambition, by receiving the democratic nomination for governor, to which position he was triumphantly elected in the fall of that year. He served with energy and ability, for four years, his administration proving so satisfactory to his partisan friends that he became the recognized leader of the democratic party in Indiana. He was that party's choice for vice presidential candidate on the ticket with Grover Cleveland in 1888, and his supporters always insisted that Gray's nomination would have insured Cleveland's election. Previous to that event, his friends urged him for the United States senate in the winter of 1886-'87, and he would, no doubt, have achieved that honor, but for the fact that he occupied the governor's chair, and could not vacate it without giving place to a republican successor, which for party reasons, he was anxious to avoid. Since his retirement from the governorship, Mr. Gray has held no office, but has been a busy leader and spokesman for his party in the state, which thinks there is no honor too high for their favorite to aspire to. Gov. Gray has a strong personality, is an excellent judge of men and their motives, an exceedingly able organizer, and a speaker of more than ordinary ability. When to this is added a handsome personal presence and courteous address, a natural talent for acquiring and retaining friends, his popularity as a party leader is easily accounted for.

ALBERT G. PORTER.— Among the self-made men of Indiana, none stand higher or have a more noteworthy career than the distinguished gentleman whose name heads this sketch. Albert G. Porter was born in Lawrenceburg, Ind., April 20, 1824. He was graduated at Asbury university in 1843, studied law, was admitted to the bar in 1845, and began to practice in Indianapolis, where he was councilman and corporation attorney. In 1853 he was appointed reporter of the supreme court of Indiana, and was subsequently elected to the same position by a very large majority of the voters of the state. He was elected to congress from the Indianapolis district in 1858, on the republican ticket, overcoming an adverse democratic majority of 800, which he converted into a majority for himself of 1,000. Two years subsequently, he was re-elected by a smaller majority. On March 5, 1878, he was appointed first comptroller of the United States treasury, which position he filled with distinguished ability until called therefrom to become a candidate for governor of Indiana on the republican ticket. He resigned, and entered into the campaign of 1880, which will ever be memorable in the history of the state. After a canvass of remarkable bitterness and excitement, in which every inch of ground was stubbornly contested, Mr. Porter was elected governor by a handsome majority. He held the office from 1881 to 1884, his administration being regarded by friend and foe, alike, as one of the ablest in the history of the state. Mr. Porter has for many years ranked as one of the ablest and most successful lawyers in Indiana, and his "Decisions of the Supreme Court of Indiana" (5 vols., 1853-6), are regarded as among the best of their kind in the state. Besides his talent in politics and law, Mr. Porter enjoys a literary reputation of no mean rank, attained chiefly from his law writings and lectures. He is especially good authority on all matters relating to pioneer history in the west, and has in preparation a history of Indiana, which will undoubtedly rank as a classic in that line of literature. At this writing (September, 1890), Mr. Porter occupies the position of United States minister to Rome, which high honor was conferred upon him by his friend, President Harrison.

ALVIN P. HOVEY.—This gentleman, who was elected governor of Indiana in 1888, has had a notable career, both civil and military. He was born in 1821, in Posey county, Ind., where he has spent his whole life. After a common school education, he studied law and was admitted to the Mt. Vernon bar in 1843, where he has practiced with success. The civil positions he held previous to the war were those of delegate to the constitutional convention of 1850; judge of the third judicial circuit of Indiana from 1851 to 1854, and judge of the supreme court of Indiana. From 1856 to 1858 he served as United States district attorney for the state. During the civil war he entered the national service as colonel of the Twenty-fourth Indiana volunteers, in July, 1861. He was promoted brigadier-general of volunteers on April 28, 1862, and breveted major-general for meritorious and distinguished services in July, 1864. He was in command of the eastern district of Arkansas in 1863, and of the district of Indiana in 1864–1865. Gen. Grant, in his official reports, awards to Gen. Hovey the honor of the key battle of the Vicksburg campaign, that of Champion's Hill. This is no small praise; also, it is remembered that military critics, in view of the vast consequences that flowed therefrom, have ranked Champion's Hill as one of the five decisive battles of the civil war, and second in importance to Gettysburg alone. Gen. Hovey resigned his commission on October 18, 1865, and was appointed minister to Peru, which office he held until 1870. In 1886 he was nominated for congress by the republicans in the Evansville district, which theretofore had steadily given a large democratic majority. Gen. Hovey's personal popularity and military prestige overcame this, and he was elected by a small majority. In congress, he attracted attention by his earnestness in advocating more liberal pension laws, and every measure for the benefit of the ex-Union soldiers. Largely to this fact was due his nomination for the governorship of Indiana, by the republican party in 1888, the soldier element of the state being a very important factor in securing his nomination, and his subsequent election. In his social relations, Gov. Hovey has always been very popular, and his family circle is one of the happiest in the state. Though a strong partisan, he is never abusive or vindictive, and at every trial of strength at the polls, he has received strong support from many personal friends in the ranks of the opposite party.

JAMES NOBLE was the son of Thomas T. Noble, who moved from Virginia to Kentucky, near the close of the eighteenth century. James Noble grew to manhood in Kentucky, and after his marriage, which was consummated before he had attained his majority, began the study of law in the office of Mr. Southgate, of Covington. After finishing his legal studies and being admitted to the bar, he removed to Brookville, Ind., and commenced the practice of his profession, and soon became known as one of the most successful lawyers and most eloquent advocates of the Whitewater country. When Indiana became a state Mr. Noble represented Franklin county in the constitutional convention, in which he was chairman of the legislative and judiciary committees. In August, 1810, he was elected a member of the first legislature under the state government, which met at Corydon, November, 1816, and adjourned January, 1817. November 8, 1816, the general assembly, by a joint vote, elected James Noble and Waller Taylor to represent Indiana in the senate of the United States. "In the senate Gen. Noble had for associates the ablest men the country has yet produced. He was not dwarfed by their stature, but maintained a respectable standing among them." He remained in the senate until his death, which occurred February 26, 1831. Mr. Noble was a large, well proportioned man of fine address and bearing. He was a good lawyer and as a speaker was very effective before a jury or promiscuous assembly. Personally he was quite popular and his warm heart and generous nature made him the idol of the people of his section of the state.

WALLER TAYLOR, one of the first senators from Indiana, after her admission as a state, was born in Lunenburg county, Va., before 1786, and died there before 1826. He received a common school education, studied law, served one or two terms in the Virginia legislature as a representative from Lunenburg county. In 1805 he settled in Vincennes, Ind., having been appointed a territorial judge. He served as aid-de-camp to Gen. William H. Harrison, at the battle of Tippecanoe, and in the war of 1812-15. On the admission of Indiana as a state he was elected United States senator, and at the close of his term was re-elected, serving from December 12, 1816, until March 3, 1825. He was a man of fine literary attainments, and a prominent political leader of his day.

ROBERT HANNA was born in Laurens district, S. C., April 6, 1786, and removed with his parents to Indiana in an early day, settling in Brookville as long ago as 1802. He was elected sheriff of the eastern district of Indiana in 1809, and held the position until the organization of the state government. He was afterward appointed register of the land office, and removed to Indianapolis in 1825. In 1831 he was appointed United States senator, to fill the unexpired term caused by the death of James Noble, and served with credit in that capacity from December, of the above year, until January 3, 1832, when his successor took his seat. He was afterward elected a member of the state senate, but suffered a defeat, when making the race for a re-election. He was accidentally killed by a railroad train while walking on the track at Indianapolis, November 19, 1859.

GEN. JOHN TIPTON was born in Sevier county, Tenn., August 14, 1786, and was a son of Joshua Tipton, a native of Maryland, a man who possessed great positiveness of character, with keen perceptions and uncommon executive ability. These peculiarities induced him to remove from his native state and settle in a home further west, where he afterward became a leader in the defense of the frontier against the hostile Indians. He was murdered by the savages on the 18th of April, 1793. Left thus early in life in the midst of a frontier settlement, surrounded by the perils incident thereto, the son inheriting the sagacity and self-reliance of his father, soon began to develop that positive energy of character which distinguished his after life. In the fall of 1807, with his mother and two sisters and a half-brother, he removed to Indiana territory and settled near Bringley's Ferry, on the Ohio river, where he purchased a homestead of fifty acres, which he paid for out of his scanty earnings, making rails at fifty cents a hundred. These early experiences laid the foundation of his future success in life. June, 1809, he enlisted in a company recruited in his neighborhood, which was soon afterward ordered to the frontier for the protection of the settlements. September, 1811, the company entered the campaign which terminated in the battle of Tippecanoe. Early in that memorable engagement all his superior officers were killed, and he was promoted to the captaincy, when the conflict was at its height. Subsequently he rose by regular gradation, to the rank of brigadier general. At the first election under the state constitution, he was chosen sheriff of Harrison county, which position he filled two terms, and in 1819 was elected to represent this county in the state legislature. While a member of that body he served on the committee to select the site for the location of the state capitol, which selection was made in June, 1820, and approved January, 1821. He was re-elected in 1821, and at the following session was chosen one of the commissioners to locate the boundary line between the states of Indiana and Illinois. In March, 1823, he was appointed by President Monroe, general agent for the Pottawatamie and Miami Indians on the upper Wabash and Tippecanoe rivers, and immediately thereafter moved to Ft. Wayne, the seat of the agency. At his instance the agency was removed from Ft. Wayne to Logansport, in the spring of 1828, where he continued to discharge the functions of his trust with fidelity and success. At the session of the legislature, December, 1831, he was elected United States senator from Indiana, to fill the vacancy occasioned by the death of Hon. James Noble, and was re-elected at the session of 1832-33, for a full term of six years. While a member of that distinguished body, he was noted for the soundness of his judgment and the independence of his actions on all questions involving the interests of the state or general government. He opposed the views of President Jackson in reference to the re-charter of the United States bank, and recognized no party in determining the line of duty, always acting from motives of public right. As a civilian and citizen, he was alike successful in directing and executing to the extent of his power, whatever purpose his conscience approved or his judgment dictated. After locating in Logansport he directed his energies toward the development of the natural resources of that town and surrounding country, and to him more than to any other man is due the credit of supplying the settlements with grist and saw-mills and other improvements, and for taking the initial step which led to the organization of the Eel river seminary, at that time one of the best known educational institutions of northern Indiana. He was also proprie-

tor of four additions to the town of Logansport, and was interested
with Mr. Carter in the plan and location of the original plat thereof.
Mr. Tipton was twice married, the first time to a Miss Shields, who
died within two years after their marriage. The second time was in
April, 1825, to Matilda, daughter of Captain Spier Spencer, who was
killed at the battle of Tippecanoe. The second Mrs. Tipton died in
the spring of 1839, about the close of her husband's senatorial career.
Gen. Tipton closed an honorable life on the morning of April 5,
1839, in the full meridian of his usefulness, and received the last sad
honors of his Masonic brethren on Sunday, April 7, 1839.

OLIVER HAMPTON SMITH, congressman and senator, was born on
Smith's island, near Trenton, N. J., October 23, 1794. He attended
school near his home at intervals, until 1813, at which time, owing
to the death of his father, he was thrown upon his own resources.
He afterward found employment in a woolen mill in Pennsylvania,
and on attaining his majority, received $1,500 from his father's estate,
which he soon lost in an unfortunate business investment. Mr.
Smith came to Indiana in 1817, and settled at Rising Sun, Ohio
county, but in a short time, moved to Lawrenceburg, and began the
study of law. In March, 1820, he was licensed to practice, and soon
afterward removed to Versailles, Ripley county, where he opened an
office, but becoming dissatisfied with the location, in a few months
he located at Connersville, thence in 1839, moved to the state capital.
In August, 1822, he was elected to the legislature from Fayette
county, and while a member of that body, served as chairman of the
judiciary committee, an important position, and one usually given to
the ablest lawyer of the body. In 1824 he was appointed prosecutor
of the third judicial district, and in 1826, became a candidate for congress against Hon. John Test, who had represented the district for
three full terms. He made a vigorous canvass, and defeated his popular competitor by 1,500 majority. Mr. Smith served with distinction
in congress, and was ever attentive and industrious in his public duties. In December, 1836, he was a candidate for United States senator, his competitors being Noah Noble, William Hendricks and
Ratliff Boon. He was elected on the ninth ballot. In the senate,
Mr. Smith was chairman of the committee on public lands, and took
great pride in the place, which he filled with distinguished ability.
In 1842 he was a candidate for re-election, but was defeated by Edward A. Hannegan, and in March, 1843, his senatorial services ter-

minated. Soon after his return home, his attention was directed to railroads, and Indianapolis is mainly indebted to him for the building of the Indianapolis & Bellfonte road, now known as the "Bee Line." In 1857 he commenced writing a series of sketches for the *Indianapolis Journal*, on early times in Indiana, which attracted much attention, and which were afterward brought out in book form. This volume is valuable as a record of early Indiana times, and contains much information not otherwise noted. Mr. Smith died March 19, 1859. As a political speaker, he exhibited much the same qualitie and powers of mastery that he did as a forensic speaker, but he was less successful on the stump, because argument and close reasoning, which were his mode of dealing with political questions, were not as popular as anecdotal and declamatory style. "As a lawyer, Mr. Smith was ever true to the interest of his client, and in the prosecution of his cases in court, he displayed much zeal and earnestness. He was an honest opponent, and very liberal in his practice, and yet very capable, and sometimes ready to seize upon the weakness or oversight of an adversary. His career at the bar was a successful one, and he well merited the high tribute paid to his memory at the time of his death." "In person, Mr. Smith was five feet ten inches in height and weighed about 180 pounds. He was broad chested, and large from the waist up. The lower part of the body was correspondingly smaller, and when he was subjected to great physical fatigue, it was too weak to bear him up. His eyes were dark, his hair was black and stood up upon his head. He had large shaggy eyebrows and the general contour of his features denoted energy, pluck and endurance. His place is in the front rank of the great men of Indiana."

ALBERT S. WHITE, one of the most scholarly of Indiana's distinguished men, was born in Blooming Grove, N. Y., October 24, 1803. He graduated from Union college, that state, in 1822, in the same class with Hon. William H. Seward, and after studying law for some time at Newburg, was licensed to practice his profession in 1825. Soon after this, he came to Indiana and located at Rushville, thence one year later, moved to Paoli and subsequently took up his permanent abode in Lafayette. In 1830 and 1831 he was assistant clerk of the Indiana house of representatives, and served as clerk of the same from 1832 to 1835. In 1833 he was a candidate for congress against Edward A Hannegan, by whom he was defeated. "He had neither the brilliancy nor the eloquence of Mr. Hannegan, but was the superior of that erratic man in education, culture and in most of the qualities which go to make up the successful man." In 1837 he was more successful, having been elected to congress by an overwhelming majority over Nathan Jackson. The year previous, he was on the whig electoral ticket, and in the electoral college, cast his vote for William Henry Harrison. In 1839 he was elected to succeed Gen. John Tipton, in the United States senate, the struggle having been an animated one, requiring thirty-six ballots divided among Mr. White, Noah Noble and Col. Thomas H. Blake. He entered the senate a young man, but his training eminently fitted him for the duties of that distinguished body, in the deliberations of which he bore an active part. He strenuously opposed the annexation of Texas, as he did every measure which was calculated to extend the area of slavery. " He was of a conservative temperament, and usually voted with the moderate men of his party, but he was conscientiously an anti-slavery man and always acted with those who strove to confine slavery to the territory it then polluted." He was active in securing grants of land, to aid in the extension of the Wabash and Erie canal, and took a prominent part in shaping legislation, to promote other important internal improvements. On the expiration of his term, Mr. White resumed the practice of law, but soon abandoned the profession and entered actively into the business of railroad building. He was president of the Indianapolis & Lafayette railroad, from its organization until 1856, and during a part of that time, was at the head of the Wabash & Western railway. In 1860 he was again called into public life, as a member of congress, where his thorough knowledge of political and state affairs soon enabled him to take high rank. He was made chairman of a select committee, raised to consider the question of compensated emancipation, and also reported a bill appropriating $180,000,000 to pay loyal men for their slaves, and $20,000,000 to aid in the colonization of freedmen. His congressional career was eminently honorable, but he failed of a renomination, mainly on account of his action in regard to the emancipation question. In January, 1864, he was appointed by President Lincoln, United States judge for the district of Indiana, to fill the vacancy caused by the death of Hon. Caleb B. Smith. He soon adapted himself to his new position, and had he lived, would have proven a worthy successor of his eminent predecessor. His term was cut short by his death, which occurred on the 4th day of September, 1864. " Mr.

White had but little in common with the typical western pioneer, and it is therefore somewhat strange that he should have reached the eminence he did. He never sunk his manhood nor lowered his self-respect, by trying to get down to the level of every man who approached him. He was in no sense a demagogue, and never sought to curry favor by pretending to be what he was not. He was always dignified and always a gentleman." In personal appearance, Mr. White was below the medium height, quite spare and had a narrow visage with a prominent Roman nose. Physically he was weak, but intellectually ranked with the strong men of the state and nation. " He was one of the first men of the Wabash country, and of the state, and his name will not be forgotten while learning and scholarship are cherished and honor and patriotism revered."

EDWARD A. HANNEGAN was a native of Ohio, but in early life moved to Kentucky, and settled at Lexington, where he grew to manhood. He received a liberal education, and after several years spent in the study of law, was admitted to practice at the Lexington bar at the early age of twenty-three. Not long after this he settled at Covington, Ind., where he opened an office and practiced his profession with flattering success for a number of years. He soon entered the political arena and ere long was honored by an election to the state legislature, in the deliberations of which he soon took an active and brilliant part. His career in the legislature brought him into prominent notice, and in January, 1833, he was elected to the congress of the United States, defeating Albert S. White, afterward his colleague in the senate. In 1840 he was again a candidate for congress, but after a very exciting contest was defeated by Hon. Henry S. Lane, afterward governor and United States senator. In 1842, much to the surprise of every one, Mr. Hannegan was elected United States senator, defeating Oliver H. Smith and Tilghman A. Howard on the sixth ballot. He took his seat in the senate on the 4th of December, 1843, and served until March 4, 1849, during which time he made several speeches which attracted the attention of the country. While a member of that body his votes were always in accord with his party. In March, 1849, President Polk nominated him for minister to Prussia, but being unfit for diplomacy by nature and habit it is no wonder that his career at Berlin added nothing to the character of the government he represented. He was recalled the next January, and with that recall the public life of the bril-

liant but erratic statesman ended. He returned to his home at
Covington, and the next year was defeated in a race for the legislature, which he took much to heart and which served to
drive him further into the convivial habits which ultimately
proved his ruin. The habit of drink continued to grow upon him
until in a fit of drunken frenzy he took the life of one whom he
dearly loved — his brother-in-law, Capt. Duncan. The two had been
drinking deeply, and angry words passed between them. Mr. Hannegan finally went into a separate apartment, but was followed by
Capt. Duncan, who applied some bitter epithets to him and slapped
him in the face. Upon this Mr. Hannegan siezed a dagger and buried
it to the hilt in Duncan's body, the effect of which was death the
following day. He was not indicted and tried for this killing, the
universal sentiment of the people being in his favor. He removed to
St. Louis, in 1857, and on the 25th of January, 1859, he died in that
city. Mr. Hannegan was warm in his friendships and had a large
personal following. His manners were elegant, and he was ardent,
impulsive and undaunted, thinking, acting and speaking with the utmost freedom. In person he was below the medium height, firmly
and compactly built, but in after years became quite corpulent. He
was a charming companion, and as an orator was more eloquent than
logical. " He was not a profound man nor a great scholar, but what
he lacked in profundity he made up in brilliancy, and his deficiency
in scholarship was largely compensated for by his quick wit and fertile imagination, and his power to express himself in the choicest language. He was of Irish descent, and inherited many of the characteristics of that warm-hearted, impulsive race."

JESSE D. BRIGHT, for twenty years a leading politician of Indiana,
was born in Norwich, N. Y., December 18, 1812, and came to this state
when a boy, locating with his parents at Madison, where he grew to
manhood's estate. He received an academic education, and after a
preparatory course of reading, was admitted to the bar, where his
talents soon won for him a conspicuous place among the successful
lawyers of Indiana. He was not profound in the philosophy of juris-
prudence, but, being a fluent speaker and quite popular with the people, he succeeded in gaining a lucrative practice, which extended
throughout the counties of the lower Wabash and elsewhere. He
was elected judge of probate in Jefferson county, and subsequently
received the appointment of United States marshal for Indiana, and

it was while holding the latter office that he laid the foundation of his political career. In the forties, he made the race for the state senate, against Williamson Dunn and Shadrack Wilber, whom he defeated, and in that body was soon recognized as the leader of the party. In fact, he was a born leader of men, and always stood at the fore-front of the line. In 1843 he was lieutenant governor on the ticket with James Whitcomb, and such was the ability he displayed in the discharge of the duties of that position, that the senators and representatives, with all of whom he sustained relations of the warmest friendship, afterward elected him to the senate of the United States. At this time, he was barely eligible to a seat in the senate, on account of his age, being the youngest man ever elected to that distinguished body. In 1850, he was a candidate for re-election against Hon. Robert Dale Owen, who subsequently withdrew from the contest, thus making Mr. Bright's election without opposition. In 1856, his term having expired, he again sought a re-election, which was granted him after a memorable contest which was decided by the United States senate in a strictly party vote. In the senate, Mr. Bright ranked high as a committee worker, and enjoyed great personal popularity. Such was his standing that on the death of Vice President King in 1853, he was elected president pro tempore of the senate, which he filled with ability until the inauguration of John C. Breckenridge, in 1857. In the latter year, when forming his cabinet, President Buchanan offered Mr. Bright the secretaryship of state, which position he saw fit to decline. He continued a senator until 1862, when he was expelled for disloyalty, by a vote of thirty-two to fourteen. The principal proof of his crime was in recommending to Jefferson Davis, in March, 1861, Thomas Lincoln, of Texas, a person desirous of furnishing arms to the confederacy. Mr. Bright organized and led the Breckenridge party in Indiana in 1860, and in stumping for the brilliant young Kentuckian gave the movement all the force and vitality it had in this state. He left Indiana soon after the legislature of 1863 refused to return him to the United States senate, and took up his residence in Kentucky, in the legislature of which state, he subsequently served two terms. In 1874, he removed to Baltimore, in which city he died on the 20th of May, 1875, of organic disease of the heart. Mr. Bright had a splendid physique, and weighed about 200 pounds. He had a good head and a good face, but was imperious in manner and brooked no opposition from either friend or foe. "He was the

Danton of Indiana democracy, and was both loved and feared by his followers."

JOHN PETTIT was born at Sackett's Harbor, N. Y., July 24, 1807, and died in Lafayette, Ind., June 17, 1877. After receiving a classical education and studying law, he was admitted to the bar in 1838, and commenced the practice of his profession at Lafayette, Ind. He soon became active in state politics, was in the legislature two terms and served as United States district attorney. He was elected to congress as a democrat in 1842, re-elected to the next congress and served with distinguished ability in that body from December 4, 1843, to March 3, 1849. He was a democratic elector in 1852, and in January, 1853, was chosen United States senator to fill the unexpired term, occasioned by the death of James Whitcomb, serving as such until March 3, 1855, during which time he earned the reputation of an able and painstaking legislator. In 1859 he was appointed by James Buchanan, chief justice of Kansas, and in 1870 was elected supreme judge of Indiana. He was a delegate to the Chicago democratic convention in 1864, and as a political leader, wielded a strong influence in Indiana in a number of state and national contests. He was renominated for supreme judge in 1876, but owing to scandals connected with the court, which excited popular indignation, he was forced off the ticket and the name of Judge Perkins substituted.

CHARLES W. CATHCART, of whose public and private history but little is now known, was born on the island of Madeira, in 1809. He received a liberal education and early in life shipped as a sailor, and after a number of years spent on the sea, located in 1831, at La Porte, Ind., where he engaged in farming. He served several years as land surveyor, was a representative in the legislature, and in 1845, was an elector on the democratic ticket. He was elected to the congress of the United States in 1845-47, re-elected the latter year to serve until 1849, and was afterward appointed to the United States senate to fill the unexpired term occasioned by the death of James Whitcomb. He served as senator from December 6, 1852, to March 3, 1853, and at the expiration of his term returned to La Porte county, where his death subsequently occurred.

GRAHAM N. FITCH was born in LeRoy, Genesee county, N. Y., on the 5th of December, 1810, and is said to have been the first white child born in that town. His grandfather was a soldier in the revolutionary war, and his father, a soldier in the war of 1812, was wounded at the battle of Queenstown. Mr. Fitch received a liberal education, and in early life, chose the medical profession for a life work, and completed a course of study in the same in the college of physicians and surgeons of western New York. He came to Indiana in 1834, and settled at Logansport, where his successful professional career soon won for him the reputation of one of the most skillful surgeons and thorough practitioners in the west. In 1844 he accepted a professorship in Rush Medical college, at Chicago, and occupied the chair of theory and practice during the years 1844–1847. Though not naturally a politician, Dr. Fitch, from force of circumstances, was drawn into the arena of politics, where his commanding talents and energy marked him as the people's choice. In 1836 and again in 1838, he was chosen to represent Cass county in the state legislature. Subsequently at the election in August, 1847, he was chosen to represent his district in the lower house of congress, holding that responsible position until 1852. During his membership he was active and efficient in the discharge of his duties, earning the reputation of a good legislator. His legislative capacity was further tested by an experience in the senate of the United States, commencing in 1860–'61. The honorable distinction acquired in subordinate legislative positions was not dimmed by his senatorial experience, and he left that distinguished body with a record of which posterity need not be ashamed. Although a democrat in political affiliations, he always esteemed principles above mere partisanship and was not slow to manifest disapprobation when his party seemed disposed to pursue a course of policy in antagonism to his better judgment. In the triangular contest for the presidency between Mr. Lincoln, Mr. Douglas and Mr. Breckenridge, he gave his undivided support to the last named gentleman, influenced thereto by a belief that his election would prevent the threatening civil war. Again when his party rallied to the support of Mr. Greeley, he manifested his dissent by supporting Mr. O'Connor for the presidency. When the war came on, he raised a regiment, the Forty-sixth Indiana, and at its head entered the federal service. He did brilliant service in several campaigns, but owing to an injury received by the falling of his horse, was compelled to leave the service before the expiration of the war. Since the close of the war, he has continued to practice his profession, not interfering in political affairs except to preserve the integrity of his inherent ideas with the vigor of his palmier days, opposing whatever he conceives to be wrong in civil and political affairs. In personal appearance, Dr. Fitch is a remarkable specimen of physical manhood, having a well knit frame and a courtly dignity which bespeaks the polished gentleman. In his prime he appeared a knight among men, and while a member of the United States senate, is said to have been the finest looking man of that body.

DAVID TURPIE was born in Hamilton county, Ohio, in 1829, graduated at Kenyon college, studied law, and began practice at Logansport, Ind., in 1849. He was a member of the legislature in 1852, was appointed judge of the court of common pleas in 1854, and of the circuit court in 1856, which post he resigned. He was again a member of the state house of representatives in 1856, and was elected to the United States senate from Indiana, as a democrat, in place of Jesse D. Bright, who had been expelled, serving from January 22, to March 3, 1863. Nearly twenty-four years afterward he was again called on by his party to represent them in the senate, to which body he was elected by the Indiana legislature, at the session of 1886–7, after a memorable struggle. His opponent was Benjamin Harrison, afterward elected president, and he was defeated by the votes of one or two independents in the legislature, who held the balance of power between the two great parties, which were almost equally divided in voting strength among the members. Mr. Turpie enjoys the reputation of being one of the ablest constitutional lawyers in Indiana, and is also graded high as a man of literary entertainments.

DANIEL D. PRATT was born at Palermo, Maine, October 24, 1813, and died at Logansport, Ind., June 17, 1877. His father was a physician and the son of David Pratt, a revolutionary soldier, of Berkshire county, Massachusetts. Mr. Pratt's early years were years of excessive toil, necessitated by the circumstances of his father's family. His early education was acquired in the district schools of Madison county, N. Y., and in 1825 he entered the seminary at Cazenovia, that state, and two years later entered Hamilton college, from which he graduated in 1831. He was a natural orator, and as a classical scholar was rarely excelled. Immediately after graduating he accepted a professorship in Madison university, and with the means thus earned began the study of law. In the spring of 1832, he decided to move west. Accordingly he set out for Cincinnati, making a part of the journey on foot, and later made his way to Rising Sun, Ind., where he taught a term of school. Subsequently he entered the law office of Calvin Fletcher, at Indianapolis, and in 1836 located in Logansport, at that time a mere opening in the wilderness. The bright promises of his early youth were soon fully realized, for no sooner was he admitted to the bar than he rapidly rose in his profession, and in a few years the fame of the eloquent young advocate resounded throughout northern Indiana. He was one who never courted notoriety, but he made himself a necessity in the field of action, and it was often a race between litigants to see who could reach his office first. At the time of his election to the United States senate in 1869, he was recognized as the ablest lawyer in northern Indiana, and his fame was not confined to this state alone, but extended throughout the western country. For twenty-five years he was without a rival in northern Indiana, before a jury. Gov. Hendricks and Secretary Thompson divided the palm with him in the south and west parts of the state. His eminent merits were recognized, and in 1847 he was nominated for congress, but was defeated by Charles Cathcart. In 1848, he was one of the presidential electors, and in 1851-53 was elected to the legislature, and soon became the leader in the house. In 1860 he was secretary of the national convention at Chicago, which nominated Abraham Lincoln for the presidency, and attracted great attention by his eloquence and commanding presence. During the war Mr. Pratt was a zealous and patriotic advocate of the Union cause. In 1863 he received the unanimous vote of his party, then in the minority, for United States senator, and in 1868 was elected to congress by a handsome majority. In 1868 the legislature without solicitation on his part, promoted him to the United States senate. It was unfortunate that he entered that body so late in life, as he was then fifty-six years of age, and with the exception of two terms in the state legislature was without public training. The artificial restraints thrown around him in the national capital disgusted him, and interfered with his splendid oratorical powers. As it was, however, he was recognized as one of the ablest men of that body during the period of his service, and although he made but few speeches, those he delivered were sound, logical and comprehensive. For six years he was a member of both claim and pension committees, and for two years was chairman of the pension committee. Millions of dollars were allowed and disallowed on his recommendation. So conscientious was he that Wendell Phillips once remarked that " Pratt is the most absolutely honest man I ever knew." Upon the expiration of his term as senator, at the solicitation of President Grant, he took charge of the internal revenue department. In 1876, the republicans urged Mr. Pratt to become a candidate for governor of the state, but he declined. Personally Mr. Pratt was one of the most cheerful and genial of men, and in his social life, and in all his associations, shed an influence around him which was like sunshine. Although he never sought literary honors, his talents could not pass unappreciated, and in 1872 Hamilton college conferred upon him the honorary degree of LL. D. In appearance he was above the average height, being over six feet, and correspondingly portly. His presence was dignified and he moved among men as one born to command. In his death the nation lost one of its faithful public servants, the state a great man, the legal profession one of its ablest members and the community one of its best citizens.

JOSEPH E. McDONALD was born in Butler county, Ohio, August 29, 1819, the son of John McDonald, a native of Pennsylvania, and of Scotch descent. Maternally, Mr. McDonald is descended from French Huguenot ancestry. His mother, Eleanor (Piatt) McDonald was a native of Pennsylvania and a woman of superior order of intellect. Seven years after the death of John McDonald, she married John Kerr, who moved with his family to Montgomery county, Ind., in the fall of 1826. Joseph McDonald was seven years of age when the family moved to Indiana, and until his twelfth year he lived upon the home farm. In his twelfth year he became an apprentice at the saddler's trade in Lafayette, in which capacity he served over five years, studying law in the meantime, for which he early manifested a decided taste. At the age of eighteen he entered Wabash college, began the study of the higher branches, supporting himself mainly by plying his trade when it was possible for him to do so. He afterward became a student in the Asbury university, and in 1842 began the systematic study of law at Lafayette, Ind., in the office of Zebulon Beard, one of the leading lawyers of the state. He was nominated for the office of prosecuting attorney before his admission to the bar, and was elected to that position over one of the prominent lawyers of Lafayette. He was re-elected prosecutor, and discharged the duties of that office for a period of four years. In the fall of 1847, he moved to Crawfordsville, which place was his home until 1859. In 1849 he was elected from the old eighth district, to the twenty-first congress, and served one term, and in 1856 was elected attorney general of Indiana, being the first chosen to this office by the people. He was re-elected in 1858, and served two terms. In 1864 he was nominated for governor of Indiana by the democratic state convention, and made a joint canvass with Oliver P. Morton, the republican nominee. At the election he received 6,000 more votes for governor than the state ticket did in 1862, but Mr. Morton was elected by nearly 20,000 votes. Throughout his entire life he has strictly adhered to his resolution to follow the law and make a success of the profession, and as a lawyer he has for years ranked among the most successful and profound in the nation. He was elected to the United States senate for six years, to succeed David D. Pratt, and entered upon the duties of that position March 5, 1875. While a member of that body he was chairman of the committee on public lands, a member of the judiciary committee, took a conspicuous part in the debates on finance, and ranked as one of the ablest lawyers in that body of distinguished men. He served with distinction until 1881, since which time he has given his attention principally to the practice of his profession, though taking an active part in political affairs, being one of the recognized leaders of the democracy in the United States. He made the principal argument for the objectors in the count of the electoral vote of Louisiana before the electoral commission appointed to determine the result of the presidential election in 1876. In the national democratic convention, held in Chicago in 1884, Mr. McDonald's name was presented as a candidate for the presidential nomination, and he had a strong following in the delegation from a number of states. He is and always has been a representative democrat of the Jeffersonian school, and believes that the true idea of democracy is to preserve unimpaired, all the rights reserved to the states respectively, and to the people, without infringing upon any of the powers delegated to the general government by the constitution. "He believes in the virtue of the people, and in their ability and purpose to maintain their institutions inviolate against the assaults of designing men." " As an orator, both at the bar and on the hustings, he is cool, logical and forcible, and as a citizen, he has the confidence and respect of all who know him, regardless of political creeds." " His views are broad and comprehensive on all questions of public interest, and his steadfastness of purpose, his honest desire of accomplishing what is best

for the people, have given him a home in their hearts and won for
him the greatest honors they had to bestow."

DANIEL W. VOORHEES was born in Butler county, Ohio, September 26, 1827, and was brought to Indiana by his parents when two
months old. The family settled in Fountain county, where Mr.
Voorhees grew to manhood on a farm about ten miles from the town
of Covington. His father, Stephen Voorhees, was a native of Mer-
cer county, Ky., and a descendant of an old Holland family,
many representatives of which were among the early settlers of the
eastern states in the time of the colonies. His mother was Rachel
(Elliot) Voorhees, born in Maryland of Irish ancestry, and married
Stephen Voorhees in the year 1821. The early farm experience of
Mr. Voorhees proved of great value to him in after life, and served
to bind him in ties of sympathy with the common people. He
graduated from the Asbury, now DePauw, university, at Greencastle,
in 1849, and soon afterward entered the law office of Lane and Wilson, Crawfordsville, and on his admission to the bar, began the practice of his profession at Covington, Fountain county, where he soon
effected a co-partnership with Hon. E. A. Hannegan, in 1852. In
June, 1853, Mr. Voorhees was appointed by Gov. Wright, prosecuting attorney of the circuit court, in which position he soon established a fine reputation as a criminal lawyer. In 1856 he was
nominated by acclamation, democratic candidate for congress, but
was defeated by 230 majority in a district previously republican, by
2,600. In 1857 he removed to Terre Haute, and the following year
was appointed United States district attorney for the state of Indiana, by President Buchanan. He was elected to congress in 1860
and 1862, and in 1864 was again a successful candidate, but in the
last election his majority of 634 votes was contested by his competitor, Henry D. Washburn, who obtained the seat. He was again
elected in 1868, re-elected in 1870, but in 1872 was defeated by Hon.
Morton C. Hunter. In 1859 Mr. Voorhees was retained as counsel
to defend Col. Cook, who was arrested with John Brown, as an ac-
complice of the latter in the celebrated Harper's Ferry raid, and his
speech at the trial was one of the greatest ever delivered before an
American jury, and it gained him a national reputation. It was listened to with rapt attention by a vast audience, and was afterward
published all over the country, and in Europe in several different
languages. Mr. Voorhees was appointed November 6, 1877, to suc-

ceed Gov. Morton in the United States senate, and has served by
successive re-elections in that distinguished body until the present
time. From his entrance into public life he has occupied a conspicuous place in the eyes of the public and at the bar, on the stump
or in the halls of national legislation, he has been a man of mark.
His powers as a parliamentary orator and a statesman are a portion
of the history of the nation, and as a party leader few if any have exercised as great an influence upon the people of Indiana as he.
" From the sobriquet of the Tall Sycamore of the Wabash, so often
applied to him, it will be inferred that he is of tall stature, which is
the case, as he is over six feet in height and weighs over 200 pounds.
He carries himself erect, and his commanding presence and dignified
bearing make him a conspicuous figure in the senate chamber."
During his term of service in the senate he has been assiduous in his
attention to the public needs. He is always present and allows no
measure of his political opponents to pass without the severest scrutiny, and with him vigilance is the price of liberty.

BENJAMIN HARRISON, one of the ablest and most successful of Indiana's party leaders, and the only one that has succeeded in reaching
the presidency, was born in North Bend, Ohio, August 20, 1833.
His father was John Scott, brother of President William Henry Harrison. The future senator and president was graduated at Miami
university, Ohio, in 1852, studied law, and in 1854 removed to Indianapolis, where he has since resided. In 1862 he entered the army
as a second lieutenant of volunteers. After a short service he organized a company of the Seventieth Indiana regiment, was commissioned colonel on the completion of the regiment, and served
through the war, receiving the brevet of brigadier-general of volunteers on January 23, 1865. He then returned to Indianapolis and
resumed his office of supreme court reporter, to which he had been
re-elected during his absence, in 1864. In 1876, Godlove S. Orthe, the
republican nominee for governor of Indiana, was compelled to withdraw from the race on account of his connection with what was
known as the " Venezuela claims," and the nomination was unanimously offered to Gen. Harrison. He accepted reluctantly, made a
gallant race against heavy odds, but was defeated by " Blue Jeans "
Williams by a small plurality. The republicans obtaining a majority in the legislature in 1880, Gen. Harrison was unanimously
nominated and elected by his party to the United States senate, in

which body he served from March 4, 1881, until March 4, 1887. He was defeated for re-election after a bitter struggle, by a majority of two votes on joint ballot in the legislature, and to this circumstance, was largely due his subsequent nomination for the presidency. At the national republican convention held in Chicago in June, 1888, after a protracted and exciting struggle, the great prize was awarded to the Indiana politician and soldier, over a host of distinguished competitors. At the subsequent election in November of that year, Gen. Harrison was successful over his competitor, Grover Cleveland, and was inaugurated president of the United States on the 4th of March, 1889.

DR. DAVID J. JORDAN.— The above named gentleman is one of the most prominent of that coterie of scientific writers who have done so much to attract attention to the physical resources of Indiana. For many years Prof. Jordan has been president of the state university. He was educated at Cornell university, and afterward studied biology under the famous Agassiz, in his celebrated summer school on Penikese island. Coming west, Prof. Jordan taught his specialty in the university of Wisconsin, Indianapolis high school, Butler university and finally the Indiana university, of which his talents eventually made him president. Prof. Jordan devoted most of his attention for many years to the study of the habits and classification of the fishes of North America. On this subject he has published over 200 papers, besides a large work which has become a standard authority on ichthyology. In enthusiastic pursuit of his favorite study, Dr. Jordan made a fine and extensive collection of nearly ten thousand specimens of fishes, reptiles and birds, but unfortunately these were all destroyed by a disastrous fire in 1883. With characteristic energy he set to work to repair the damage, and soon had a better collection than ever. He has been a voluminous writer on scientific subjects; the greater part being devoted to his specialty, the fishes of the western states. He has gathered around him at Bloomington, a school of students who have grown up under his care, imbibed his tastes, and greatly assisted him in his scientific researches. The result of their conjoint labors and writings has been to make the state university the center and authority on subjects relating to biological work.

PROF. JOHN COLLETT, the most distinguished of Indiana geologists, is a native of this state, having been born in Vermilion county in

1828 and graduated at Wabash college in 1847. He has taken an active part in politics, having been state senator, state house commissioner, state statistician and state geologist. But his chief fame and his chief claim upon the gratitude of his state, are based upon his work as a scientist. Prof. Collett's life has been studious, useful and laborious. He has devoted most of his time to the study of the geology of Indiana, and has done more than any other person to make known the natural resources of the state, especially to advertise to the world the value of its coal measures and stone quarries. Chiefly through his efforts, the building stone of Indiana has been introduced to commerce, and is now used extensively for the construction of public buildings in all parts of the Union. He proved its superiority by a series of tests. From 1880 to 1884, he was state geologist, and for many years previously, had served as an assistant in that office, to which he contributed his most earnest labor and the riches of his well stored mind. In 1884, he published the first and best geological map of the state ever issued, and has written voluminously on all subjects relating to the geology of the state. There is not a county he has not visited and studied, nor one with whose geological history, dating far back into the dim twilight of the prehistoric periods, he is not so familiar as to be able to trace and read like an open book. Prof. Collett belongs to that useful class of citizens which, while not obtaining the passing applause and glittering fame that is conferred upon the politician in high office, confer more lasting benefits upon mankind, and are of more actual value to a state than all its politicians put together. Indiana needs more John Colletts and fewer "statesmen" of the Col. Mulberry Sellers and Senator Dillworthy type.

MAURICE THOMPSON.— There is no more picturesque personality in the Hoosier state than the poet, naturalist, essayist, story writer and publicist, whose name heads this sketch. A native of the south, he possesses all the frankness, ardor, geniality of disposition and fervent feelings so characteristic of the warm latitudes. His home, however, since the war has been in Indiana, with whose institutions and people he has become thoroughly identified. Mr. Thompson's tastes are literary, and his occupation and fame lie in that direction, but occasionally he takes an excursive flight into politics, more by way of diversion than otherwise. He has served one or two terms as member of the lower house of the legislature, and one term also as state geologist by appointment of Gov. Gray. He prefers, however, to wander over the fields and woodlands, watching the habits of birds, and studying nature in all her varying moods. On these subjects he writes most entertainingly in stories, in poems, and in magazine essays. He is a born naturalist and is never so happy as when studying the interesting flora and fauna of his adopted state. He views nature with the eye of an artist, and describes her charms with the heart of a poet. One of his books covering these subjects, entitled " Sylvan Secrets," is as charming as an Arabian tale. " The Red-head Family " is a bird sketch of the most delightful description, in which the imaginings of a poet, and the word painting of an artist are mingled with, and give color to, ornithological information of the most exact kind because gathered by a student of nature in actual contact with what he describes. Bird song, nest building, bird anatomy, the loves, hates, trials and habits of the songsters of the grove, are themes which this poet-naturalist has enriched with the appreciation of a Thoreau, and the descriptive powers of a Goldsmith. One of his articles, a gem of its kind, describes the habits of the mocking-bird in his native southern haunts. Mr. Thompson says, what is not generally known, that the mocker sometimes sings as it flies, after the manner of the skylark, and he dwells at length on one of these "descending songs," which the mocker poured forth' as he fluttered on ecstatic wing from branch to |branch, and finally by slow degrees, to the earth where he fell exhausted with the efforts to produce his own exquisite melody. Mr. Thompson is a voluminous magazine writer and covers a wide variety of topics with unflagging ability. He is a conspicuous member of that galaxy of literary stars who have shed such lustre upon Indiana since the war period, and contributed so much to give her high rank in the world of letters.

JAMES WHITCOMB RILEY.— Some fifteen or twenty years ago, there commenced to appear in various papers of Indiana, poems in dialect, relating to homely phases of human life and touching on those domestic topics that are common to every fireside. At first they only attracted the attention of a few, but by degrees, their fame spread as they were more and more appreciated, and people began to enquire the author of such pieces as " The Old Swimmin' Hole," " When the Frost is on the Punkin and the Fodder's in the Shock," " The Flying Islands " and other gems, the characteristics of which were a gentle humor, always accompanied by a rich vein of tenderest pathos. Usually these poems purported to be written by " Mr. Johnson, of Boone," or some other bucolic individual unknown to fame. Most of them were published in the various newspapers edited by the late George C. Harding, himself a universal genius of the first water, and always in sympathy with rising literary talent which he did more than any other newspaper proprietor of the state, to foster and develop. By degrees it leaked out that the author of the popular dialect poems was none other than James Whitcomb Riley, a young man of Hancock county, who from the rude life of a farmer boy, found himself drifting irresistibly into rhyme, like the noted Mr. Wegg. In the course of time, Mr. Riley's fugitive pieces were collected and published in a volume, which was succeeded at intervals, by others of a similar tenor, all of which were warmly welcomed and generally read by lovers of that kind of verse which deals with lowly human nature, and as it comes from the heart of the writer, goes directly to the hearts of the readers. Soon Mr. Riley had a state reputation, and was welcomed everywhere with affection as the typical "Hoosier Poet." It was not until the national meeting of authors in New York, in the winter of 1886-'87, that Riley's fame spread across the state lines and extended to boundaries that are touched by the two great oceans. The select critics of literature in the east fell easy victims to his genial personal address and platform ability, and when the meeting adjourned, Mr. Riley was by general consent, placed high up on the temple of fame, alongside of the most popular American poets. After that, he figured conspicuously on the lecture platform, as a reciter of his poems, and has been much sought after for concert and lyceum work. Mr. Riley is a distinctive Hoosier product and his poems are rich with the flavor of the soil from which their author sprang. He has done much to give Indiana high rank in the literary world, and for this, as well as for the intrinsic merits of his compositions, enjoys a warm place in the hearts of his fellow citizens of the Hoosier state.

LEWIS WALLACE.— Though a soldier of distinction in two wars, it is not as a military man that Gen. Wallace has achieved his principal fame. It has been rather with the pen than the sword he has conquered, and no Indianian has carved his name so high on the literary temple as the distinguished subject of this sketch. A son of Gov. David Wallace, he was born in Brookville, Ind., on the 10th of

April, 1827. He received a common school education and was studying law when the Mexican war roused him from his reveries. He served in that war with credit as a first lieutenant, and at its close resumed his profession, which he practiced chiefly in the cities of Covington and Crawfordsville, Ind. He served a term of four years in the state senate, but never took kindly to politics. At the breaking out of the civil war, he was appointed adjutant general of Indiana, soon after becoming colonel of the Eleventh Indiana volunteers, with which he served in West Virginia, participating in the capture of Romney and the ejection of the enemy from Harper's Ferry. He became a brigadier-general of volunteers, in the fall of 1861, led a division at the capture of Fort Donelson, and displayed such ability as to receive a major-general's commission in the following spring. He participated conspicuously in the fated field of Shiloh. In 1864 he was assigned to the command of the middle department, with headquarters at Baltimore, Md., with 5,800 men. He marched to the banks of the Monocacy, and there offered battle to the overwhelming forces of Gen. Jubal A. Early, who, with 28,000 men, was marching triumphantly upon the national capital. On the afternoon of the 9th of July, hard by the railroad bridge that spans the Monocacy near Frederick, Md., was fought one of the bloodiest engagements of the war, in proportion to the number engaged. Gen. Wallace was entrenched behind stone fences that stretched along the heights near the bridge and at right angles with the river. McCausland's cavalry, which led the vanguard of Early's army, crossed the stream and made a vigorous assault upon Wallace's lines, but after a very spirited and bloody engagement, they were forced to retreat, but took up and held a position in the rear. Soon thereafter a long line of infantry were seen fording the Monocacy, and filing right under cover of hills and trees, to a position in front of Gen. Wallace's center. These troops were the famous "Stonewall brigade," formerly made immortal by Jackson, but now consolidated with other seasoned veterans, into a division commanded by Major General John C. Breckinridge. They deployed and were ordered to advance directly to the assault of Gen. Wallace's main position. The onset was furious and the fatalities on both sides, many hundreds in a few minutes. The Union troops resisted stubbornly, but were finally forced to give way, and the hundreds of dead bodies observable on the field after the fight, showed how bravely they had endeavored to stem the tide of invasion. Though defeated, Gen. Wallace and his troops had accomplished the important duty of delaying Early until reinforcements could reach Washington. Gen. Wallace was second member of the court that tried the assassins of Lincoln and president of that which convicted Wirz of the Andersonville prison horrors. In 1878 Gen. Wallace was governor of Utah and served from 1831 to '85 as minister to Turkey. He has lectured extensively and is one of the most popular of the platform speakers of the day. His chief fame, however, rests upon his authorship of the religio-historical novel, "Ben Hur: a Tale of the Christ," of which over 290,000 have been sold without diminution in the demand. It has already become an American classic, and takes front rank among the imaginative works of the world. Other popular works by Gen. Wallace are, "The Fair God," a story of the conquest of Mexico, "Life of Benjamin Harrison" and "The Boyhood of Christ." No other Indianian has done so much to give his state high rank in the field of polite literature.

SCHUYLER COLFAX, statesman, and vice president of the United States, was born in the city of New York, March 23, 1823. His grandfather, Gen. William Colfax, was a native of Connecticut, and served with distinction in the war of American independence. His father died before his son's birth, as did also a sister, and thus he became the only child of his widowed mother. The early years of Mr. Colfax were spent in his native city, where he attended the public schools and afterward became clerk in a store. In 1836 he came to Indiana, and located at New Carlisle, St. Joseph county, where he again entered a store as clerk, and in 1841, he became a resident of South Bend, in which city he subsequently received the appointment of deputy auditor. In 1842 he was active in organizing a temperance society at South Bend, and continued a total abstainer throughout his life. At this time he reported the proceedings of the state senate for the *Indianapolis Journal*, and in 1844 entered the political arena as a public speaker for Henry Clay. In 1845 he became editor and proprietor of the *St. Joseph Valley Register*, of which he was also founder, and he continued its publication for a period of eighteen years. He was secretary of the Chicago harbor and river convention in 1847, and in 1848 was elected secretary of the national whig convention, at Baltimore, which nominated Gen. Zachary Taylor for the presidency. He was a member of the Indiana constitu-

tional convention of 1850, and in 1851 received the whig nomination
for congress. His opponent was Hon. Graham N. Fitch, an able
politician and a fine speaker, with whom he engaged in a joint canvass, during which the two men traveled over a thousand miles and
held over 70 discussions. The district was strongly democratic, yet
Mr. Colfax was defeated by only 200 votes. In 1852 he was a delegate to the national convention which nominated Gen. Scott for the
presidency, and in 1854, was elected to the Thirty-fourth congress,
by the memorable majority of 1,776 votes, although the same district
in previous years gave a democratic majority of 1,200. In 1858 he
was again triumphantly elected to congress, and served as a member
of that body by successive elections until 1869. He was elected
speaker of the house in December, 1863, and on April 8th of the following year, he descended from the chair to move the expulsion of
Mr. Long, of Ohio, who had made a speech favoring the recognition
of the southern confederacy. The resolution was afterward changed
to one of censure, and Mr. Colfax's action was generally sustained by
Union men. On the convening of the Thirty-ninth congress, Mr.
Colfax was again elected speaker by 139 votes, his opponent, Mr.
Brooks, of New York, receiving but thirty-six. March 4, 1867, he
was for the third time chosen speaker, and his skill as a presiding
officer, often shown under very trying circumstances, gained the applause of both friends and political opponents In May, 1868, the
republican national convention at Chicago, nominated him on the
first ballot for vice president, Gen. Grant being the presidential
nominee, and the ticket having been successful, he took his seat as
president of the senate, March 4, 1869. In August, 1871, the president offered him the position of secretary of state, for the remainder
of his term, but he declined. In 1872 he was prominently mentioned
as a presidential candidate, and the same year he refused the editor-
ship of the New York *Tribune*. " In 1873, Mr. Colfax was implicated
in the charges of corruption brought against members of congress
who had received shares in the credit mobilier of America. The
house committee reported that there was no ground for his impeachment, as the alleged offense, if committed at all, was committed before he became vice president." " He denied the truth of the charges
and his friends have always regarded his character as irreproachable."
His latter years were spent mostly in retirement at his home in
South Bend, and in delivering public lectures, which he frequently

did before large audiences. The most popular of his lectures was that on "Lincoln and Garfield." He died at Mankato, Minn., January 13, 1885.

ROBERT DALE OWEN was the son of Robert J. Owen, a celebrated English reformer, who was born in 1771 and died in 1858. He was born near Glasgow, Scotland, November 7, 1801, and after receiving a liberal education in his native country, came to the United States in 1823, and settled at New Harmony, Posey county, Ind. In 1828, in partnership with Mrs. Frances Wright, he began the publication of a paper called the *Free Enquirer*, which made its periodical visits about three years. He afterward moved to New Harmony, Ind., where he was three times elected to the Indiana legislature, and in 1843 was elected to congress, in which body he served until 1847, having been re-elected in 1845. When in congress, he took a prominent part in the settlement of the northwest boundary dispute, and also was largely instrumental in establishing the Smithsonian institute at Washington, of which he became one of the regents, and served on the building committee. He was a delegate to the constitutional convention in 1850, and no one bore a more prominent part in the deliberations of that body than he. In 1853 he was appointed *charge d' affaires* at Naples, and in 1855 was minister at Naples, holding the position until 1858. During the civil war he was a firm supporter of the Union, and one of the first to advocate the emancipation of the slaves. Mr. Owen was a firm believer in the doctrines of spiritualism, and was fearless in his advocacy of the same. He inherited the communistic notions of his father, who had failed in numerous attempts to carry the system into practical operation, and he also signally failed in his attempts to accomplish a similar purpose. His scholastic attainments were of the highest order, and he possessed a mind well stored with general knowledge. He was indeed a man of transcendant ability and may justly be regarded as one of the greatest, as well as one of the best men Indiana has ever claimed. He contributed largely to the literature of his day, and the following is a partial list of his best known works: "Moral Physiology," "Discussion with Original Bachelor on the Personality of God, and the Authenticity of the Bible," "Hints on Public Architecture," "Footfalls on the Boundaries of Another World," "The Wrong of Slavery and the Right of Emancipation," "Beyond the Breakers," a novel, "The Debatable Land Between this World and the Next," "Treading My Way," an autobiography. Mr. Owen departed this life at Lake George, N. Y., January 24, 1877, aged seventy-six years.

RICHARD W. THOMPSON, ex-secretary of the navy, is a native of Virginia, born in Culpeper county, June 9, 1809. In the fall of 1831 he emigrated to Indiana, and taught school in the town of Bedford, afterward establishing the Lawrence county seminary, which he conducted about one year. Abandoning school work he embarked in the mercantile business in Lawrence county, and while thus engaged began the study of law. He was admitted to the bar in 1834, and the same year he was elected a member of the Indiana legislature, in which body he not only displayed great ability and foresight, but was also instrumental in shaping much important legislation. In 1838, he was returned to the house, and the following year was chosen state senator, of which he was president *pro tempore* on the occasion of the resignation of Lieut. Gov. Wallace. In 1841 he was elected to the United States congress over Hon. John W. Davis, but declined a renomination to the same position, and in 1843 removed to Terre Haute, in which city he has since resided. He was a presidential elector on the Harrison ticket in 1840, zealously supporting Gen. Harrison in public speeches, and by his pen, and was a defeated candidate for elector on the Clay ticket in 1844. In 1847 he was again elected to congress by the whig party, and became prominent in national legislation during this term, but at its expira-on retired from public life. In 1849 he was appointed United States minister to Austria, by Gen. Taylor, but declined to accept the honor, and was also tendered several other appointments by the general government, all of which he saw fit to refuse. During the war for the Union he was active and rendered valuable service to his country, was commandant of Camp Dick Thompson, near Terre Haute, and also served as provost marshal of the district. He was again a presidential elector on the republican ticket in 1864, and a delegate to the national conventions of that party in 1878, and 1876, in the latter of which he nominated Oliver P. Morton for the presidency. In 1867-9 he was judge of the eighteenth circuit of the state, and on March 12, 1877, he entered President Hayes's cabinet, as secretary of the navy. He served nearly through the administration, but resigned the position in 1881, to become chairman of the American committee of the Panama Canal Company. Mr. Thompson has written many political platforms, and obtained a reputation for his ability in formulating party principles. He is an eloquent and effective speaker, and a man of benevolence and unassuming manners.

COL. FRANCIS VIGO, whose name is prominently identified with the early history of Indiana, was born in the kingdom of Sardinia in 1740, and died at Vincennes, Ind., in 1836. Until 1778 he was a resident of the Spanish port of St. Louis, where, as an Indian trader, he acquired the title of the "Spanish Merchant." He removed to Vincennes a short time previous to its capture by Gen. George Rogers Clark, whom he was instrumental in assisting, for which he was afterward arrested by the British as a spy. In the Illinois campaigns of 1778 and 1779, Col. Vigo rendered valuable service to the army of Clark, by advancing large sums of money for food and clothing. Through his patriotism and self-sacrifice, he served the army and gave victory to the cause of the colonies in the west. He was made commandant of the militia of Vincennes in 1790, and in 1810 was one of Gen. Harrison's confidential messengers to the Indians. His name will ever be associated with the early history of the Wabash valley.

JOHN W. DAVIS, one of Indiana's most noted public men, was born in Cumberland county, Penn., July 17, 1799, and died in 1859. He was well educated and graduated in medicine at Baltimore in 1821, shortly afterward removing to Carlisle, Ind. He was soon embarked on a political career and graduated for the purpose in that universal and popular school, the state legislature. He served several years in that body, and was chosen speaker of the house in 1832. In 1834 he was appointed a commissioner to negotiate a treaty with the Indians. He was elected to congress by the democrats, and served from December 7, 1835, until March 3, 1837, was re-elected, and again served from 1839 until 1841, and from 1843 till 1847. During his last term he was speaker of the house of representatives, having been elected on December 1, 1845. He was United States commissioner to China in 1848-'50, and governor of Oregon in 1853-4. He presided over the convention held at Baltimore in 1852, that nominated Franklin Pierce for the presidency. Mr. Davis was a strong man and a party leader of long continued popularity and well recognized ability. He was also a decided feature of the list of self-made Indiana publicists.

www.ingramcontent.com/pod-product-compliance
Lightning Source LLC
Chambersburg PA
CBHW020943120726
47905CB00008B/2651